GEARED FOR PLEASURE

GEARED
FOR
PLEASURE

RACHEL GRACE

HEAT | NEW YORK

THE BERKLEY PUBLISHING GROUP
Published by the Penguin Group
Penguin Group (USA) Inc.
375 Hudson Street, New York, New York 10014, USA
Penguin Group (Canada), 90 Eglinton Avenue East, Suite 700, Toronto, Ontario M4P 2Y3, Canada
(a division of Pearson Penguin Canada Inc.) • Penguin Books Ltd., 80 Strand, London WC2R 0RL,
England • Penguin Group Ireland, 25 St. Stephen's Green, Dublin 2, Ireland (a division of Penguin
Books Ltd.) • Penguin Group (Australia), 250 Camberwell Road, Camberwell, Victoria 3124, Australia
(a division of Pearson Australia Group Pty. Ltd.) • Penguin Books India Pvt. Ltd., 11 Community
Centre, Panchsheel Park, New Delhi—110 017, India • Penguin Group (NZ), 67 Apollo Drive,
Rosedale, Auckland 0632, New Zealand (a division of Pearson New Zealand Ltd.) • Penguin Books
(South Africa) (Pty.) Ltd., 24 Sturdee Avenue, Rosebank, Johannesburg 2196, South Africa

Penguin Books Ltd., Registered Offices: 80 Strand, London WC2R 0RL, England

This book is an original publication of The Berkley Publishing Group.

PUBLISHING HISTORY
Heat trade paperback edition / March 2012

Library of Congress Cataloging-in-Publication Data

Grace, Rachel, (date)
Geared for pleasure / Rachel Grace.—Heat trade paperback ed.
        p.   cm.
ISBN 978-0-425-24566-8
I. Title.
PS3601.L3545G43   2012
813'.6—dc23
2011042879

150142767

For Cookie—Love is the reason. Thank you for moving into Theorrey with me for the duration, and for being my science guy. For Kate and Roberta, who allowed me to play air pirate and believed in me enough to make this happen. And for Robin L. Rotham, who is eternally patient and always there.

Most important, to the Smutketeers: Eden Bradley/Eve Berlin, Crystal Jordan, and Karen Erickson. As well as Lilli Feisty. For more than three years you have been my friends as well as the story in my head. I am lucky to know all of you, and to have been able to create the powerful female characters you inspired during that one fateful phone call—and place them all in my crazy, topsy-turvy clockworky world. All for one and one for all.

Contents

EARTHLY DESIRES

Chapter One

Find the Deviant. Trust no one but its captain with your identity and your secret. Everything depends on you.

Dare lifted a hand to her temple and grimaced at the rough and unpleasantly aromatic material of her woven glove. She needed to quell the turmoil in her mind and focus on her mission, but the task was difficult.

She had prepared as much as she could for this leg of the journey. Her borrowed clothing—from mangled cap to worn boots and pungent gloves—ensured she would not stand out, much less be recognized as one of the queen's elite shield guards. She need only lose herself in the milling crowd, make her way through the outer edges of the city toward the docks, and, fortune willing, find the ship she was searching for. It was a task that had, this morning, seemed as fraught with unknown dangers as a journey through the Avici desert. Yet thus far she'd encountered not a single obstacle.

The ease with which she had concealed her departure stirred her with ire rather than instilling her with confidence. She had believed the palace—indeed, the entire community of Queen's Hill—to be impenetrable. Granted, the security detail focused on keeping the unsavory elements out, not in. Nevertheless, the lack of vigilance was unacceptable.

In light of all she had witnessed in recent weeks, she acknowledged that her escape might not be the fault of inattentive guardsmen alone. No. More powerful forces and far more dangerous games seemed to be at play.

So *why* was she abandoning her post?

She glanced over her shoulder where, high between the peaks of the Twin Mountains, the Copper Palace's glimmering domed rooftops beckoned to her. From here, Queen's Hill was awe-inspiring. Distant. The place that had been her home for most of her life had never seemed farther away. But she could not falter now.

She took a steadying breath and walked slowly into the throng of Trader's Square, weaving between the long rows of wooden stalls crowded with people and supplies. Though the goods often changed with the seasons, the stalls were stationary. They'd been built long ago to cater to those who worked and traveled on the elevated rail.

Dare looked up. The views of the spectacle from the palace windows had not prepared her for the crisscrossing webs of rails that merged above her. Or for the sheer size of the transport swinging subtly as it waited to be boarded.

The governors and nobles visiting Queen's Hill often spoke of traveling the vast distances cradled in the comfort of the transports' grand salons. She could not fathom how the sturdy vehicles, laden with cargo and humanity, did not bend the narrow bars. Instead, they hung as light as fruit from a metallic vine high above. How was it that they flew through the air with such ease and with no apparent regard for the natural laws that kept the rest of humanity grounded?

However the marvel was managed, it succeeded in helping travelers avoid the dangers of the uninhabitable and forbidding places that lay between Centre City and the rest of the queen's domain. Only the truly prepared or the incredibly foolish would risk crossing the marshlands or black desert any other way.

Her gaze followed the rickety wooden stairs leading up to the rail's loading dock, which was held aloft by thick posts of ironwood and steel. There was a small crowd waiting to enter the transport. Above them, she could clearly see two men perched on top of the tram, on either side of the large engine that powered the machine. One man with long braided hair and a beard was armed with a rifle to protect the travelers. The other, stout and bald, methodically filled a furnace with fuel.

The machine bellowed like a great beast. The steam that belched from its smokestack darkened the sky above her and reminded her of winter clouds. It began to move slowly away from the raised platform, scraping along the suspended track as it headed for its unknown destination.

Where was it going? The small but bustling city of Newgarren on the edge of the desert? Two Moon Bay? Or perhaps this tram went all the way to Faro Outpost, on the other edge of the continent alongside the treacherous western sea. Her friend and fellow guardsman Cyrus had been handpicked from Faro and brought to the palace. She imagined it an exotic place, full of adventure and wonders, but he rarely spoke of it and, sensing his reticence, she never pressed him for details.

The idea of travel was fascinating, but no matter how intriguing those destinations sounded, Dare had no desire to book passage on the rail. Solid ground, even on a dangerous path, sounded far more secure than tempting fate in the air . . . or on the sea.

The sea. She stiffened her spine. She would do all that loyalty and duty demanded of her. If that meant boarding a sailing ship, so be it.

Though first she had to find her way to the docks through this boisterous crowd.

Dare cringed. The wonder that drew her gaze had not stopped her other senses from intruding. Rich smells of cooking meat lingered thickly in the air, filling her nostrils. She couldn't see where the scent was coming from, and her rumbling stomach protested. But the aroma was not the only thing upending her equilibrium. A cacophony of human and animal life assaulted her ears. The chatter of men and women of all ages and attitudes, the mournful baying of the prized threehorn cattle sold on the edges of the square, all combined into a din that played an unwelcome melody on her senses. That tune, as well as the grating emotions of the horde of unaware Theorrey citizens, warred for attention inside her.

She had not imagined their feelings would be so darkly complex. Far more distracting than her surroundings.

Avarice, aggression, lust, and desperation . . . The chaos of it all dizzied her, every inch of her skin aching at the crush of it. Yet again, she was tempted to return to the silent serenity of the Copper Palace. Although she could no longer find peace there, it was still her home.

The vying calls of aggressive sellers refused to be ignored. The sellers of Trader's Square were of a different ilk from the merchants allowed to peddle their wares inside the stormgate. Louder. Coarser. Lacking in respect and hygiene.

Having spent her life traversing only the levels of the protected Queen's Hill, a community in itself, Dare felt entirely out of her element. She had studied in the libraries of the scholars. Wandered the lush gardens of the nobles. Trained with the Wode on duty there, shield guards and protectors of Theorrey and its rulers. And on each market day, she would go down to the lowest level, close enough to hear the hum of the charged outer gate, to choose a special trinket from a polite and officially licensed merchant. A trinket she always hoped would make the queen offer her one of those rare, honest smiles.

That was the world she knew.

She'd often silently agreed with those who insisted that Queen's Hill held every wonder worth having. That the rest of the city, the rest of the world, could only hold disappointment after such perfection.

Cyrus and the queen did not share that view, and as she continued to wander through the open marketplace, she thought she could better understand their reasoning. It was difficult *not* to marvel at what she beheld. Not to feel the excitement of a kind rarely encountered on the Hill. So much life.

This place was raw and dirty, yes. Intimidating? Most assuredly. But the ingenuity of these citizens *was* impressive. They traded in more than necessities. Even in their poverty they were not unlike the artisans on the Hill. They also traded in fancy. Their imaginations seemed to have no limit, and had more experience to draw from.

There were devices she could not begin to describe alongside produce and sweets she could not recognize or guess the flavor of. Her stomach rumbled again, attempting to convince her that it would rather have a taste of the produce than study the mechanics of the windup wonders.

She took several more steps, avoiding a steaming pile of animal excrement—which instantly allayed her appetite—before spying a vendor who sold alabaster house idols the size of her palm. They were all carved in the image of the eternally young queen, each so accurate that it was hard to believe such perfection could be replicated by hand so many times and without flaw.

Another stall held a jumbled pile of mechanical arms and legs for those who had lost limbs and needed a viable replacement. She recognized them, but she'd assumed they had been created solely for the Wode. She'd seen several elder shield guards use the clunky devices nearly as effectively as an undamaged appendage. A few could even use the different switches to change their "fingers" into tools to tighten bolts or heat steel, allowing them to maintain their usefulness.

Of course, there were those who spoke of augmentations that would turn their new arms into powerful weapons for combat, but she doubted the veracity of those barracks stories. They did, after all, include the use of theorrite, a gem the members of the Theorrean Raj thought too rare to waste on wounded veterans. Theorrite was to be used only for "the betterment of Theorrey." The science ministry believed their intellectual advances were far more important in that regard than an injured Wode's pride.

Near the end of the row, her attention settled on a stall where a trader sold pendants of swirling desert glass. The beauty of the jewelry stilled her steps. The unique pieces were scattered amongst other treasures. Polished ivory horns that had been hollowed out and filled with alluring, colorful spices. Spiral daggers made of sharpened bone and leather. She believed the objects must have come from Newgarren until she saw what was beside them. Her lips parted. *Wings.* Small wings spread out to glide, made to catch the wind, and engineered out of what appeared to be tanned animal hide and brass. Dare had never seen anything like it. Surely they weren't for actual use? They were far too small to hold a man's weight.

The markings painted on their surface gave her an answer. The symbols weren't of human origin.

Felidae.

Dare recognized one or two from the old journals that the scholars loved, though she would never attempt a guess at their true meaning. She knew of few who could. It was said even the Felidae themselves had forgotten generations ago. Yet these wings had been recently made.

The slender male trader noticed her studying his goods and

frowned. "Don't hover 'round my stall if you can't pay, boy. Felidae artifacts ain't easy to come by, and I don't mean to give 'em away for free."

She heard a barked-out laugh before a bearded man stepped into her line of vision, blocking her view as he addressed the trader. "Hah! If those are genuine artifacts, I'm a bloody nobleman's son. Everyone knows them Spotted Spines never had no culture, 'cept mining or stealing. They never made nothing but more of themselves to feed. Scavengers, not inventors, the lot of them." He paused and studied the items more closely. "What do you want for that knife?"

Dare lowered her head and walked swiftly away before they noticed her again. *Boy,* he'd called her. Despite the coarse conversation, she bit her lip to hide her smile. Her disguise was working.

Queen Idony would love this. To walk freely amongst the people, unrecognized. Even the disguise would no doubt make her laugh with delight. The unusual sights, the raucous sounds, the dank, musky smells . . . she would love all of it. If only she were here to share it with Dare.

She frowned, recalling the unusual messenger that had found her in her palace rooms the day before, just as her own suspicions about the strange goings-on in the palace had become too strong to ignore.

Not human, the messenger had instead been a flying insect made of aged copper. Its wings were colored with old, weatherworn patches of blue, green, and gold. It looked like the paintings of dragonflies she'd seen in the queen's rooms, though this one was much larger.

It appeared to act of its own accord as if it were alive, landing on the ledge of the balcony outside Dare's quarters. Faceted crystalline eyes had followed her movements with a strange ticking sound and the unmistakable grinding of gears. It seemed to be watching her, though she knew that was impossible.

When she'd reached out to touch it, the warm metal vibrated with a unique resonance beneath her fingers. A hidden panel on its back had opened to reveal a folded parchment stamped with the queen's personal seal: the sword and chalice.

There was no doubt it was her sigil. More than its design convinced Dare. The queen had showed her long ago how to confirm the authenticity of her mark. She had made the lesson a game, leaving parchment filled with clues around the palace. Clues she would need to follow to find whatever it was Queen Idony had hidden from her that day.

The trick for this particular game was queensfruit, the most abundant fruit in Theorrey. The pale pink rind had to be peeled and its juice dabbed on the red wax sigil to cause a unique transformation. The vertical broadsword that seemed to pierce the heart of the chalice would turn a light silver while its jeweled hilt darkened to amber and brass. The chalice itself became silver as well, the darker brass used to outline the lotus design etched on the outside of the cup.

Only the queen's wax, her personal mixture, could create that reaction. It meant whoever had sent this had her approval and followed her command above all others. A true ally.

For Dare, the note on the parchment confirmed and doubled her suspicions, the stunning news leaving her no time to investigate the mechanical insect. Not that it gave her a choice. Its job completed, it had shuddered to whirring, clicking life and taken off into the air with the grace of a living bird, disappearing too quickly for her to gauge its direction or learn anything further from it.

The instructions it had delivered had been precise and emphatic. She was not to go to the ruling body. About this, the Theorrean Raj and the Wode commanders were not to be confided in or informed. It had been an unusual command, but Dare's loyalty was first and foremost to her queen. It always had been, even before she had been chosen as the Queen's Chalice. Her father had made sure of it.

The missive had posited a truth that Dare had confirmed for herself that very night, though it struck her even now as impossible. However, it could not be denied. *Her* queen was no longer within the protection of the palace. Something insidious and untenable was going on, and Dare was on her own.

Hopefully this captain of the Deviant had answers she did not. Or, at the least, knew how to communicate with her mysterious, message-sending ally for more information.

"Welcome to Trader's Square."

Dare stopped short, digging the heels of her scuffed, borrowed boots into the dirt. That was the queen's voice. It was tinny and unnatural, but it was hers.

She looked over the crowd to find the source of the cheerful announcement. There, seated on a throne of limestone, nodding to the passersby, was a life-sized automated replica of the queen coated in delicate copper leaf. A crank key at the base turned slowly as the figure moved through its sequence of operations with clockwork precision. A nod. A wave. An expression of serenity.

It was a masterful likeness. Dare had seen other such automatons before, most as they were being built. The artisans told her that people loved to feel the queen was watching over them wherever they lived, which was why they were sent out to all of the cities in Theorrey. In this way, everyone could be as close to her divine presence as possible. In spirit if not in truth.

This one was the best yet, forged with such attention to detail that Dare had to move closer.

Queen Idony the Ever Young. The artistic engineer had captured the eternally fourteen-year-old monarch perfectly; the mischievous smile, the large, deep-set jeweled eyes, wise and knowing beyond her apparent years. Even the distinctive shining hair was exact—made of fine, individual strands of white gold. It fell to her shoulders, drawing attention to the necklace that always adorned her graceful neck.

The Nymphaea Infinitum.

Dare had been a much younger, newly chosen Chalice the first time she saw the amulet. It had fascinated her ever since. Its strangely shaped gears, made of a metal unlike any she'd seen before, surrounded a lotus whose many petals were crafted from the valuable greenish-blue theorrite. What made it all the more unusual was that it seemed more than an ornament. It appeared to be grafted to the queen's skin. As much a part of her as her own flesh.

"The symbol of my rule," Queen Idony had told her with a small, ironic tilt of her lips.

The immense sadness emanating from her when she'd said it had made Dare—naïvely foolish and unaware of protocol—ask her why. Father had warned her not to share the knowledge of her gifts with others, but he couldn't have meant to include the queen. Surely she, of all people, already knew. She knew everything.

"You dare to presume what your queen is feeling?" Idony's smile had grown, and real amusement rolled off her in pleased waves. "I think you will be my favorite Senedal, Demeter. And I know we shall be friends. Though I'm not sure such a stodgy name will suit you. What *was* the commander thinking? I believe I will call you Dare."

A scratchy, female voice interrupted her musings and brought her back to reality with a jolt. "Pretty version ain't she, boy? We've been needin' a new one for years. Got her in a few weeks ago though, surprised if this is the first time you've seen her."

Dare couldn't tear her gaze away from the moving statue as it nodded in regal welcome. She knew she had to acknowledge the woman who had appeared beside her lest she seem odd or out of place, but it was not easy to look away from the dearly familiar queen.

She tried not to flinch when she finally glanced up at the thin, taller woman's face. One half of it was smiling. The other half, mal-formed from some terrible misfortune, was pulled into a grimace.

Dare forced herself to speak. "I've been ill. A . . . friend was looking after me."

The scarred hand patting her arm stilled for a moment, and Dare sensed a jarring edge of suspicion from the woman. "Ill, you say? That's too bad. But you look healthy enough now. Young and strong. Though I'm guessing it must be a tender throat that has you still sounding like a girl at your age. Friend, huh? Don't have any family to look after you, then? No one who would care that you walk through the square untended?"

Dare tried to deepen her voice. "Yes. My throat. And I'm old enough to be on my own. I need no attending."

Suddenly, Dare could barely hold back her tears. All the emotions around her must be affecting her control. A member of the Wode did *not* cry. She'd learned that long ago, when her father had first left her at the palace. She was a warrior, a soldier. Bred to be a companion and guard. Love and family were not for people like her.

Yet she *did* have a family of sorts in Queen Idony and Cyrus. An Arendal, Cyrus was Dare's counterpart, the Queen's Sword. They had arrived at the palace on the same day, replacing generations of their predecessors as the queen's companion guards. Her Arendal and Senedal. Her Sword and Chalice.

She hadn't cried when, months ago, she had been informed that Cyrus was missing, presumed dead. She hadn't cried when she discovered that the queen . . . No. She could hardly admit the truth, even to herself. It was too horrific.

She could not cry now.

Dare tugged the brim of the large woolen hat farther down, to hide her expression. She wasn't quick enough.

"Oh my," the young woman, who looked to be around her age,

tutted. "Here you'll be thinking Lucy Thrice is ugly *and* mean. Put my foot in it, did I? I'm sure you are perfectly capable of attending yourself. Nothing could scare a brave lad like you, eh? But that throat and those watery eyes have given Lucy an idea. Tell you what, I have a special grain tonic that'll ease your troubles. My own creation. Good for all that ails you. I won't charge you a thing for a taste."

The queen's automaton tilted her head. "Welcome to Trader-der-der-der-*Dare-Dare*-Trader's Square."

Dare's heart stuttered along with the replica's vocal recording. Had it just said—? No, that was preposterous. It had to be a coincidence.

A man walked by and kicked the platform, the hollow thud making Dare cringe. He no doubt believed, as anyone with good sense would, that the gears within had jammed. As he passed, one of the queen's metal eyelids lowered over a jeweled eye, which was emitting a soft blue glow. It looked decidedly like a wink. Impossible.

"The artist'll be hearing about that little glitch I'll wager. Come on, now. Time for my famous remedy." The woman tugged on her arm but Dare shook her head. Seeing the queen's likeness had only increased her urgency and reinforced her determination to complete her mission. Visiting with this pleasant unfortunate had no part in it.

"You are kind, Miss—"

"Thrice, is me. Lucy Thrice."

Dare nodded. "You are kind, Miss Thrice." She politely but firmly disengaged herself from the woman's grime-covered grasp. "Unfortunately I must be on my way."

"Listen to that," a male voice drawled behind her. "If I closed my eyes, I'd be sure a lady from the Hill had come to visit with those sparklin' manners, instead of a dirty lowborn boy."

She saw Lucy's mud-brown eyes narrow. "So would I. The lady part leastwise. I'm thinking we've found our special bird. Though you two are here early."

The man snorted. "We're right on time, with you *just* thinkin' that.

Had you fooled for a tic did she, Thrice? Thought you were the smart one. But then, you don't have the right parts to sniff out the difference like we do. Bet she'll fetch a price worth claiming at the docks."

The brazen comment was followed by a wave of disdain and lust that crawled over Dare's skin like snakes, telling her it was time to move on. She turned to find not one, but two squat, heavyset men, both of them looking at her with a cruel intent that matched the energy they were sending without restraint in her direction.

Dare held up a hand, not out of fear, but obligation. Wode protocol demanded she warn them. Even the lowest-born criminal deserved that much before punishment was meted out. "Step aside now, and I won't have to hurt you."

In answer, the men laughed and lunged for her.

Perhaps she would have been wiser to duck away from their grasping hands and run. It would be more in keeping with her disguise than her ultimatum had been. But she found herself growing angry instead, unable to keep up the pretense in the face of her outrage.

This was still Her Majesty's land. Could a person not walk through it unaccosted? A mere boy? A woman alone? And where were the Wode charged with maintaining order in the square? They were meant to protect the innocent. To ensure safe commerce.

The first man tore her frayed jacket sleeve and half her shirt with one sharp tug. "Lookit 'er skin. So white and soft. Bet 'er tits and bits are just as fine. We should sample 'er before we sell 'er."

Sell her? To whom? A red fog colored the edges of her vision at his words, but she tamped it down. She may be outnumbered and outsized, but her formative days had been spent training with men *and* women far bigger and stronger. These lowborns made a mistake to underestimate her because of her small stature.

The sleeve of her jacket dangled, and she let it drop to the ground, revealing the pearl-handled dagger strapped to her right forearm.

Cyrus had shown her how to conceal a weapon for an instance such as this. An instance when fighting fairly would get her killed. One twist of her wrist and it was in her hand. Then her body tensed, prepared for battle.

The shorter man's eyes narrowed. "Nettles, she has a knife. Watch yourself."

He took a step back, though he was still blocking her avenue for escape. Surprised but unconcerned, Nettles licked his lips, and Dare sensed a twisted, more sinister thread running through his emotions. *He enjoyed the idea of hurting her.*

Dare glared scornfully, making it clear she doubted his abilities. He sneered at her expression as expected, and attacked. It was obvious in moments that this would not be a difficult fight. His big body was lumbering and slow. It was fair to say he was no match for her.

She ducked beneath his hands and struck his midsection with the hilt of her dagger, knocking the air from his lungs. Spinning low to the ground, she swept her leg out and snagged his booted ankles, felling him like a thick oak.

Before the dust could settle around him she was kneeling on his chest and slamming the heel of her hand into his nose. He howled with rage as it gushed blood, flinging up an arm to protect himself. Dare grabbed his wrist in a ruthless grip and bent his arm back on itself until it snapped with a satisfying crack.

The man bucked in agony, but before he could toss her off, she had her dagger behind her back, pressing it threateningly against the seam between his legs. She spared a glance for the man still standing. "He would *not* thank you if you took a step closer."

She flinched at Nettles' suffering when it reached her senses, but did not allow herself to be distracted by it. He deserved no pity. "I apologize for your pain, though I should unman you for your wicked thoughts." She let every ounce of loathing she felt show in her voice and her eyes. "Instead, I will leave you for the authorities, safe in the knowledge they will agree with the punishment I have dealt. A reminder not to touch what does not belong to you. If a shield guard learned you sought pleasure with an unwilling partner again, you may wish you'd turned away when you had the use of both arms."

Dare felt a sharp prick sting her neck and covered it with her free hand. Turning in shock, she saw Lucy Thrice beside her, holding a tiny thorn-shaped needle between her dirty fingers.

"What have you done?"

The woman shook her mane of tangled brown hair. "You should have come to have a nip with me, child. Your head wouldn't ache so much after if you'd had my tonic instead. And if your family had been smart, they'd have told you that the Wode in Trader's Square can be bought for a sip of my more pleasurable mixtures . . . and that you ought not to walk around alone."

When Dare swayed, the woman cooed, "It'll be all right now, Lucy Thrice is here. You want to experience something new? A better life?" She tsked. "You came to the wrong place. If you think about it, I'm really doing you a favor."

Dare's cheek hit the dirt beside the groaning Nettles, and she felt her body twitch as she struggled to move. Her limbs were going numb, her mind scrambling in panic.

The other man turned her onto her back, wrenched the dagger from her hand, and knocked off her woolen hat with his boot.

"By the two moons!" Lucy crowed. "Special bird indeed. You'll make twice the fortune for Lucy Thrice as she thought. Damn Wode," she added, a look of true disgust crossing the unscarred side her of face. "Shields, they call themselves. Break most of the rules they imprison or kill us for breaking, don't they? And yet one of those bastards must have had his way with someone outside his line to make such a small, strange-looking thing as you. No wonder you fight like you do. Come by it natural, eh?"

Then she smiled down into Dare's eyes. "Now you *will* thank me.

Someday you surely will. Best life you could have if someone was to
see what you were here, bastard and all, would be a vessel for their
hate. Least this way you'll get paid for it and have a decent chance of
surviving after."

The horrifying picture the woman painted was the last image
Dare saw before the world went black.

Chapter Two

She woke when a cool, damp cloth was brushed across her forehead and placed over her eyes. Was she home? Her body ached as it did whenever Cyrus decided to show her a new sparring maneuver, and she was on a bed with sheets so soft they *could* have come from the palace.

But Cyrus was gone, and she was nowhere near Queen's Hill. Or her queen. Dare would have sensed her presence as she always had before.

Her head throbbed, still recovering from whatever had been at the end of that needle. Unless she missed her guess, Lucy Thrice had succeeded in "saving" her. A favor Dare would pay back in kind as soon as she could.

Someone stood beside the bed, her thoughts and feelings in no way as convoluted as Lucy Thrice's had been. Though still soft. Another woman, if Dare had to guess. She opened her mind and sensed only open curiosity, guilelessness, and compassion from the stranger. A fellow prisoner? A sympathetic servant?

Dare frowned in confusion. She knew there was only one other in the room, and yet she could hear voices. Male and female voices. Laughter. Soft moans.

When she tried to reach up to remove the cloth from her eyes, wondering why her mind was deceiving her, she realized that her wrists were bound.

Her head jerked and knocked the cloth loose, sending it sliding onto the pillow beside her in a wet heap. Dare looked up at her left wrist. Chains. An attempt to move her right arm proved just as fruitless.

She was chained to the bed. The cuffs were lined with velvet, but there was no mistaking the iron it covered. Why would anyone go to so much trouble to make handcuffs comfortable?

Dare shifted beneath the cool white sheet. Her legs were free, which was a blessing, but she noticed an added impediment to the escape she was already planning—her nudity. All she owned had been stripped from her, including her weapons. She should never have turned her back on that manipulative tonic seller. Or thought her kind on the basis of her unfortunate face.

"There now. I know it looks bad. I told the boss my own self that he might've gone too far, you being as little as you please, and passing out from weakness and all. I told him a girl who looks like you should be treated decent for once in your life. But when he sets his mind to something, not a one of us can change it."

Dare turned her narrowed gaze on the woman beside her. Her accent indicated she was from one of the smaller farming communities. It was clear the long-limbed girl meant her words to be supportive. Kind. Her blonde hair was fashionably upswept with violet ribbons, and her body was barely covered in a thin dress of darker purple. She wore her corset on the outside of her gown, and it pressed her tiny breasts up so that Dare, or anyone else who was looking, could see more flesh than modesty should have allowed.

She smiled at Dare. "They call me Lavender. The boss told me to watch over you until you came to."

"My name is Dare and I'm pleased to meet you, Lavender. Now that we've been formally introduced, would it be possible for you to release me?" She tried to keep her voice calm as she subtly tested the thickness of her bonds.

Lavender's mouth formed a moue of apology but she shook her head. "The boss was firm on that. When he realizes you couldn't be a threat to anyone, I know he'll make sure you are welcomed more warmly. This isn't how he behaves as a rule. He's been tense since he returned from the mainland on his errand, and I'm guessing rescuing you and tossing out one of his own men for accepting money for an unwilling girl made his day that much worse." She patted Dare's hip soothingly as she spoke without taking a breath. "Never you worry, Dare. Those two men who trussed you up to bring you here would be wishing they had been assigned to the mines . . . if they were still alive to wish. And if they were Felidae, of course. Neither of which is a possibility, is it?"

The mainland? Rescued? She must still be under the influence of Lucy's drug. Nothing made sense. Perhaps if the sounds around her could be muffled, she could think. "Lavender, if I may ask, *where* is that noise coming from?"

The moaning had gotten louder, the voices rising as if in pain, yet Dare saw no one but Lavender in the room. Felt no presence but Lavender's.

"You're not afraid at all, are you? Just curious. I like that. The noise . . ." Lavender's smile grew mischievous and knowing. "Since most of the private rooms are being used, and he isn't willing to put you in the women's suite yet, the boss decided to place you in the Echo Chamber. He has a wicked sense of humor."

Dare stared at her blankly. "The Echo Chamber?"

In answer, Lavender placed another pillow beneath her head, affording her a clearer view of the room. It was luxurious, as lavish as any palace suite. She could see the finely crafted vanity and wardrobe, an exquisite hand-knotted rug on the floor, and red brocade curtains draping the walls, no doubt keeping out the light to ensure she could not gain her bearings.

Lavender pointed with one hand as the other slowly caressed Dare's hair in a tender, almost absent fashion. "Do you see the statue in the corner?"

Dare studied the sculpture with a combination of awe and horror. What at first appeared to be a plaster jumble became arms and legs, breasts and hands. Three men surrounded a voluptuous woman, all caressing her as she rose nude from large waves frozen in time. "I see it."

"There is a different statue in every corner of this room. When I first brought a man in here, I was near surprised as you. I mean, they don't move at all, but it still seemed like they were watching." She shrugged. "They *are* definitely listening. I'm not certain how they work, I only know they do. We can hear every bedroom from this spot, no matter where it is. 'Cept the boss's, of course. And ours. No profit or pleasure to be had from listening in on *our* day-to-day. Boss already knows all our secrets."

"The noise is coming from other *bed*rooms?" Dare felt the heat as blood rushed to her face. Those were not screams of pain, then. What kind of place *was* this?

Lavender laughed, not unkindly. "Some men enjoy doing, some watching. Others, for whatever reason, prefer the listening. When the last is true, we bring them here."

Dare's voice sounded high-pitched, even to her. "We? How many women has this boss of yours *saved*? Are you all forced to share yourselves against your will? Forced to indulge in perversions with strange men?"

The young blonde sighed blissfully. "He would never force a woman to do anything she had no desire to do. Not our captain. A hero, through and through, he is. He doesn't care what side of the Hill you were born to, every woma—"

Dare felt a pang of guilt as Lavender fell into a limp heap on the floor. She had used the momentum gained from freeing her wrist to knock Lavender between the neck and shoulder, rendering her unconscious. She would have a headache when she woke, but no more than that.

There could be no help for it. It had to be done if she was going to escape this place. Wherever she was.

Dare rubbed one aching wrist thoughtfully, grateful that the cuffs had not been difficult to overcome. The lining's material had made them easier for her to slip her way out of.

She rolled off the bed and stepped gingerly toward the wardrobe, forcing her bruised body to move. She must have been tossed around like a bag of feed while she was unconscious. Or Thrice had let the men get a few hits in. Was that why she still felt so sluggish?

Dare shook her head. Clothing first, then answers.

Lavender called her boss a captain, but Dare refused to believe he was the one she was looking for. The one she was told to trust. The Deviant *would* be an apt name for a ship made to indulge the sort of debauchery that was obviously occurring here, but Dare hardly thought any loyal servant of the queen would ally themselves with criminals.

A sound of frustration escaped her lips. One garish sarong the color of a blinding sunrise. Long enough to wrap around her, nowhere near enough material for adequate covering. She would use the sheet but it was far too voluminous to allow for freedom of movement, and Lavender might awaken if she were to attempt to remove her dress. Not that she had the height or narrow frame required to wear it. The sarong would have to do.

Duty first, Dare. She had to get out of this room, find her weapons, or any that were handy, and confront this arrogant captain. A male shout of satisfaction echoed off the walls, covering her bare limbs in a full-bodied blush and hastening her movements.

This "boss-captain" had *much* to answer for.

She wrapped the fabric securely around her, braiding her thick mass of hair while heading for the door. She'd known it would be locked, but with no keyhole in sight, it also appeared impenetrable.

A whirring, distinctly mechanized sound had Dare spinning on her heel, arms raised in self-defense. Bluish-green light emanated from a square-shaped seam above the bed. Another room?

She stepped atop the plush down of the mattress and reached up to slide her fingers along the opening. Air. She could feel it on her skin. Not another room, then. Better. A means of escape.

Prying the panel open proved simple enough, and relief rushed through her when she realized it was a shaft big enough for her to crawl through.

The light was moving away from her, beckoning her to follow. Had she seen the fluttering of tiny wings? Dare hefted herself up into the opening, feeling the cool, smooth metal beneath her hands. The snug confines did not engender a sense of security as she began to crawl through the length of the shaft, though anything was better than being chained and helpless.

"Follow the light, do not think," she muttered under her breath.

But she had to. What *was* it? Far too small to be another dragonfly, yet eerily reminiscent. The more important question had to be, was she on a ship? Was it at sea or still stationary at the docks? The mere idea that they could be away from land at this very moment made her queasy.

She soothed herself with thoughts of her personal patch of garden on the palace grounds. Her hands deep in rich soil, the sun warm on her face, and the queen teasing her from the balcony for dirtying her Chalice uniform.

The buzzing light brightened and lifted out of her sight. What was it? Or who? It moved with purpose, staying just out of view. And then it disappeared altogether.

The shaft must continue upward. Did up mean out? It had to. Dare reached up with one hand, seeking purchase, something to grasp to aid her climb. She found nothing. She stretched farther and heard the groaning give of the thin metal she knelt on. Time seemed to slow, long enough for her to guess what was happening, but not long enough for her to escape her fate.

It collapsed, buckling beneath her, the jagged edges of the broken shaft scraping her thighs and hip as she followed the pieces down into the room below. Pain radiated throughout her body at the jarring landing. Nearly blind with it, she reacted instinctively to the sound of masculine cursing above her body.

Her foot flexed and her leg kicked out behind her forcefully. A sense of satisfaction soothed her discomfort when she connected with muscle and bone.

The man beside her swore with more vigor and stepped back, but Dare didn't take the time to study her victim. Rolling to her feet, she ran toward the floor-to-ceiling window and froze.

"How—?" A memory blinded her for a moment, replacing the incomprehensible vision before her eyes. In her mind she was in one of the turret courtyards of the Copper Palace, searching for Queen Idony at her favorite spot. She'd been winding up an odd-looking toy that Cyrus must have brought back from one of those special missions the queen was always sending him on. She'd set it in the small pond in front of her just as Dare arrived.

"Look," she'd said.

Dare had sat down on the ground beside her obediently, smiling as she watched the ship shuttle across the water. When it started to sink, she reached for it, believing it defective, but the queen stopped her. The ship submerged and continued to make its way around the pond, this time *beneath* the water.

Queen Idony had told her it was called a submersible. "Someday, Dare," she'd whispered. "Someday you and I will travel in one the size of a small city. We will have a grand adventure under the sea."

Dare recalled her laughing reaction. "My queen, when that day comes you should take Cyrus instead. You know I prefer dry land. Besides, I cannot swim."

She blinked rapidly, her awareness returning along with a wave of sadness that swiftly turned to nausea. Black spots filled her vision. "Oh my."

She wasn't in a ship *on* the sea. She was beneath it. There was no way out.

"I find it intriguing that a pocket-sized package with such a talent for escape and violence is afraid of a little water."

Dare strained her neck trying to look at the man standing behind her, and *not* the wall-to-wall, floor-to-ceiling glass holding back the sea.

The wall he currently had her facing.

At least he'd put her in a comfortable chair before he'd bound her to it with the silken curtain cord. Still. She would much rather be looking at *anything* else. The view was disorienting to say the least.

He was, she assumed, the infamous boss Lavender had told her about. Her attempted escape had ironically led her directly to his private chamber.

She'd lost consciousness. She wished she could blame it on the remnants of Thrice's drug, but she knew better. She had fainted at the sight of the sea consuming her, much to her chagrin. Apparently she had been out long enough for him to restrain her once more. Now her arms were bound tightly against her sides to prevent movement or escape.

Lavender had said he was kind to women. A hero. Where was his kindness now? Why was he forcing her to face something that he knew terrified her? Not that she should admit to that weakness. Not to him. Not to anyone.

"I am not afraid of, how did you put it? A *little* water? There is more than a puddle outside your window, sir." She shuddered as she looked up at the endless, watery dark. "Any being without fins would be surprised were they to awake to this view. I am not sure how far we are from Centre City, but I demand you release me. Find the nearest shore. If you require compensation I can arrange it once I am back on land, and I will tell no one of the crimes you are now complicit in."

His chuckle caressed her bare shoulders. Had he come closer? "Why would I do a thing like that? Release you after witnessing the carnage you wrought on Nettles before he caught you? On poor Lavender? And only moments ago, on my leg. I am no fool, *my lady*."

The timbre of his voice was low, disarmingly attractive with the hint of an accent she could not place. It was odd and unfamiliar, and it only intensified her sudden desire to turn around so she could see the face that belonged to the seductive rumble and the complicated puzzle of feelings he was exuding. He was not as easy to read as the others she'd come across since she'd left the palace. That did not bode well for her. Not in her current state.

She shifted in her bindings and winced. The shards of metal must have scraped her legs on her way down. Added to the bruises from her capture, the fog still lingering in her head, and the knots in her stomach brought on by the sea surrounding her, she knew she was not at her best. She would have to be careful not to give too much away.

"My sincerest apologies for harming Lavender. I believed, chained as I was, that I had no alternative. But I am once again confined, and therefore no danger to you or yours. I understand you dispatched Nettles with far less mercy than I, regardless."

His voice hardened. "I did. Perhaps I was too hasty, but I am ever impatient with the ignorant. Kidnapping is not my business. If anything, it endangers my reputation. Thrice and her ilk may have been unaware of that before, but no longer." He hesitated, his voice gentling. "Lavender is fine. In better shape than you. Truth be told, she is in awe of your skills with handcuffs and hopes you'll explain how you did it when you're feeling better. She believes some of her regular visitors would find that little trick . . . stimulating."

She heard the sound of water being wrung out of a cloth and then he was at her side, sliding the warm, damp washrag over her injured thigh before he spoke again. "You are not a prisoner. Not officially. You were confined until I could determine who you truly are and why you are here. Your attempt at escape did not help your cause. I am now more curious about you than I was before. More intrigued."

Dare lowered her chin against her shoulder, catching a glimpse of dark hair as he cleaned off her wound. The same man who bound her was now tending to her? For what reason? "Your curiosity will not be satisfied with me, sir. I have no secrets worth telling." Not unless he was the captain she'd been looking for.

She could feel his attention intensify as his touch slowed. "You are very beautiful. Soft but disarmingly strong. You mentioned compensation. What kind did you have in mind? Are you a runaway? Or did they steal you from your virgin's bed on the Hill? Is there family or a lover who would pay a ransom to see you again?"

Dare's body jerked at the unexpected question. She had to tread this murky water carefully. *Water.* She swallowed weakly. She was *under* water. She attempted a careless shrug. "You are the first to look at me and think me highborn. Before I answer your questions, may I request an answer to mine? Where am I? And who are you?"

He stood again, backing away, but could still sense his stare and that feeling again. The one she wasn't used to. *Excitement. Arousal.* It had to be coming from him.

He hummed, considering. "I suppose that's your right, though I am irrationally insulted that you haven't heard of the Siren. She is one of a kind, after all. But then, secrets are her trade. Inside of her all deeds dark and dangerous are recorded for posterity. Not usually a place for a woman of high birth. Unless, of course, she has a taste for something different. Something base and untamed."

The Siren. This ship was not called Deviant. He was not *her* captain. Relief was quickly followed by regret. She was on the wrong vessel, still no closer to her goal, and she could not tell her captor the truth as to who she was. If he—if *anyone* but the Deviant's captain— were to find out what had happened to the true queen, least of all anyone of the criminal persuasion, anarchy would swiftly follow.

Queen Idony was the light that held the world together. The people's faith, as well as their knowledge of her ever-presence, kept Theorrey running smoothly.

In order to get back on dry land and find the vessel she'd been originally bound for, she would have to attempt to be what Lucy Thrice believed her to be. A shield guard's bastard. Anything more and he would surely use her for his own personal gain. Anyone with noble connections could be bartered for. But a lowborn was quickly forgotten, could not be used because she had nothing to lose. Could make her own bargains.

She relaxed her fists where they'd tightened at her hips. "You have seen me, sir. You know what I am. You know a ransom would be pointless. It is cruel for you to continue to pretend otherwise while lurking in the shadows behind me."

She heard him swear behind her and felt the rope give as he cut it before tossing the knife on the ground at her feet. She eyed it for a moment as she rubbed feeling back into her limbs, but there was not time to reach for it. Large hands gripped her arms, lifting her out of the chair and twirling her around to face him. "I *have* seen you. The color of your eyes, your hair. And I know what you *should* be. The unwanted child of a lusty Wode and a defenseless citizen. Too small for service, too distinctive for anything else. So why do I not believe you are who you seem?"

As soon as the room stopped spinning, the light shining from the sconces along the wall provided her with her first good look at the infamous boss.

He stole her breath.

Had she supposed all criminals would look like Nettles and Thrice? That their foul deeds would somehow show through their inheritance and onto their skin? If so, she would have been wrong. This man was impressive. Imposing. His back and shoulders rivaled her fellow shield guards' massive physiques. If not for his midnight black hair, she would have thought he was one of her own.

She'd always believed Queen Idony the most striking being she'd ever seen, but this man . . . His face . . . She doubted an artisan would be able to truly capture his appeal.

No one on the Hill would say he was handsome. Not in the way the nobles measured such things, with full cheeks, perfectly symmetrical features, and fair skin. His attractive qualities were not that easily defined. He was too hard, his features sharp and chiseled as though by a rough hand.

She studied his strong, currently unshaven jaw and cheekbones. His nose, which must have been broken more than once, and his lips, firm with resolve and frustration. His skin was darkly bronzed, which was not an unusual coloring in itself, but it made those light, crystalline eyes all the more dramatic. Stunning, really. In fact, she could not remember seeing eyes so light a hue before. They were as difficult to fathom as his thoughts.

Unique.

She tore her attention away from his face with difficulty, only to discover his body was just as distracting. He wore a white collarless shirt that was half unbuttoned beneath his burgundy vest, and black pants so snug she should think them vulgar. Instead Dare felt herself struggling for breath again. Who *was* this man?

He laughed at her expression, a deep rich sound that heated her blood. "Are you ready to deliver your judgment? Do I not look the proper part of dangerous criminal? Owner of the *Siren*, nefarious gaming den and brothel beneath the sea? If it helps, you in no way fit the mold of helpless victim, *or* one in my employ, despite your revealing attire. And you seem too clean and taken care of, too healthy and strong—apart from your recent injuries—to be a half-breed from the lower levels."

Dare swallowed the gasp she'd been fighting since his admission. She'd had suspicions, but now that he'd confirmed them she was shocked. The moans of pleasure from the Echo Chamber, Lavender's clothing, the words of Lucy Thrice—it all made sense now. Brothel. An old word for a forbidden business.

From Dare's observations, she knew that on occasion pleasure was sought and given between unsanctioned couples, nobles and lowborn alike. As long as it was consensual and did not result in offspring, the law and its shield guards turned a blind eye.

But there were a few unbreakable rules. No one was to take pleasure from the unwilling. No one of any caste was to cohabitate or produce offspring without the proper protocol and inheritance blood testing. That law was more difficult to enforce, though stringent census records were kept in every city and community in Theorrey. The penalties, if discovered, were severe. Most children born without permission were taken, tested, and placed in lifetime apprenticeships in other cities.

There was also no selling or trading of pleasure permitted—at least, not outside the boundaries of the island chain of Maithuna.

Maithuna was set apart. It existed outside the laws by the grace of the Theorrean Raj. Its production of potent medicinal flowers and herbs, as well as its connection to the nobility in Centre City and beyond, ensured its autonomy.

It was a sinful fact of life that was never spoken of in more than whispers inside the palace walls. Certainly not in front of the queen. Dare herself only knew of its existence because of the stories Cyrus had heard from other Wode who had been, in their opinion, lucky enough to be sent to guard product shipments or visiting nobility.

This was *not* Maithuna, which meant the *Siren's* existence was a violation of the highest order. Whether or not he believed, as everyone else seemed to, that she was born from a violation, she would not allow herself to be purchased or touched by a stranger. "I am no whore, sir."

He leaned closer and his scent surrounded her. A spicy, masculine scent that she found herself inhaling in spite of the situation.

His lips quirked. "I can see that. Though I would argue that none of the women aboard the *Siren* are whores. They are gainfully employed. Free, in fact, to choose whom they wish to pleasure instead of having that choice taken from them."

"Whom, not if. A convenient distinction. And your definition of freedom is difficult to believe from my current point of view." Dare glanced down at the rope lying at her feet, his hands gripping her arms, and wished he would move away. He was too distracting.

"The *Siren* has a schedule to maintain." He sounded reasonable, but she could feel that she had insulted him. That her judgmental tone was doing nothing to alleviate his suspicions. "Her current voyage has just begun."

Bargain with him, Dare. Focus. "Of course, but surely you will need to resupply. If you allow me to leave at your next rendezvous, I would be grateful." She shifted in agitation, sighing heavily. "This place does surface on occasion?"

His broad palms cupped her shoulders, fingers reaching behind her to loosen her braid, and he nodded. "Yes, she surfaces. And I must admit, the prospect of your gratitude is fascinating. Would it come with answers? You introduced yourself to Lavender. Is Dare your true name?"

He was still touching her. Why was he still touching her? "It is the only one I answer to. And your name?"

"Bodhan."

It was dark and exotic. It suited him. She leaned closer instinctively, the heat of his body warming her. What was wrong with her? Why was she so affected by his nearness? And he was affected by hers, as well. That, at least, was obvious to her usually faultless abilities. But he still doubted her.

He tilted his head. "You say you're not of noble birth, yet you are naively arrogant as only a noble can be. I am having difficulty with all the ways you don't add up."

"Ways?" She swallowed, staring at his lips, his chin. Anywhere but into his eyes. He was too observant. Too attentive. She might almost believe he had her abilities, that he could sense she was hiding things. Lying.

Bodhan's thumb traced her ear lightly, and she could not hide her reaction. She shivered.

He smiled. "This way for one. You are not used to a man touching you, not like this. Such a shame. Your skin is soft as cream, unblemished by work or hardship. All others of your claimed station are scarred by life inside and out. And your speech—"

She inhaled sharply, and indignation momentarily quelled her reaction to him. "*All* others? Are you claiming to have met many like me? That the queen's shields, the Wode, are regular offenders of helpless, lowborn women? That they break Theorrean law with impunity?"

He moved as a predator would, pressing her back against the

cool glass, his mouth a breath away. "I see I've angered you. What an anomaly you are. I have met no one like *you* in all of my travels, Dare. Though I have come across dozens of half-breeds hiding cowardly in alleys. Shorn-headed vagabonds begging for passage aboard the *Siren* to escape their plight. Not a one of them would be offended by the hint of a slight against the blue-haired militants the Theorrean Raj unleash on the population. Not a one of them would say the word 'lowborn' in that condescending, elite tone. None but you."

Her breathing was too rapid, her heartbeat too fast. She wished it were anger at his assessment of her rather than a reaction to his nearness, but she knew better. She needed to regain some semblance of control. As much as any woman could in her position.

His fingers threaded through the hair he'd just insulted.

Indigo hair. It was an inheritance marker within all Wode and their descendants, pure-blooded or not. It was not something that could be hidden, but Dare's father had always taught her to be proud of what she was even when the other young guards soared above her in height and ability. And she *was* proud, especially when, at eleven years old, she'd been officially called to become the Queen's Chalice. It was an honor she was never completely sure she deserved. Now more than ever.

A tug on her hair drew her gaze to those glacier blue eyes. His emotions were conflicted but stronger than before. Suspicion mixed with a new protectiveness, curiosity tangled with increasing desire. *Desire.*

She had never sought pleasure before. What she'd sensed on several occasions at the noble galas and shield guard barracks had always been disturbing enough to discourage her curiosity.

There was a time when she'd considered how attractive the Queen's Sword, Cyrus, was when he trained in the gardens. He was, however, too much like a brother to her. They had both been isolated from the world, she more so than he. Still, she imagined Cyrus as much a novice as she was. It had always been impossible to tell since, being one of only three humans in all of Theorrey aware of her ability, he'd always kept his emotions in tight check around her.

Dare hadn't understood what she was missing, the strength and intensity of feeling that existed outside of her isolated experience. In truth, she had felt more raw emotion in the last few days than she had in a lifetime. It was overwhelming, but it also made her feel alive.

Bodhan made her feel alive.

She had known him for the space of a conversation. She was, in point of fact, his prisoner, despite what he said to the contrary. Yet the way he was looking at her, the weight of his body against hers, and the emotions emanating from him, made her tremble. It was not an unwelcome feeling.

His body was hard and hot where he was cradled between her thighs, the silk band of cloth and his pants not barrier enough to keep her from responding. She scolded herself for the reaction. This was not what she was here for. She could not forget that.

"May I have your word? You will let me leave at the soonest opportunity?" She hesitated, then whispered, "Please?"

His brow furrowed, though he did not pull his gaze from her lips. "Please, she says. And with such heartfelt urgency. What is out there for you that is worth the danger you would surely find? That you would wish so desperately to leave perhaps the safest place you could have stumbled upon?"

She pressed her lips together, surprised to find herself tempted to tell him everything despite her resolve only moments before. His stare was mesmerizing, his mouth was close, and his words were so disarmingly kind and sympathetic—too kind for a criminal to utter with any sincerity.

"Bodhan," he said quietly.

"What?"

"Say, 'Please, Bodhan.' You aren't in my employ, so I cannot threaten you with financial loss. You are not my prisoner. If, as my guest, you won't answer my questions, then I would at least have the pleasure of hearing my name on your lips when you beg."

Dare would have told him she didn't beg, that she never had, but his mouth covered hers, stealing her breath for a third time. Her eyes closed and her mouth parted instinctively at the gentle pressure.

Curiosity and something else shimmered to awareness inside her. This was no sloppy, invasive touch, yet it was no cold, lifeless peck, either. Nothing like the kisses she'd witnessed in the past. This was different. A sensual question. A carnal greeting.

If it had been an action of force she would have fought him, bitten his lips, his tongue. Instead Dare found herself straining to get closer, following his mouth, mimicking the movements of his tongue with her own. It was as if something else had taken over her body. Someone else.

Bodhan.

One of his hands came up to touch her cheek, angling her head to deepen the kiss. He moaned against her lips, and Dare felt a rush of excitement that he was as affected as she.

Was this how it always was? This floating sensation? This fire? Her lips felt swollen from his thorough ministrations, her skin tingling everywhere he touched her.

Dare tangled her tongue with his, savoring the taste, the texture of his mouth. It was addictive. Dangerous.

She felt the air caress one of her nipples and pulled back with a gasp to see he had tugged down the too-bright sarong to cup her curving breast. She'd always felt her heavy bosom was a hindrance in a fight, and she'd usually kept herself bound beneath her gold and white Chalice uniform. It had never occurred to her that she could derive pleasure from being touched in this way.

She glanced up to watch his eyes as the ice melted, the blue darkening at the sight of her flesh. Looking down again, she bit her lip, seeing the untouched skin, the tightening nipple through his eyes. She could feel the fine tremor in his fingers as he circled the hardening bud, and its color changed to that of a newly blooming rose.

He growled, lowering his head toward her chest, his breath hot and shallow against her skin. "Perfect."

She arched against him, a cry of surprised pleasure escaping her at the sharp sensation. He closed his teeth around her, tugging lightly before sucking her deeper into his mouth. Fire flared from her breast to her womb, her sex heating as his hips ground into hers. She couldn't think, couldn't breathe.

The palm that had lifted her breast to his mouth slid down her side, calluses scraping sensually over her hip. He shifted, his fingers slipping between her legs to trace a line along her inner thigh.

She lifted her arms to pull him closer, then stilled. She did not know this man. Only moments before he'd had her tied to a chair. What was she doing?

Bodhan must have felt her tense against him. After one last lingering lick, he lifted his head. His narrowed gaze studied the stubborn set of her jaw, the cheeks she knew were flushed with newly awakened passion.

He stepped back and Dare squirmed, covering her damp breast with the sarong, wishing he would look away. Wishing he hadn't stopped. She wanted to be angry, to ask if this was how he sampled all his merchandise. But she could not be a hypocrite. She had wanted him to kiss her. She had wanted more.

She wished heartily she could appear coolly unaffected. Instead her voice trembled like the novice she was. "Please, Bodhan."

His nostrils flared and she looked down, her eyes widening when she noticed the fit of his pants. He was erect, every detail of his shaft outlined in sharp relief against the fabric. She swallowed hard past the tightness in her throat.

"Are you certain? You are a sensual creature, Dare, in spite of your obvious inexperience. A natural. You could do well here." He watched her carefully and shrugged when she raised her chin to glare back in stony silence for reminding her where they were and who he was. "The Siren's loss then. We will not surface until we reach Two Moon Bay. That is a four-day journey. If, at that time, you still wish to leave, you are free to go."

Four days until they surfaced? She blinked rapidly, taking deep, slow breaths. She would *not* faint in front of him again. "I will."

He nodded. "So I've gathered. I must insist on your obedience until then, and your silence as to what you see while you are here. Our clientele pay me handsomely for their privacy."

"I swear by Queen Idony the Ever Young, I will keep your secret."

He smiled. "I notice you do not swear to obey me. You are a puzzle, Dare. I would solve you before this is done." He brushed her breast with the back of his fingers, making her shudder. "Yes," he murmured as he noticed her reaction. "A beautiful puzzle."

He turned to walk away from her, stopping before he opened the door. "You are far beneath the ocean, with armed guards stationed outside. I will send Lavender back to release and clothe you, but do not attempt to leave or use your wiles on my men, or our deal will be null."

"I have no wiles and no wish to use them. You will hardly know I am here."

His low laugh wrapped around her like an embrace. "Dare, you must trust me, if only in this. Every moment you are here, each breath that you take on the Siren . . . I will know."

Dare watched him leave, listening as his low voice gave directions to whoever was standing outside. Her guard. She wasn't as angry as she thought she would be; her relief at his promise was too great.

Would he keep his word? For some reason, she believed he

would. She was not sure why the desire to trust him was so strong, or how she could have reacted to his kiss, his caresses, the way she had. As soon as he touched her, she'd lost her ability to reason. Lost her ability to feel his emotions because her own were overwhelming. It was oddly liberating.

Bodhan was an enigma. He could not have missed her arousal, yet he did not press her. He could have taken her easily—she would not have denied him if he had continued. Yet she was thankful he had not reveled in her weakness. The blow to her pride would have been too great had he taken the last illusion of control she had left.

Her thoughts raced ahead. Four days. In four days she would be in Two Moon Bay. According to the Wode who had been stationed there, it was a favorite port for sailors and traveling traders alike. Surely someone there would know of the Deviant and point her in the right direction.

Then her first kiss beneath the dark, mysterious waters would be nothing more than a memory.

Chapter Three

"She smells like fresh sweets. Tasty. I may save my profit for once to have a lick of *that* treat."

The sultry voice made the small crowd of women surrounding Dare laugh. Even the guard stationed in the open doorway chuckled. She could only be grateful he was facing the other way.

Lavender grinned at her in the long mirror's reflection and Dare tried to return the expression, grateful the woman sported neither bruises nor hard feelings from their earlier encounter. Her smile contorted, interrupted by the gasping need for air as Lavender tightened the laces of the corset she'd brought for her to wear.

"Be good, Seraphina. I think our Dare is shy, in spite of her name." Lavender leaned closer to Dare, the scented oil in her hair and face paint all seeming to blend perfectly with her name and the color of her dress. She whispered in her ear, "Never you mind her, love. She teases everyone. It's just her way. Only been here a few days longer than you this time, and as usual, you'd be thinking *she* ran the place instead of the boss."

The woman in question came closer and Dare turned to greet her, as well as evade the infernal corset session for a few air-gulping moments. When she finally faced her, the hairs on her arms lifted, her skin heated, and she had the oddest sensation she had been punched in the chest.

She was *nothing* like the others. Standing out in the crowd, not simply for her defiance of the women's color-coordinated fashions. Her curved hips were covered in a black crinoline underskirt that she wore instead of a dress, and her full breasts spilled out of a jade corset embroidered with, of all things, golden dragonflies. They drew Dare's gaze, but not nearly as much as the dark oval spots that lined the outside of her arms, disappearing up her neck, behind her subtly pointed ears and short tousled hair that was the shade of a dark ruby when it caught the light. But the spots . . . Dare knew those spots. Knew she would find the same markings up her spine.

Seraphina was a Felidae. A female Felidae with no shame in showing her markings. Showing most of her body, for that matter.

Dare had only been this close to one other of her kind. The queen's personal maid, Nephi. Nephi was a shy, slightly older female, though still quite beautiful. She had always covered her ears with a lace cap and her body with a high-necked, long-sleeved gown. Even on the warmest of days, she'd refused to reveal her markings. The queen adored her, and it was clear Nephi shared her feelings, but to Dare it seemed she was an anomaly. A Felidae who enjoyed the company of humans. Seraphina was obviously another.

The rest of their kind did not usually enjoy mixing outside of their species. With their keen vision, agility, and desire for isolation, they chose to work in the mines and the processing factories that bordered their settlement near the mountains framing Centre City.

Dare knew the queen did not approve of the settlement's borders, fortified as they were with stormfence—the same technology that, with the turn of a crank, electrified the massive entrance gate to Queen's Hill. Neither did Idony approve of the shield guards monitoring the Felidae's comings and goings, or the pending alternative recently put on the table by the science ministry: that they should all be brought in to be tagged as a census alternative.

The Theorrean Raj had never disguised their disregard for the Felidae as a species. They annually denied the settlement elders' requests for improved living standards. For the opportunity to trade fairly. The decisions disgusted and enraged the queen in every instance.

But not enough to disagree.

In fact, since she'd been in the palace, Dare had never heard Idony speak a word aloud in protest. Not when the Raj members, the nobles, and the queen had their annual meeting to discuss Theorrey's future. Nor when the governor from Maithuna brought his harem of chained Felidae females—declawed, tails clipped, and obviously drugged—to the Hill when he was called to negotiate a change in trade conditions.

Idony had hated every moment she was forced to take part in *that* official visit but willed herself to remain silent. Only Dare, because of her abilities, had known the queen's heart. Had felt enough that she knew not to ask her why.

Seraphina's voice brought her back into the moment. "Get a good enough look, pretty girl? Count every silky spot? If you're nice to me, I may even show you my tail."

She came closer, until her cheek was flush against Dare's. She smelled of sex and something unique. Some alluring aroma that made Dare feel strange, liquid. She thought a female's pheromones only affected males of the same species.

Seraphina pressed a soft kiss against her jaw, her tongue slipping out to caress Dare's flesh.

The rough, wet texture made Dare shiver and she leaned closer, hardly aware of her movements, of the fact that she was asking for more.

Seraphina cupped Dare's bare shoulders in her hands, turning her back toward the mirror where she could see them both reflected in the beveled glass. The heat of her bare breasts pressed against Dare's back enticingly.

Dare's eyes, indigo blue to match her hair, were wide and dilated. Her hair had been left down, curls flowing toward the middle of her back in a wild, abandoned style that was so unlike her usual tight braid.

Beside the gloriously colorful Seraphina, Dare should have felt dowdy and plain. But as she studied herself in the mirror, the silver threaded corset that cinched her waist in tight, her own not insignificant breasts plumping above the fabric, she felt intensely female. Powerful. New.

Seraphina lowered her voice, her lips brushing against her teasingly. "But just so you know. If you're *not* nice? I'll show you my claws instead."

The threat left Dare oddly unafraid. There was something in those exotic, kohl-lined green eyes that reminded her of Nephi. Something she trusted instinctively.

"Save it for the men, Phina. Help me get her dress on," Lavender prodded, shattering the moment. Both women lifted the gown, made of the same silver and white material as her underthings, and lowered it over Dare's head.

"My, my. The boss must think to make a fortune on the virgin market. This dress is fit for the eternal queen herself. Maybe you *are* the reason he went off all mysterious." The woman who'd spoken looked at the others, who were nodding thoughtfully.

Dare held up her arms, jerking as Lavender started yet another round of lacing. She missed her Chalice uniform more with each passing moment. It was loose and comfortable. Sexless and laceless.

She would be able to breathe.

"You are mistaken." She gulped her denial along with another quick breath. "I have no idea where he was before I woke up in this place, but it had nothing to do with me. I was taken by a woman named Lucy Thrice and her oafish twits against my will."

Another younger woman in pink came forward with a vigorous nod. "It's true. Our handsome guard, James Stacy?" She blushed as she mentioned his name to the women around her, her gaze darting toward the eavesdropping guard. "He told me Thrice's latest sidekicks drugged and trussed her up, but they'd claimed they had no other choice. She had beaten the two men soundly. Broke a nose and one of their arms. James said the boss shot them both when he found them dumping her, naked and tied up onshore. He let Lucy go free, being that she's a woman and all. You know what a gentleman he is."

She had only beaten Nettles, but Dare wasn't going to contradict the story, not when the women began looking at her differently. When she could feel what they felt. *Admiration. Curiosity.* Emotions preferable to the pity and detached judgment they'd sent her way when Lavender had first brought her to the suite.

It was a dormitory of sorts, still richly decorated but with narrow beds made only for sleeping, the sitting area, and a few small windows revealing the deep water that encased them.

Dare noticed something else. The sconces along the wall emitted light but did not flicker. Neither did she detect the scent of fumes. It seemed the *Siren* was not only offering illegal services, but its entire construct was criminal. Theorrite was the only explanation for a submersible containing the kind of power that was reserved for scientific and royal use alone. How had Bodhan stolen enough to create at this scale without attracting attention?

The women gathered round, peppering her with questions. Where did she learn how to fight? How did she break such a big man's arm? They wanted to know every detail.

All but Seraphina. She stood back, arms crossed, staring at Dare with a challenge in her expression. "The element of surprise will not always work, regardless of your size. You beat the man but you underestimated the woman." She shrugged. "I know Lucy Thrice. She is dangerously clever. A mad chemist with poisons and sleeping draughts, that one. She has enviable survival instincts and is . . . sexually energetic if the mood is right. She was by far the greater threat. All you were in danger of from Nettles was a disappointing prick."

Dare lifted her chin, oddly hurt that this woman she was so drawn to seemed to be mocking her. And ashamed of herself for not being more suspicious of Lucy Thrice. "He would have forced himself on me. No man should take away a woman's control."

Seraphina's exotically slanted eyes glittered like emeralds. "Not in that scenario, of course. Still, my heightened instincts say you would enjoy the wonder of submitting to another. Allowing yourself to be thrown over a man's lap, your skirt tossed above your head as he spanks your sweetly glowing cheeks. No?" She chuckled at Dare's blush. "I admit it isn't *my* first choice. I would much rather be the one giving the spanking, since I've yet to meet a man who is my match. You'd be surprised how easily the biggest toughs fold when I get them alone. How they like to bend over and have me—"

"Well, I think Dare was very brave," Lavender interrupted as a few of the other women laughed bawdily. "I also think she doesn't need to hear about your infamous escapades. Not today."

Seraphina smirked. "I tease, Lavender. You know how I love to tease." She met Dare's gaze, curiosity a living thing in her eyes. "So fair Dare of the bluest hair, if it wasn't for your sake, then why do *you* think our boss disappeared for days without letting anyone know where he was going?"

Dare tilted her head, wondering why everyone was so fascinated with Bodhan's actions. It was, however, a fascination she shared. Everything about him interested her. Intrigued her. Worried her. "How long was he gone?"

"Five days," the lady in pink piped up. "And James said he'd been sure he heard the boss mumbling about treasure, but he came back with his pockets empty." She smirked. "And an armful of you."

Dare's senses went on alert with the information. The treasure she'd made an oath to guard—Queen Idony—had disappeared in that time frame. Could Bodhan have anything to do with the theft of Theorrey's heart?

It was horrifying to think she could have kissed a man, fantasized about a man, who was capable of such villainy. He was a criminal whose trade was based on divining the desires of others. Yet even as those thoughts crossed her mind she doubted their substance.

She would have felt malice in him. Darkness. Surely it would have been clear.

"Look at the gears turning in that brain of hers." The redheaded Felidae licked her lips, meeting Dare's gaze with a speaking wink. "Smart *and* sexy, with a name like Dare? I definitely need to keep my eyes on you."

"Seraphina."

The deep voice startled Dare out of her daze. Seraphina rolled her eyes. "He always interrupts my fun. Look lively ladies, our lord and master has come a-calling. Do I get my whip back tonight? I promise I'll behave."

Bodhan only smiled. "You promise that every night."

Dare watched the vivacious female sway toward where Bodhan stood in the doorway, the guard now gone from view. The movements of Seraphina's hips were more pronounced than they had been moments before. Feline.

She gestured toward Dare with a sweep of her arm. "How true, but she should know that is why you keep taking me back, smart man that you are. Speaking of men, if you were aiming to scare all the exciting clientele away, you have succeeded. You've covered all our new girl's biggest selling points in your best virginal finery."

Dare bit her lip, looking down at her clenched hands, knowing

Bodhan scanned every inch of her, from her silken slippers to her modest bodice with off-the-shoulder sleeves. The outfit did belong more to a ball on Queen's Hill than a brothel. Although her bodice was still lower than she would like.

She refused to meet his eyes. She would not allow him to practice his charm on her once more. A little over three days and she would be free. She doubted their paths would cross again. Surely she could resist this unnatural and decidedly unwelcome attraction until then. And perhaps she could discover his secret. Discover whether or not he was connected to her mission.

The room was filled with silent speculation. Dare could sense the women studying them, wondering at the obvious tension between their boss and the new arrival.

Seraphina chuckled, breaking the silence. "I can see we have all left him speechless. Perhaps we should take Dare downstairs where she will be more appreciated." She moved toward Dare, where she stood by the mirror, but Bodhan's touch on her elbow stopped her.

"That was why I disturbed your privacy. The Siren's parlor is full of men vying to appreciate all of you. As usual, Seraphina, you and your whip are much in demand." His gaze included the other women. "I appreciate the warm welcome you have given our guest, but you are all far too beautiful to stay hidden in your rooms."

He guided them out the door, and Lavender murmured behind her, "He called you our guest, Dare. That means you won't be joining us tonight, more's the pity. You *do* look pretty."

"Dare and I have business to discuss. Don't worry, Lavender, I'll take good care of her." Bodhan followed the group of flamboyant women to a curtained balcony, while Dare and Seraphina lagged behind.

The sounds of muffled male revelry could be heard beyond the velvet drapes. Dare could hear music and the sound of glasses clinking. How many men were down there? Curiosity made her reach out to pull the curtains aside but Seraphina, whose back had been turned away from her, caught her hand before she could touch the fabric.

She shook her head and glanced over her shoulder. "If they see you, catch a glimpse of that lovely head of hair, tonight's free pass will be over. He will be obliged to present you. I am sure neither you, nor our handsome proprietor, would like what happened next."

Bodhan went to the far end of the balcony, where the railing was missing, and pushed a long golden lever forward. Dare heard the distinct sound of gears grinding, and a spiral stairwell appeared, rising from somewhere down below.

The men had obviously taken that as a sign that the night was about to take a more enjoyable turn. The appreciative shouts and applause grew louder, the perspective customers clearly enjoying the drama of the moment. As were the women around her. Dare could feel their expectance, their arousal. She was suddenly grateful she was no longer tied up in the Echo Chamber. Now that she knew the women, listening to their cries of pleasure would be that much more disconcerting.

When the stairs clicked into place, Bodhan turned to face the women once more. "Remember, you are in control. You choose whom you wish to pleasure, whom you wish to pleasure you. If any man's advances are unwelcome, if they offend you in word or deed, I and the Siren's guards are standing by to protect you as always. Now go enjoy."

That didn't sound like the speech of a vulgar seller of flesh. Dare studied the women. They were all gazing up at him as though he were too good to be true. A paragon who was even now directing them to descend the stairs and find a man to seduce.

She shook her head.

Seraphina sauntered past him, looking down at his formfitting trousers before licking her lips. "You are unwise to hide such a talent this far beneath the sea. With your gifts and knowledge, you could run the world. Don't you think so, Dare?"

Dare had a feeling she was not merely speaking of his oratory skills. She decided silence was the most sensible course of action.

Bodhan and Seraphina shared a speaking look before she shrugged, walking slowly, tauntingly, toward the stairs. Try as she might, Dare could not make out her tail beneath the bustled skirt.

When they were alone, Bodhan met her gaze. "Seraphina can be aggressive. I hope she did not distress you."

Dare shook her head, too distracted to hold her tongue. "Not at all, sir. Truly, I am more fascinated than distressed."

His smile was sardonic, his strong jaw shadowed with stubble. It gave him more of a rakish air. "You are not alone in that. I have never seen another female so enjoy her work. This visit she is more voracious than usual. It seems she wishes to sample every pleasure the *Siren* has to offer before the month's end." He came closer. "And I believe I told you, my name is Bodhan."

"Very well, Bodhan."

He held out his arm gallantly. "Good. I enjoy hearing the sound of your voice. So distinctive. As a rule, I've only heard that style of speech from those educated on the Hill. Is that where you were raised?"

She placed her hand on his arm, feeling the muscle beneath her palm, and bit her cheek to hold back a smile. The interrogation had begun, but she could sense the lightness of his mood. She was in no danger at the moment. Though she should have known he would not readily give up.

"Yours is far more distinctive than mine," she demurred. "So distinctive I cannot place it. Will you tell me where you are from as well? If you have been there recently?" His silence made her lips tighten. "Regardless of where I came from, I am here now. I believe

I would have remembered if anyone requested references before tying me up like wild game for a feast."

His arm tensed beneath her fingers, but he didn't argue. She did not ask where they were going. In fact, touching him was once again making it difficult for her to concentrate. She should be taking in every detail, every door and hallway. Yet it seemed a pointless endeavor. There was nowhere to escape to as long as they remained submerged.

After a few moments walking in the opposite direction of the staircase, past the women's suite and farther down the hall, they stood in front of a narrow door she had assumed led to a water or utility closet. When he opened it she looked inside and inhaled sharply.

She attempted to pull away from him. "Unhand me. I had your word you would take me to Two Moon Bay."

He turned his arm to grip her hand in his. "And I will. What is it, Dare? Is the view truly that terrifying?"

The view was an iron gangplank that led to . . . nothing. The abyss. Water above and below and on every side. There was no purchase. No balance. She wondered how she was breathing at all. Why the sea was not crashing in around her . . .

He huffed a surprised breath. "You are shivering. Breathe, woman, and take a closer look. The sides and ceiling are clear, but they are there. The illusion can fool you." He pointed with his free hand. "See there, at the end of the walkway? There is a latch for a door. And can you make out the brass framing a small lit-up room beyond? That is the Siren's lift, a room that takes us up or down, to other levels on the ship. There is even a cushioned bench inside it for you to sit on while you travel." His fingers squeezed hers securely. "I meant to surprise you, to show you something I'd imagined you would enjoy. To show you how beautiful the Siren could be. Not for you to think I—what? Had decided to sacrifice you to some sort of angry sea gods?"

"The thought had crossed my mind." She placed her free hand on her chest, feeling her heart race. A lift. It was merely a lift. She had seen several that led from the Copper Palace to the Theorrean Raj's inner sanctum and science labs below. But this was . . . "How? How does it work? How can mere glass hold back so much water? And I see no winches or wires. What makes it move?"

There was a smile in Bodhan's voice as he guided her down the walkway. "Inquisitive but not confused," he murmured. "Interesting. In answer, I can tell you there is nothing *mere* about my *Siren*. The windows, the lift, every rivet on her frame is unique. The glass is of a special resilience not used or known of in the world above. She is more than she seems. She reminds me of you in that way."

Now that she had regained a few of her scattered wits she noticed the filigreed brass and wood handrail along the plank that led through what seemed to be a short glass tunnel. The watery view was intermittently broken by the delicate brass framing each pane.

His hand on her lower back led her into the small glass room that was the lift itself and closed the door behind them, sealing it with a nerve-inducing finality. Dare looked down, relieved to see a solid floor beneath her feet. Despite the rail and floor and the few latches that dogged the door, she felt as if she were in a soap bubble. Insubstantial. Capable of floating away at any moment.

Breakable.

She had almost no sense of movement when their descent began, save for the hall she'd walked through soaring away overhead and the steel sides of the *Siren* rushing past her as they dropped.

Heightened by the close proximity and the adrenaline of fear, her senses were sharply enhanced. She inhaled his darkly masculine scent, an aroma that was more intense than Seraphina's had been. Spicier.

Dare had a sudden, overwhelming urge to lean against him, to touch him. To bury her nose in his neck and breathe him in. A ridiculous but tantalizing notion, in spite of her current circumstances. Was this den of sin compromising her principles so swiftly, then?

Or was it him? Bodhan, alone, who did this to her?

His thumb caressed the flesh of her hand and she shivered. Perhaps her initial instincts about his abilities with mesmerism were correct. How else could she explain her reaction each time he was near?

She watched him flip open the clasps of the wide leather brace at his wrist, saw a telling glow beneath the fingers of his free hand, and remembered herself. That was no timepiece, but more proof of his criminal behavior. Bodhan, too, was more than he seemed. She would need all of her faculties to discover just how much more, and what, if anything, it had to do with Queen Idony.

"You aren't looking, princess." Something locked into place as the lift stopped mid-journey. "The Siren deserves to be admired."

"I would rather not, thank you. Where are you taking me?"

"On a tour as my guest. We are now in a singular spot on the lift. The spot where you can see the entirety of my lady love and replace your fear with awe. Or have you changed your mind? Would you rather join the others for the evening?"

His threat was subtle but perfectly clear. She could obey, or she could earn her passage with the rest of the women.

Dare followed his instructions and her mouth opened in astonishment. "Impossible."

Someday you and I will travel in one the size of a small city.

The queen's words echoed in her head. The size of a small city, indeed. Though this was no simple windup toy. It was, she had no doubt, more immense, more unique than any ship that floated on the surface above it.

"Not impossible." Bodhan's voice was deep and rich behind her. Close. "The Siren is one of the unsung wonders of the world. Ten stories of wonder. She is a magical marvel of invention created, as everything should be in Theorrey, to be desired and enjoyed."

He might have been describing a lover, the way he spoke of his Siren. But Dare could only agree. She *could* see everything from this vantage point.

A dome of colorfully stained glass topped the decadent vessel like a jeweled crown. Beneath it, light poured out from rows of large brass-framed viewing windows and small round portholes that ran the height and length of the ship. It also pulsed from what had to be the engine room at the far end of the submersible, housing the soul of the beautiful beast.

The iron Leviathan stretched and curved for what appeared to be miles on either side of the lift. Perhaps it was magical, or it could be an illusion of the dark sea—either way it was impressive. The entire submersible seemed to shimmer with light and life. And so much movement.

For a moment she forgot to be afraid, leaning forward against the glass like an eager child and looking up to study the dizzying motion of the utterly improbable brass rings that slowly circled around the girth of the ship's midsection.

An image of the gyroscope in the old scholar Steele's study sprang to mind, though she doubted even he had imagined a version of this magnitude being used. Certainly not for any illicit intentions.

"Who was the Siren's architect? Did you steal this from the science ministry?" She knew the moment she spoke the words they were ill advised. In an instant her tenuous situation and the fragile barrier that trapped her between a tensed male body and certain death seized control of her heartbeat, causing it to race.

His hand slid out of hers, but he didn't step away. "The Siren belongs to me. As a child I watched each bolt fastened, each room

built. We grew up together, she and I. The Theorrean Raj"—he spit
the words as if they soured his tongue—"and all who blindly do their
bidding, are too narrow to *dream* of her. Too focused on themselves.
All charts halt at the reef they call Theorrey's End, in fear of what
lies beyond. They are hypocrites, not creators."

She knew he was watching her closely, could feel his gaze burning her, but she needed him to speak. She had only felt his honesty.
Honest desire. Honest curiosity. And now, honest loathing. "Why
would you say such a thing?"

His hands were caressing her arms almost absently. "Would it
surprise you to know that many of your Raj and their ministers,
when they don't holiday on Maithuna, frequent the Siren?"

It would. They were, after all, the ones who made and amended
the laws without the need of the queen's approval. Was that why
Idony so distrusted them? Why Dare herself was finding it difficult—
since she'd left the safe confines of her home—to obey the laws she'd
been raised to protect?

"Hypocrites, indeed, if it is true. I suppose you hate our eternal
queen as well." Enough to commit treason by kidnapping her? Or
worse? She held her breath, waiting for his answer.

It was sincere. "I love Queen Idony, may she be as ever-blessed as
she is wise. I am *not* fond of those surrounding her. Those that hoard
her light for themselves. None of us—" He cut himself off and
changed subjects abruptly. "But why should we speak of politics tonight? The dress suits you. Seraphina was right. You look like a princess trapped in a tower."

The words took Dare by surprise and she turned to look up at
him for the first time since they entered the cramped confines of the
lift. "I cannot help but feel trapped in this lift, in my current situation, but I am no princess."

His uniquely pale eyes were unnerving, his gaze instantly homing in on the bare flesh of her neck and shoulders. "And I am no prince. Still, you *are* lovely."

She took a deep breath, the action pushing the mounds of her breasts higher above the cut of her gown. It was not as revealing as Lavender's, and was far more modest a design than Seraphina's garb, yet she felt naked. Vulnerable.

"It is near impossible for me to believe you are as untouched as you seem, unless you *were* hidden in some secret, windowless chamber until yesterday." He ran a frustrated hand through his dark hair. "My job is to read people. Who they are. What they desire. You confound me, Princess Dare. I know you are hiding something, but what?"

His job was to read people? She knew he could not have the abilities she had, or he would have acted on her conflicted emotions by now. "Nothing. I am hiding nothing."

He shook his head at her words. "You and I both know better. A suspicious man would believe you a spy sent to drive me insane before you steal my secrets. But which ones? I am in possession of so many."

Dare had not foreseen that her own suspicions would be turned on her. He thought *her* a spy? "You're very open about your secrets with a suspected spy. If I *were* one, I would be an incompetent at best not to get what I wanted from you. However, there is a flaw in your suspicions. Unless my plan included skillfully stumbling into an assault and abduction in order to be brought into your presence, allowing myself to be drugged and manhandled, handcuffed and trapped in this cage of a dress for just the chance to speak to you." She shook her head. "I can assure you I did not ask to be taken so far away from the safety of solid ground and all I know. When we arrive at Two Moon Bay I will depart this admittedly luxurious deathtrap and you'll have no cause to see me again."

His brow furrowed. "I will pretend you did not call the Siren a deathtrap because I know you cannot mean it. Are you on the run, Dare? Is someone after you? If you tell me I might be able to help."

"Other than Lucy Thrice?" She raised one challenging brow, determined not to be swayed by his concern. "Once again, I would be more inclined to answer your questions if you would answer one of mine. Where did your five-day errand take you when you left the Siren?"

Bodhan smiled at her quick rejoinder. It was a wide, wicked smile that should have sent frissons of fear through her body. But it wasn't fear that made her quiver.

"I see you have been speaking to the ladies. They do love a good secret. I, however, know every answer, or lack of same, comes with a price. And at this moment, it seems neither of us is willing to pay." He gestured to the cushioned bench beside them, reminding her of its presence. "If you will not answer my questions, and I will not answer yours, we are at an impasse. Come and sit. The view from here serves more than one purpose. I would show you why pleasure is no crime before you leave us."

She took an instinctive step back, as much as she could, and his smile disappeared. "At some point you will stop treating me as you would Nettles. As though I would hurt you. And then perhaps you will recall that you said you would obey me if I let you leave. My ship, my rules. Will you not honor your word?"

Dare told herself she had to do it for her queen, and it was true. But as she slid around him and lowered herself onto the bench, watching him remove his vest with slow, methodical movements, she silently admitted that it was not the *only* reason.

"*What* are you doing?"

He arched one eyebrow in feigned surprise. "The room is warm, don't you agree? I simply wish to make us both more comfortable."

Bodhan let his vest fall to the floor and she shifted in her seat.

What he was doing had the opposite effect of comfort. She bit her lip. "I have no idea what you mean," she lied, a heated blush spreading across her chest. "My clothing is *far* more constricting than yours and *I* am fine."

He knelt beside her, so tall his light, piercing eyes were nearly level with hers. Mischievous. "You are? That *is* odd, because if anything, I am warmer than I was a moment ago." His hands reached for the top buttons of his shirt.

"Wait." She didn't sound very commanding, but her words were enough to still his fingers.

He chuckled. "Keep breathing, princess. My sense of humor, I've been told, is not as well-honed as I imagine it to be." He reached for the cushion beside her and lifted the hidden lid beneath it. "There is something I want to show you."

She studied the open neck of his shirt longingly and noticed the muscles of his forearms bunching, revealed by his rolled-up sleeves. His hand disappeared for a moment, emerging moments later gripping an odd-looking device.

"What is *that* for?" She knew she sounded breathless, but how could she be blamed? Bodhan was at her feet, his dark cheeks flush with sensual knowledge and his arousal washing over her skin like heated oil. It was too much to ask that she resist.

His graveled voice sealed her fate. "Let me show you."

Please.

Her only saving grace was that she had not uttered the plea aloud.

Chapter Four

"Adjust the lenses."

Dare licked her lower lip, attempting to do as he asked despite her many questions.

Another stolen item. It had to be. The ocularia devices were used exclusively by the Wode. She'd used one herself, to observe the comings and goings around Queen's Hill. Though it had been more for Idony's amusement than true surveillance.

Yet this, too, like the gyroscope, was far more advanced than any she'd seen. Or used. Its clarity through this amount of moving water was fascinating. So it had been stolen and then modified? A part of her wanted to ask, wanted to demand a direct answer. Surely if she did, his defenses would raise and this intimate tension between them would cease.

Was that why she remained silent?

He'd placed the ornate brass device on her head and over her eyes, adjusting the leather straps to fit to her comfortably before she could study the layers of multi-hued lenses. His warm, strong hands over hers, he showed her how to adjust it for the clearest view. Dare did not admit there was no need.

She pushed one lens down, and then the other, seeing the world blur and tightly focus accordingly. She looked past the spinning rings and gasped. Life. The sea was full of shadowy moving figures. How had she missed them? In particular, how had she missed the long, sinuous hunterfish and their smaller, more viciously fanged companions that swarmed in schools, hovering just outside the rings? They stayed away as though there were a physical barrier around the Siren, holding them back as the submersible slowly moved through their domain.

Bodhan's body pressed against her knee, and she could feel his heat through the full fabric of her skirt. "No fear, princess. The sea monsters the sailors shy away from, as well as the fish they hunt, would not survive my Siren's song. Her tune repels them. The design is so ingenious I am envious I did not invent it. Now, look toward the windows, and tell me what you can make out."

Dare found the closest window and looked inside. One small adjustment to the ocularia and it was as if she were right outside, peering in. "Oh my."

His palms were on her thighs now. Had he moved closer? "Describe what you see."

"A lady from the rooms. The one in pink—"

"Coral," he interrupted. "We call her Coral. Is she alone?"

"N-No. There are two men with her. One looks just like . . . Well, he's dressed as a noble. The other is one of your guards." She shouldn't be watching this. She knew it.

And she knew the noble. The youngest son of the Heinwald line. His family would be disgraced if they knew he was in a brothel, shedding his clothes with such swift, shameless haste as Coral and the other man looked on, smiling.

"I should not be watching them."

Bodhan chuckled. "But you are. And despite your protestations, you aren't turning away. Interesting. You have stumbled upon the perfect view, Dare. We wouldn't want to shock you your first time out with Lavender's acrobatics or Seraphina's whips. And yes, you should watch. I will forgive my man James, who is undoubtedly taking his off-duty time to share in Coral's pleasure with her customer, if you do." His voice deepened. "No matter what you see, Dare. What you feel. Do *not* look away. What are they doing now?"

No matter what she felt? By watching them? Or the sensation of Bodhan's own rising arousal as he gripped the fabric of her skirt in his hands?

"They are kissing. The men, both of them, are kissing her. Coral. Taking turns." She took a flustered breath. "She is sitting on a table and James is letting the other man have his turn while he . . . Oh, her skirt . . ."

What was he doing? James had lifted Coral's skirt, spreading her legs as he sat down at the table between them . . . Was he kissing her there? In so intimate a place?

Dare's body was on fire. A part of her knew she should close her eyes, but she could not. She had to watch. Coral's ecstatic expression told Dare that she enjoyed the attention. Reveled in it. In fact, it seemed to inspire her to lean toward the noble who stood ready beside them and kiss his lean, pale torso.

"Dare, before I pressed my lips to yours, had you ever been kissed?"

"Never." Her answer had come quickly. Been too emphatic. But she was far too distracted for caution. For coherent thought. No one had come close to attempting what she saw happening before her eyes. Perhaps it was her duties as Chalice and close ties with the queen. Or her unusual size for a shield guard that kept men away as the Siren repelled the creatures of the deep.

She had never imagined this, let alone wanted to experience it for herself. Until now, she'd had not the first inkling that this kind of world, these types of feelings, existed. "Never," she repeated in a soft, regretful whisper.

Bodhan's fingers caressed her lips tenderly, one slipping just inside her mouth to touch her tongue. It was instinct that closed her lips around him. That sucked in her cheeks and tasted the salt of the sea and something uniquely male. Uniquely Bodhan.

He growled. "I will not lie and say I'm sorry for that. May I kiss you again?"

She tried to turn her head to study him, forgetting the device distorting her view, but he used his palm to keep her facing the noble's room. "Keep watching. You don't have to answer. I can see what you want, Dare. Your skin is flushed, your lips are parted . . . You enjoy watching. I'm glad. It's something we have in common. You want my kiss as well. Another desire we share. Tell me no if you must, but I find I need to taste you, all of you, more than reason should allow."

He wasn't lying. No longer difficult to read, his lust was blinding inside her, merging, intensifying with her own. How could she deny them both? She did not say no, instead moaning softly when he pushed her skirt up to her waist and she heard the tear of the fabric that concealed her sex beneath.

She wanted what he wanted. What Coral was experiencing on the Siren, her back arching off the table as her hand pressed the guard's head greedily against her.

Just once to not be what she was. To be woman, not Wode. To be Bodhan's to do with as he would.

She watched the threesome caress and debauch each other, the experience enhanced by Bodhan's hands sliding up her thighs, spreading them wider for his view.

"Smooth and pale as cream, you are. Nothing to obscure my view. You say you've never been kissed? Here as well? Then I will be the first." He inhaled sharply, his strong body shuddering slightly against hers. "You smell delicious, princess. What are they doing now?"

It took more time than it should have for her to respond. "Coral is . . . Her mouth is on the noble's . . . Bodhan, *please*."

She wasn't sure what she was begging for. For him to touch more of her, to kiss her the way he'd described, or to order her to look away. Either one would be a relief. But he was in no mood for mercy.

"Sucking his cock? James must be jealous. I'm told she can send a man smiling to his grave with that mouth of hers. Can you imagine what it feels like, Dare? To have that power over a man? It *is* power. Most men would spill every secret, toss away every treasure for that kind of pleasure. Trust me, I know."

Her breasts were heaving as she struggled to catch her breath. "Would you?" She remembered the hardness she had felt pressed against her. Would he want that from her? Want her to take him in her mouth? Why did that thought not horrify her?

Bodhan's rasping timbre scraped along her spine. "Do not taunt me, Dare. Not when you're this close, this open." His fingers slid up the damp slit of fabric and his knuckles pressed against her bare sex. "This wet. I think it's time for that second kiss. Watch them, but feel me."

She felt his breath and gasped before his tongue replaced his hand. Was this what James had done? How Coral had felt? Her vision blurred as all her attention centered on the spot where his mouth touched her sex. Licked and sucked her flesh into his mouth, groaning against her skin as though he had never tasted anything as sweet.

Controlling her emotions, separating them from the external so she could use her ability to best aid and comfort the queen, had always been a part of her training. What Bodhan's mouth was doing to her now took away her control.

She prayed he would continue. He must. She knew there was

more. Just as she'd known the first time he touched her. Hadn't she been imagining it since then?

She gasped, focusing once more through the ocularia, unable to resist her curiosity. Coral's mouth had left the noble's body, and James had lifted his head from between her thighs. None, it seemed, was done with the other, despite the satisfied flush on Coral's cheeks.

James stood, the panel of his pants spread open, and Coral locked her legs around his waist, pulling him closer.

Dare's stocking-clad legs had lifted as well, seemingly of their own volition, to rest on Bodhan's broad shoulders. A reaction he showed his approval of with hands that tightened on her skin, his tongue plunging deeper inside her. *Yes.*

James had lifted Coral in his arms, her hips pumping the way Dare's were, even as the other man came into view, standing behind the girl in pink. "Oh . . . *Oh my.*"

Bodhan lifted his mouth, his breathing heavy, his forehead pressed against her thigh. "Good girl. You're still watching." She felt his smile on her skin. "Pleasure for pleasure's sake, my princess, debauched and unlawful, leads to endless combinations. Endless delights. She can have them both, take them both. And she loves it."

She shifted on the cushions, unable to conceive of such an embrace. Bodhan's hands moved, two thick fingers filling her sex, another sliding lower. "Bodhan?"

"You would love it, Dare. You are as passionate as I knew you would be. As curious." His teeth lightly scraped her thigh and she moaned aloud, her face heating when the sound seemed to echo off the walls of the glass room.

"Unfortunately, I do not share with other men. But there are ways." His fingers curled inside her, lifting her off the bench in reaction. "Ways I find myself longing to show you. Positions you've never imagined. Devices that could simulate the sensations . . . Dare, are you doing that on purpose? Trying to distract me?"

Bodhan swore when she thrust against his fingers, all decorum, all shame gone as she matched the rhythm of her hips with the throbbing beat of the need inside her.

The two men were pumping into Coral's willing body with abandon, each of their expressions a study in carnality. She could not feel them, but Dare knew their desire was no stronger than hers. Bodhan's words, his touch, combined with the story line playing out before her eyes took her to a desperate place. She was close to something. To what she'd experienced the first time he'd touched her. More.

He lowered his head once more and his tongue tangled with his fingers to fill her, to give her what she needed. Dare's hands reached down to grip his thick, black hair, seeking purchase in a world turned upside down. His soft, short curls tangled around her fingers while she watched Coral find her ultimate release.

Dare could not help but follow.

She shouted Bodhan's name, lightning arcing through her body as though she'd touched a stormwire. Yet even as the waves washed over her again and again, she knew there was more pleasure to be had. She wanted to touch him, kiss him the way he'd kissed her. She wanted what she'd seen . . . but with Bodhan. Only Bodhan. She did not want to share him, either.

Her hand reached up to take off the ocularia, her head turning as she tried to remove it so she could kiss him. Show him without words what she wanted. Before she could remove it her gaze landed on the largest window of the Siren. The one that she recognized as being in Bodhan's private suite.

And saw Seraphina.

Dare was still quaking, Bodhan drinking in every last drop of her reaction, thoroughly distracted. It took her a moment to register what she was seeing.

The Felidae's presence, her fleet movements, shocked Dare back into her pleasure-addled body like a cold shower of seawater. What was Seraphina doing?

A flitting bluish-green light buzzed around the room, looking chillingly similar to the one that had guided her through the airshaft. It did have wings. What *was* that thing?

Seraphina pulled a pin from her hair and unlocked Bodhan's desk, rifling through the papers within.

Bodhan himself was making his way up her body, his thoughts where hers had been moments before, his hands reaching to move the viewing goggles out of the way.

Seraphina chose that moment to look directly at Dare as though she could see her without aid, even from this distance. She held up one finger to her mouth and winked, disappearing from view with the fluttering light before Dare could blink again.

Bodhan removed the ocularia, his mouth opening passionately on hers. Dare melted against him, giving in to what he was feeling. What he made her feel. How did he distract her with such ease?

He lifted his head. "Let me spend the night seeing how much pleasure you can take. How many firsts I can give you. Come to my bed, Dare."

"No!"

They both froze, neither prepared for her emphatic rejection. Dare had the sudden desire to bury her head in her shaking hands. She'd wanted to say yes more than she should have. But her survival instincts forced her to deny him.

What if Seraphina was still inside? What if she'd found something that told her why he had been gone? If he knew of Queen Idony's whereabouts.

Her body, her heart did not believe he had anything to do with it. He had been sincere when he'd declared his love for the queen. Sincere in his need for Dare.

Her rational mind had a harder time trusting the head of an

unprecedented criminal operation. One with enough funding, trained men, and technical skills to accomplish the deed.

Seraphina's appearance had reemphasized her situation. Reminded her that she needed to stop allowing herself to be distracted. Her objective was too important, not just for herself, but for Theorrey.

All she felt at that realization was regret. "I'm sorry, Bodhan. I-I'm not—"

But he was already standing, reaching for his shirt with a humorless smile. "Not ready? Trying to con the con, princess? I've no wish to be vulgar, but you, my dear, are as wet and ready as a marsh cat in heat."

She flinched, but he wasn't finished. "You are correct, nevertheless. I have no desire to force my attentions on an unwilling woman. This was a bad idea. I'm certain we should get you back inside where it's safe. The Siren is never short of willing company. If I need it, I will find it elsewhere."

Dare's gaze dropped to the straining fabric of his pants. The idea of another woman touching him was untenable, but what could she say to stop him? She had no wiles, no clever retorts. She could do nothing but allow him to grip her elbow, a gentleman's instinct no more personal than a stranger's touch, and set the lift in motion once more to return her to the women's suite.

His grip tightened when she slowed near the door to the women's suite, his strides taking them past. "Isn't this—?"

Bodhan shook his head, his eyes narrowed on the passage ahead. "Despite your protestations of innocence, princess, even you must know I cannot leave you so unattended for your voyage. The women deserve their privacy and my trust. You've earned neither."

Dare shivered. His voice was hard. Devoid of the tenderness and passion it had held only moments before. Her only consolation was that his emotions were not violent. Tightly reined in and frustrated . . . but not violent.

Still, she had to know. "Will I be bound again?"

Bodhan's jaw tightened. "I trust that will not be necessary."

They arrived at his room and he curtly nodded to the guard at the door before pushing his way in with her close to his side. Dare instinctively looked up. The shaft she'd fallen through had already been mended, as if it had never happened. Not that she would choose that route again, but it also meant that, with a guard stationed at the door, Seraphina must have found another way in.

Her body jerked as Bodhan continued forward, his grip still firm on her arm. He did not stop until he'd passed the large, decadent bed and reached the wall on the far side of his bedroom. It was covered with a life-size painting of a woman rising from the sea, reminding Dare of the statuary she had seen when she'd first awoke aboard the Siren.

The sensuality in the painted face seemed to mock her, scorning her rejection of the pleasure she could have had with Bodhan. Dare knew he was not planning to force her. Still, being here with him, in his rooms, her regret for her hesitance grew with each passing moment.

She watched his free hand caress the golden frame, his thick fingers gliding across the grooves with a lover's touch. She'd known that touch for a moment. She wanted it again.

The clicking sound startled her, as did the sudden opening that appeared when the painting slid to the side on unseen hinges.

A room. The painting hid a room?

There were no other ways into the space that she could see. But if there was one hidden alcove, perhaps there was another.

"You'll sleep here," Bodhan interrupted her musings.

Dare studied the stark room. The feather mattress was thin and the furniture spare, but not overly so. There was a high shelf with some strange devices and a single sconce offering dim light. It was the size of her wardrobe at the palace.

She looked up at him, her chin jutting defiantly. "Is this my punishment for refusing your bed?"

She felt her barb hit him, though only a small tic at his temple revealed any outward reaction. He smirked. "I had hoped to spend a more enjoyable evening learning all your secrets, it's true. I do have a reputation to maintain after all." He lifted one shoulder carelessly. "This is merely a room. No prison. You would have stayed where I could keep an eye on you, regardless. You are a mystery I haven't solved yet, princess. I cannot take the risk of leaving you too long with my loose-lipped, overly curious employees."

She recalled something Lavender had said about the bedrooms being safe from the sound devices in the Echo Chamber. "Because you don't spy on the women's suite."

His chuckle was telling. "You see? You already know more than you should." He released her arm and ran a hand through his hair with a rough sigh. "A smarter man would have held you in the lower decks near the guard's bunks. I am in no position to play nursemaid at the moment, there is too much at stake. But in this case I'll have to make an exception."

Nursemaid? Her fingers curled into fists at the implication. "Make none on my account, then, since I am no child."

Suddenly he was close, so close she could feel his body pressing against hers, his still-hard shaft pushing against her stomach and the doorframe digging into her back.

He snared her gaze. "No? Your reactions tell a different story. You don't seem to know what to do with passion when you feel it. And I know you feel it, Dare. Unless, of course, you've changed your mind?"

Had she? Even now, when his words stung her like pinpricks, when he obviously meant to keep her confined, she wanted more of what she'd experienced in the lift. Wanted to experience the ecstasy she'd observed through the ocularia. But did she dare?

Her momentary hesitation took the decision away from her. She felt his self-disgust and disappointment as he stepped back. "Ignore the vulgarity of your host, princess. I will not force my attentions on you again. I can assure you you'll be safe here."

He waited until she took a tentative step into the small room. "The guards will bring your meals, and you can use my facilities to wash. Other than that, I'll have to ask you to endure the cramped quarters for the rest of our journey. For your safety."

As he closed the door Dare thought she heard him mutter, "And my sanity." But she couldn't be sure.

She sighed as she looked around her new quarters. A secret room in a secret brothel beneath the ocean. How far away the Copper Palace seemed now. And how different she felt.

Dare could hear nothing on the other side of the door, but when she focused, she could still feel him. His frustration and his suspicion. His attempt to tamp down his desire.

All emotions she shared.

She should explore the room, find out everything she could about what secrets Bodhan was keeping. Perhaps she could find a way to communicate with the Felidae about what the woman had been after.

But not tonight. Tonight she just wanted to sleep. To shrug off consciousness in hopes that it would ease the ache in her heart, the heat still lingering in her limbs. Perhaps when she woke she would remember that her mission was more important than her emotions. That desire was not in her plans.

She took a deep breath and flinched, realizing there would be no sleep until she figured out how to get out of this corseted contraption without aid.

And until she could get Bodhan out of her head.

*   *   *

The rotund science minister blanched and Bodhan's lips curled into what he knew would be a threatening smile. "I trust you know what I do to those guests who cross the line with a woman in my employ, Minister Jens?"

The minister swallowed, his gaze darting around Bodhan's room as if expecting assassins in every shadow. "I have heard rumors, sir. Only rumors."

Bodhan ceased shuffling the pile of blank papers on his desk and stood abruptly, causing the older man to gasp. He smiled. He enjoyed some parts of his job more than others. "I have heard rumors as well, Minister. Interesting rumors about your *special* experiments. Pet projects that not even your sponsoring Raj member knows about. Isn't he the one who has to approve all your test subjects?"

It was plain that, until this moment, the man had believed he was being dressed down for his aggressive behavior with Ivory and Grey, his regular favorites. Bodhan watched the horror transform the usually powerful man as he realized the knowledge the brothel owner somehow possessed. And what he could do with it.

"We are friends." Bodhan shrugged, his gaze narrowing on his prey despite his casual movements. "We don't need secrets between us, do we?"

"No. No, we don't." The minister wet his dry lips. Waiting.

"Friends respect each other's property and employees, each other's secrets." Bodhan moved closer. "Friends are also willing to be honest. I will start. You can return to the Siren's pleasures. I will ask the ladies to forgive your impropriety and I will *not* send the parchment and proof of your personal experimentation." He paused meaningfully. "If you grant me a favor in return."

The minister's watery eyes were nearly popping out of his head. Bodhan would feel sorry for him, if he weren't quite so disgusted. "Of course, Bodhan. What favor would that be?"

He smiled again. "I haven't decided yet. I will let you know as soon as I do."

"Sir, may I have a moment of your time? My apologies for the interruption, but the matter is urgent."

Bodhan raised one eyebrow without acknowledging his guard. "Minister, we understand each other?"

Minister Jens bobbed his head as though boneless. "Unmistakably."

His sense of satisfaction as he watched the man leave lasted only moments before he was pacing again. It was a habit he had picked up only last night, and already he seemed to be wearing down his carpet. He did not pace. He never paced. But now that he knew Dare was on the other side of the wall, no doubt sleeping the early morning hours away without giving him a second thought . . . He paced.

"Sir?"

He turned toward the head of the Siren's security detail with a terse nod. "James. Before you bring your urgent matter to my attention, I feel the need to share one of my own. I hope you enjoyed yourself the other evening, because if we don't solve this particular problem before we surface in the next few days, I'll be inclined to leave you landlocked on Two Moon Bay."

James stood taller, his expression alert. "Yours to command, sir. Who needs killing? If it's the minister, I'll admit I wouldn't consider that a punishment."

Bodhan chuckled, leaning against the edge of his desk and crossing his arms. "Always admired that about you, James Stacy. It's one of the reasons I put you in charge. Though I've noticed of late your efforts have been half-hearted. I will assume the other half is directly connected with your prick and therefore, the lovely Miss Coral." He shrugged. "Still, even a partial effort should have ensured the security of my suite. A security that has now been breached not once, but twice in the last week alone."

James's cheeks stained with embarrassment or ire, Bodhan wasn't sure which. "Sir, we replaced the broken air shaft, and had 'em bolted up as much as we could . . . Did you say twice, sir?"

Bodhan nodded. "Twice. Last night while you and your lady were getting free jollies off young Heinwald's coin, someone pilfered through my desk. Nothing was taken, since nothing of value is left here when I am not present, but the intent was clear."

He was thinking about her again. She was so close. She had attempted escape once before, but he knew it couldn't have been her. Even if she hadn't been with him all night. And he knew she hadn't left her room. He'd woken at every sound, certain she had found a way to open the door's hidden latch to join him in his bed, only to find himself still alone. Dare was no thief. He'd stake everything on it. She was too honest. Too innocent. Damn it all to the edge and back.

"I need a revised list of our clientele and the men we've recently added to our employ just to be thorough, though I have a suspect in mind." He sighed. "Add a stiff drink and your invaluable insights into why I continue to let Seraphina back on my Siren, and we'll talk no more about your free rides."

James Stacy practically saluted, a darkening on his cheeks that might have been a blush. Yes, he was definitely blushing. "For what my opinion is worth, sir, Seraphina's never pinched from a friend. From you. She knows you'd never let her back on board. We'll find whoever's done this, but so you know . . . I don't aim to cheat you or the ladies, either. Coral and I are in love."

Bodhan turned his back on the besotted guard. "Fine, yes, of course. But before you decide to leave my company and have pinkly hued babies, you should at least know the girl's real name. It could come in handy someday. Now what was it that was so urgent?"

He looked over his shoulder in time to notice James glancing curiously around the room. By now the Siren's staff was no doubt abuzz with ideas about what he'd been doing with their special "guest." His actions were doing nothing to quiet their curiosity. He had requested breakfast for two this morning from the galley before the minister arrived. He hoped it would get here before Dare woke. "Please tell me it has nothing to do with my personal life."

James Stacy shifted uncomfortably but shook his head. "No, sir. You wanted me to keep you informed about the movements of a particular customer. He's made his special request for this evening, sir. The chair and two females, as you expected."

Bodhan felt satisfaction welling inside him. Finally. "Then we shall give him a fine private show, won't we, Mr. Stacy? Exactly what he wants, with an extra guest, of course. He should be pleased to find the Siren's owner a fellow voyeur. Then we'll discover what he knows about the people who've gone missing this year, yes? And who is behind the kidnappings. You know what to do."

James tilted his head. "Which women, sir?"

"Leave that to me. Just make sure the room is properly prepared and attended. And make a batch of our special two-tiered brandy. But first, bring me that list."

His guard nodded and disappeared without another word. Bodhan's grin quickly returned to a grimace. Which women? The customer in question was never easy to please. His first thought was for the free-spirited Seraphina. She was no easy one to control, but business increased tenfold when word spread that she was on board.

Though the Felidae was as well known for her sticky fingers and eavesdropping abilities as she was for her skills at seduction, she had never taken from any in his employ. Her qualities could be used to his advantage in this situation. Especially if she suspected he was aware of her trespass. He couldn't trust her but he could motivate her by offering her something she wanted. In that way, Seraphina was predictable.

If only he could say that about Dare. He had no idea what she wanted, other than off his Siren.

What was he going to do about her? Just release her to her own devices once they reached port? How could he do so with a clear conscience? She was such a tiny thing, ill-equipped for the world around her, despite her surprising strength. Her honest surprise as she discovered each new aspect of her current situation was proof of that. The world was full of dangerous people who would take advantage of her naïveté.

Yet what were Dare's alternatives? Staying here was just as fraught with danger. She could share pleasure for her living, though the idea of anyone laying a hand on her made him reach instinctively for the theorrite pistol concealed in a clasped holster at his thigh.

She could stay with him. An indefinite guest who would soon become privy to all his machinations. The bribery, the secrecy. His secrets shared, while he still knew close to nothing about hers. He suspected many things, but had no tangible proof.

He had ways. It was his business, after all—other people's secrets. A family business he had been proud of, until this one small scrap of a woman looked at him with scorn. Still, he could use his connections to discover the truth about who she was, where she'd come from, without her knowledge.

That would certainly woo her straight into your arms, his inner voice mocked him. He couldn't take away her choices any more than he could accept the authority of the Theorrean Raj. And he wanted *her* to tell him. Strange though it sounded, he wanted Dare to trust him. Not to flinch when he came close, or read dark intent into his every word and action.

Why did it matter?

There was nothing for it but to let her go when the time came.

His life was complicated enough. Each year, each new lost girl in need of a job, each man in need of a second chance or fugitive from the Raj's laws needing to find sanctuary, brought him more complications.

In the beginning his job had seemed so simple. Long-term, but simple. And honorable. Where had he gone wrong? Why had he, unlike his clever predecessor, been stuck collecting so many strays? And why now, of all times, had the confounding, utterly distracting, and inexplicably vulnerable Dare arrived on his Siren? Tied up like a gift meant for him alone.

Or a trap.

Big movements were afoot, rumors he could hardly fathom, and danger for those he cared about at every turn. The news his cousin had shared with him in Newgarren after he'd left the Siren to save him from those greedy, thieving thugs was difficult for him to believe. An old myth was stirring to life in the desert.

Right now, all he could do was focus on his latest target, whose odd proclivities and running mouth would hopefully be his downfall, as well as turn him into Bodhan's involuntary informant.

He ran a hand through his hair. He dared not take the wrong step in this. He needed more information, reliable information that he could use about where the missing had been taken. All shapes, sizes, and genders in every town they frequented. The stories of abductions made no sense. Had no reason he could discern.

Granted, most of them were half-breeds or lowborns who wouldn't be missed as much as the higher castes. But traders were not safe, either. It wasn't unprecedented that the Wode who worked for the science ministry would take people into custody indefinitely, but this was different. People were being taken from their beds, from street corners.

Dare was lucky it was Lucy Thrice, an ordinary criminal, who had taken her for profit. It could have been much worse. She could have simply vanished.

More and more had been disappearing over the last few months until finally, in an action Bodhan could not countenance or forgive, someone had been taken off the Siren itself. A tall, slightly banged-up, self-confessed Wode half-breed who had found his way on board for a short trip, and ended up with more than he'd bargained for.

Bodhan's eyes narrowed, staring out the window at nothing. Wode.

That man had appeared near as dazed by his surroundings as Dare, though he'd hidden it a hell of a lot better. He'd also come of his own volition, with goods to trade and the knowledge of how to contact the Siren. Bodhan recalled it being suspicious that the man had seemed surprised it actually existed.

He frowned. Apart from his height and shaved head, the half-breed seemed more like Dare than chance should allow. Intelligent. Curious. And he didn't fit, either. How had that comparison evaded him until now? Was there a connection between them?

His door opened and Bodhan whirled on his booted heel, grabbing for James's collar a bit too roughly. The paper in the guard's hands rattled. "Our missing passenger a few months back. The Wode bastard. Do you remember his name?"

James chuckled nervously. "What? Oh, sure. Of course. The boys and I took him under our wing, it being his first time on and all. Almost asked you to hire him, he'd looked so down on his luck, but then he disappeared."

"I remember, James. Clearly. His name," Bodhan spoke through gritted teeth, reminding himself that he was known for his patience. Famous for it. "What was his name?"

"C-Cyril? Or Silas I think? No, *Cyrus*. That's it. I remember because the night we got him drunk enough to talk to Grey and Ivory, who were both giving him the eye, he went and bragged about having a cock the size of a sword." Bodhan let James go and the guard took a nervous step back, a wary smile on his face. "Cyrus the Sword, he called himself. We told him dagger or sword, it's still all about skill."

Bodhan shook his head absently. "I was distracted during that trip, but he was a bit of a prig, wasn't he? More like the nobles who refuse our services than an abused stray."

James Stacy's shoulders relaxed and his eyes sparkled. "He was nice enough that he didn't deserve to be taken, but he was upright and tight for a certainty. He ended up turning down all comers and drove Seraphina herself crazy. I seem to recall her sniffing after him. She loves a challenge. But even I was surprised at how often *he* rejected *her*. She's not used to that, you know."

Yes, Seraphina had been on board then as well. And just as interested in Dare now as James said she had been in the man. Damn. More than chance indeed. He now knew for certain that Seraphina would be one of the women he chose for the evening.

"James, I've changed my mind. Whoever it was sneaking about my suite has nothing but the knowledge that I leave sweets and customer complaints in my desk. We'll worry about security after we surface."

Another guard knocked on the door, balancing a tray of food delicately in his large, awkward grasp. Bodhan offered the man a genuine smile. "At last. It looks good."

He hoped Dare thought so.

James and the guard exchange knowing smirks, and Bodhan scowled at them. "Is something amusing?"

"No, sir." James' smirk disappeared and the other guard made a hasty exit.

Bodhan lifted an eyebrow. "Spit it out."

James Stacy shrugged. "Coral said everyone is talking about you and the girl . . . I mean, the way you and she . . ." He raised his hands as if to ward off Bodhan's expression. "Women do love to speculate, sir."

"The women aren't paid to speculate. They are paid to distract and please our passengers and indulge their whims. Let them know that in the future, restraint concerning speculation about me is strongly recommended."

"Did you still want that drink, sir?"

Bodhan took a breath, offering an olive branch. "Relax, James. I am not myself today. And this food will do to soothe your beast of a boss. You can go now. I'll let you know when I've chosen the women I'll need for this evening."

"Yes, sir. I'll just leave this with you." James set down the paperwork he'd been asked for and headed out of the room once more.

The door had no sooner closed behind him than the female voice that haunted his dreams spoke up behind him. "I volunteer."

Chapter Five

Dare felt his surprise through the blood pounding in her ears and the intensity of her own emotions.

She'd barely slept, too aware of the man on the other side of the hidden door. Too tempted to join him. Instead, she'd found one of his shirts in a small chest in the corner of her sleeping chamber and put it on after working her way out of the layers of her gown and corset. Then she'd proceeded to study every inch of the room, the devices on the shelves, and each seam of the wall for an alternate entry point.

It hadn't taken long to discover the latter. Minute metallic shavings beside the narrow vent that allowed air to circulate through the room was all the proof Dare needed. Seraphina must share her penchant for climbing through air ducts. She was, however, far better at it than Dare had been. There was no way she could imagine squeezing through the narrow aperture, yet Seraphina had done it. For folly? Or something more nefarious?

The devices were unusual and varied, one seeming to have no relation to the other. At least, none she could discern. They certainly gave her no clue as to what this room was used for.

There was a small board that seemed to be a puzzle game. Its strange, maze-like structure and miniature steel ball that journeyed through it had distracted Dare for half the night without being solved.

Another device looked to be more dangerous. It was made of smooth swirling desert glass, similar to the jewelry she'd seen at the square, only this piece was long and thick as a bottle's neck. When the small brass key was wound at the base, the shaft's tiny internal mechanism began to hum and flicker with life, giving off a shock that reminded her of the stormgate technology. When her fingers touched it, however, it did not cause pain. Just a strong tingling sensation that spread throughout her limbs. If it was a weapon, its smoothly rounded end made it an awkward and ineffectual one. But what else could it be? Without context the devices told her nothing, held no secrets. She was no closer to understanding Bodhan or his activities than she had been yesterday.

When she could wait no longer, she had studied the door, finding the latch to open it from the inside without much difficulty.

So he'd told the truth. This wasn't her prison.

She'd heard voices as soon as the painting began its silent slide to the side. No one noticed her. Bodhan had been too busy threatening a science minister when his guard had come in, concealing the sound of her arrival.

Dare had stayed half hidden by the painting, her heart in her throat as she was thrown by one revelation after another.

Bodhan already knew someone had been in his room. Already suspected Seraphina. More importantly, people had gone missing, and he was planning on entertaining a man he believed had information about them. Were the abductions related to Queen Idony? If so, Bodhan's desire to know more surely proved his innocence. Didn't it?

She'd almost revealed herself the first time James disappeared, but something stopped her. She wasn't sure she was ready to face him, and not just because of her state of undress.

Dare felt vulnerable. The intensity of Bodhan's emotions were heightening her own. She'd felt sure he would hear the shortening of her breath, her heart pounding. Sure he would turn around and see her in the shadows. But he didn't.

When James returned Dare was thankful she'd remained out of sight. They mentioned Cyrus. It had to be her companion guard. Had the Queen's Sword been aboard the Siren in disguise, and then taken away against his will?

The instant she'd heard his name her resolve returned. She was Wode. More than that, she was the Queen's Chalice. She may be underwater, but she was never helpless.

When he remained silent she lifted her chin and raised her voice. "I said, I volunteer."

Bodhan did not pretend to misunderstand, though his expression was dubious. "Blushing virgin to whore overnight? Were the accommodations that uncomfortable, or have I underestimated the Siren's seductive call?"

She blushed, thankful he had turned, offering her his back as he uncovered the platters of food on the desk methodically. "I believe there is an old saying about making decisions on an empty stomach. Surely it applies to such a dramatic change."

She stepped closer, drawn by her desire to help as well as the aroma of freshly baked bread. "You said people have gone missing? Taken against their will?" People that included Cyrus. She was no whore, but there was much she would risk to save her companion guard.

His chuckle caressed her. "I knew I should have confined you below. Though I can only imagine what the guards discuss down there." He glanced over his shoulder, slipping a wedge of queensfruit between his lips and chewing. "As to my private conversation, abductions happen all the time, princess. You are proof enough of that."

"These are different." She could feel the truth in her words, knew from what she sensed in him that she was right. "And someone like me was taken off the Siren. You just said so."

He turned back, his expression sobering. "Someone very much like you. Curiously so. Although, he was never in any danger of being deflowered or harmed. A man of his size could more than handle himself. At least, that was what I mistakenly believed. You are a different story. Regardless of what you did to your captors, to me, you could not protect yourself from every male on board were I to reveal you to them."

Had he moved closer or had she? "Just one. I could protect myself from one man. And I do not believe you would allow anyone to hurt me."

Did she truly believe that? Did she trust that he would protect her? She barely knew him, and what she did know should have made her wary. He was a rogue, a thief, and a seller of pleasure. And more than that, he was one of the last people to see Cyrus alive.

Could he still be *alive*? After all this time? Was it fate that had thrown her so far off course—perhaps the queen herself, guiding Dare to find her Sword, to ensure her own safe return?

Bodhan shook his head. "You must have been sent to test me. Or damn me. You stand here, in nothing but a man's shirt with your hair wild from sleep, and attest to my honor. You trust me to protect your virtue and yet share none of your secrets." He sighed. "Of course you are correct. I would never let anyone hurt you. But tell me, Dare . . . who is it that will protect you from me?"

She smiled. She could not help herself. It seemed he was going to give in. "James Stacy?"

He pulled out his desk chair and guided her to it, setting a full plate of food in front of her. "Never wager on it. Eat. Before I change my mind and throw you back in your room. It is lucky for you, this particular gentleman doesn't enjoy the physical act itself. He only requires the performance, preferably between two women. Two unique women. And if there is one thing you are, Dare, it is unique."

Dare choked on the piece of bread she'd been hungrily devouring. "Two women? Together?"

Bodhan's expression heated, making Dare intensely aware that she was naked beneath a thin, white shirt that smelled of him. "You volunteered." He winked, leaning over her to steal a slice of cured meat. "But if it eases your mind, Seraphina can be gentle if the occasion requires it of her."

Dare paled, recalling the Felidae's provocative behavior. She could only hope Bodhan still held possession of Seraphina's whip, and that her own lack of skill was not too apparent. If there was a man aboard who knew Cyrus's fate, she would find out tonight. One way or another.

"Lesson one, fair Dare, is to not seem quite so terrified by my presence. Some men enjoy fear, but you will take all the fun out of *my* evening, I can assure you."

Dare blinked, startled. She'd been staring again, not at Seraphina but at the contraption in the center of the room beside her.

The chair.

"I am not scared of you. I am just unused to—" She made a weak gesture toward the offending object, then toward herself, unable to find the words.

Seraphina licked her lips. "Fornication? Debauchery? Lust? Any of those will do."

Dare nodded and crossed her arms protectively over her breasts, once more pushed up and out in an unnatural fashion by the corset she'd been given to wear when she was escorted to this guest room. That, along with a sheer pair of lace-trimmed bloomers completed her degrading ensemble.

Was this what Bodhan had wanted her to wear? In front of other people? Other men? She supposed after her eager plea to participate in seducing information out of one of his customers, he had no reason to think she would demure.

"I'm sorry, Seraphina. I'll do my best."

Stunningly green eyes sparked with laughter and the Felidae smiled. "I'm sure you will. You can call me Phina, Dare. We will be getting to know each other much better, after all, and I prefer it. No need to be formal, not you and I, yes? Certainly not now, when I know you kept my secret."

Dare watched the woman place one of her long, agile legs on an arm of the chair, unclasping her garter and rolling down her stockings to reveal the smooth, leanly muscled limb. "Secret?"

Phina lifted her eyes to the ceiling and shook her head. "You saw me in his suite at the same time I saw his head buried between your pretty pale thighs. Bodhan has a suspicion it was me but he's not sure. I could smell it. That means you did not tell him I was the one who found my way into his rooms. You could have, but you didn't. If I were an honorable sort I might think I was in your debt."

She smirked, but Dare felt the bitterness beneath her words. "Alas, I'm just one of those Spotted Spines. You know you can't trust me to pay you back. I do, however, know how to give a good time. And I can play tamed pet, which is, I believe, what your Bodhan wants me to do with you tonight. But it's not because I am doing him any favors. His goals and mine merely coincide this evening."

Dare forgot her nerves and shook her head. "You are more than that. And he is not *my* Bodhan."

The tilt of Phina's head made her look like a true feline, as if she were scenting the air around her. "You believe half of what you say and wish the latter was a lie. You don't have to wish, fair Dare. He wants you more than a man in his position should."

She finished removing her stockings, leaving herself clad in nothing but a thin, emerald chemise that fell to her knees. An oddly feminine choice for her that made Dare wonder if they'd each dressed in the right costumes for tonight's performance.

"I'm someone new," she muttered. "He does not know my secrets yet."

"The boss has never been with any of us, you know. Not even when we were new. Never shown the slightest interest apart from brotherly concern." Phina turned and Dare could see the bulge of her tail, as well as the dark spots painted up her spine. "I always swore he was either impeccably discreet or a windup automaton."

Dare lifted her brows in disbelief but Phina just shrugged, turning to lean against the chair. "It's true. I usually have to use my whip to keep the men at bay. It's a lovely curse of mine. But not him. He is a stickler for rules. As long as he is the one making them, of course. Since I can practically taste your unaccosted purity, you no doubt have him twisting for it. Especially after the tease you gave him last night." She chuckled softly again and lowered her voice. "You can use that to your advantage."

"Use what?"

Phina studied her. "Come closer and I'll tell you. I promise neither the chair nor I will bite. Yet." When Dare obeyed, coming close enough to smell the arousing aroma that always seemed to hover in the air around the Felidae, Phina lifted one hand to caress her cheek. "His lust for you. Other than a sharp blade, a man's lust is the best weapon a woman can have outside of Centre City. *If* you are as curious about the boss as I am." Her face took on a playful expression. "And I know you are. He is full of delectable secrets. His last disappearance is just one of many since I've known him. I'd believed he was having a scandalous and secretive affair, but now that you're here—now that we both know that we are giving a performance tonight for someone Bodhan cannot stand—I can see I was mistaken. You could discover the truth for all of us with a wink and a flash of skin. Lust loosens lips faster than the expensive rot they serve downstairs."

The Felidae's green eyes glazed over for a moment, lost in thought. "Lust can blind us all at times."

Dare shook her head, her smile shy. "Lust is your weapon, not mine. I have no training."

Phina lowered her hand to Dare's hip and squeezed. "Something we can remedy with ease."

"Bodhan, you've picked the two players well. They are so eager they have begun without us."

Seraphina shifted her body so most of Dare was concealed. An oddly protective act that she could only be grateful for. As soon as she heard the stranger's grating voice, she'd been frozen by anxiety. How would he react when he saw her? If everyone's warnings were to be believed, her hair alone could cause him to change his mind about what he wanted for tonight's performance.

She could hear a smile in Bodhan's voice, but the tension no one but she could feel was doing nothing to ease her nerves. "Have I ever failed to deliver, Lennis? Sit, and allow Seraphina to pour you a drink. I must see to my special surprise."

Seraphina did not move until Bodhan arrived to take her place, successfully keeping Dare shielded from the new arrival. His hands cupped her shoulders, tightening to a near painful degree when he realized what she was wearing.

His voice was low and dark. "Who put you in this?"

She licked her lips and swallowed past the dryness in her throat. "The guard that brought me. He said the women had assured him it would fit me."

He swore under his breath. "I should never have agreed to this. I can call in James to take you out. Get another girl. There is still time."

His concern washed over her like a warm breeze and stopped her shivering. Even with how much he felt was at stake, he was willing to protect her from this.

But there was no more time.

Lennis, the client, had apparently run out of patience. "I demand to be shown my surprise, Bodhan. You know how I hate to be kept waiting. Who will our dirty Felidae be tormenting for my pleasure?"

Dare forced her breathing to slow. Forced herself to remember that this was for Cyrus. For the queen and all her subjects who had been taken against their will. She took a step back, away from Bodhan's touch, and he lowered his hands with a hesitation she could feel as if it were her own.

"Lennis, you love the rare and unusual. Tonight, I think you will have to admit I have surpassed even your expectations." He stepped to the side, his shoulders relaxing and roguish, sensual smile returning. "This . . . is Dare."

She forced her hands to remain at her sides and kept her chin up by sheer force of will. His shock hit her before her eyes could even focus on him. He wasn't a noble. At least, not from any family she recognized. Though he did try and dress the part. His suit hung on his slender form. His long brown hair draped dully over narrow shoulders and framed a face made up to look healthy with rouges and tonics. But Dare could still see the yellowish tint to his flesh that he'd worked to hide.

Cyrus could have crushed him with one hand. How could he be connected to the abduction of the Queen's Sword?

Lennis grinned, his body shifting with excitement like a bouncing child's. "Bodhan, you are a wonder. How do you do it? Look at her. No scars. All her hair and teeth. You found yourself a half-breed that looks like she's never been touched. The infamous Felidae

Seraphina and an almost-Wode. All for me. I should have tried the tables before we came up for the night. Luck is with me."

Dare watched Seraphina rub herself against the insipid man as though he were irresistible, though Dare believed she was beginning to understand the Felidae's ways. She was ensuring he received the full affect of her pheromones. That he was appropriately dazed.

She purred into his ear. "She doesn't just look the part. She *is* an innocent. You know I can tell." She parted her lips to show him her sharp, white teeth. "As soon as you give me permission I will be the first to introduce her to passion. For you."

The man rubbed his hands together and Dare cringed. Her only solace was in knowing Seraphina knew how to play this game, and that Bodhan was jealous of how Lennis was ogling her.

"Seraphina." Bodhan's voice was harsher than she was used to. "Put her in the chair."

Oh, Idony. What was she to do? She bit her lip, tasting blood. Whatever she must to get out of this situation intact, to give Bodhan the time he needed to steal his secrets.

Was it mere days before that she was one of the highest-ranking Wode, esteemed above all others for her duty and honor to the queen? She'd had no idea this world existed, and now she was a part of it. A voluntary part of Bodhan's deceptions.

The two men sat in comfortable loungers, a large bottle of liquor on the table between them as Seraphina took her hand and led her to the intimidating contraption.

The chair was made of copper and wood. It had arms and a seat with leather padding, but it was the legs of the chair Dare was focused on. Were her feet supposed to go there? Spread out like that?

Seraphina growled softly in her ear. "Just hold on tight and follow my lead. If you're a good girl I will tell you everything they are saying. I do owe you after all."

The men were speaking in low tones Dare could not discern. She

could feel the sick, cloying lust of Lennis, as well as the more complicated layers of Bodhan's emotions, but she couldn't hear a word.

A Felidae, however, could not only see through water, she could
hear for miles. Dare nodded, allowing Phina to guide her into
position.

Once her legs were on the wooden slats that extended from the
chair, Phina pushed a lever on the side. The action triggered something that caused her legs to spread further apart, completely revealing her to the men's view.

Her fingernails dug into the chair's arms as her flesh heated with
embarrassment. All that stood between their gaze and her bare flesh
was the thinnest of materials. She may as well have been naked.

Lennis made a high-pitched noise of pleasure. "Tear that fabric
open and let us see if the half-breed has any cunny curls."

Seraphina purred and held up her hand, allowing him to see her
sharpened nails extend. "Of course, handsome. Let me get her comfortable first."

She leaned over Dare and pushed another lever behind her.
"Don't listen to him," she breathed sensually. "Just enjoy what I'm
going to do to you and think about how crazed Bodhan will be while
he watches. I can smell him, fair Dare. He's hungry."

The chair leaned back far enough that, unless Dare lifted her
head, she wouldn't have to stare at Lennis. Without knowing what
was going on, all she could do was feel.

The sound of tearing fabric followed by a cool breath on her sex
told her Phina had done as the man had requested. In the brightly lit
room, all eyes were on her. Seeing what no one but Bodhan had had
seen, had tasted, in the lift. The bare skin that surrounded her sex.
Bodhan's desire and possessiveness blew against her like a heated
breath of air, making her shiver.

"Hmm, just like a pure Wode, then." Lennis almost sounded disappointed. "I always hope the inheritance mix'll make them different

somehow. I know your Felidae has fucked her share of full-blooded Wode before. Maybe your novice tastes different than the others, eh, Bodhan?"

He wanted to kill the little man.

Bodhan's feelings had become so intense she could hear them clearly. With every moment that passed he had to control his desire to maim, though Lennis would never know it from their conversation. "Delicious idea. Seraphina, give her a thorough tasting while Lennis and I enjoy the view."

Dare's head lifted at that, snaring Bodhan's icy blue gaze from across the room. Despite her abilities, his words still hurt her. That he could let someone else . . .

A subtle tightening of Phina's fingers around her thighs drew her attention. "The show, Dare. Pretend to enjoy it until you do." Phina's smile was sensual. "I know I will. Pretend and let him work without worrying he's scarring you for life."

Phina placed soft, open-mouthed kisses on the skin of her thigh, now bared for all to see. Dare whimpered, closing her eyes. It felt . . . good. Gentle. Feminine. Warm.

Phina's voice vibrated against her skin. "You taste as unique as you smell, fair Dare. Wonderful. And Lennis is already drunk and distracted. Bodhan knows just how to start his bragging. He's telling him how good he is at acquiring people for the Siren."

Dare moaned when Phina's rough tongue stroked the crease of her sex. Bodhan had done this. Tasted her like this. And now he was watching her. Wanting her. Wanting to taste her again.

"Touch your breasts, Dare. Touch them and show them you are responding to me." Phina shifted position, the sound of her chemise shifting Dare's only warning before the soft fur of her tail was caressing Dare's arm. "Trust me."

Her eyes opened halfway, feeling hooded and heavy as she watched the tail wrap around her wrist. It felt heavenly. And Phina's emotions were kind. Wary but kind, with an intriguing thread of true arousal. It was a tantalizing combination. She would do what the Felidae asked.

Dare reached up to caress the bare skin above her corset and sensed Phina smile against her flesh. "That's right. Touch them the way you want him to. The way you need him to. Bodhan is struggling now. But he's done enough. Lennis cannot stop talking about his use of independent procurers. How much money he's been given to be careful, to never choose the same place or same person to carry out their deeds twice. How he and his partner Mul—"

Phina stopped talking, her tail stiff and trembling. Dare's senses picked up Phina's sudden rage. She wasn't sure why, but she knew without a doubt that Seraphina was going to leap across the room and kill the perverted Lennis. She had to stop her.

Dare reached down and, with far more courage than she was feeling, tangled her fingers in Phina's hair. She raised her voice so the men could hear. "Do that again, Phina. *Please*. It feels so good."

Phina's green eyes widened, then narrowed suspiciously. She'd been doing nothing. Dare tried to send a warning expression. They needed to know about the people involved. Needed to know where they were being taken.

But Dare had distracted Lennis. "What did she do? Let me see it again. Better yet, can we fuck her with something? Seraphina can fill her with her tail. Or we can use one of your special devices, yes, Bodhan? One of those stormcocks made of glass that would give her all those heavenly little shocks."

He stood up, weaving a little as he moved away from Bodhan's restraining hand and attempted to unbutton his pants. "I'm tempted to do the deed myself, and damn restraint. How often does one come across such an undamaged half-breed? Such pretty blue hair and so small she couldn't put up much of a fight. How much more will it cost? I will pay any price."

Phina got up slowly, keeping her eyes on Dare, who shook her head. For some reason, she did not believe Phina would be able to restrain herself. Whatever he'd said to set her off felt . . . personal. Bodhan was hardly faring better. The idea of this man touching her enraged him.

"Unfortunately, that was not a part of the arrangement, Lennis. You know the rules."

Dare sat up and watched Bodhan walk toward the drunken man, his movements wary but his smile still firmly in place. "Though you don't need my Siren. From what you've told me you could have the most skilled procurer go out and get you any virginal flower you desired."

Lennis frowned like a petulant child and backed away from Bodhan. Closer to the chair. "They aren't for me, you simpleton. I'm paid to bag them not bring them to my bed. I'm not allowed to touch them. Sure, we can rough 'em up if they struggle, but for the most part, we're just meant to send them to the Avi—well, to get them. I don't know where they go from there, but it certainly isn't home with me."

His feelings were confused. He wasn't sure why he'd said so much. He'd almost told them about the desert.

Dare slid out of the chair, heedless of her state of disarray, and moved around the dangerously still Phina to face him. His eyes were dilated, hard to read, but his emotions were strong enough for her to hear the confusion of his thoughts. And they were confused, too much so from one simple drink.

Dare looked up at Bodhan in shock. "You drugged him."

Phina put a hand on her arm but Dare shook it off. "You drugged him, and whatever it was, it was too much. His mind is jumbled and he's too muddled to think, let alone control himself. But he was lying. He knows exactly where they take them."

"And how, by Theorrey's End, did you figure all that out while sitting in that damned chair?" Bodhan's growl was intimidating, as were the suspicions she could feel slicing her skin like lashes from a whip.

"Trust me. I just do." She looked up at Lennis. "You and your partner. Where do you take the people you abduct? You said Avi. Avici? The desert. Do you just dump them there or is there a reason? Do you leave them on the black sand to die?"

Lennis was looking panicked, his head shaking so vehemently that his hair went flying. "How do you know about the desert? Spying? You were spying on me?"

Dare had to take a chance. "Do you know who was responsible for abducting the man from the Siren? Did they take him to the desert as well?"

She focused, willing him to panic. Willing his emotions to strengthen so she could read them more clearly.

Not him. He didn't know. Not him.

Dare sighed, her heart aching. "It must have been his partner. He had no idea."

Lennis raised his hand as if to strike her. "How dare you! I will show you how a half-breed should speak to her betters."

Before Dare could raise her hands in defense, Bodhan was there. Dare saw the blood pouring from the other man's nose before he fell to the ground and was surprised that she hadn't needed to defend herself.

"Seraphina, back away."

Dare looked up to find Bodhan standing over the prone Lennis, his hands up to ward off the growling Phina. "He's a murderer, boss. We've heard enough. I'd just like to pay him back in kind."

"Not tonight. My ship, my rules, remember? Dare, the blanket on the back of my lounger. Cover yourself. *Now.*" Bodhan never took his eyes away from the Felidae, but he raised his voice. "James Stacy."

Dare instinctively obeyed as the door slammed inward and James and several guards poured through the opening, swords and guns in hand. "Sir?"

Bodhan kicked Lennis with his boot. "Pour a bit more of our special brew down his throat and post a guard at his door in case he wakes. I want him unconscious with no memory of what happened tonight until we surface, is that understood?"

James nodded. "Perfectly, sir. Anything else?"

Bodhan's expression was grim. "Yes. Seraphina will be returned to the women's suite for the duration. No customers, no special requests, no exceptions. Dare will be taken below, where I entrust you personally with her safety and care. A hair is touched on her little blue head and everyone will pay. Again, am I understood?"

James paled, but nodded again. "Yes, sir." He hesitated. "Are you sure?"

Dare wrapped herself protectively in the blanket, hating the expression in Bodhan's eyes when he looked at her. So much distrust. He'd been truly concerned for her safety when Lennis attempted to strike her. She had the strangest sensation it was that emotion that had made his decision, more than the way she'd behaved.

She'd said too much. Asked too many questions. Both Phina and Bodhan were looking at her as though they had never seen her before. They could not know about her abilities. No one could.

His lips barely moved. "What I am sure of is that I don't pay you to question my orders. Take her. And get her something decent to wear."

She saw Seraphina shake her head in stunned surprise as James led Dare out of the room. Was she surprised he had sent her away? Or that he had not allowed Seraphina to question her the way she now obviously wanted to?

Only three things were certain. If Lennis's partner had abducted Cyrus, he had been taken to the desert. Seraphina, from the turmoil and guilt inside her, knew more about the disappearances than she was admitting. And Bodhan? It seemed the more she trusted him, the less he trusted her. She hadn't been prepared for how much that bothered her. How much she wanted to please him. To be near him.

Land could not come soon enough. She had to find Cyrus and the queen. There was no time for distractions. And Bodhan was a dangerous distraction. Dare couldn't help but feel that with Bodhan she was sinking. Her feelings, like water, were rising above her head.

And she had never learned to swim.

Chapter Six

"You go on in now, Dare. And if you'd take this in with you, I'd be thankful." James Stacy shifted impatiently before handing her a bottle of amber liquid. "Let the boss know I'm off to the engine room to make sure Massen stays awake for the ascent this time and won't have our ears poppin' and bones rattlin'." He noticed her expression and his grin wavered. "No, I mean, it's perfectly safe. Your ears won't bleed or nothin'. Massen is the best. Honest."

He turned and started to walk away, muttering to himself under his breath.

Two days of waiting for Bodhan to visit her. Two days spent learning more about James Stacy and his love for the young Miss Coral than she'd ever cared to know. He was a good, honest man. And he did love to talk.

She'd managed to get him to share more about the goings-on aboard the Siren. James believed his boss could do no wrong. It seemed to be an epidemic on this ship, putting Bodhan on a pedestal. According to James, there was nothing he wouldn't do for his employees, nothing he wouldn't risk to help an innocent. The way the guard described him, Bodhan was more hero than sinner. As virtuous as the eternal queen herself.

So why had he not come? Not even to question her about her apparent knowledge of the abductions? Why had he waited until they were about to surface to send for her?

And why did she care?

"Come in, Dare."

She had been so distracted by her inner turmoil that she hadn't noticed the door opening. How had she missed it?

Bodhan made an imposing figure framed in the doorway, the light behind him throwing him into shadow. He took a step back, gesturing with his arm to invite her in.

Willing her feet to move, Dare let her gaze flit from the panoramic view of the sea to the luxuriously inviting bed beside it. A bed she had once been invited to share.

Had he done what Phina said he never would? Had he chosen one of the other women to fill his bed while she was stuck playing sticks with the bored guards? The voluptuous Ivory perhaps?

She took a deep, slow breath, telling herself she was not interested in his bed, his sexual proclivities, or his reasons for staying away.

"Dare."

She whirled to face him, and it became clear there were sights far more dangerous for her peace of mind than his bed. Shirtless, irresistible sights.

Having an unobstructed view of Bodhan's muscled chest and broad shoulders made Dare feel as though she was still trapped in her constricting corset. She had imagined him like this for days, but he defied all her fantasies. Surpassed them.

She let out a long, shaky breath and let her gaze drift over the lean, chiseled angles of his chest and stomach. The broad shoulders and back narrowing to his waist. His skin like dusk, with a sheen of sweat making him glisten, making her mouth dry with the need to press her lips to his skin.

There were scars on his left arm and side. Jagged and deep. She opened her mouth to ask how he'd gotten them, but was distracted by the brand on his right arm. It was . . . unusual.

She knew most members of the Wode, as well as particular tradesmen, had distinctive brands on their skin as a source of pride. Some had more than one, branding their arms, enhancing the scars with colored dyes to show their alignment with a special group inside their caste. It was their way of setting themselves apart.

Dare and her companion guard were not permitted branding when they were given their Arendal and Senedal names. In fact, they were the first Sword and Chalice to be without that honor since the creation of the post.

Several members of the Theorrean Raj had instituted the ban as a new safeguard upon Dare's arrival at the palace. They'd stated the queen's companion guards, with their intimate knowledge of Her Majesty, could be punished or used in some way to harm the queen. Without identification, they cited, one shield guard looked much the same as another. In keeping this change secret, they protected themselves, and Queen Idony, that much more.

Dare envied his mark but did not recognize the design. Was it unique to owners of submersible brothels? Or merely meant to draw her attention to his lean biceps?

She swallowed. If the latter, it was effective. And focusing on the clothed parts of him did little to ease her anxiety. He still wore his black buckled boots, his dark, fitted pants and, if she was not mistaken, the gun strapped to his thigh.

That made her heart race for an entirely different reason.

"You wished to see me?" Dare subtly changed her stance, readying herself in case she was wrong about him. In case her current belief that, despite his criminal behavior, he had nothing to do with Idony's disappearance, was incorrect. Wouldn't James Stacy be surprised if Bodhan disappointed so dramatically?

The "boss" was taking his own inventory of her outfit, and whatever he saw made him grin. "I hadn't realized I'd hired a guard so short in stature. I told them to clothe you, but I had no idea they would give you a uniform. Who did you talk into getting you that?" He held up his hand. "Don't tell me. James is ready to leave Coral for you and will do anything you ask."

Dare's chin rose defensively. "Never. *He* is too loyal. He simply knew I would be more comfortable. There was no reason for me to dress in finery for myself. Certainly no reason for me to stay in that revealing costume around the guards." He stiffened at her reference. "I could have been wearing Ministry robes, for all it mattered. Your men kept me well hidden."

"That was for your protection." He stepped closer, his smile turning sensual. "I like you in finery." His gaze dropped to the formfitting, but not confining, uniform. In particular, the front seam of her pants. "Then again, there is something to be said for this look on you. Less a princess and more a little warrior. In fact, one might say you look too comfortable in a guard's uniform. As if you were born to it. Though we both know there is no way you could have been. Anyone can see by looking at you that you are only half Wode. Correct?"

Her cheeks warmed again and she tugged her brown buttondown jacket self-consciously. Perhaps this had been a bad choice of outfit, adding fuel to the flames of his suspicions, but she felt more prepared to face her departure than she would have in flounces of lace. "One might also say that your look is too comfortable as well. Should I wait outside while you finish dressing?"

He chuckled. "Then you admit you were looking. I thought you were too proper for that, princess."

She grimaced. He was right, she *had* been looking. "I admit to nothing. Perhaps you could tell me what it was you wanted to see me about instead? And why now?"

"I wanted to apologize."

She hadn't been expecting that. "For what?"

How had he gotten so close?

"For taking you aboard the Siren instead of waiting for you to make a choice. For allowing you to wake in a strange environment in chains. For making you a part of my parlor games and putting you in danger, despite my better judgment . . ." His voice trailed off as his hand reached up to finger a button on her coat.

Dare licked her dry lips and made an attempt to seem unaffected. "I volunteered for that. I wanted to help."

Bodhan's jaw tightened. "You did. In fact, because of your actions I believe I learned more secrets than I'd planned on."

She hesitated. "Are you sorry for what happened in the lift?" Why had she asked that? If he was, she had no desire to know it. It was a memory she wanted to hold on to after she was gone.

His ice-colored gaze snared hers. "No. Never for that. That is the one thing about this particular journey I will not apologize for."

He had no regrets about what happened between them? Despite his misgivings about her? Her secrets? "Oh."

"Oh, she says." His head bent until his lips were a breath away from hers. "I can only hope you will remain this biddable for my next request."

"Request?" Was it wrong for her to hope he would ask her for a kiss instead of her silence? "Would this have to do with our arrival at Two Moon Bay? I promise I will breathe no word about the Siren, though it seems I am the only one living who had no knowledge of its existence."

Even Cyrus had known. James had talked about him, too. He *had* been here. Cyrus Arendal had come to the Siren in disguise, and somehow, between his last night aboard and the passengers disembarking, he'd gone missing.

Dare now knew it was Lennis's partner. She also knew Seraphina had been attempting to seduce Cyrus. She had to talk to the Felidae once they were freed. Had to find out everything she knew. Surely Phina would want to help. Unless she'd been an accomplice.

Bodhan's response was slow. "Not the only one. But no, my request has to do with my curiosity. I'm afraid it must be satisfied before I can let you leave. You were too capable with Lennis. Uncowed by his threats, too sure of his incapacitation. You know more than you should for being so unschooled in so many other areas. Very like the last *half-breed* I had on board and I simply have to know why. To know if I'm right and that you are not at all what you seem to be." He stepped back abruptly, his expression closed. "Take off the jacket, Dare."

"Pardon me?" His words held no seductive timbre. This was no request. It was a command. Did he suspect she was pure Wode? A palace shield guard? Connected to Cyrus? She should have never left the safety of his hidden room. Regardless, he could not learn her secrets. The queen's life depended on her. Everything did.

"Take. Off. Your. Jacket." His fingers tapped out a warning against his holster. Was he threatening her?

Her ire was as intense as it was unexpected. This was not the gentleman the women fawned over and the guards idolized. This man was a bully. "I see. Do you intend to finish what Nettles started then? Or Lennis? Did you allow me safe passage, keep me hidden with the guards so I would feel beholden to you? So that I would experience more humiliation when you finally demanded your compensation?"

The lift of his eyebrows was subtle, but the burst of true surprise and confusion she sensed from him was as clear as desert glass. *It had never even occurred to him.*

He raised both hands, palms up, in her direction. "I have told you before that I have never, nor would I ever, force a woman. I believe you should know *that*, if nothing else about me, from our short acquaintance. I could have seduced you fully in the lift. Could have taken you the other night. Believe me, it crossed my mind, all the ways I could have had you." He shook his head. "You have been safe aboard the Siren as I promised. How can you still think so little of me? There is a reason for my request, but it is not your humiliation."

"Too late for that." She turned on her heel, her unblinking eyes focused on the door. "If you will please excuse me."

He was there before she could reach for the brass knob. "I cannot. I do apologize, sincerely and profusely, but I must insist. No matter what you think of me afterwards, right now you must remove your jacket, no more than that, and then I will let you leave."

Dare was shaking with rage, disappointment, and regret. The last was the hardest to take. She had been safe with him. She'd begun to trust him. And then he'd locked her away, only requesting her presence to prove something to himself. To steal some of her secrets.

She lifted her hands to the top button of her jacket, knowing Bodhan was watching her every move. She thought of what Phina told her. She had no clue what he was attempting to do, why he had made such an inappropriate request, but perhaps she could discover it for herself. Loosen his lips for her own purposes.

She took a long, calming breath and her fingers slowed, releasing the first catch. She glanced up at him from beneath her lashes and, recalling an expression she'd watched Seraphina use with some success, attempted a coy smile.

A vein pulsed in his temple, and with it, Dare felt the change come over him. Emotions that had been consistent, if tempered, sparking to unrestrained life.

Distraction. Desire.

She could do this if she could keep her own feelings under control, not allow her own fantasies or desires to take hold. There was nothing for him to find that would reveal her identity. All she had to do was focus.

She released the second button, knowing she wore nothing beneath but a thin muslin band to restrain her breasts. Would he be shocked by it? As aroused as he had been in this very room, when she'd worn nothing but a strategically wrapped scarf? When he'd had her bound? Perhaps he would take her breasts into his mouth again, or change his mind about whatever it was he was trying to do.

Perhaps, in lieu of that, he would be distracted enough to remove himself from her path of escape. She could return to the safety of the guard barracks below and wait to surface.

The idea was not as appealing as she'd imagined it would be.

Need. There was no disguising how each newly revealed inch of her flesh increased his arousal. The vulnerability beneath his desire.

Bodhan's mercurial behavior made Dare waver as she unhooked the last button. What was he really after? The truth he'd said. But what truth? That she wasn't to be trusted? That she was Wode? Or that he could resist the feelings she could clearly sense. Feelings she shared.

She held the edges of her jacket together with clenched fingers, unable to hold her tongue. "What is it you expect to find? Why are you armed against someone you know is no threat to you? Someone who arouses you? Someone who helped you? You have yet to tell me what you learned from Lennis."

Had she truly said that aloud? Despite her embarrassment, she refused to look away when Bodhan let go an open-throated laugh.

"I have one less question, my princess." When her brow furrowed he elaborated. "Your name. Blunt, thy name is Dare. How could you be called anything less?" He unstrapped the holster on his thigh and set it behind him on the desk. "I learned he has a partner named Muller, and that neither are the brains behind what is happening.

Whoever *is* has unlimited funding and resources, but Lennis has never met them in person. You were the one who confirmed the people had been taken to the Avici. As to the pistol, I'd forgotten I had it on, princess." His grin was distracting. "I would never *dare* . . . You would no doubt break my arm before I could take aim, warrior that you are."

He chuckled again, and she felt oddly insulted. He'd lost his tension. Was he laughing at her? "You are amused at my expense?"

"No, no of course not." He shrugged. "This is more at my own expense. I am a hardened criminal after all." His voice sounded mocking to her ears. Dismissive. "My kind sees conspiracies and spies where none exist."

Why was she not relieved? "You don't believe I could fool you?"

"I don't believe you mean harm to me or mine. I don't believe you would fool me. It isn't in your nature. You will omit, you will distract, but you do not hide your feelings well. You would never be a very good spy, princess. I am paying you a compliment. You are most certainly keeping things from me, but you are no sabateur or threat. You are too much of an innocent."

Dare dropped her arms and let her jacket fall to the floor, feminine satisfaction coursing through her limbs at his stunned reaction. "All things I believed I told you when we first met. And innocent or no, I think you'll find me a quick study."

Bodhan's stare burned through the loosely woven fabric and Dare's body reacted, her nipples hardening to a near painful degree.

She took an unsteady breath. "What were you looking for?"

He groaned. "I swear by the stars I do not recall." He stepped away from the door and gripped her shoulders in his hands. "You were alone with my guards with nothing on beneath that jacket? With your body so on display?"

Her body on display? She was covered more modestly than any of the women on the Siren. "I have been in a sheet, a scarf, and in that foul, pointless chair of yours in less than I'm wearing now. Why does that matter?"

"Don't remind me about the chair, princess. I may have it confined to my quarters. Or burned." The flat of his palm slid from her neck to the rise of her breast. "I could release them all from service for seeing you like this. Every man apart from James. He is too good to replace. I will offer him Coral in return for his silence."

Before she could take in his words he'd lowered his arms and gripped her hips in his hands, lifting her until her lips were level with his. Dare reacted out of instinct, her arms and legs wrapping around him as he groaned into her mouth.

This made as much sense as the dreams she'd been having, but Dare was long past caring. It felt like years since he'd kissed her, since she'd been close enough to feel his arousal mingling with hers, stoking hers.

He turned and walked with long, sure strides, her in his arms. Her back was still bouncing off the fluffed mattress when her boots hit the floor. Bodhan raised his lower body so his fingers could spar with hers on the buttons of her pants before he dragged them down her legs, revealing the bare flesh beneath.

Bodhan inhaled sharply. "Now I just might *have* to kill them. Unless you kill me first. Did you not think to ask for underthings?"

Dare had no ability to argue. She wanted him too much, was overwhelmed by the ferocity of his actions and the strength of his need.

She could use left over exposure to Seraphina's pheromones as an excuse, but that would be a lie.

Bodhan had been seducing her from the moment she'd fallen—literally—into his lap. The days spent surrounded by guards who spoke freely of pleasure, her time with Phina and Bodhan, every moment on board the Siren had led her here. Into his arms.

This time she wanted to do more than pretend. More than watch.

And this was her last chance before she was set off the ship. Her last chance for Bodhan to be her first, if not her only. Who knew what would happen if she couldn't fulfill her vow? Couldn't find the Deviant.

He gripped one of her wrists in his fist, guiding her hand to the hardness pressing heavily against his pants. Against her. She didn't need to be told what to do. Her fingers trembled and slipped in their rush to release his erection.

Coral had described it to her when she'd brought her food, or rather, when she'd come to visit James Stacy. The heat and smoothness of a man's phallus. How well it responded to the slightest touch. She'd laughingly teased Dare, saying, "Long and slender, short and stout, all men love when you tug it out."

Bodhan lifted his mouth to study her when he felt her lips quirk upward. "Something funny, princess?" he growled. "I warn you, laughing at a gentleman in my condition is unwise."

Dare's hand reached in to the now-open panel of his pants and wrapped her fingers around as much of him as she could. "Oh my."

His eyes narrowed to heated slits. "You are forgiven, and those are swiftly becoming my two favorite words. Let's see if I can make you say them again."

She was melting from the inside out. The feel of him in her hand was burning her palm, making her ache. None of the women had mentioned that touching him would do anything to her.

Were these *his* feelings inside of her or her own? It was insanity, wherever, whomever it was coming from. They were connected, skin-to-skin, emotion-to-emotion, yet it was not enough. The only coherent word in her head was *more*. She needed more of him. His smell. His touch. His mouth on hers.

More.

"You should never confine this. Never have to hide this beauty." He reached up to loosen her hair and huffed out a rough chuckle at her surprised expression. "There is no reason to. We have established that you would never succeed as a spy. You are too much of a distraction, even without all these maddening curls."

She moaned as he lowered his head and closed his mouth over her nipple, his tongue dampening the cloth that she wished would disappear. "Please."

He nipped her with his teeth. "Love that word as well. The next time, I will have enough control to draw this out. Long enough that you will be hoarse from your pleas."

Dare struggled to gasp for air at the first thrust of his fingers inside her. Yes, that was what she wanted. What *they* wanted.

Bodhan's mouth kept returning to her breasts, his fingers slipping through her sex, making her squirm. Dare squeezed his shaft, marveling at the sensation of iron swathed in silk. Physically, she could feel every ridge and vein, the beat of his heart. Emotionally, she could feel his impatience.

It was an emotion she shared. With her free hand she reached up and tugged on his hair until she got his attention.

Those eerily beautiful blue eyes looked into hers, dilated and unfocused with arousal, and she smiled, knowing just what to say.

"More. Please."

The vein throbbed at his temple again. And again. And then he shuddered. A fine tremor that sent a matching vibration through her entire being.

"Good girl." His growl was close to indiscernible, but she understood. And so did he.

He reached over her head, slipping beneath one of his pillows and pulling out something strange. She tried to focus, but it was hard to see. "Another invention?"

"Think of it as my way of protecting you from breaking Theorrean law." He sighed as he took her hand away and lifted himself off her. Dare whimpered in regret.

She watched Bodhan take a thin sheath of clear material and slide it over his shaft, and was reminded of a hand being covered with a glove. Her heart stuttered at the sight of his erection. She'd known its impressive girth from touch, but the full view filled her with a sense of excitement . . . and trepidation.

He paused, his hand gripping the base of his shaft, even now giving her a chance to change her mind. She had no intention of letting him stop. She may be intimidated, but she knew Bodhan would take care of her. She trusted him. With her body, if not her secrets.

Her arms wrapped around his neck and she pulled him down for a speaking kiss. She wanted him, no holding back, and he would know it before she was done.

He hummed against her mouth and gripped her hips in his hands. Dare inhaled sharply with the first press of his erection at the opening of her sex.

"Dare," he muttered against her mouth. "You're so wet. Relax, princess, and breathe. I have to—"

She cried out as he stretched her, slowly filling her as he stared into her eyes. Dare's gaze clung to his, and she allowed his utter satisfaction to wash over her, easing her body's own tension. That sharp prick of pain that was no match for her arousal.

She never realized . . . never knew it could feel like this. This was more than a tool for procreation. This *was* life. Some pain but mostly pleasure. Indescribable pleasure. All-consuming and as necessary as breathing.

When his hips were flush against hers he buried his face in her neck. "Dare . . . Dare you feel . . ."

She knew. She could feel everything. "Bodhan . . ."

There were no more words once he started to move. It was a rhythm she seemed to know despite her inexperience. Her thighs tightened on his hips, her own lifting off the bed to meet him. Each thrust was made easier with the slickness of her arousal, intensified by the clenching muscles of her sex.

She was perfection. He'd never felt so lost in a woman. Never been so close this swiftly. Only her.

His thoughts. If they were powerful enough, feelings often found their voice in her mind. Did he truly think that? About her?

He slung his hips with enough force to drag her halfway across the bed and she lost the ability to think entirely. Dare's fingers curled into his back and he snarled, closing his mouth over her shoulder.

Shameless cries and groans of need sounded around her, whether from the movement of the bed, the surfacing of the submersible, or her own throat, she could not guess. She didn't care.

"I knew you would be like this. Knew you would feel like this," Bodhan rasped. "Dare, please—"

He was begging *her*? He was the one making her wild, the one rocking deep inside her, his rhythm escalating. *Yes . . . deeper.* She never wanted it to end, wanted to stay connected to him forever. But how much longer could her body take this? She felt charged, inflamed. Combustible.

"Bodhan." What was happening to her? To them? Her voice broke as she called out his name again.

"Let go, Dare. I'm here." He braced his hand over her head and pressed his forehead against hers. "Come with me."

Feel me.

She did. She was. His adrenaline, his arousal, spiked and shattered in shards of raw passion around her. His strong body pumped against her as he groaned his release, taking her mouth in a ravenous kiss that sent her flying out of the salty water and into the atmosphere.

Not one feeling, *every* feeling. Every sensation. For one blissful moment she was everything. With Bodhan.

Her body was still shaking with the power of it when she felt him move. For a moment, she tightened her arms and legs around him. Unwilling to let him go.

"Shh, Dare. Let me take care of you." He lifted her off the bed long enough to pull down the covers.

Through vision blurred by the power of what she'd just experienced, she watched him finish undressing. Her hand lifted to her breasts and she sighed. She was still wearing the muslin and Bodhan had still been in his boots. How could her world have been so radically altered that swiftly?

A cool cloth between her legs made her flinch. Bodhan took the hand that rose in protest, kissing the back of her knuckles as he washed her. Soothed her. "Trust me. This will ease you. Make you more comfortable."

A few moments later he'd set the cloth aside, sliding in beside her. He kissed her fingers, her chin. He was sated. Solicitous. "Do you need anything else, Dare? Did I hurt you?"

She shifted on the bed. She ached, but it was not unpleasant. Her skin, her sex still tingled, and jolts of desire continued to pulse along her nerve endings. "I feel lovely."

He laughed softly. "You are lovely. Of course, I haven't seen all of you yet." His fingers went to her waist, making her giggle and teasingly resist until she allowed him to turn her onto her stomach. He began to place soft kisses up her spine until he reached her nape, pushing her hair over to one side.

One of his fingers started to trace a featherlight design along the left side of her back beneath her shoulder blade and she sensed a small jolt from him. Surprise? Bemusement? The feelings made no sense, so she focused on the physical sensation of his touch on the small raised area of skin.

Her birthmark. She had tried to glimpse it more than once, when she knew she would not be disturbed, but to her it looked like nothing more than a blurred circle of blue.

Her father had been adamant that she never let it be seen by another living soul. "You have many strikes against you in the Wodes's eyes, Demeter. Your size disturbs the other shield guards. They whisper that your inheritance is flawed. If they knew you were marked as well, you would not be able to fulfill your destiny. They would not accept you as a Senedal. As a Chalice for Queen Idony." He had patted her head, his expression grim. "You will hide this as you hide your ability, daughter, or I cannot protect you."

"Lovely, Dare," Bodhan whispered, bringing her back to the present. "You are not what I expected at all. How did you stumble onto my Siren?"

They both knew what had brought them together. Chance. An accident of timing. An opportunity for greed. Dare buried her face in the nearest pillow. The real question, the one she had no clue how to answer was, why was there a part of her that did not want to go?

He curved his warm, muscular body around her, tugging the plush coverlet over both their bodies in the lingering silence.

Dare bit her lip, fighting back tears. Had she ever felt as safe as she did at this moment? As full of life?

But what right did she have to feel this way? She was born for one purpose, to be the queen's companion protector, her Chalice. Idony could be suffering far away from Two Moon Bay, from Centre City. She could be in pain and suffering . . . though not dead. Dare would have sensed it.

And within the palace? A betrayal of which the magnitude was still too enormous for Dare to completely comprehend was fomenting. In more ways than she could count, she was running out of time.

Knowing that truth, bearing that burden, had not stopped her, if only for a heartbeat, from thinking that she never would have felt this, would have met Bodhan, if Idony had not been in danger. If Cyrus had not gone missing.

Perhaps this moment with him, this taste of pleasure, had been the greatest mistake of her life. Because now she knew what she was missing. What her blessed, isolated life in the palace had lacked. As she let herself relax against him, Dare knew this was something she should not allow again, yet she could not bring herself to regret it. There would be time enough for that once they'd surfaced.

Chapter Seven

She wasn't sure how long she'd slept when a strange noise woke her. Not the external machinery of the Siren. It was footsteps inside the room. Several pairs.

Tension. Impatience.

Footsteps and emotions that did not belong to the man sleeping heavily beside her.

"Had a feeling she would do the trick. *I* am good, but Bodhan was made of stone until she came on board. Who knew he had a fetish for virgins with secrets?"

Seraphina? Why did she sound like she was talking through a teakettle? Dare tried not to move, feigning sleep along with Bodhan. She hoped it was pretense. How could he sleep through this invasion? She supposed it was up to her to determine whom Phina was talking to, and how they had gotten past his guards.

A hard female voice spoke in hushed tones. "Phina, we have to hurry and we are out of options. It's not here. There's *nothing* here. You still aren't sure where he keeps his high-profile imprints. The bribe-worthy kind."

Phina sounded defensive. "How dare you doubt me? I found the imprints, even fondled the sweet guard who never gets to leave his post. There is nothing in them we don't already know. He must have hidden it when he disappeared from the Siren."

The other woman sighed. "Then we have no other choice. Freeman will bring him with us, and I can get it out of him on the move."

It's not here. What Phina had been looking for when she broke into the room? They were taking him. Whoever they were, Dare could not allow them to hurt Bodhan. She tensed, alert and ready to move if they took one step closer.

Phina's chuckle was delighted. "Fair Dare of the bright blue hair. You may have held the boss' *sword*, but I have his gun aimed at your pretty head. Do not think you can fight me. I like you, you tasted sweet, and I have no desire to use it on you, but I will. Now sit up and turn around. No need to cover up on our account. You look scrumptious."

Dare did as the Felidae asked, though she dragged the sheet with her to cover her breasts, her back still to the intruders.

She was angry. And sick of being taken places against her will. "You've been a part of the abductions all along then, Seraphina? Are you the reason Cyrus was smuggled off the Siren? How many victims did you seduce for them?"

She felt the pistol against her back. "I could kill you for suggesting that."

"Wait." The other woman swore. "Something you forgot to mention, Phina? How could you not tell me about her? Do you think this is a *game*?"

Phina's voice was sober, every trace of amusement and ire gone as the gun fell away from Dare's back. "I swear I had no idea. I mean, I knew she was *something*, but her scent is confusing." She paused. "I assume we have another passenger?"

"We do. Get her dressed, and swiftly. The gas you released into the crew's quarters only works for a few hours. That goes for the head knocks I gave to the outside guards. It's nearly dawn. They could wake at any time." Dare heard her sigh. "Freeman, get that fancy bastard to the Deviant. Leave the note on his desk and keep your masks on."

Phina hummed. "I love a bossy woman. And see how she worries. Come now, Dare. I will forgive you if you forgive me and get dressed."

The Deviant. That was the name of the ship she had been looking for when Lucy Thrice interrupted her search. The name of the ship she'd been planning to seek out when they'd surfaced. Had it found her instead? And was it filled with more criminals?

Despite the queen's seal, Dare was beginning to doubt her messenger. These people were thieves who could not find an object on an enclosed submersible. Why would she believe they could help her find her queen?

Unless she had been wrong about Bodhan. Had she just had the most profoundly powerful experience of her life with the man who had taken Idony?

No.

She did not believe she was wrong. Not this time. This man was what James believed him to be, what they all believed him to be, she would stake her life on it. She picked up the jacket Phina had thrown over to her side of the bed and spoke without turning to face them. "I demand to be taken to the Deviant's captain."

Phina tossed her boots, just missing Dare's thigh as they bounced off the wall. "Lucky Dare. That is the plan. Just promise you won't give me any trouble on the way. I have grown rather fond of you, you know, despite your accusations."

She nodded, adding a silent caveat. No trouble. Unless they hurt Bodhan.

Dare studied the two dimly lit figures in the distance. The man was the size of a mountain, with hair that glinted gold in the breaking dawn. He had a Bodhan-sized bundle over his shoulder, making her imposing lover seem no heavier than a sack of grain.

His slow, rhythmic glide kept him even with the woman beside him. She had dark hair that fell straight to her waist, her long black coat billowing out behind her to reveal a silver shimmer. She wore a sword at her side.

Dare wished she had a weapon.

These were crewmembers of the Deviant? And how was the Felidae beside her, the one still holding Bodhan's unusual pistol, connected to them?

Dare took in her surroundings. The Siren had surfaced off an isolated cove, a long metal gangplank extending from the submersible to the shore. She could see the lighthouse used to guide sailors that was perched on a jetty along the sharply curved shoreline that gave Two Moon Bay its name. She could hear the birds that followed the ships at sea pleading for scraps nearby, but she could see no people. She'd surmised the women and other employees of the Siren were either knocked out by the gas they'd spoken of or by the hostile woman striding ahead of them. But where were the paying clientele? The guards who were supposed to be ready for any eventuality?

"Why is he unconscious?" She glanced at Phina. "If you aren't connected to Lennis, why would you need to do this? Is he hurt?"

"Bodhan? No, he's just resting. Trust me, it is the only way he'd leave his ship for ours. See this?" Phina lifted the arm not holding the gun and shook her wrist, the jangling sound directing Dare's attention to her bracelet. At first glance it seemed like an ordinary trinket. A slender copper bracelet layered with thin gold and brass cylinders creating a unique design.

"The brass holds darts coated in poison and the sweet, shiny gold ones contain a sleeping draught. Big men will either die or take to bed, depending on which trigger I press." She folded her fingers toward her palm, indicating what Dare had believed to be dangling clasps. She hummed playfully. "I believe I hit him with a gold dart . . . but in the heat of the moment you can never be sure."

When she noticed Dare's expression she stopped smiling. "You are no fun to tease. He will wake up in a few hours, I promise. I told you I knew Lucy Thrice, and she knows her tonics." Dare remained silent and Phina huffed. "I refuse to accept responsibility for this. You were *not* supposed to be in his room. He put you down with the guards. One of the more foolish decisions I have seen him make. You should have woken up near sunset with the others, feeling as though you'd had a tipsy night with the girls, and then you would be free. But no, you had to have your fun without me. Any day other than this I would say good on you for seducing the boss." She fingered the pistol's barrel absently. "Any other day and I would have joined you both and made sure you thanked me for it. I was disappointed, to say the least, that we weren't able to finish our performance. Speaking of that, in case you were wondering about Lennis? He is no longer a danger to anyone."

The way she'd said that, and the satisfaction Dare could feel rolling off her, made it clear that she'd killed him. Seraphina had killed Lennis. More difficult to swallow was the knowledge that Dare wasn't sure she wouldn't have done the same, given the chance.

"I prefer being conscious, just the same, thank you." Protecting Bodhan and getting closer to the Deviant. Phina, however, still hadn't given her much to go on. "Why are you doing this? Why to him?"

Dare felt the sand turning to hard, dry dust beneath her boots as they moved further away from the sea. She could see the angled rooftops of the coastal town and recalled how excited she'd been to come here, to be on land again, but not like this. Not at gunpoint.

"Bodhan has always been good to me." Phina shrugged, her brilliant green eyes narrowing in thought. "Let me come and go as I please, scratch my itches while lying low. But I won't apologize for this. My loyalty lies elsewhere. Some secrets he has to share, for all our sakes."

Loyalty. An image of the queen laughing at something Cyrus had said flashed in her mind. They were where Dare's loyalty should lie.

Why, then, when she was closer than ever to her goal, was Bodhan's well-being all she could think about?

They headed farther inland, away from the town. And the bay. "I thought we were being brought to the Deviant."

The feline smile that first made Dare shiver returned to Phina's lips. "We are, Dare. Trust me."

She took Dare's arm and turned off the path into the tree line. She felt the wide, waxy leaves of palm bend and break as they brushed past. The terrain grew rougher, and with every step Dare grew more confused.

When they reached a large outcropping of rock, barren of growth, Dare noticed four new arrivals, men weighted down with large barreled rifles, swords, and other assorted weaponry standing guard. What kind of battle had they been waiting for?

"We got company? More women. I like it. Hope one of 'em cooks." The dust-coated man with the long braids in his beard smiled when he spoke, but it did not improve his appearance.

The man beside him was nervous. Twitchy, with shifty eyes and a piercing voice that hit Dare's ears like bullets in the early morning air. "I thought the plan was to steal *things*, not people. I was against it. You know that, right? Against poking at the Siren in the first place. Bodhan is near scary as you, Captain. What if his men come after us? You know they will. You don't think they'll find us? You'd have to be pretty thick to believe tha—"

Dare jumped when the woman he had been walking toward whirled in the dirt to face her. Without a word she reached out to pull Bodhan's pistol from Phina's already outstretched hand and spun back around in one graceful, elegant action.

In an instant the two men who'd spoken were dead on the ground, their insides revealed by gaping holes in their chests, as Dare attempted to process what she had witnessed.

She had never seen a theorrite pistol before. No other explanation existed for the focused emerald light that had blazed from the steel barrel like a bolt of green fire.

Of course it would belong to Bodhan. Was he hoarding a cache of the material? It should be no surprise to her after her trip in the Siren. Most of the critical systems in the submersible, from what she had observed, contained more than gears, cogs, and hydraulic power.

But the weapon itself was not the issue. The unexpected use of deadly force was. The remaining men had lowered their weapons, their faces pale with fear and respect.

The woman handed the gun back to Phina without turning, her attention focused on the perfect, seared circles the pistol had created.

"Clean and to the point. I like it. However, I still prefer my sword," she said, seemingly unaffected by the bodies. "Does anyone else feel compelled to comment on my judgment and irritate me in general, or do you remember your terms of service?"

The men lowered their heads in acknowledgment, and Phina caressed Dare's arm, whispering with a tone of admiration in her voice. "New crew never last long on her ship. One of the men still standing has been with her for years, loyal to the Deviant. The fate of the other is still any man's guess. He looks a little green around the edges. Freeman and Gebby, though. She trusts them . . . as much as she trusts any man."

Her ship. *This* was the captain of the Deviant? The woman who, though at the moment appeared to be without her ship and two of her crew, held Dare's and Bodhan's life in her hands. And hopefully information on the true queen's whereabouts.

From the edge of the flames into the fire, Dare mused, thinking of the infernal bit of flying clockwork that had started her on this journey. To date, she had been kidnapped, seduced, and then kidnapped again. The Wode guard had no clue of the current danger lurking in Centre City, and Dare was consorting with increasingly dangerous criminals. She had no weapons, no assistance, and no idea what would happen next. There had to be a way for her to gain the upper hand in this.

"I can feel you eyeing the pistol in Phina's hand, Blue, but there is no need. Believe it or not, we are on the same side." The captain turned and Dare got her first full view of the impressive beauty.

When she held out her hands, her jacket lapels opened to reveal a black choker made of velvet and a blooming ivory flower pendant resting against the base of her throat. She wore a man's dark vest with matching pants and boots, as well as weapon holsters on her hips and thigh.

It struck Dare that she dressed as though she meant to be a shadow to be overlooked or a patch of weather to steer clear of. Her uniquely jeweled and shimmering sword, the flower that was her nod to femininity, and her flawless, heart-stopping face, however, made her stand out like sunlight through the storm.

Phina was exotic in a sensual, fiery way. Bodhan and Idony were singularly exceptional. This captain? She was art. From her thickly lashed hazel eyes framed by perfectly arched brows, to her shimmering, lush lips and stubborn chin. All the more frightening considering the offenses she had committed only moments before. An angel of death without mercy or remorse. And she had none—Dare could sense no traces of regret in her.

"I have seen no proof of our similarities," she said, indicating the bodies with a wave of her hand. "Quite the contrary, in fact."

The woman's expression acknowledged Dare's words. "And yet I received word to expect a certain blue-haired someone with a birthmark I could not mistake, from a messenger whose seal I honor." She raised one of those perfectly arched eyebrows, acknowledging the spark of surprise Dare felt pass through her. "I assume you know of what I speak."

Birthmark? Who *was* this messenger and how did he know about her birthmark? "Yes, I—" Dare's words caught in her throat as Bodhan moaned, shifting on the larger man's shoulder. Her heart leapt into her throat. Was he in pain? She had to get him back to the safety of his Siren. "We were supposed to meet, and here we are. That man is no part of this. Release him."

The captain's expression hardened. "Do not think to question my decisions or command me. It is no matter to me who or what you are. For the time being that man is my prisoner; he has something I need and he will not be released until I have it in my possession."

She stepped forward, fear for him renewing her courage. "Until? But then he will be returned unharmed?"

The captain put her hands on her hips, her disappointment in Dare obvious even without her abilities. "Emotions are weakness, Blue. But of course, if the flesh peddler gives me what I need, I will land near a cozy shoreline where he will be free to contact his ship." She shrugged tightly. "If he resists, no promises. Be satisfied—that is the only assurance I will give."

She raised her voice so the men behind her could hear. "Lash up and stow the landing dodger, then bring up the moorings. I want us well on our way before the locals are done with their morning adulations."

Her mind reeling, Dare watched them all move with determination and purpose toward the rocks. The only phrase she'd understood was morning adulation. At sunrise and sunset, every civilized population in Theorrey turned their collective gazes toward the location of the Copper Palace. Toward Queen Idony. Or the nearest house idol or automaton facsimile of Her Majesty.

The Wode of her regiment had done it without fail, and she along with them until she'd arrived at the palace herself. Her father had told her it was done in remembrance and reverence. To bless the eternal queen and the peace she had brought out of the chaos of the old world. Here, in Two Moon Bay, they had no idea that they were looking in the wrong direction. The palace had a resident, but it was no longer the true queen.

Phina nudged her with her hip, still dressed in her sensual Siren uniform. "If you stare at your boots for too long you will miss the show. Bodhan thrilled you with the view of his tin bath toy, yes? Be prepared to witness the Deviant. She is the true beauty."

Dare shook her head, but lifted her gaze obediently. "Do the mixtures in your bracelet induce delusions as well as sleep and death? I see nothing but men clambering atop rock and over corpses on the ground."

"I knew that would bother you." Phina fingered Dare's jacket, distracting her. That she could affect her in this stress-filled situation was a testament to her skills at seduction. No, not skills. Talent. It just came naturally for her to emit sensuality, even when she was speaking of killing.

"I would say the captain is not vicious, but we'd both know I was lying. She is hard and colder than ice on a good day. She is also a good judge of character. Those men were new and they were already balking. They would have run to the nearest alehouse or crowded corner smelling of fear and dripping gossip. The reason the captain is so good at what she does is that only a handful know of her. Know of the Deviant. She does what she must. But if it makes you feel any better, I doubt she has any intention of hurting Bodhan. They are more alike than you know."

Dare was only partially listening, her heart wrenching a bit at the sound of Bodhan's name. But it was hard to concentrate on anything but what was right in front of her.

Nothing she had been through thus far had prepared her for all she'd experienced in recent days. The Siren. Ministers purchasing pleasure under cover of the dark and dangerous sea. A Felidae who mingled with humans as an equal, freely and without judgment or impediment. Her first attempt at pretense and seduction and her discovery of intimacy and passion with Bodhan.

And now this . . .

Perhaps she should have expected to be astounded, though how anyone could expect to see a beautifully ornate, full-size sailing vessel appear out of thin air was beyond where her rational mind could take her.

Not only was it nowhere near the water, but the pile of rock that had stood there only moments before was disappearing as the Deviant came into view.

It was a grand ship made of ironwood, with fin-shaped sails folded against its side and a fanned tail for a rudder—a design that could surely sail the sea with ease, if it were meant to. A contraption reminiscent of a long fluffy cloud floated restrained in thick webbing above the Deviant's length. It looked nothing like a main sail to Dare.

She squinted, seeing one of the still-breathing members of the crew standing on a high deck near the back of the vessel. His face was red, his arms straining as he worked a braided rope hoist, and his actions caused Dare to notice something else. A curved brass bar elegantly encircled the entire ship. The bar was lined with small rings that appeared in even increments as the illusion dissipated and the real object was revealed. It was an optical illusion, an elaborate one that Dare was at a loss to explain.

The ship's name, Deviant, was etched deep in the bow and inlaid with gold, making it clear to Dare that this was indeed the ship she'd been sent to find. The woman *was* the captain she'd been encouraged to trust.

She stumbled as she stepped closer, and Phina put a comforting arm around her. "There now, fair Dare, I've got you. Amazing, yes?"

Dare nodded. "How did they do that?"

Phina tugged her forward, toward a rope ladder that had dropped from the ship, which hovered only a few feet off the ground. *Hovered.* Dare felt the blood leave her face and her mouth go dry.

The Felidae didn't notice. "You mean how did a rock become a ship? Would you believe me if I told you this magical invention uses the blood of ancient monsters? No? Well, the skin then. Ancient Felidae would, no doubt, weep for the lack of respect." The grip on Dare's arm tightened for a moment. "I choose to think that this way they get to fly while they help to hide our more nefarious doings. That is respect enough."

"Monsters? Phina, what are you—"

"Seraphina Felidae, get your tail on deck before I leave the both of you behind. Maybe the Siren's guards will forgive you for their leader's loss. Maybe the Wode who walk the bay's perimeter won't mind the two dead men beside you. Are those chances you want to take?"

"Just my tail?" Phina grinned at Dare playfully but hurried her up the swinging ladder, following closely behind her. "I know how fond of it you are, Captain, but there are other parts of me worth saving as well."

The captain made a sound of aggravation, pushing away from the wooden railing and disappearing from view—too swiftly to see Phina's hand reaching up to pinch Dare's behind.

"You have nice parts, too, Dare," she teased. "But the entertainment, as well as the grand tour, will have to wait. Our fearless leader is in a snit. She will feel better once we're sailing and your lover is awake for her to question."

Bodhan. Her lover. Her first. This morning had turned out nothing like she'd imagined. But then, had anything since she left the palace?

Solid ground was further from her grasp than ever.

Bodhan's head throbbed and his body felt as though he'd been banged against the spire reefs at Theorrey's End. What parts he *could* feel, that was. His hands were numb, no doubt from the shackles digging sharply into his wrists as they were forced to hold the weight of his limp body.

At least someone had the presence of mind to put on his pants.

He'd been sure he would wake with the same sense of peace, of bone-deep pleasure he had fallen asleep to. That Dare would still be in his arms. That she would say yes when he asked her to stay. Or tell him a truth he already knew. As small of stature as she was—Dare was Wode. Training and all. And he would wager she had lived on the Hill until she'd arrived on the Siren.

Dare. He had *not* expected what he found after they'd shared their pleasure together. He'd been looking for the mark of the Wode, not that. Just when he believed he had her figured out, that he understood what she was, a new mystery arrived to bedevil him.

If anyone had harmed her . . .

"Are the accommodations as luxurious as you're used to?" A honey-eyed voice that did not belong to Dare spoke on the other side of the room. Bodhan kept his eyes closed, attempting to gather his wits before he faced his abductor.

She had no need for his acknowledgment. "I hope you enjoy it. Think of it as my gift. Now you can tell the innocent you bought and defiled that you, too, know how it feels to be chained against your will. Fair is fair."

That brought his head up. He opened his eyes and squinted in pain. Too bright. A large circular window with a view that consisted of clear, unfiltered, sunlit sky greeted him, making it difficult for him to focus.

He sensed the familiar hum beneath his feet, felt the sway and knew. He was in the air, and the elevated rail did not climb this high.

That left two options, neither of them promising. Luckily, if he was right, he'd found his way to the lesser of two evils.

He forced himself to smile, though every tooth in his mouth hurt at the action. Whatever they'd given him had been enough to fell five men. "Captain Amaranthe. As ever, your etiquette is only matched by your ever-present good humor. And beauty, I see. The rumors never do us justice, do they?"

She remained silent. Did she think him so uninformed? If conversation kept her off balance, perhaps he could discover if her reference to Dare meant she, too, was on board. Discover what it might take to get to her and get them off this floating boat in one piece.

"My business is information, you know that." His tone was reasonable, giving him time to slowly get accustomed to the exceedingly well-lit room and put more weight on his feet. It eased the pain in his wrists slightly. "And before you say it, allow me to correct myself. A *portion* of my business is information. It is a portion I am known for excelling in. Hence, the successful relationship we have shared over the years. Distant though it may have been."

She took a step closer, her face coming into focus. Despite his words, her beauty had surprised him. Her expression of judgment did not. Her first mate, however, completely lived up to his mythical reputation.

The captain squinted, her hazel eyes nearly disappearing in the process. "What is wrong with your eyes? They have no color. Are you ill or have you just spent too long underwater?"

"No need to be rude. My eyes may be bloodshot but they were still blue the last time I checked. And I may be a bit worse for wear, but I can hear perfectly." Bodhan nodded toward the silent, hulking shadow. "I suppose I've him to thank for my current condition."

That got a quick response from the captain. "As if you could match him. He carried you like a sleeping babe to the ship, made sure you were as decent as a man like you *can* be before I could welcome you personally. You should thank him."

Though her reply was defensive and protective, the man seemed more than capable of handling himself. The intelligence in his eyes, as much as the mass of his body, told Bodhan the stories did not do him justice. Not just muscle beneath that mop of yellow hair, then.

He looked respectfully into eyes the color of river gold. "I humbly thank you for my pants, sir. Man to much larger man, you'll understand if I never spin the part of this yarn where you carried me with such ease. Some stories do not need to be told. I have a reputation."

Her first mate's lips quirked, but Captain Amaranthe snarled and pulled a jagged-toothed dagger from the sheath on her thigh. That would make a painful mark. "Are you still doped on Phina's damn dart juice? Do you think for a moment that your situation could not get worse?"

Bodhan's smile grew. He was getting to her. He *was* good at his job. He allowed his anger to hone his wits, to soothe him. "Seraphina. *That* is a piece of information I didn't have before. That she is part of your crew. That would clear up the mystery of why she broke into my suite the other night. And this morning, of course. Does she add anything particularly noxious in her sleeping elixirs? Because they certainly pack a punch."

He would have to remember to pay her back for that. "I must be losing my touch. I would not have taken the merciless Captain Amaranthe for a come-as-you-please employer. Had you figured for the in-for-life-or-dead type. I also thought you were smarter."

She, too, had calmed. He had heard she was at her most serene with a blade in her hand. "You know nothing about me. And we have no time for pleasantries. I brought you here for a reason."

He shook his head. "We always have time for pleasantries, my lady captain. And I obviously know more about you than you thought I did. Though I would love to know why you felt the need to steal me from my ship. I would also appreciate knowing the how. Security, you understand."

He let his expression harden, his gaze narrow on hers. "This is not how this long distance relationship usually works, Captain. Our mutual friend believes it best to strive for inconspicuous as opposed to sloppy. Or have you forgotten?"

She refused to look away. "I haven't forgotten anything. I have no loyalty to you. I disagree with what you do. With what you force women to do for you. And now, you seem to be forgetting your end of the bargain. This relationship, as you call it, was based on a sharing of information." Her dagger came up to tap his chest lightly. "*All* information. You have been keeping more than your share of secrets from me. Not the least of which is Phina's little blue-haired friend. Any idea who she is? Or did that not matter when you decided to fuck her?"

Bodhan was no longer in the mood to play this game. He rattled the short chains of his shackles when he leaned into the tip of the dagger. The prick of pain was worth the surprise in her eyes and the pinpoint break in his skin. "Where is she?" When she didn't answer he growled. "I swear by our queen, you'll get no answers from me until I see her with my own eyes."

A behemoth-sized hand touched the captain's shoulder and she turned toward her first mate, locking her gaze with his in silent communication.

She stepped back, lowering her dagger and shrugging off the masculine touch. She appeared shaken, but she tried to hide it with a snide, "If there were more time I might make you wait for entertainment's sake alone. It was my understanding the infamous Bodhan was too clever to allow his emotions to rule him. But there is no more time. You have what I need, and I have what you want. Perhaps a trade can be arranged."

Bodhan inhaled sharply. "I wonder what our friend the Khepri would say if he knew one of his best operatives had gone rogue."

Captain Amaranthe's frown transformed into an expression he could only describe as smug. "Bodhan, you *are* off your game. Maybe you should retire. Who was it, do you think, that pointed me in your direction?"

Chapter Eight

The undeniable truth of her situation had been easier to accept than she'd initially imagined. Perhaps her days in the brothel beneath the sea had affected her on more than one level. Or maybe it had been all of the queen's magical stories over the years that enabled her to accept her new circumstances. She was, in fact, a passenger on a sturdy vessel that skimmed the waves of the air, instead of the water below. This was no illusion.

It wasn't wires or rails that held the Deviant aloft, but the strange cloud-shaped tube hovering above the ship. Phina had pointed to it as they'd started their vertical ascension and told Dare it was a singular creation known as an aether cocoon. An inventive chemist's mixture filled and formed the specially sealed fabric, making the Deviant lighter than the air. As buoyant as wood on water.

But that wasn't what powered it. Sails and steam and something more pushed it forward. The captain had given the order to run silent until they were over unpopulated land, and Dare had not heard the telling chug and belch of a steam-based engine. She would be willing to lay wager to the fact that this, too, like the Siren, contained contraband theorrite.

The logical conclusion, that theorrite could not possibly be as rare as she had always been led to believe, was inescapable. It was also last in the latest string of lessons that had sent a ripple through her foundations. How many other truths would she discover to be lies?

The gears of Theorrey did *not* run smoothly. Sexual depravity was not limited, controlled, or merely excused on the islands of Maithuna. And—she thought of Bodhan and her body warmed—it was not always depraved. It could be beautiful for pleasure's sake alone.

Neither were the Wode inherently honorable. In fact, many of her fellow shield guards must have shown quite a different face for the queen's citizens to accuse them so often of forced intimacy, or infer their abuse of power. She thought of the cruelty she had endured as a child in the barracks. Perhaps their behavior did not come as much of a surprise to her as the other realizations in her new reality.

The Theorrean Raj. The queen's council who held her up as a symbol of their will while enforcing laws she did not introduce or approve of. Whether they had anything to do with the queen's current disappearance, they were hypocrites beyond imagining, and her mysterious messenger was correct in ordering her not to trust them.

The final sword prick that burst her illusory bubble? Invention and imagination were the province of criminals rather than scientists. Weapons made of light instead of lead or steel, ships that flew above the clouds and swam beneath the sea. These things that her sovereign would applaud and embrace—these things were hidden.

Surely the science ministry could have spent their time focused on marvels such as these instead of their obsession with things unseen. Blood inheritance and its markers. Deciding who would and who would not procreate. Longevity for the nobility, enhanced intelligence for those born into scholarly families, and strength for the Wode. How did their obsession uplift the entire Theorrean population as they so often claimed?

The answer was simple. It did not.

Was nothing in her world true?

Dare looked down and noticed a break in the clouds. From this vantage point she could see so much land. Glints of life set fire by the sun, so miniscule she had to squint to make out any movement. The Wode barracks and shipping community of Two Moon Bay was swiftly disappearing. She knew there would be smaller communities separating the black sand of the Avici desert from the marshlands and the sea. Perhaps this ship, similar to the ones that floated on water, had a monocular she could use.

"Lean too far over the rail, lady, and you'll fall into the dodge. Don't think the captain is ready to lose you yet, else you'd a been tossed."

Dare looked over her shoulder at the balding man who had so wisely held his tongue when she'd first arrived. "Does she do that often?"

"Captain Amaranthe?" The second man stood mid-deck, coiling heavy rope around his deceptively scrawny arm. He was tall and lanky, his cheeks hollowed and his eyes so deep-set he reminded Dare of a corpse she had once seen prior to its placements on a pyre. "Ever hear the fisherman claim females aboard are a curse to the catch?" He did not wait for her answer. "Female captains seem to be a curse to the crew. Especially ones like our captain. Gebby here has lasted the longest, not counting the big mute who rarely leaves her side. Sooner or later, every man who works aboard this beauty meets his doom. Some get rot-drunk and fall over the rail. Some die during one o' the tussles we get sent into. Some, as you seen yourself, she kills outright 'cause she can."

Gebby shushed him, his face stern. "*Some* live to a ripe old age 'cause they keep their gape shut and never speak ill of the fine captain. The captain and first mate could run this ship alone if they had a mind to. *Some of us* should remember that."

Dare knew it was time to change the subject. "What does dodge mean?"

The older man scratched his cheek, as if deciding how much he should say. Dare imitated Phina's smile. "Please tell me. No one has had time to give me the grand tour yet. Too busy with their hostage, I believe." She hoped she sounded charming. "I think they also forgot to give me your names."

She noticed the blush appearing through the stubble riding high on his rounded cheeks. Amazing how quickly that worked. She would have to remember it.

"Name's Gebby. Sour mouth over there is Wen. I heard Lightfoot call you Dare, and just figured she'd told you about us 'fore she left you on our watch." He tried to stand a bit straighter. "I apologize for the poor manners. Don't have much need for 'em up here."

"Lightfoot? You mean Seraphina?

Gebby chortled. "In *some* circles. Depends on which town we're in, what the weather's like there, and if she's made an admirer or an enemy." His dark eyes sparkled. "Other 'an the captain, *we* call her Lightfoot 'cause of her skills at gettin' in and out of a place without a soul bein' the wiser. She's the best I've seen at robbin' people. Anytime Lightfoot's on deck, I know we're in for adventure."

"Oh." Dare blinked, hoping he would see it as a flirtatious batting of her lashes as opposed to surprise at his obvious admiration—not for Phina's feminine appeal—but her thievery.

"You were going to tell me what a dodge was?"

"That I was." He joined her at the railing's edge, leaning his arm down with a grunt of exertion. "Put your hand down where mine is. Careful, you'll get a touch shocked."

She hesitated for a moment, following his lead and sliding her hand down the wooden beams of the ship until her fingers slid against something . . . slick. Like slime. An arc of energy made the tips of her fingers tingle, but there was no pain so she didn't move

her hand. She leaned a bit farther and saw a shimmer akin to a
bucket of soap-filled water catching the light. She could still see the
ground through it, but it was distorted. So distorted it made her
queasy. "What *is* that?"

Gebby chuckled. "*That* is dodge. Same stuff that's in the landing
dodger—where the Deviant looked like part of the ground?" Dare
nodded in remembrance and he continued. "Well there's a mast, of a
kind, that swings clear 'round the bottom, stem to stern. The dodge
is rigged to that mast and we pull it out whenever we have a need."
He waggled his bushy eyebrows humorously. "Which we always do."

She bit her lip. "I am not a natural sailor, sir. I had no idea this
existed. To be truthful, I'm still confused."

He shook his head kindly. "A natural sailor would be scratchin'
his head just the same, Miss Dare. The dodge on the Deviant is the
only of its kind that I know of. Most ships don't need to hide the way
we do. Fish never notice them coming anywise. You see?"

Not at all, she thought. "So the dodge is what hides you? How do
the mechanics of it work? What is it made of?"

"I pay Gebby to follow orders, not answer questions." The captain's voice made Gebby's friendly grin disappear along with the
natural color in his cheeks.

Dare acknowledged that her own anxiety matched his. The
woman had certainly made an impression.

"Miss Dare. Captain Amaranthe." Gebby nodded at both of them,
excusing himself without another word.

Dare met the captain's gaze, lifting her hand slowly from over
the railing, as if to ensure it was not seen as a hostile act.

The woman sighed. "You have nothing to fear from me, Blue.
I've told you we are not enemies." She tossed a square of fabric at her,
which Dare caught without thinking. "Wipe your hands now. The
dodge can have corrosive qualities when it comes into contact with
sensitive flesh."

Why was she not surprised? She did as instructed, watching the captain catalogue her features as though she were something beneath a science minister's microscope. "Where is Bodhan? Is he awake?"

"He is." The captain crossed her arms. "You and I have a few matters to discuss before I stop torturing him and let him see you. Follow me."

She turned and moved with long, determined strides, forcing Dare to rush to keep apace. They passed the shining bright work and freshly scoured deck that seemed to mock the skeleton crew with its daunting size, and headed toward a door that led below.

The helm's deck sat above the door and her eyes widened when she noticed the wheel moving to and fro with no one to guide it. She paused. "Shouldn't someone be steering?"

The captain shook her head and mumbled before lifting her voice so Dare could hear. "Phina will explain it to you later. I do not have time to give sailing instructions."

They reached the door and the captain opened it and started down the steps. Bodhan was down there. She'd seen the captain's muscle-bound companion disappear with him. Phina, too, had followed shortly thereafter, muttering something about a change of clothes and leaving Dare with instructions to wait.

Dare was still confident of Bodhan's innocence, inasmuch as it pertained to Queen Idony. Whatever he had done to this captain, he did not deserve to suffer. She would not let it happen.

The captain began to speak without looking back or slowing her forward momentum. "For the sake of your curiosity, I will answer one question, though I am sure you would rather not know. What you were touching is made from the skin of a dead deep-water beast. So rarely seen we don't have a name for it. Alive, it has properties that allow it to hide in plain sight on the surface of the sea. It becomes whatever its prey needs to see to feel safe. Then it traps and digests them. Slowly.

"We call it dodge, and we use it in a similar fashion. Add a little jolt of static from the engine, and if our prey needs to walk by and see rock, they see rock. If they look up and expect to see the sky . . ."

"They see sky," Dare finished softly, equal parts fascination and horror vying for dominance inside her. Phina's earlier words made sense. The blood of monsters. But who on Theorrey would think of inventing something so deviously macabre? So ingenious?

Now she just needed to discover if the Felidae's instincts about Bodhan's treatment at the captain's hands were accurate as well.

She entered a long hall full of closed doors that led, she assumed, to living quarters and storage rooms. At the very end, Dare could see a ladder descending to a lower level. From the opening, a barely discernible rhythmic hum rose into the air like a heartbeat. It was similar to the sound within the walls of the Siren. She'd been right. The engine was enhanced with theorrite, though perhaps not used as extensively as it had been aboard the submersible. The Deviant hadn't the need of as many creature comforts.

Dare focused and sifted through the emotions she could sense in the air around her, hoping she could home in on Bodhan's, but the captain restrained her with a hand on her arm before she could take a step past her down the hall. "We can talk in here."

She opened a door on her left, revealing a room that appeared to be an armory—or a torture chamber. Blades of every shape and size imaginable hung from the wall, all polished and displayed as if they were artisan oil paintings. Or trophies. There was also an impressive array of rifles in a locked rack made of the same ironwood as the ship.

The captain, it seemed, while lacking in crew, had no lack of tools with which to arm them. Though Dare had a feeling Captain Amaranthe preferred not to share.

The clicking sound of metal grinding on metal made her glance back to watch an automatic locking mechanism seal the door behind them.

Dare concentrated on keeping her expression neutral, which made Captain Amaranthe's lush lips twitch. "Welcome to the captain's quarters, Blue. The only place I'm sure Phina cannot break in to interrupt us. My personal palace."

Dare's lips parted in shock. Her palace? She studied the room with a more discerning eye, noticing the red- and gold-tassled hammock in the corner by the circular window. It was stacked with mismatched pillows, and beneath it were several piles of well-worn tomes and a tapered candle that was melted half down. They were more than parchment manuals for lowborn education. More than Theorrean lore. These were the kinds of books the scholars placed on their highest shelves, guarding them as one might a treasure. Had Phina stolen them for the captain from noble homes?

An unobtrusive desk was riveted to the floor beside the hammock, across from the narrow door Dare could only assume was a water closet for washing and other essentials.

The desk was small but intricately carved. Wood inlaid with solid ivory . . . or bone. The design etched into the inlay depicted the Deviant, its sails unfurled. On either side of the carving was a symbol she recalled seeing etched into the dragonfly's metallic skin—a different kind of insect, round with wings folded against its body.

Bodhan's leather wrist brace sat on top, still glowing with a telling pulse.

Neither object belonged in this stark, barren room. "You *sleep* here?"

The captain sat on top of her desk, obscuring Dare's view, and startling her once again with her youthful beauty and shimmering long dark hair. She lifted one shoulder absently. "Like a newborn, if we are sharing personal habits. This is where I come to relax. Where

I think when things refuse to add up." She reached behind her and lifted a two-sided dagger off the wall without looking to ensure she would not be cut. It was of a design Dare did not recognize, the markings on it indistinguishable from this distance.

Captain Amaranthe began to twirl it with dexterous fingers, and Dare could feel the action soothe her. "You and Bodhan, for example. Phina shared how you came to be in his bottom-feeding Siren against your will. From your reaction when we met, I know that you received word to find your way to me, just as I was told to expect you."

Dare held her breath, attempting to keep her mind trained on the captain's words and not her intimidating actions. Though handling the blade continued to calm her, it was having the exact opposite effect on Dare's peace of mind. "Speak your mind, if you please. I was told to trust you, but I do not follow orders without cause. What you said earlier . . . how did you know of my birthmark?"

Captain Amaranthe smiled and Dare exhaled in admiration. It was a radiant transformation that intensified the flecks of gold and green in her eyes. Disarming. "I like you, Blue. I admit I would have more respect for you had you not bedded a man who trades women with the ease that a herder trades threehorns—but I'm sure you had your reasons. Seraphina always does."

She stood, tossing the dagger behind her shoulder where it embedded itself in the wall beside its original hook. "The Wode are not exactly my allies. Even half-breeds could work for my enemies. The Khepri told me your birthmark would be an unmistakable sign that you could be trusted. Simple as that."

Truth. Dare could sense it. The captain, for all her posturing, was not attempting to deceive her.

But nothing was that simple. Dare still had no idea how this "Khepri," whoever he was, had known about it at all. But it was obvious that the captain had other things on her mind. "I have it on unquestionable authority that Bodhan is keeping a secret he is not sharing with us. Knowing his reputation, more than one. I thought it was an object, a recording, or an incriminating parchment. Phina was sent in to retrieve it, but she could find nothing that related to . . ."

Dare had the strangest sensation of falling. She had to know. "Related to what?"

"To whom. To the queen we both serve." Captain Amaranthe sent her a pitying look. "If there is a potential threat, you and I are the people who root it out, regardless of our personal feelings. But you know that, else we would not have been brought together by our mutual friend."

"Mutual friend?"

"The Khepri. The person whose message brought you to me. We are supposed to help each other. Trust each other." She reached out to grasp Dare's arm. "You can start by advising your lover that his life depends on his honesty. Our association has been beneficial to both of us until now, but I need to ensure that no one has the chance to endanger the queen. Not even the infamous Bodhan."

Dare wanted to drop where she stood and say, "No more." Up was *not* down. Night was *not* day. A moon had *not* fallen from the sky, leaving only one in its place.

The captain, this woman who shot her men down without regret, who employed deception with ease and countenanced thievery, was a loyal defender of the throne. She believed her words with the force of a sword's blow, Dare could sense it, but she was wrong.

The plot Captain Amaranthe was rushing to quell had already been set in motion. She could not know who or what Dare was. Did not know what she knew.

This messenger, this Khepri, must not have told Captain Amaranthe the whole truth. The truth he'd known and proven to Dare. Why? Did he not trust *her* completely, or did he intend to let Dare reveal it?

The captain's facts were wrong, but the danger was very real.

And information was something there was no doubt they needed more of.

Bodhan. At every turn, she wanted to trust him, decided to trust him, only to be confronted by another doubt. Another whisper. Whether he was aware of it or not, he must know something. With all the powerful highborns who congregated inside his Siren, he *must*.

She had no choice but to discover, once and for all, which side he was on. As a woman, she prayed it was the right one, for the sake of her heart. As the Chalice she wished the same, for the sake of her queen.

Dare took the captain's hand off her arm politely, allowing her to see the resolution in her gaze. "Let me speak to him alone."

She watched the silent mountain of a first mate use a key that seemed too small for his fingers to open the bolted lock on the outside of the door. While he did she studied him in silence.

Unlike the rest of the people on the Deviant, she had not heard him speak once. She wondered if he was capable. Even his name, Freeman, was unusual, but everyone had aliases, so that told her nothing of value. Neither did his clothing or features.

He wore a roughly textured long-sleeved shirt the color of parchment and simple brown pants and boots. There was no weapon holstered to his side or thigh. His size indicated that anything he wore would have to be made especially for him, so that was telling in itself. He *chose* to downplay his more intimidating attributes.

His face was as hard as the rest of him. Not unattractive—quite the opposite, in fact—just unbending. It struck her that he was far more beautiful than he seemed. A golden statue of an angry old god. Yet something about him, something Dare could not quite put her finger on, seemed kind. His emotions were serene. At the moment.

If what she'd sensed from him whenever he was near Captain Amaranthe was any indication, there was much more to him than he wanted to be revealed.

More secrets.

Freeman's enigmatic countenance was, perhaps, a wise strategy considering the woman he worked for. The blade-loving captain closed herself off for a reason. The emotions *she* betrayed felt tumultuous. Dangerous.

Another complicated character. Dare sighed. Was it wrong to long for someone, anyone, who was exactly what they appeared to be?

As Freeman turned the door's handle she steeled her spine. Knowing what she thought qualified as personal quarters, Dare could only imagine the type of accommodations the captain believed a prisoner deserved.

Though to be fair, the room she'd been told she could sleep in was near as decorative and lush as the ones on the Siren. It seemed Captain Amaranthe did understand the difference between others' preferences and her own. She simply chose to embrace a rougher style of life.

When the door opened, she kept her head down, staring at the tray of food she'd brought from the galley. It might not be his usual fare, but the hank of charred meat and grilled marsh onions were all he would be allowed until he was freed. It would nourish him, regardless of its taste.

"Sir? Could you bring in the basin and cot, please?" Dare watched Freeman nod and step outside, coming back with a familiar-looking basin resting on a pedestal in one hand, and a long uncomfortable-looking cot in the other.

She went to the window across from the door and set the tray down on a wide ledge, along with several drying cloths. Freeman stood the copper basin beside her, and Dare searched for the turn-key, grateful to have something to focus on aside from the man she had come to see.

As she manually wound the simple device, she heard the soothing whir of the gears turning. At last, something familiar. The deep copper bowl was topped by a pitcher of the same material, connected with slender conductive rods. The water began to flow from the pitcher to the bowl and back again, and Dare knew it would warm quickly, and stay warm as long as it the gears turned.

The Wode used these in the barracks, and on exploratory campaigns into more forbidden areas when luxuries were scarce.

She heard the scrape against the floor and the jangle of metal behind her that told her Freeman had placed the cot into position against the wall and loosened the length of Bodhan's chain. When she'd been told he was chained to the wall she had insisted he be given the basic comforts. She told the captain it would help her attain their mutual goal.

It was a well-reasoned argument. She saw no need for anyone to know her personal emotions had more to do with her demands than logic. She refused to watch Bodhan suffer. It was as simple, and as complicated, as that.

Freeman left, closing but not locking the door behind him. Dare glanced back out the window, noticing a flock of birds, their violet and burgundy wings spread wide, soaking in the rays of the setting sun as they shared the air with the Deviant. It was a beautiful sight.

Still, taking everything into consideration, she would have preferred to see it from the ground.

"I remember seeing the partial plans for the Deviant years ago. I can't say I believed it would ever get airborne. I'm impressed." Bodhan groaned and she heard the chains rattle again. "I have a sneaking suspicion that I needn't have worried about your well-being. You seem to have adapted rather quickly. Unless I was wrong about your ability as a spy?"

Dare bit her lip. His tone was mocking, but with no true venom behind it. "You were unconscious and your pistol was aimed at my head. Should I apologize for not being chained beside you? I don't believe you're in any danger. If I did—"

"Dare." His voice compelled her to turn around, and when she did her heart dropped. Her relief at seeing him unmarked by one of Captain Amaranthe's sharp objects was tempered by the sight of him bound to the wall.

He'd relaxed his shoulders, slowly sitting down on the cot she'd brought for him. A small groan of relief escaped from between his lips. He glanced past her toward the window, squinting at the light. "I never believed you responsible for this. And you are correct, I am in no danger. Not from Captain Amaranthe, despite her threats. My hunger is the only excuse I can muster for my rudeness. Is this a new form of torture, or am I allowed to eat what's on that tray?"

"Oh." She turned and swiftly grabbed the food, walking across the room and delivering it to his waiting hands. They were still restrained, but he had enough freedom of motion to eat on his own.

He lifted the meat to his lips, chewing for long moments before grimacing as he swallowed. "It *is* torture. One bite and I'm exhausted. And marsh onions? Insult on top of injury. You'd think she could hire a cook with all the loot at her disposal."

"Do you know Captain Amaranthe well?" How well? Had all the vitriol the captain had spewed about Bodhan been based on romantic history instead of a general dislike of his profession? She *was* a beautiful, if frightening, woman.

Bodhan looked up at her and she sensed his astonishment. His wariness. He was not as unaffected as he pretended to be. "Didn't she tell you? I'm surprised. How can you be expected to gather information without any of your own? Did she tell you, at the very least, what it is she *thinks* I have in my possession that is worth all this? That way, if I have the answers she seeks, I can offer them. Alas, logic doesn't seem to be her strength, does it, princess? I'm sure she's just trying to let me know her sword is bigger than mine." He winked. "That is how we criminals play this game after all. Not that a shield guard from Queen's Hill would know that."

Oh yes. He was upset. And he knew. At least, knew she was Wode. Despite her size and lack of marking, despite her denials, he knew.

It no longer mattered.

She moved to the basin and dipped one of the towels in the now-warm water. Her heart raced as she wrung the fabric out. Because of his nearness or the circumstances? She already knew the answer. Both. Hearing his voice, looking into his eyes, reminded her body of the last time they were together. What he had done to her. What she'd wanted him to do again.

"Did the poor rag offend you? Whatever its crimes, I don't think it deserves to be strangled. This meat on the other hand . . ."

His dry wit was oddly soothing, propelling her back to his side. She knelt hesitantly on the cot beside him. His body was dusted with dirt and sweat, no doubt from being wrapped in a rug and hauled about like a bag of lifeless goods. And who, other than Phina, could know what those drugging darts had done to him?

Dare inhaled. Strange. His scent had only become more compelling. More arousing than it had been before. How was that possible? Her cloth-covered hand cupped his shoulder and his movements stilled.

He licked his lower lip clean and spoke softly. "As much as I would wish you were doing this solely out of concern for my care, I can't help but feel you are still keeping something from me."

She studied the shimmer of his lip, absently stroking his neck and back with the wet cloth. "I am." She swallowed, knowing she had to give something to get in return. "In the lift, before you—what I mean is that I saw Phina in your room, but I kept it from you."

He was expressionless. "Because you were helping her by keeping me distracted?"

Dare knew she had to tread carefully. "Before I was taken by Lucy Thrice I received a message to trust no one but the captain of the Deviant. A captain I did not know and a ship I believed to be seabound."

"And the message?" His voice was lower, rougher, and she realized he had set down his tray, his hands clenched in fists as she washed the sides of his ribs, his chest.

Why did she feel so breathless? "It was stamped with a trusted seal."

Bodhan exhaled on a shaky sigh. "A seal I know well. Cryptic bastard couldn't take into account you might be confused. Or you might end up with me instead of Amaranthe. And now he has her convinced that I'm being stingy with something she needs."

"He?"

Bodhan leaned his head against the wall. "*He* is our connection, princess. The captain's and mine. Or I should say, the Khepri is," he muttered, almost as though he were speaking to himself. "What game is he playing at? He knows how rabidly she fulfills her duty. It's an admirable quality, until you find yourself in chains."

The knowledge that he, too, knew this Khepri, that he'd been in communication with him, was an important piece of the puzzle she was forming in her mind. Though not apparently enough of a revelation for her to stop touching him. She was not sure she could. It was getting harder to concentrate, but she had to. This was too important.

"I was told to trust her, but I want to trust you as well, Bodhan. I *have* trusted you." His jaw clenched at the reference and she shivered with memory, determined to continue before she lost her reason entirely. "The captain was told you have something, some information on a plot against the throne. I believed you when you spoke of your love for our queen, and it's one we share. If you tell the captain what you know, she promised to give you safe passage back to the Siren."

His chains clanked against each other as he reached for her, pulling her close until she lost her balance. Her breasts pressed against his chest. "There is *always* a plot against the queen. The ministry, the nobles. The more they drink, the more they plot. Most merely fantasize, taking their frustrations out in other ways. Ways I allow them for a fee. Any more than that I share with the lovely captain through our mutual friend. What she does with the information after that I leave to your imagination." His thick lashes fluttered down until his eyes were nearly shielded, and he tightened his grip on her. "You are going to have to give me more, Dare. You haven't even told me whether or not I'm right. You are Wode, and yet, you're not. Is your name even Dare?"

"Yes, I'm Wode." She had no more breath to answer, to tell him all of it. That she'd had no knowledge of the Khepri. That she'd had no idea that all this lay outside of the gates of Queen's Hill. She could not speak, but she could feel his breath against her lips. Perhaps relief had stolen her air.

There had been no fear in him at being found out. No panic or anger. All she felt inside him was righteous frustration and increasing desire. It convinced her that trusting him as much as she had was the correct decision.

And that he still wanted her.

She parted her lips to answer him, trying desperately to remember the question, to ask more of her own, when his mouth took away her ability to speak entirely.

Yes. Her body curled into his, knowing what it wanted, recalling what he could do to her. She felt him attempt to lower her to the cot beneath them but he stopped with a jerk, swearing against her mouth. The chain's length had hindered him, reminding them both of their current situation.

Dare did not want to be reminded. Not yet. She pressed her hands against his chest and used her strength to push him back against the wall, her lips opening more aggressively over his.

His approval was clear in his low growl, and elation filled her that she could have this sway over him. She had no true skills at seduction, nor Phina's unique pheromones. All she had was desire. But she hadn't lied to him. She learned quickly.

She slid her mouth away from his and opened it against his neck, her tongue instinctively testing the flavor of his skin. Salt and heat. As earthy, dark, and alluring as his scent.

She recalled once more the effect Coral had on her noble and guard when she'd kissed their skin. The sound Bodhan had made when she'd asked if he would like to be kissed in that way. Could she bring that type of pleasure to him now?

Dare peppered soft, gentle kisses along his collarbone, stopping to investigate the base of his throat where she could feel the rapid pulse that matched her own. His need matched hers as well, but he hadn't moved since she started her exploration. Hadn't told her to stop.

She studied her hands on his chest, her pale against his rich bronze. The smooth skin of his chest let her palm slip lower with ease to the ridges of his muscled stomach, revealing the hard, dark nipple that had heated against her hand to her fascinated gaze.

Would his body react as hers had? Would he feel the same fire and lightning sensations when she sucked the skin between her lips? Bit them gently?

There was only one way to find out.

Chapter Nine

His hips bucked up instinctively when the sharp, perfect white pearls of her teeth closed over his left nipple. He had not believed it an erogenous zone for a man. When her tongue lashed lightly across the tougher flesh he shuddered, man enough to admit that he'd been wrong.

Could the intense reaction have something to do with his current position, chained and out of control? It was a first for him, being in a situation of this sort. He'd been in rough scrapes before, life-threatening negotiations and brawls where the odds were stacked against him. *This?* It was not a battleground he understood.

He knew of many women who enjoyed being in power. He couldn't do what he did without understanding those dynamics. But, though he'd never admitted it aloud, Bodhan secretly found the men who craved that sort of role reversal lacking.

He took control. Women submitted to *him*. He gave them pleasure that left them weak and wound them up so tightly they had to beg or they would shatter. It was what he had been planning to do to Dare, but his need for her that first time had been too great. His feelings too tender. What had passed between them had been beyond simple pleasure or control.

Now he'd woken up chained to a wall, unable to process the changes in their situation, the information she had given him before their lips met.

The last thing he wanted to admit was that he enjoyed this. Dare's innocent oral exploration. The painful ache in his cock as he waited for her curiosity to take her lower. By the two moons, *lower.*

He bit his lip hard enough to taste the copper of his blood. He would not beg her.

Not yet.

That soft, sweet mouth was on the skin above the top button of his pants, her fingers releasing him buttonhook by agonizing buttonhook.

He relived those moments he had been inside her. He'd seen her reactions when she touched him, her surprise at his size. Would she hesitate now?

No. Not his Dare. His Dare had a need she barely understood but embraced without question. Her passion shook the earth around him, and her courage drew him to her in a way that had left him reeling, stunned.

In an elemental way he chose not to study too closely, he recognized his claim. Whoever she was, whatever her purpose or accident of fate that had brought them together, did not matter. She belonged to him.

And he was her prisoner, in more ways than one.

He hissed at the near explosive reaction he had to her touch. She gripped the base of his erection, her mouth a kiss away, her breath bathing his skin in fire.

"Dare?" *Please, my love. Do not make me beg.*

Her voice was a caress on his sensitive flesh. "I do not mean to tease. I'm just not certain how—I couldn't tell how Coral had—"

He banged the back of his head against the wall, wishing them somewhere else. Wishing his chains away so he could take her now.

"There is no way for you to fail, princess. Not at this. Unless you torture me to my death."

He caught the quizzical look she sent upward and groaned. "Put your mouth on me, Dare. As if you were kissing my lips, savoring the taste of my skin. Kiss me as I kissed you in the lift."

The memory of her addictive taste only increased his desire, the agonizing hardness between his legs. Her mouth opened lightly on the head of his cock and he ground his jaw together, holding his hips still with all the willpower he possessed.

"Yes," he growled. "Taste me. There's no need to be that gentle. You can take more . . . take it all."

His encouragement was all she needed. The silken indigo of her braided hair slid over her shoulder, allowing him to watch her mouth widen to accommodate his thickness.

She would kill him before she was done.

Her cheeks hollowed as she sucked him in deep. Her tongue swirled around his shaft. How did she know he loved that? It seemed she could read his mind, that he no sooner fantasized an action than she mimicked it with her mouth. An intensified arc of pure need traveled along his spine, and he knew he would not last long.

Not like this. He opened his mouth to tell her what he wanted. Her astride him. Her cries of delight joining his. But it was too late. His body defied him, hips lifting off the cot until the head of his cock touched the back of her throat as he found his release.

Dare moaned in surprised delight, swallowing his seed with greedy abandon. He shouted hoarsely, shocked at the intensity of his satisfaction and the depth of emotion that followed. He'd only come this hard once before.

With Dare.

He closed his eyes, lost in the pleasurable aftershocks of her ministrations. His limbs trembled enough to rattle his chains, a vague reminder of their current situation. A situation he was fast beginning to conclude was the realization of his greatest fear.

Dare lifted her head to kiss him and he caressed her lips tenderly with his own. For her, he would risk being wrong. He would give the captain what she'd asked for. Answers. Hopefully he would get some of his own in return.

A familiar voice rose in irritation on the other side of the door. "Again? Have you no shame? No idea how cruel it is to taunt a Felidae with the scent of fucking and not invite her in?"

Dare pulled her mouth away from his with a gasp, blushing deep pink from the roots of her blue hair to the top button of her jacket.

Bodhan smiled grimly. "A little late, Seraphina. Was there anything else you wanted?"

He could hear her grumbling but she didn't open the door. "I was being polite by volunteering to come down here. The least you could do is return the favor." Her tone changed, from petulant to clipped and alert. "Our unexpected passenger pick-up put us behind schedule. Both moons wane tonight. We have to make an emergency landing and set up camp. The captain wanted to leave you in here but I convinced her that Dare would no doubt protest."

Bodhan felt his entire body tense. It did not occur to him to make a remark regarding the inconvenience of his abduction. Not now. "I appreciate the heads-up, Seraphina."

Phina's smile was evident even through the door. "She only agreed once I told her we could keep you in shackles. I'm not sure why . . . she still has not fallen prey to your charms."

He studied Dare's wide, wary gaze until he heard Phina's footsteps fade away down the hall. "Love, I'm going to need your help cleaning up before they come in to get us."

She looked down, blushing again and jumping off the cot to soak another cloth in the warm basin water, returning to gently wipe his stomach and his still-erect cock.

He wanted her again. It would have to wait.

"Something is wrong and you know what it is, don't you?" Dare's voice was whisper-soft. "Are we in danger?"

His thoughts were grim. He knew the story too well. It had been passed down through the generations as long as any living being could remember.

When the two moons waned together, when Theorrey was blanketed in shadow, no man or beast dare take to the air . . . save one. One beast that was not a beast and a man that was not a man. To most it was a story told to keep children inside, safe from the dangerous beasts of the wood and marsh. But Bodhan knew the threat was based in reality. Captain Amaranthe knew it as well.

"Yes." He snared Dare's gaze, his own unblinking as he attempted to convey the seriousness of the situation. "Stay close to me once we land, Dare. And keep sharp."

Dawn could not come soon enough. There would be no rest tonight.

Dare sat on the surprisingly comfortable chairs Freeman had brought out for them, Bodhan beside her, short-chained iron shackles still binding his wrists. She frowned. They had not offered him a shirt, and she could see several small welts had formed on the bronzed skin of his back from the bug bites they'd endured between the ship and camp. He had yet to complain about them.

She would say this—Freeman and the other two male crewmembers had made the small, elevated patch of dry land nearly as livable as the Deviant. A difficult accomplishment in the marsh.

It had to be something frightening indeed to have sent this hardened lot into such a spin. Their landing had been her first clue to their state. It *was* a landing. The ship was no longer hovering the way it had been at Two Moon Bay.

The lower dodge had been furled against the sides along with the sails and it was bobbing, like an ordinary vessel on a deep pool of marsh water.

They'd released the aether mixture from the cocoon and the fabric had deflated, floating down like an enormous bedsheet to blanket the deck. The captain had shut off the engine and any power routed to the living quarters along with it, which, by the look in Gebby's eyes, was not something they did without serious cause.

They'd been guided off the ship to a spot where they could remain hidden by the tangled web of vegetation, but were still able to keep an eye on their transport.

Captain Amaranthe appeared edgy, fingering the hilt of her unusual sword as a touchstone and pacing the perimeter made by the sloping hill of their open-air camp, and the repelling device set up near the stove. Just as the immense version had kept sea creatures away from the Siren it surrounded, this smaller version seemed to be keeping the stinging, chirping bugs at bay. But the captain still acted as though she were ready for an attack of some kind.

Phina, too, seemed different. More than just her outfit had changed since Dare had seen her, though the new look was startling. She had changed from her fancy corset and daring skirt, but the Felidae's clothing was even more provocative. A feat Dare had not believed possible.

Thigh-high boots made, Dare would guess, from the butter-colored leather of the threehorn, complete with brass buckles along the side, covered most of her legs. Her upper thighs were encased in ruby red tights that nearly matched the richness of her hair in color, and the snuggest pair of leather short-pants in existence.

Her red corset had no design, other than the buckles up the front that seemed to match her boots, with slats for small silver arrows.

Weapons that reminded Dare of the dangerous bracelet Phina still wore on her wrist. The arm-length bracers and the whip coiled at her waist completed the predatory fashion statement. This was a thief's garb? Dare could not imagine *not* being noticed in such an outfit, much less sneaking past security and shield guards as Gebby had insisted she did so often. Still, with her tousled hair glowing like a beacon and her bright clothing, Phina stood out.

She also looked more like a wild thing than she had before. Crouching atop her chair, spots visible along her arms, her long, entrancingly mobile tail flicking behind her and her emerald eyes watchful, she was pure Felidae. In her current state, her feelings were less complex, easier for Dare to translate. She did *not* like this place.

Dare knew there were several areas of Theorrey, particularly in the south, that contained marshlands similar to this one. She herself had been taken blindfolded and left in the marsh at the edge of Centre City with only a simple dagger when she was eight. As part of her shield guard training, her goal was to procure a rare white lotus for the queen . . . and survive until she found her way out.

She had not thought of that in years, nor of the trauma of learning firsthand about the stalking techniques of the animals that dwelt in these unpopulated regions. Years of ease and isolation with the queen may have softened her more than a Wode should admit, but Dare felt nowhere near the anxiety she was sensing from the men and women around her.

What could have caused this kind of reaction?

She asked them bluntly, and they all looked at her with suspicion. She tensed. Was this something she was supposed to know?

"Miss Dare no doubt wants a story to go with our campfire. Haven't told it in a queen's age, pardon the expression. May I?" Dare looked up at the balding Gebby with a grateful smile, thankful that he was attempting to spare her embarrassment.

She found herself riveted to Gebby's animated tale of the black sky ship and the crew who brought death in their wake. Of the immortal Scarlet Lord who ruled them and stole people from their homes when the two moons waned. His features glowed in the light of the small, smoking stove that sputtered soothingly in the center of the base camp, his hands casting expressive shadows.

Idony would love this story. She would no doubt appreciate Gebby's lavish embellishments. There was nothing that brought the queen more enjoyment than telling a story. Still, it did not ring any truer than the Wode tales told around the campfire to scare the young cadets. It certainly sounded nothing like the explanation she'd requested.

She tried to maintain her smile for Gebby's sake, but she was dubious when the humorous man finished with a dramatic flourish. "This is why we've landed? Because there is another ship that sails the sky, hidden by darkness instead of dodge? And this captain, the Scarlet Lord? A child's story could not have a more impossible villain. If no one wants to tell me the true reason we have landed, then I will not ask again, but do not patronize me."

Phina's laugh was short and derisive. "Impossible? You believed sailing the sky was impossible not a day ago, fair Dare. That traveling beneath the sea was impossible. Tell the truth now, you had no knowledge of a prick's shape before you found one in you."

Dare flinched and the captain stepped toward Phina in silent warning. "You'll forgive Phina's crudeness; this is not her natural habitat. Though she has a point. Your naivety about the most ordinary things would be amusing if it weren't so disturbing. Point of fact, the more I know you, the less I understand why you are here." She tilted her head, hair tumbling around her shoulders as she looked down on Dare. "I had expected more when I saw your mark, but we no longer have time for riddles."

She turned her chin to her shoulder and spoke to the men behind her. "Gebby. Wen. Get your boots wet and make sure our girl won't drift. Keep your eyes open."

The two men shared a speaking glance before obeying in silence, disappearing from the dim lights of camp. Dare watched Gebby smacking the back of his neck when the bugs descended on him before he disappeared from view, Wen tromping along beside him.

Dare could feel expectation thicken the air. All of them: Freeman, Phina, and the captain. They had forgotten about any information Bodhan might have about the queen and focused on her. Even Bodhan wondered about her—she sensed it, though she felt him reach out to place his hands on her knee for comfort. His wrists were still shackled, yet he thought of her comfort.

Trust the captain.

She did. And she trusted him. It was time to show them the proof. Dare stood, letting Bodhan's touch slip away as she stood at her full, if not impressive, height. She was glad she wasn't facing him for this. "I am called Dare but that is not my true name, and I am not a half-breed or a bastard. I am Wode."

"You don't smell of pure-blood Wode," Phina snorted, but her tail stilled behind her. "I've been with more than one shield guard, fair Dare. Male and female alike. All of them as tall as two of you put together," she sighed lustily. "Legendary stamina, and a very distinctive scent."

Dare pressed her lips together and nodded. "You are not the first person to notice my differences. But I was raised Wode and lived in the main barracks until I reached my eleventh year."

Bodhan stood abruptly, angling himself so he stood between Dare and the captain. Dare bit her lip to hide her surprise. He was protecting her? Even now?

The captain's eyes rolled. "Please. Stop. Your masculinity may overwhelm me." She turned to Dare. "You said until you were eleven you lived in the barracks? Did no one notice the differences in you before then?"

"They noticed." Dare's voice was grim. "My father was a commander, but I could not be protected from all of their scorn. I never knew my mother, was told she had been posted far to the north, so the others were free to spin any yarn they wished to explain my anomalous attributes. There were many. But I believe it was those same traits, along with the esteem my father had always been held in, that led me to my posting."

Dare took a breath, taking comfort in the thin blade hidden in her boot. She had armed herself before they left the Deviant, and if these people were not what she sensed them to be, she would have to use it.

"I am Senedal. Demeter Senedal. The Queen's Chalice."

The captain paled and Freeman took a subtle step closer to her side, ready should she need him.

Phina leapt from her chair and moved toward Dare, her head cocked and eyes narrowed in suspicion. "You tell us you are a Chalice but if it's true, you're one who isn't guarding your queen. I'm guilty of many crimes, most of which I don't regret, but none of them are treason."

Dare clenched her fists at her sides. She forced herself to say aloud the horror she had been holding inside for too long. To speak the words that, even now, made her ill. "I serve the true queen, Idony the Ever Young. Not the mockery that wears her face and sleeps in her bed in the Copper Palace."

The captain drew her sword in response. "Traitor."

Dare inhaled sharply, but stood her ground. "I did not want to believe it, either. My message from your Khepri confirmed my greatest fears."

Her memories blurred her vision, the emotions and her sense of loss returning in a rush of pain. "I have spent more than half my life by Queen Idony's side, privy to her mannerisms, her thoughts, her emotions. She has been my monarch and my friend. One day, without warning, I was locked out of her rooms. Kept away, with unfamiliar Wode brought in to protect her in my stead. After I received the missive I snuck into her rooms against her orders and learned the truth. The woman who wears the crown has flesh but no feeling. She is *not* the queen I know. Someone went to unthinkable lengths not only to take her but to replace her. Lengths that I believed included killing my companion guard. There is no rumor of a possible plot, Captain Amaranthe. Though Bodhan may have information that could help us that he is unaware of, you should unchain him immediately. I speak the truth. Queen Idony has been taken."

The captain shook her head, backing up until she bumped into her first mate. "Why would the Khepri not tell me when he obviously told her? He pointed me toward the Siren instead of bringing me directly to her side. Instead of scaling the walls of the Copper Palace itself. Why waste all this time?"

An odd, out of place whirring grew closer, as if in answer, and they all turned their attention to the darkness.

"He certainly knows how to make an entrance doesn't he?" Phina's voice held a trace of admiration, despite her restlessness. "Though on a night like tonight, I'd rather it didn't glow like the rest of those bugs he's so fond of sending to guide us. He should understand our need to stay hidden."

Glowing bugs? Dare thought back to her initial attempt at escape from the Siren, and what she'd seen in Bodhan's room with Phina. Was this what it had been? The Khepri guiding her? Them?

"Who *is* this Khepri? And why does he bear the queen's seal?"

Bodhan lowered his voice, his eyes on the blue-green glow moving toward their camp at a rapid pace. "He is, without question, the most brilliant inventor Theorrey has created. He is the leader of our unusual consortium, such as it is, and the queen's right hand."

The queen's right hand? She had never heard that title before. Surely she would know him. No one knew those filling the queen's palace better than she. Unless he wasn't in the palace.

Another memory struck Dare with a sudden, almost physical blow as the glow brightened.

Queen Idony standing on her enclosed balcony, a strange light bathing her. She was speaking in a hushed tone, but when Dare knocked to announce her entrance, she'd laughingly confessed she had been talking to herself.

She'd thought she knew every secret the queen had. Apparently she'd been mistaken.

"Khepri's hummingbird," the captain murmured. "Freeman, hang one of the blankets on a sturdy branch behind us."

Dare watched the big man move with surprising swiftness before returning her attention to the brass bird hovering just out of reach. It did hum. She could hear it, perhaps because of the rapid, barely visible flapping of its mechanical wings.

It darted toward Dare and she stepped back instinctively for fear of being hit by the tiny brass bird. But it did not attack her; instead it hovered in front of her, its clear crystalline eyes full of seeming impatience.

Then the copper and brass marvel did something truly odd.

It tilted its head to one side and glanced down at Dare's right hand while she looked on, uncomprehending. After a moment it fluttered down until it was even with her fingers, before lifting to her eye level once more. It did that twice before Dare, utterly fascinated, began to catch on.

She lifted her right hand slowly, palm up toward the busy automaton. She trembled with the excitement of discovery as it instantly landed on her skin, the cool metal buzzing with clockwork life. She could also make out a closed panel on its rounded chest etched with that strange segmented bug again. The symbol for the Khepri.

She heard Phina snort softly. "I think it likes you."

It folded its little wings against its sleek body, and the panel opened, revealing a circular depression within its clicking inner mechanism that seemed to be missing a gear.

Bodhan bent down at her side, leaning close to study the opening in the dim light of the fire. He must have seen something she didn't because he straightened and spoke to the captain, his tone urgent. Anticipatory. "Captain Amaranthe, did you bring it as I requested? My wrist brace?"

Freeman slid the device from his pocket and walked closer to hand it to Bodhan, who instantly began to tap the largest theorrite crystal in the center with a definitive rhythm. "The Khepri sent me something ages ago, along with some of his more florid prose. I'd nearly forgotten about it." A loud click came from Bodhan's device and the gem turned clockwise on its own. "The basic meaning seemed to be"—he caught Dare's gaze with his light blue stare and winked—"keep this close until the right one comes along."

He lifted the theorrite crystal out and placed it in his pocket. Between the conductor of his brace and the leather, there was a small compartment. He stepped closer to Dare so she could look into it. It was a copper gear. Miniature but intricately precise, though a closer look revealed unusual grooves etched into it like the rings of a tree. The perfect size for the bird's missing piece.

"What is that?"

"I think it's yours, princess." Bodhan nodded toward the Khepri bird. "More precisely, yours to put into *that*."

Dare frowned in confusion, but the bird seemed to understand, turning its head to study what Bodhan held. With her left hand, she reached for the small mechanical piece carefully, praying she would not drop it onto the soft, wet ground beneath their feet.

Before she could touch it, she was stung by a type of static charge that arced across the space between the gear and her skin.

"Ouch." Dare looked down at the improbable creature in her hand, relieved that it appeared unaffected by the jolt or her surprise.

Her fingers tingled as they did when she'd touched the dodge on the ship. She flexed them and made a fist to regain sensation. Now prepared for the shock, she touched the gear with her fingertip and gently withdrew it. It was so light it clung to her skin.

She brought her new acquisition toward her right palm and the open panel of the automaton. As she moved the gear closer she felt a force, like that of a magnet, cause the gear to wobble, then spin off her finger and snap into position inside the bird's chest.

The gear and its surrounding clockwork began to turn and the panel shut with a decisive click. The messenger's wings flexed and stretched, humming into flight once more, this time heading toward the blanket that Freeman had put in place.

Hovering beside the fabric, the automaton beat its wings faster than it had before. She heard a crackling sound much louder than the fire and felt a static charge building in the air around them.

Traces of the energy began to coalesce around the body of the bird and arc between its wingtips. Its crystalline eyes started to flash with bright white light, the energy seeming to pool in its head. Its beak opened and the flashing light shot from its eyes onto the blanket, creating flickering images that Dare prayed everyone else could see.

"Queen Idony," she gasped. A grainy image of her queen like the one taken by an artisan's amphitype. Only this was not a single smiling queen frozen in time. Each flash of the bird's eyes changed her expression in the tiniest of increments, until she appeared to be speaking. Her mouth moving.

"The beak is an opening for sound, I believe." Bodhan's low whisper sounded close, but she couldn't look away. "It is a message, Dare. A recording made by the queen herself."

A recording? Like the automaton at Trader's Square? A voice, sounding metallic and far away but still recognizable, echoed around the small camp. "If you have retrieved this message then my Chalice is in your company. Her unique markers alone could initiate this recording." Dare watched the queen's smile wobble in the shuttering pictures. "What we knew would be has come to pass. I have been taken from the palace against my will. The Theorrean Raj, selfish and greedy though they may be, could not have done this on their own. But they are deceived if they think he will share power if he is allowed to reign again."

If *who* were allowed to reign again? Dare took a step closer to the bird, straining to hear every word.

"There is too much to tell, and too little time to explain. Captain Amaranthe, you will need more than your Freeman and Seraphina, no matter their talent, to man the Deviant now. Bodhan of the Siren may be your greatest ally in this. Trust him."

Dare could feel the captain and Bodhan's tension at the mention of their names, but she could not look away from her queen's flashing face. There was such sadness in her eyes, and it broke Dare's heart to see it.

"Go north and send my regards to those within Tower Orr. They can help."

"Dare . . ." The voice paused and the queen seemed to look directly at Dare. "The life of my Chalice is precious to me. No harm must come to her." The recording skipped for several anxiety-ridden moments. "I gave my Arendal Sword a dagger before he went missing. Find it if you can. Find *me* if you can. I can endure, but my time may soon be winding down."

The beak closed and the bird's eyes ceased to flash. Her queen was gone. Again.

"Damn it, what happened? Why did it stop?" Phina had walked toward the blanket, her hand touching the fabric where Idony's face had been. As if she could maintain the connection by will alone.

The captain ran a rough hand through her dark hair. "That is all we have to go on? A dagger and a tower I have no knowledge of? She knew more than that, I could hear it. Why wouldn't she just tell us?"

Bodhan's low voice was thoughtful. "Perhaps she knew someone was listening and was unable to say more."

Dare rubbed her temples, trying desperately to think. What was it she was trying to say about Cyrus? She'd given him a dagger? If it was so important, why had she sent him away with it in his possession?

She had just seen proof that Idony knew of Captain Amaranthe and the Siren. She had called Bodhan an ally. Her faith in him had been justified, not that she hadn't already learned to trust him. To trust what she felt about him.

So why did she feel as though her heart was splintering? As if she never knew the queen at all?

And who was the man she spoke of? The one who had fooled the members of the Raj?

Agonized screams broke through the group's silence, and all of them flinched in surprise when a blood-covered Wen pulled down the blanket and appeared before them.

Wen dropped to his knees. "Gebby. I told him we shouldn't have come here. It took him. Biggest marsh cat I've ever seen bit his arm clean off and dragged him into the marsh. Please, he was cryin'— beggin' me to help him. Captain, *please*."

Dare turned to reach for the blade in her boot but stopped when she saw that the hummingbird, its mission complete, had disappeared the same way the dragonfly had.

The captain strode into the darkness, shouting orders. "Freeman, with me. Phina, in the trees now, I need your eyes. Wen, stay with Bodhan and Dare. We will return as quickly as we can."

"I could help." Bodhan lifted his hands, grimacing at the clinking of metal that kept them connected. When the captain disappeared as if he hadn't spoken, he muttered, "Perhaps not. She is just doing this for spite now."

Dare wanted to talk to him about what they'd just witnessed. Wanted to run after Captain Amaranthe and help Gebby. The kind crewman did not deserve such a gruesome fate. She knew of more than one marsh creature that had the ability and the aggression to kill a man.

"I think I should help them," she said. "Just let me—"

The distinctive cock of a pistol closed her throat. She looked up in time to watch Wen, now on his feet with a calm expression transforming his features, raise another cocked weapon and aim it at Bodhan's heart.

In the chaotic moments before, she hadn't sensed what she did now. Intense delight. *He'd laughed while slitting Gebby's throat and covering himself with the stupid man's blood.*

She swayed at the strength behind his sadism. "You killed him."

Wen's smile dimmed. "Lucky guess." He steadied his aim. "Three guesses what I'm thinking now, *Chalice.* Come on," he wheedled. "I *dare* you."

Chapter Ten

Dare mentally brushed away the negative feelings swarming round her head like insects and focused on her options.

Bodhan was vulnerable, still shackled despite the queen's words. The captain and the others were searching for Gebby, believing him alive. Dare was livid, but she was Wode. Though she hadn't had much use to practice those talents in the confines of the palace, they were a part of her.

She was no longer trapped beneath the sea or hovering over Theorrey in a flying machine. She was on solid ground.

Here, rage could enhance her abilities. Wode were of the earth, they said. Strong and numerous as the mountains and as molten at the core. She had taken down Nettles, and this man was a lanky half-wit compared to him. Only his aimed guns gave her cause for hesitation.

She could hear Wen's heart racing with the thrill of his success. Could sense Bodhan's nearly imperceptible movement as he edged his way toward something he could use to protect them.

"Either you are brighter than I originally gave you credit for, capable of overcoming all of us with nothing but two rusty pistols and your wits," Bodhan said derisively, "or you are a pawn in a bigger plan. I'm laying my wager on pawn. And pawns never play alone, so how about you tell us where your friends are?"

He was using the opportunity to distract their attacker. Clever. She would think he had done this before.

Dare's gaze narrowed on Wen's unsteady grip on his weapons. "You're right, Bodhan. I can feel others. Not the captain or Phina. Strangers. And the marsh has gone quiet, a sure sign we are no longer alone."

Wen paled. "It's true then? You are what my lord has been searching for? The blood in the chalice who can read minds?"

Bodhan laughed. "Ah, blessed ignorance. Do not tell me it was your idea to volunteer to crew for the bloody Captain Amaranthe as someone else's spy? You don't have to read minds to guess what she does to spies. Let's just say it takes time. Quite a bit of it, so I've heard."

Wen shuddered, his eyes blinking rapidly as if he feared he'd faint. He attempted a weak sneer. "Cursed bitch won't get the chance. I sent out the beacon. He knew she would come, don't you see? Knew *I* could get close. So I'll take little Miss Dare here, get my reward, and the rest of you can meet my other shipmates."

His lord. His ship. Was Wen implying he was a crewmember of the *other* airship? The fictional airship?

Bodhan seemed to think so. And his worry for her was tangible. It was also unnecessary. The gun aimed toward him, along with the glimpse she'd been given of the queen, had been the catalyst that reminded her who she was, and why she was here.

Bodhan would not be harmed.

She caught his eye, wishing for an instant he could feel what she felt for him. That he shared her ability. That he knew.

"You know what I love most about our campsite?" she asked.

He lifted one eyebrow, perhaps thinking she'd lost her mind as she took several steps back. The land dipped until she stood beside one of the trees that sprouted up through the wet grass.

Dare grinned. "You don't need Phina's senses to know that the heavier you men are, the louder your boots splash in the muck."

In an instant, she'd kicked out behind her and ducked to avoid Wen's reflexive shot. She heard a loud curse as she and Wen both hit the attacker lurking in the tall grass and darkness. The sound of a large body splashing as it sank into the marsh music to her ears.

Her leg was still high in the air and she deftly reached back with one hand to pull the slim blade out of her boot.

"Are you sure you're pure Wode? I have never seen a move like that from someone without Felidae blood." Bodhan's impressed tone pleased Dare immensely, though she knew the reaction was inappropriate to the moment.

"Just Wode," she assured him. "What I lack in size I make up for with other abilities."

He had moved as she spoke, using her as a distraction. He reached Wen's side and brought the metal on his wrists down hard on the skinny man's head. Wen crumpled in a boneless heap and Bodhan crouched down low to grab a pistol, tossing it toward Dare before reaching for the other. "Indeed. Remind me never to make you angry, princess."

The sound of the shot had sent the others out of hiding. Dare counted perhaps ten pairs of boots running toward them in the darkness. These men were not trained to move silently, which she found odd. Surely stealth would be a requirement for those who crewed the mythical shadow airship.

She hoped the captain had heard the commotion as well. Quiet or not, the numbers were against them. Dare moved strategically toward the center of camp, closer to Bodhan and higher ground.

They appeared through the mist and the darkness, men who varied in weight and size, but wore the same dark clothing, the same stripes of red painted across their faces like bloody claw marks.

The same distinctive weapons.

Dare narrowed her gaze and made a quick mental inventory of their raised hands. Every man she could see wore the same fingerless black leather gloves. Each glove was fitted with sharp retractable blades attached at each knuckle. Simulated Felidae claws? She had been expecting guns similar to Wen's, but these men were nothing like the skeletal deckhand.

They charged Dare and Bodhan with loud roars, fists high. She fired one-handed into the mob, holding her blade up and ready with the other.

She moved to stand directly in front of Bodhan, noticing as she did that their attackers seemed to be scattered, closing in from every side.

Dare opened her mouth to order him to turn around and fight back-to-back with her as Cyrus had taught her, but he was already moving into position, shooting his nearest attacker as she did the same. "I prefer being front-to-front with you," he quipped, "but I suppose this will have to do for now."

His teasing was short-lived as a clawed hand came close enough to scratch the fabric of her jacket and a small patch of skin at his side. She heard the useless clicking of his pistol and he swore. "I also prefer not to be shirtless and chained without *my* pistol when costumed marsh devils attack." He grunted as his fist connected with someone's flesh. "I am a simple man."

Dare sympathized. Wen's guns were far from reliable.

She blocked one clawed, beefy fist with her forearm and used the butt of the pistol to break the closest man's nose. It might not shoot but it was still good for something.

It seemed as if there were more of them coming. There was no way she could fight them all off. She felt the pressure on her back increase and whipped her head around to see Bodhan with the short chain connecting his cuffs wrapped around someone's neck, choking him until he lost consciousness.

He noticed her and snarled a smile. "And you thought I was just a pretty face."

His enthusiasm was contagious, but she had no time to respond to his banter. Arms nearly as thick as her torso wrapped around her chest, lifting her in the air and scratching her arms in the process. The sharp blades stung her flesh, and the scent of her own blood in the air around her only increasing her adrenaline.

Dare dropped her chin against her collarbone and then banged it back with all her might. The action caused her head to ring with pain, but it was effective. The oaf dropped her in surprise, falling back into the men behind him while cupping his bloody face.

Captain Aramanthe's voice reached out of the darkness. "Need any help, or should I sit this one out?"

A bubble of relieved laughter built in Dare's chest as Bodhan replied, "And deprive you of your fun?" He stepped on one prone attacker's wrist and twisted until they all heard the audible crack, then lifted his arms to deliver a two-fisted blow to a yowling adversary. "Any chance you brought my pistol, Captain?"

Captain Amaranthe's wicked smile was her only response as she drew her weapon, heading Dare's way.

Her sword was truly a thing of beauty. The steel glinted sharply even in the dim light. Almost too quickly for the eye to see, the captain's free hand pressed what had appeared to be a decorative gem on the hilt, then the silver sword began emit an eerie tone, a vibration Dare could feel in the air around them. In her skin. What in the name of the queen . . . ?

Captain Amaranthe grinned at Dare's expression, her hazel eyes sparkling. "Let me show you why this one is not on the wall. Get down!"

Dare obeyed instinctively and the captain's sword sang as it swung in a swift, perfect arc through the air. A male shout of horror cut off midstream before the blade returned to its owner's side, no trace of blood marring its pristine polish.

Looking over her shoulder, Dare saw that the other men had paused as a unit to stare down at the one who had fallen. Both pieces of him. He'd been split neatly down the middle and the halves had fallen in opposite directions on the spongy earth. The sickly smell of a singed animal tainted the air, and Dare preferred to think it was from the man's black fur cloak rather than the man himself.

Dare swallowed with difficulty and stood. When this was over she might swoon, but the Wode in her knew there was no time for that.

The men did not. She could feel their horror strong enough to read them clearly. *They had not expected this type of magic.*

Magic?

She used their distraction to her advantage, diving headlong into the crowd of flustered assassins. Dare lashed out at the nearest attacker with the heel of her boot, using her slender blade to slice through his shoulder and into the muscle, rendering his clawed hand useless against her. When he howled in pain but still lunged for her with his working hand, she had no choice but to plunge her dagger into his throat.

Phina's wild cry pierced the air and Dare knew she had joined in the fray. Now that Bodhan was no longer fighting alone, Dare allowed herself to focus on the remaining men. Hours or perhaps mere moments later, she whirled around, dagger high, and found herself face-to-face with the captain.

Stepping closer, her face glowing from exertion and the joy of battle, Captain Aramanthe panted, "Not so useless after all, are you, Blue?"

Dare wiped her blade on the leg of her pants, hoping she looked as at ease with actual fighting as the others did. A lifetime spent sparring had not prepared her for the reality of death. For blood. For the instant of frightened awareness in the enemy's eyes, in their hearts, before she dealt a killing blow. But she knew enough not to expose her weakness to this powerful woman. "Useful enough that you'll call me Dare?"

The captain lifted one elegantly arched eyebrow. "Perhaps. If I do, then I will reciprocate and allow you to call me Nerida. But only in private." She paused, taking the time to adjust the hilt of her sword until the sound and tactile vibration halted. "I suppose this new stage of our relationship means I have to release your beau and return his pistol." Her tone turned hopeful. "Unless you prefer him in chains?"

They turned back toward the wreckage of the camp. Freeman and Bodhan both watched them with something akin to admiration and—Dare opened her mind and reached toward them with her senses—lust.

She shook her head, fighting a bemused smile. "I'd prefer him free."

If he chose to be with her, he would do so while neither of them was under duress.

They were walking toward the men, stepping over the small island of dead or unconscious bodies left in their wake, when Dare noticed Phina. She was kneeling on the moaning Wen's chest, her body unnaturally still.

Bodhan spoke up with a cheeky grin, "We now have two prisoners for the price of one, either a fine replacement for me."

Dare glanced at the struggling stranger on the ground. Bodhan's boot pressed firmly into one forearm, Freeman's into the other, effectively rendering the man's upper body immobile.

Phina made a clicking sound with her tongue, drawing Dare's attention once more with a negative shake of her tousled ruby red hair. "Only one prisoner for you. Wen is *my* trophy." She leaned down until her nose was touching his. "He killed Gebby. Funny. Happy. Gebby."

Dare took a step closer, worried at Phina's odd tone, but the captain stopped her with an outstretched arm. "Gebby was good crew. Wen had no cause to kill him. From the look of the body, he snuck up on the old man. Prickless coward gave him no chance to defend himself."

Phina put her fist to Wen's chin, the clasps of her bracelet jangling out a warning. "I have a special kiss for you." She nipped his nose with her teeth. "It lasts for hours, makes you burn. You deserve a kiss, don't you? Gebby would want me to spare you." Her smile was broad, her lips thinned to bare her sharp white teeth. "But he's not here to stop me, is he?"

Wen looked terrified. "My lord will protect me. He knew *she* would come to the Deviant with her long blue hair and her magic. Knew I would be here. He will protect me." But he was no longer certain.

"Dare."

She looked up at Bodhan, unsure of how she felt about such a lack of mercy despite Wen's murderous actions. Bodhan held her gaze, giving no quarter in his expression. "He meant to take you away from me. Meant to kill us all."

Wen's sounds of agony were real now, telling Dare that Phina had used one of her poisonous darts on the man. She turned at the sound of scrabbling fingers digging at earth and crushing grass. Phina had taken her weight off his chest and Wen had rolled onto his stomach and was crawling away into the marsh. No one made any attempt to stop him, knowing his freedom would be short-lived.

Dare could not look at Phina. Though she understood her reasons, the turmoil of her emotions, she was uncomfortable with the Felidae's methods. But one man was fascinated. The wide-eyed prisoner, still easily held by two large booted feet, had been watching what Phina did with something akin to adoration.

Captain Amaranthe moved closer to him, blocking Dare's view. "I'll protect you from the Felidae if you tell us why so many of you came after us, if more are on their way, and why."

The man curled his lip. "Protect me? I pray to my lord that you allow me the sweet sting of her kiss. A free Felidae, not imprisoned by the cruelties of the usurper's rule? Let her claws penetrate my heart and send my soul to bliss."

Dare's lips parted in surprise, and everyone around her wore similar expressions. Phina most of all. Dare could feel her confusion at his declaration, but it made a certain sense. It explained their attackers' markings, their choices of weapons. These men emulated the Felidae, or attempted to. Emulated and perhaps obeyed?

She came closer, and he followed her movements with avid eyes.

"Is your lord Felidae?" She kept her voice soft, inquiring.

He smiled, the expression on his face akin to an adoring child or a fanatical cult member. "No. He looks human as we do so we may hear the truth. That the Felidae came from him as we did. As we all do. They follow him and soon is the time when he will lift them up to rule."

Phina growled, a sound more animal than human. "Queen Idony rules. The Felidae follow the queen. Are loyal *to the queen*. The moons must have addled your brain."

The prisoner winced as Freeman shifted more of his weight onto the man's arm in silent warning, but he still shook his head. "He promised you would not have to suffer much longer. He loves you.

He lifts your yoke as we speak." His gaze darted back to Dare. "But we need the stars to align. The third moon will burn the sky red and the river will run with gold. We need the blood of the earthbound Chalice."

Bodhan bent down to grip the strange man's hair in his hand, yanking hard. "Wen said that as well. Blood of the Chalice. I swear by the two moons I will carve you into small, bite-size pieces and use you as bait if you do not explain *precisely* what that means."

But Dare knew. The man felt it so strongly, believed it with so much of his being, that she was surprised no one else could hear.

Sacrifice. They needed sacrifice and there would be more than one.

She was trembling, not sure she should share what she'd learned with the others. Not with everyone so on edge. They would interrogate him, no doubt kill him in the attempt, but Dare knew they would receive no more information. This man was a true believer. He was no mastermind. He was simply obeying the will of his lord.

A cry echoed across the marsh, breaking the tense silence. Dare and the others whipped around in time to see Wen's severed head fly freely from his body and roll toward them on the small, bloodied hill.

Bodhan straightened and took a step toward the women. "There are more of them. Get me out of these damn cuffs. *Now.*"

The prisoner shouted in premature victory as he attempted to use their distraction to his advantage, rolling to his feet and taking a few panicked, stumbling steps toward her.

There was no need or time for Dare to lift her thin blade. Freeman reached out with one hand and dragged his flailing body back, snapping his neck as though it were no more than a twig before letting him drop. He nodded at Dare without a word, his attention returning to the head . . . and the sound of slow, unsteady footsteps splashing through the watery landscape.

And whistling. It was out of tune. Why did it sound so familiar?

Dare watched a tall, broad-shouldered shadow emerge from the darkness, his sword sheathed as he cupped something carefully in his hands. Another body part?

The low light of the fire that still blazed began to define his features. His head was shorn and covered with scars and fresh cuts as though he had shaved it himself with his blade, without the benefit of a reflective surface.

At some point his shirt may have been white, but now it was caked in mud and dried blood and torn in several places.

Dare's body shook visibly. She knew it but she could not seem to stop. She looked down at his hands, unwilling to focus on his face. To hope.

He was cupping a white lotus.

Bodhan strode toward him, rage and a frustrated desire for violence radiating off him like hot rays of the sun.

"Bodhan, wait! Don't hurt him." She ran ahead of him, making sure the man was blocked from the others. "Cyrus? Cyrus, is that you?"

He stopped whistling abruptly and indigo eyes, dilated but still so like her own, looked up at the sound of her voice.

Dare covered her mouth with her hand, tears spilling freely down her cheeks as she studied him. The skin around one of his eyes was cut and swollen with infection. His gaze was feverish. Confused. Both of his lips were cracked and raw with dehydration.

She would recognize him anywhere. "You're alive."

He lowered his chin to study the flower in his hand. "I found it. Some beast just tried to take it from me but I chopped off his head." He squinted. "I think it's the right color. Her favorite color. Will she forgive me now?"

He stumbled over a dead body and dropped hard to his knees, carefully steadying the lotus in his hand. "Keep it safe. I have to keep it safe for her."

Dare knelt down beside him, trying to bear all his weight as he tipped to the side, unconscious. "Help me. One of you, help me, *please.*"

Bodhan joined her, shouldering the slumped body despite her initial resistance. He lowered his voice. "Cyrus is the Arendal Sword, isn't he, Dare? Your companion shield guard to the queen is the same man who was taken from the Siren."

There was no surprise in his voice. Dare nodded, her voice ragged as she replied, "The queen blamed herself when they told us that he was gone. She would never have put him in harm's way. She loved him as much as I—" A sob welled up from her chest, choking her words.

The small group was somber as they studied the man who had carried a sacred flower into the remains of their carnage.

Phina broke the silence. "He is *not* the Queen's Sword. You are mistaken. You have to be."

Dare looked up swiftly, protective anger flaring inside her. "I have known Cyrus since he *became* an Arendal. He is like a brother to me. I lived more than thirteen years at his side. He *is* the Queen's Sword. He's alive and we . . . we need to get that ship off the ground and get him medicine and—"

Bodhan interrupted her, his attention on Freeman. "How quickly can you get the Deviant back in the air?"

Freeman glanced at the captain, who nodded in answer. He turned toward the ship, his long and powerful strides making short work of the distance.

"It won't be long," the captain murmured. "I'll stay on the alert until he's done."

"Captain." Bodhan sounded adamant even to Dare's distracted ear. "I do not mean to overstep, but I believe Phina needs to help your first mate with the ship."

Phina snarled but Bodhan was not deterred. "Perhaps it will cool her head. Allow her to think before she speaks."

Captain Amaranthe narrowed her gaze suspiciously but she complied. "Phina, go. Now."

When Bodhan nodded, Dare turned back to Cyrus, lifting her palm to his overly warm cheek. "He's sick, Bodhan. But he's alive. Cyrus is alive."

"I know, princess. I know."

Dawn was just breaking on the horizon when Bodhan allowed himself to relax and slip his pistol back into its holster. It was beautiful.

Had he ever enjoyed the feel of direct sunlight warming his skin until this moment? No. It had always been a reminder of his separateness, his secrets. But now he embraced the early morning light, knowing he had never had as much to lose. The secrets he kept? The people he was responsible for? The Siren that he so loved? None of it mattered as it should anymore.

Not as much as Dare.

He had lost his heart to the Queen's Chalice. Looking back, perhaps it had been from the moment he'd carried her on board his Siren. She *had* been locked in a tower all these years, along with the Ever Young queen. And a part of him had already known that.

His suspicions about the Siren's other half-breed arrival, Dare's improbable naivety and unquestionable integrity . . . It all made sense now. Though he was not sure if his feelings ever would.

She was like no one he had ever known. Rare and precious and far more than the owner of a brothel and procurer of information deserved.

It was unbelievable to him, to think that if things had stayed as they were, he would have never known she existed. For him, it would have been a lifetime of longing for something, unable to put his finger on the what—or the who—he was waiting for.

A low male voice brought him out of his musings. "The medicine

I keep on board broke the fever. All he needs now is sleep. And possibly a growing pot for his flower. Even in sleep he would not let that damn thing go."

Bodhan acknowledged him with a sober smile. "He speaks. I'm honored. Thank you, Freeman, Dare must be relieved. I also appreciate that you had Captain Amaranthe remove my chains. I know it was not her first choice."

The large man leaned against the rail and nodded. "The queen trusts you. It is enough for me."

Bodhan's smile grew. He understood the first mate's meaning. Their love for the queen and respect for the Khepri was what brought them all together. The one thing they had in common.

And Queen Idony's love for Dare could not be questioned after the revelations brought by Khepri's hummingbird. "After last night, I think Dare would have found her way without me. She is small but resourceful. I'm not sure I could have stopped her from escaping were we not underwater for the entire journey."

"You protected her."

Bodhan feigned surprise. "According to your lady captain, I had my way with her. I suppose it depends on how you look at it."

Freeman didn't smile. "The Chalice was unfamiliar with the Khepri until this happened. How could that be true? Her birthmark is . . ."

He sighed. "I know what it is. And what it might mean. I don't believe she does." Bodhan shook his head. He had no idea why it had been done. Why she had never been told. It was no ordinary mark. "There can be no doubt that she is important. But I'm not sure now is the time to address it. She's been through so much."

"The captain won't want to wait."

Bodhan nodded. "Perhaps you can suggest we give her a little more time and head to this—what did Queen Idony call it? Tower Orr?"

Freeman looked out over the horizon, his normally enigmatic

expression tinted with concern. "I would chart the course if I knew the way. North is not the most specific of directions. Hoping Dare or her Sword companion have our answers."

Bodhan leaned tiredly on one hip, knowing his next suggestion wasn't going to go over well. "The queen said I could help, and I can. Whatever is coming, the Deviant needs more men. And men, I have."

The laughter that escaped Freeman's lips was as disturbing as it was surprising. "Amaranthe is not going to like that."

"But you'll tell her."

Freeman met Bodhan's gaze, understanding passing between them. "I'll tell her. She'll see the truth in it." He paused as if unsure whether or not he should continue. "As to your truths, I suggest you sleep on them in Dare's room. She needs looking after, now more than ever."

Bodhan felt his hairline rise with his brows. "When you speak you don't mess around, do you? Before I take your advice, there's one more thing the captain should be aware of. Phina has seen the Sword before. As have I. He was on the Siren passing himself off as a half-breed." He'd stopped smiling now, lost in thought. "She's more than seen him actually, and they disappeared around the same time. Her tail was a bit bent out of shape when she realized who he was last night so I'm thinking . . ."

He let the sentence hang in the air, but they both understood. Phina had no doubt done what she always did, brought the man to ecstasy then robbed him blind.

"Damn it all."

Bodhan nodded. "She may be looking for an escape hatch soon, just so you know."

"No." The first mate shook his head. "Phina is as loyal to our queen as you or I. She won't be going anywhere. To be honest, I am more concerned about what the Wode will do when he wakes up and sees her." He rubbed one callused hand along the back of his neck in frustration. "Maybe he won't remember."

Bodhan sincerely doubted it. He had yet to meet the man who had run afoul of Seraphina Felidae and forgotten who she was. But she was the captain's crew, not his. Her crew. Her problem.

He stood straight and began walking toward the wooden door without another word. Freeman was right. He needed to be with Dare. His energy returned at the thought of touching her again.

Her body, her heart . . . protecting those was his new job for the foreseeable future. Not because she was the Chalice, but because she was his. He just had to convince her now that she was no longer on his ship. No longer alone. Now that she was free to decide how she truly felt about him.

Chapter Eleven

Dare let her damp hair hang over the edge of the claw-foot tub she'd found waiting for her in her room. It looked heavy, made of stone with copper conduction bars lining the outside—very similar to the baths in the women's suite of the Siren, though those had been bolted in.

Freeman must have done this for her. Her initial instincts about him had been correct. He *was* kind.

The water that filled it was steaming, and Dare had no thought to resist its lure. She toed off her boots and shed her grime-covered clothes before lowering herself in its soothing depths.

She tried to piece all that had happened together in her mind. All the wonders and horrors she had seen, along with the queen's words. Cyrus was alive. Her other half. Against every odd imaginable they had found each other this far from the palace. It was a relief, if she were honest. Cyrus was a true leader. He would know the next steps they needed to take to save Queen Idony.

Would he understand what Dare had done? What she had risked and the company she'd kept since last they met?

He had always been the most honorable of the both of them. Had always followed the rules of Wode. Would he hear her when she explained the truths she'd discovered about the Raj members and their science ministry?

She bit her lip, sinking lower into the heated water. Would he forgive her for Bodhan?

Since she had seen the queen's message from Idony's own mouth and her companion guard had appeared, Dare felt pulled in two directions. Her old life beckoned with its security, the family she'd always known, and a lifetime of memories.

Though her adoration and dedication to the queen could not be questioned, and she knew she would find a way to restore her to her throne or willingly sacrifice her life in the process, she was no longer sure that she could return to her former self.

This life called her, too, despite its chaos and her lack of balance. Perhaps because of it. She still needed so many answers. Why the queen had kept so many secrets from her, why people reacted so strangely to the mark she'd been born with. In fact, the only thing she didn't question was Bodhan. A man full of secrets who was never what he appeared to be. Yet, from him, she had received only honesty. Felt only truth and passion.

He was real. What she felt for him was real. She had no inkling what future there was to be had with the owner of the Siren, but she desired it. *Wanted* there to be a way. The knowledge was as frightening as it was freeing.

She wanted to be with him.

The door creaked open and she sensed him without opening her eyes. His relief at the sight of her. *Desire.* She smiled. "Bodhan."

"I think we need to clear the air between us." A boot fell with a thud to the floor and she knew he was undressing. "Our queen has commanded I share my greatest secret with the captain, and I will, but I wanted you to know me first. I *need* you to."

He sounded serious, and she opened her eyes as the second boot banged on the floor. "If we are being honest, I am not sure we will both fit in this bath."

Bodhan smiled. "Trust me, we will. Since you shared your secrets in the marsh, I thought it was time to return the favor. Have you ever wondered at the mark on my arm?"

"Of course. I thought trader's caste, perhaps . . ."

"It is no trader's caste I belong to."

Her brow furrowed. "What *do* you belong to?"

"Other than to you?" He slipped the large shirt Freeman had loaned him over his head, revealing several cuts and bruises from their recent skirmish. "The answer is not what, it is where. But perhaps that is the wrong place to start."

Dare gasped when he dropped his pants and swept her out of the water in one smooth move. Her body chilled in the cooler air of the room but warmed instantly when he stepped inside the tub and lowered them both until she was sitting in his lap, her legs on either side of his waist. "Oh my."

His cock hardened against her stomach. "Do not distract me with your love words," he muttered. "You know what I'm feeling as well as I, don't you?"

He raised his eyebrows at her shocked expression. "I heard the queen. And I'm no idiot, Dare—I already knew you were special. Special enough that you knew what Lennis was thinking. What all of us were feeling. Enough that there can be no secrets between us. Not on my end. So you know that everything I say to you is true. Which makes my usual mysterious charm irrelevant."

He relaxed into the water, his fingers gripping her hips, making it difficult for Dare to concentrate. Though she sensed that he needed her to, that what he had to tell her was important.

"I am what I've always claimed to be. The owner of the Siren. My father, however, is a master inventor. He built her when I was a young man, with help from the Khepri. An uncle of mine ran her until I came of age, and then passed her secrets and her guardianship to me." He paused. "The kind of political and personal secrets you can only get from taking down a man's guard. Putting them in compromising situations. The kind that would ensure we could keep the queen safe . . . and our people hidden."

"Your people?"

Bodhan's eyes darkened as they gazed into hers. "My people. People who live without caste. Without the laws of the Theorrean Raj or the enforcement of their laws by the Wode. It is paradise, my home, Dare. Beyond description. I do what I do, protect who I can, for them. The Khepri has his way, the captain hers . . . the Siren is mine."

How could that be possible? The Wode had outposts in every habitable corner of the world. No one was beyond the law. Yet the way he described it was intriguing. Paradise. It sounded far more welcoming than the world she'd come to know. "This is your secret that the queen wanted you to share? Your people? And Queen Idony and the Khepri both know of this place? These people?"

He nodded, his fingers caressing her lower back, her hips. She pressed her palms against his chest, reveling in the resistance of his powerful body.

"I believe we were the ones she was referring to in her message. If the men of Aaru knew she was in danger, nothing—not fear of discovery or death—would stop them. My people love and honor the queen. When the others look to the Copper Palace and bless the queen, the people of Aaru pray for her freedom."

Her freedom? But she had not been taken that long ago. Bodhan read her expression. "You have felt it yourself, Dare, you know you have. The palace is a cage. Beautiful and gleaming, but still a cage. Since you have been her Chalice, has she left it? She may have uttered no word against the ever-increasing control of the Raj, but surely you felt it?"

She had. Her limbs began to tremble as she felt the truth in his words. A truth that had crept into her awareness over the last few days. Had it only been days?

She had accepted, without question, what she had been told to. She had wondered why the queen would remain silent when she disagreed with each new law passed by the Raj. Wondered but never dared question. She felt unworthy of being the Chalice.

He swore. "Dare, I am an ass. This was not what I meant to— I wanted to tell you everything. To share what I am with you. All that I am. So you would know that I wasn't a criminal. That I am as loyal to the queen as any on this ship. As the companion guard you love. I have no cause nor the ability to pass judgment on you and neither does the queen. Look at all you have risked searching for her. To save her. Is it any wonder she would love you?" He lifted her chin with the fingers of one hand until she was looking into his eyes once more. "That *I* would love you? That I would hope that you could find a way to love me in return?"

His words broke through the darkness that had been crowding in on her. He loved her. And she knew now that, even when she'd believed him nothing more than a criminal, she had desired him. Loved him.

Her mind was spinning again. She had a feeling that was a sensation she would have to get used to. Her world had changed but she was now living in it. A part of it. No more secrets or riddles or games. It was hard, but it was real.

Now all she wanted, all she had, was this moment, was this. Touching him. Loving him. Feeling his love for her. "Perhaps we could save any new and life-altering sharing for tomorrow?"

Bodhan studied her face intently for a long moment and then his smile returned. "Whatever will we do with ourselves until then?"

"You could give me another first."

A growl rumbled in his chest and his cheeks flushed with arousal.

Dare reached down between them, taking him in her hands and lifting her hips to guide him inside her.

"First time in the bath or on top?" Bodhan's voice was raspy. Breathless.

She lowered herself onto his erection, leaning forward until her words brushed his lips with her own. "The first time I tell you I love you, too."

He kissed her and Dare melted into him, her body alive with sensation, on fire with need. He filled her so completely, so perfectly. As if he had been designed for her body. Created for her pleasure. Born for her to love.

The world could wait for them. For this. It could stop for this moment. Just this once. As long as his hands kept hold of her hips while she rocked against him, water splashing from the tub onto the floor with the power of her thrusts. As long as he continued to kiss her, sucking her tongue into his mouth and moaning at her taste. As long as he loved her.

He tore his mouth from hers with obvious difficulty. She was so close to that remembered feeling, so close to breaking apart in his arms, that it took a moment for his words to register.

"I love you, Dare. Senedal or no. You are my Siren. The only woman I cannot resist."

Dare bit his jaw, rocking her hips against him and crying out as her movement started a deep, powerful quaking inside her. "Am I your first?"

His fingers tightened almost painfully against her flesh. "You are. In every way that counts. You are my heart. My only. Love— *Dare.*"

He dragged her against him and took her mouth again. When he joined her in oblivion, his shouts mingling with hers as they shattered together.

It was not until they were lying in her bed after hours had passed that Dare could form a coherent thought again. "I feel bad for Coral and the others. For James Stacy. They must be worried for you. Wondering what happened."

Bodhan lifted his lips from her neck, where he'd been gifting her with slow, tender kisses as she lay in his embrace. "They know."

She lifted herself onto one elbow, feeling her eyes widen with her surprise. "How?"

He grinned. "My cuff is connected to the Siren, princess. They could find me anywhere as long as it was turned on. And it has been since we left. I tapped out a message before I removed the theorrite in the marsh." She nodded and he continued, "I received their reply just before dawn. James and a few of the others are on their way. Captain Amaranthe's newest recruits until I can get word to Aaru."

She could hardly believe it. "They're leaving the Siren to come here?"

"Some will stay, though I've given orders that we are out of business for the indefinite future." His expression sobered and he reached out to cup her cheek with his warm palm. "Did you think I—that *any* of us—would leave you alone in this, Dare? Did you imagine I could? The Siren is at the queen's command, along with the Deviant. At *your* command, Chalice. We will find her together."

Dare's vision blurred. She was not alone. She and Cyrus had allies now.

She had Bodhan.

It was impossible for her to know how her companion shield guard—her friend—would react to the news when he woke. But one thing was certain. Once again, nothing would ever be the same.

For Dare, loving a man like Bodhan would ensure it.

FIERY TEMPTATIONS

Chapter One

"So little to drink, so much time."

Seraphina uttered Gebby's favorite salute to the empty air before pressing a bottle to her lips and tipping back her head. She swallowed the final moss-colored drop, set down the empty container on a wooden chopping block in the galley, and glared at it in morose consternation.

"Absencea," she scoffed. It refused to deliver on the promise of sweet oblivion it had given her in the past. Two bottles into the noble's beverage of choice and her tail was still on edge. Now, nothing of the finer liquor remained on board. She would have to drink the rot they had left in the cupboards.

The crowd of Siren guards who had invaded her safe haven had no doubt drained Freeman's private stock. Not exactly welcome guests. As of last night, the Deviant had been overrun and was flying in circles. Two of Phina's lives, the ones she'd kept separate for so long, were merging into singular chaos.

She needed another drink.

She had served Captain Amaranthe on the airship Deviant as a part of her crew, a consummate thief and—should the situation prove dire—assassin. Her service on the submersible Siren was in an entirely different capacity.

Each ship gave her its own brand of satisfaction and release, but the Deviant was her home. The only place she had true purpose. She served Queen Idony. In her own unique fashion.

The queen. Phina owed her everything, loved her with a ferocity of emotion she had never allowed herself to feel for a human before. Without her, she would have been lost long ago. To the mines. To beatings from the Wode for her rebellious nature. Or worse, killed for the treason she had been coerced into committing, the ignorant accomplice in the abduction of the Queen's Sword.

Since she'd sworn her allegiance to Queen Idony and aligned herself with the captain and the Khepri, Phina had never looked back. Her confidence in her skills and wits, as well as her ability to squeeze out of tight places, had never faltered.

Until now.

She should have known Dare was the Queen's Chalice, regardless of her unusual scent. She should have searched Bodhan's infernal wrist cuff, the one device he'd kept close to him at all times on the Siren. Though even if she had, they would have never been able to use it without Dare.

She should have known that damned stubborn man she'd used all her wiles to seduce when he arrived on the Siren was the last man she should have trifled with. Or let trifle with *her* before leaving him to his fate.

Above all of these things she should have known, the queen's jeopardy was the most difficult for Phina to deal with. She should have returned to the Copper Palace for their annual late-night visit instead of throwing herself into the distraction of sexual play aboard the Siren. Sexual play meant to distract her from a certain blue-eyed Wode. The fact that he had been taken. That she had been complicit in his disappearance.

Phina grabbed a full jug of the homemade rotgut and left the galley, her thoughts no longer entirely on her queen. She could smell *him*. His scent was distinctive from the other males aboard, and it was all over the damned ship.

Cyrus. The Arendal Sword. The Queen's Sword. He smelled like the first snows on the mountains. The clean cold air that occasionally cut through the factory fog. The fire and sweat in the air when a mating occurred in the Felidae settlement.

The scent was stronger than it had been in days, making her hair stand on end, her flesh heat, and her lips curl back in instinctive reaction.

He was awake now. He would see her. Know she was on board. How would he react? With remembered pleasure for a night of passion, or rage?

She stopped in the hallway, aware that she'd been heading to his room, gravitating there as she had each time she allowed herself belowdeck. She'd watched him while he'd slept and healed. Where had he been? What had happened to him since she'd last seen him?

Phina now knew a few of the players involved in his abduction—one of them was dead, and one of them would be for tricking her into being an accomplice. But not right away. First he would direct her to the true villains behind the abductions. Once she found them? They would suffer. Not only for what they had done to Cyrus, but for ruining her life by sending him back to *her*. To the Deviant. Making her think about him again and see him in the flesh. As if looking into Dare's identical indigo eyes had not been enough of a reminder of her guilt.

She turned back to the galley, focusing on the stained glass behind the cooking stove as soon as she walked through the door. Sunlight sent shafts of colored light through the flowers and vines. It was an addition to the Deviant she knew the captain had chosen herself, though she had no idea why. Nerida Amaranthe was not the flower type.

Phina bent her knees and leapt up onto the copper conductors. She slid the latch that kept the window closed open and pushed the glass outward. Her other hand still held a firm grip on her jug.

It took no effort to evade the sticky dodge that shielded the ship from ground view. Looking up, she saw the rope that dangled just out of reach. Human reach. But as she had been reminded most of her life, Seraphina was no human.

Tension coiled in her thighs and then she was flying. She felt an instantaneous jolt of adrenaline before her fingers and tail wrapped around the thick fibers of the rope. She loved the feeling. It was—on occasion—better than seeking her pleasure with a willing man. Or two.

Her climb required less thought than maintaining her hold on the liquor. When she lifted her body over the rail and rolled, she crouched low on the helm's deck between the autobinnacle that guided the ship when Freeman was not piloting it manually and the thick decorative railings. The aether cocoon shifted softly in the rigging above her, the only witness to her spying.

A small crowd of men stood in a loose circle on the deck below. They were watching something she imagined not a one ever expected to see in their lifetimes—the Sword and Chalice of the ever-young queen sparring on the deck of a ship that should not exist.

Not that the fact stopped them all from shouting advice and offering criticism. Men did love a good fight.

Phina inhaled deeply. The Sword was healing, but a lingering infection remained. The smallest of traces, but still there. And something else that she didn't want to think about. A scent that reminded her of how completely she'd wronged him, however inadvertently.

She grimaced. What man would be fool enough to push himself this hard before he was ready? The others may be conned into believing he was in perfect condition, but Phina knew better. She could hear his heart racing and see the waves of heat coming off his body from his exertion.

Dare, in contrast, was holding back. Phina had been so drawn to the strange, special girl—even before she knew who she was. Her scent and taste had been unique. Her fighting . . . she had never seen a Wode female use anything other than her brute strength. Certainly never known of one who seemed to be able to—though lacking in height and strength—fight with such intuition and instinct. Such awareness.

She was not merely Wode. She couldn't be. Dare was something more.

Her old "boss" from the Siren had noticed Dare as well. Phina bit down on the cork that stoppered her jug, tugged it out, and spit it into her palm. She wrinkled her nose as she took a swig of the bitter brew, squinting at the sight of Bodhan attempting nonchalance on the sidelines of the fight. He was *not* doing it well, despite his eyes being hidden by the oddest-looking covering. He called them shaded spectacles or lenses. The man had interesting trinkets.

How he must hate this. Watching his lover grappling with another man, innocent or no. It was clear the two knew each other well, could communicate without words. Their sparring match was more of a dance, and Bodhan wanted to cut in as much as Phina was tempted to.

He was smitten, that was clear. His usual distant demeanor was gone, as was his obsession with his work. The man had shut down the Siren for this mission. For Dare. He must really believe he loved her. It was the only conclusion Phina could find that would excuse the exceptional man's change in behavior.

From her hidden perch above the fray and the banter of the new crewmen, she studied him. His dark skin and black-as-night hair. He lowered his chin to look over his lenses and she was struck, as she always was, by those distinctive light blue eyes she had only seen in one or two others in her lifetime. Usually in traveling traders.

He should have been her type. Someone who understood and embraced debauchery in all its forms. Someone who did not judge her for her nature. She may have felt a twinge of regret that she had not fallen for Bodhan, had not swayed him from his respectfully self-imposed rules and seduced him into taking a lover from those in his employ. But she was never truly drawn to him in that way, and he had never shown an interest in anyone. Until the innocent Dare.

Still, she was a lucky little Wode. Bodhan was a good man.

Thinking of *how* lucky brought her attention back to the newly awakened Cyrus. He had been a truly inventive lover. Tireless and unwilling to play her domination games. She was panting for breath at the mere thought of how he'd laughed at her whip. At her suggestion that he let her take control.

The long hours of delight that had followed.

She took another swig of the rot. He had not been truthful with her, either. He had told her he was a half-breed when she could clearly scent his lie. He had told her he was wandering and shiftless when she could see the agenda, the determination in every move he made.

Had his lies made it easier for her to justify her actions?

Watching him spar now, his movements confident, cunning, and ruthless, she wondered at how anyone could have believed his disguise. Just as Bodhan had sensed Dare's secret almost from the beginning, she had known Cyrus was a bad liar. Which had been, in itself, a surprise. As a rule she knew that most men lied.

In her experience everyone did, and she saw nothing wrong with it as a rule. Though she'd always noticed that women were not as quick to lie as those creatures in Theorrey blessed or cursed with a prick. Lies seemed to come with the appendage. Inherent to their sex. Cyrus was different. He did not enjoy lying. And he was the kind of man who would have a hard time forgiving those who did.

She lifted the jug once more.

"Early to be drinking."

The male voice behind her was soothing. No accusations, just commentary. A deep, rich, melodic commentary that instantly lowered Phina's hackles. At last, a familiar port in her current storm.

She looked over her shoulder. "Freeman. How is it that someone near as big as the ship could sneak up on a Felidae?"

A momentary smile relaxed his features. "If the Felidae in question is distracted by drink and an overabundance of pheromones, it is not as hard as one might imagine."

She leaned her head against the polished wooden railing and batted her eyelashes at him playfully. "You have such a beautiful voice, Freeman. You should use it more often."

Yet, he never did. As far as she knew, Freeman only spoke at length to the captain and herself. And recently to Bodhan, which only made Phina like the brothel owner more. Freeman was the best judge of character she knew. Still, apart from trading supplies and hiring the occasional crewmember, he had chosen silence over verbal communication. And people believed *she* was talented at misdirection.

Phina knew that others, more often than not, believed Freeman a big, hulking, slow-witted mute. It was his own form of the dodge. The illusion he projected to the world as Captain Amaranthe's first mate. And it was a good one.

Men were easy enough to understand as a rule. Most clothed themselves in selfish needs, spoiled and longing for approval. Easily threatened. In the rougher parts of the world, you could be small and brilliantly silver-tongued, or large and stupidly obedient, but anything outside that expectation—indeed, anything more complex— was viewed with suspicion. The people the Deviant crew needed to work with did not trust complexity.

Freeman was truly intelligent, strategically brilliant, a gifted healer and pilot. He could also crush a man's throat with the fingers of one hand and no doubt memorize a scholar's book of poetry while doing it.

He was a dangerous enemy and an irreplaceable ally. Not even Captain Amaranthe understood his complexity. And Phina knew if Freeman had his way, she never would.

His eyes, more golden than brown, twinkled, disrupting her train of thought. That was another thing the captain never seemed to notice. How handsome he was.

"I should speak more and you should flirt less. Each is as likely as the moons rising in the morning." His strong, square jaw tightened as he nodded in the direction of the men on the main deck below. "Why are you hiding? No one is a stranger to you here. Unless there is something you have yet to tell us about our new arrivals. Any irate victims or broken hearts I should be wary of?"

She avoided his knowing gaze and took another fortifying gulp of the jugged courage. Swallowing, she forced herself to offer a careless shrug. "I dislike change. The Deviant can practically fly itself, no offense to her pilot, yet we are filling up on crew, and the Siren is currently out of commission, leaving me to search for distraction elsewhere. My kind is inherently predisposed against change."

He tilted his head, the dark gold of his shaggy hair falling over his forehead. "You are rarely this poor a liar, Seraphina. Are you taking responsibility for her disappearance? The queen was *theirs* to protect. If anyone is at fault it would be them." He was silent for a moment, as though contemplating his own words. "However, I cannot blame them, either. They have both had a rough time of it. And it seems Queen Idony and the Khepri kept secrets from all of us, even her closest companion guards. No matter how powerful the ship, no one can fly it blind. We need to find this Tower Orr. And we need to question Dare's companion about the dagger."

Phina turned to study Cyrus once more. He had removed

his shirt and his back was uncovered for her view. His skin had been darkened by the sun since last she'd seen him like this. It appeared harder. Battle-roughened. Her lips tightened. It had also been whipped. The long, deep scars crossing his back said he hadn't enjoyed it.

She wanted to taste it. Kiss it better.

In the last few days his hair had grown, an indigo shadow covering the scars on his head. Phina recalled gripping that head, fighting to keep her claws retracted as he took her to the brink only to leave her there, beginning her torment anew.

Freeman lowered his voice in warning. "Do not growl or they will find you out. No one has told him you are on the ship yet. That will happen soon enough. The captain allows them this moment to relieve their tension. For the Sword to prove he is fit to fight. But her patience will not last. I'm surprised she has restrained herself this long. To have so many men on her ship, to let so many know what we are doing . . . it's not easy for her to obey this particular request from the queen. It would help if she had more information. A direction. I believe she thinks the Queen's Sword will be the key."

Phina would get it for her if she could. But she had a sinking feeling that she was the last person Cyrus wanted to see.

Alive.

"I taught you better than this, Senedal. Unless your intention is to shame me in front of this new crew."

Dare rolled her blue eyes at Cyrus playfully, her cheeks glowing from their invigorating match. More than invigorating. Dare, it seemed, was just warming up for more. Cyrus, on the other hand, was ready to lie down once more. Or have another cup of that hot, restorative tea that monster of a first mate brought to him twice daily since he'd arrived on this unique airship.

Dare shook her head. "You think I hold back, Arendal?"

Cyrus grunted, evading a low dagger strike with a swift side step. "I know you do. I believe over a decade of training you have given me insight into how you think. You still let your thoughts and feelings distract you."

She stepped back, a strange expression on her face as she looked over his shoulder. "Perhaps you are correct." Dare bit her lip in a telling gesture that Cyrus recognized from when she was a child. She was unsure. He lowered his weapon.

Her shoulders squared and she raised her voice. "Seraphina? Cyrus believes I am too tenderhearted to give him the sparring match he desires. I think you would be a better opponent for him, don't you?"

Cyrus turned as if in slow motion, noting the pity, the apology in Dare's gaze. His hand instinctively tightened on the hilt of his borrowed sword.

He saw the tall first mate standing on the higher steerage deck, looking down at something, or someone, at his feet. The man shook his head and took a jug away from a slender hand connected to a feminine arm.

An arm marked with unmistakable Felidae spots.

When the woman stood and turned, Cyrus watched as the distinctive limb became a figure. A curvaceous, nubile body barely covered in a tight corset and topped with a wild mane of fiery red hair. His heart began to pound. It beat out an angry rhythm in his head. In that rhythm was a name.

Seraphina Felidae.

There were images that had sustained him under the burning heat of the sun and plagued him during the long, cold nights he was away. They had kept his rage alive and focused his energy. They'd helped him escape his shameful fate and arrive, insensate but alive, at the Deviant.

All of those images had been of her.

Her bare breasts filling his hands. Her sharp teeth digging into his flesh. Her cries when he'd licked one velvet marking on her spine, his hips pounding against her again and again.

The look in her emerald green eyes when he'd asked her to stay the whole night. Desire and regret. She'd kissed him and he'd felt the sharp sting of a dart piercing his flesh.

In those moments before he lost consciousness, he'd cursed her, and himself, for being taken in. For believing the power of the need between them was real enough to risk his mission. To make himself vulnerable. His own desire had betrayed him, but she had dealt the killing blow to his pride and opened the door to the enemy while he was at his most vulnerable.

Seraphina Felidae. She was here. On the Deviant.

He snarled. "I accept your replacement, Dare. Gladly."

His gaze was trained on her every movement, noticing her hesitation. Her tension. It seemed she did not want to fight him.

He would have to change that. "How did she convince you to let her on board?" he asked to the group at large. "She must have given someone as hard a ride as she gave me. She is talented in that area. Almost as talented in bed as she is at deceit."

"Cyrus." Dare whispered the admonishment, but he would not listen. She couldn't know what he'd been through.

"You forget my abilities, brother. I know what you are feeling. Just remember, she is loyal to our queen. Our ally."

"She is loyal to no one but herself." He knew Seraphina could hear him and saw her tail stiffen at the insult. "How could she be? We all know what she is."

He was a bastard, but he could not help the elation that coursed through him as he watched her leap over the balustrade and onto the deck. Adrenaline raced in his bloodstream despite his fatigue. Rage gave him strength.

He was Wode.

She held up a hand and caught the two daggers someone tossed her way with an ease that had Cyrus licking his lips in anticipation.

He smirked. "No whip, Felidae?"

"You're injured. Being what I am, even I would not kick a wounded babe for sport. Besides, I need no whip to beat you. We all know what you are as well."

They circled each other and to Cyrus it seemed everyone else disappeared. Only she remained. Her intoxicating scent. Her body.

Her betrayal.

"What a reunion to wake to." He chuckled bitterly. "James Stacy and his friends, the brothel owner, and now you. Am I to believe I'm back on the Siren? That the past few months were merely a nightmare? Or did you all want another chance to sell me to the highest bidder?"

Seraphina flinched, her body tense. Wary. "Much as I'd love to blame them, you and I both know they had nothing to do with what happened to you. Why waste all that passion on people who have not earned it?"

"Why, indeed." He strode closer to her, his sword out, leaving himself wide open. "You want passion? Fight me."

She made no move to strike him, though he noticed her knuckles were white around each dagger's hilt. He wanted her to. He wanted a reason to release all that was pent up inside him. All that pain. All he had been through. And all the while the people he loved in danger because he allowed this woman to come to his bed. "How much was I worth?"

"What?" She shifted, taking a step back.

Cyrus moved closer, unwilling to give her a chance to escape. "The Queen's Sword must have been worth something. They went to so much trouble to take me out of a heavily guarded submersible. That is no easy feat."

"If only, Arendal." Bodhan's voice was condescending, a grating and unwelcome interruption. "The Deviant's crew plucked me out of my bed without a single shot fired. The Siren's security has been lacking of late."

James Stacy groaned behind him. "I've apologized for that, sir. It will not happen again."

He wanted them gone. Wanted their silence. If he had a gun . . .

Seraphina inhaled sharply. "Keep out of this, all of you. This is between sword boy and I, isn't it, Cyrus? I tied him up and dragged him unwillingly to my bed. I personally gave him each new scar on his body." She smiled and licked her lips, taunting him. "Oh and did I mention? I thoroughly defiled innocent Dare in front of Bodhan and a paying customer."

Cyrus could not stop the raw sound of outrage that escaped from his chest. She knew. Knew the words to rend his control from his grasp. To shred it to pieces until he was more animal than man. She had done this to him. Made him this beast that couldn't think. His head was clouded, his body aching and his heart fighting to explode from his chest.

Her fault. Seraphina Felidae.

He dropped his sword and reached for her, taking her to the ground with an ease that should have given him pause. His legs pinned hers while one hand gripped her wrists above her head.

The other curved threateningly around her throat, applying momentary pressure.

"Fight me," he growled. Why was she lying there? She had the strength to buck him off, to claw at him and force her release.

Her green eyes were huge. As mesmerizing and exotic as he had remembered, with an expression he'd never seen in them before. Regret. Her breath against his lips was sweet with drink and the flavor that was hers alone.

He caressed her neck, silently cursing the marks he could see forming on her silken skin. Why did he care? Felidae pheromones inspired lust, not guilt. She had sent him to his end. Or believed she had. She'd taken everything that made him what he was. Why did he suddenly want to beg her forgiveness?

"Fight me," he repeated harshly.

He felt a sharp point pressing his chin upward until he caught the captain's eye. He hadn't noticed her approach.

Her expression was chilling. "*I* will fight you, Wode. In fact, if you are not off her before I press this colorful gem on the hilt of my sword, I will fight both pieces of you that remain. I doubt, either way, that it will be a challenge."

Cyrus got to his knees and stood swiftly, his hands out to show he meant no harm. What had come over him? No matter how livid he'd been when he'd seen her, there was no excuse to harm a woman. "My apologies. Her presence surprised me."

Captain Amaranthe hesitated, then sheathed her sword and studied the silent crowd. "As for the gawkers. That is enough sport for the morning. Despite what Bodhan may have told you, this is no pleasure cruise. We need to post watches fore and aft, and I expect the deck and all its workings to sparkle." Her hazel eyes darkened. "If I must sustain you with food and drink, and, it seems, all of my best liquor, you will earn your keep."

He noticed her expression soften as she reached out a hand to help Seraphina to a standing position. "Shall I kill him for you?"

The pale Felidae shook her head and he thought he heard her whisper, "I've done enough."

He watched her turn to walk toward the lower cabins, stopping when she reached Dare's side.

His companion guard reached for her. "I *am* sorry. I did not believe he would react so strongly."

Seraphina took her hand and squeezed. Cyrus frowned. Did

Dare trust her, then? How was that possible? With her abilities how could she?

"He is not himself. They did more than wound him. Vayun," Seraphina muttered loud enough for him to hear as she pushed Dare's hands gently away. "*He* smells of vayun. Remnants only. If given in excess it can still be detected for several days. He is no doubt suffering withdrawal along with the last of his illness."

Was this a trick? *She* was defending *him*? Cyrus stepped forward swiftly. Too swiftly. "How do you know what they gave me?" His laugh was bitter. "Oh, I beg your pardon, I forgot. You were the one who fucked me, stuck me, and handed me over to them."

He wove, unsteady on his feet. The day's activities seemed to crash in on him at once, along with the knowledge that he was about to show his weakness to them all. Again. "No."

"Cyrus, are you unwell?" Dare's concern felt too much like pity. He refused to accept it.

He growled. "I just need a drink. And a few more answers about what we're doing to find the queen."

Captain Amaranthe patted him on the shoulder too firmly to be mistaken for sympathy. "And they say there is no such thing as coincidence. Answers are what we need as well. Freeman? Make this man a stiff cup of tea while I show him to my quarters for a little chat."

On her lips the word chat sounded unmistakably like interrogation.

Seraphina was walking away, her head down, her tail gently stroking her thigh as if she were unconsciously offering herself comfort.

He swore. A distraction sounded like a brilliant idea right about now.

The men dispersed, all eyeing him with equal parts judgment

and fear, when Dare returned to his side. Cyrus waited until Bodhan and the others had followed the captain before speaking to her.

"You knew she was here? You know what she did to me?" Unable to look at her, he stared over her shoulder at the clouds rushing past.

"I know she was trying to find you. And yes, I knew you were missing. Bodhan was trying to find yo—"

His expression of disbelief halted the words on her lips. "The whoremonger was trying to save a half-breed? You expect me to believe that? And Seraphina was aiding him, I suppose. Overwhelmed with guilt for drugging me so her friends could have me stuffed in a trunk and shipped off to . . . Never mind. You have no idea what kind of people you're dealing with, Dare. You have to trust me. Have I ever been wrong?"

Her answer shocked him. "You know how much I respect you, have always respected you, but yes, you have." She sighed, whispering in a low voice so no one else could hear. "I was not prepared for this, Cyrus. Neither of you prepared me for *this*."

He stepped back to lean against the ship's railing, reeling as much from her words as his body's damnable weakness. She was not wrong. He'd had enough time to think about it when he was away. About all the things Dare did not know. How he had left the safety of Queen Idony to unprepared palace Wode. His overconfidence in his own abilities had been thoroughly routed.

He thought about what he'd learned this morning. That the queen's worst fears had been realized while he had allowed himself to be shamed beyond redemption as a prisoner. That they were on an airship with a non-Wode contingent that were, nevertheless, loyal to the queen.

Dare had found her way here alone. She had risked her life's blood while she believed herself without allies. Had been without allies. It was much to take in.

But he was here now.

And so was Bodhan, captain of the Siren. And it was obvious, even in his current state, that he was involved with the Queen's Chalice. The way he looked at Dare brought every one of Cyrus's protective instincts roaring to life.

Cyrus could not deny it vexed him. Dare was his family, the Chalice he had been trained to protect, along with the queen, for as long as he had been Arendal.

"I am sorry for all you have suffered due to my incompetence," Cyrus began hesitantly. "I can understand your loss of faith in me, but I admit I cannot fathom your recent choices."

Dare tilted her head, her indigo braid sliding over her shoulder as she peered up at him. "You mean Bodhan."

Cyrus shrugged. "I am grateful that he cared for you when I could not, but he is—"

"More than you know," Dare completed his sentence, interrupting him. "He is so much more than you know. Queen Idony may have entrusted you with more of her secrets, but not all of them. Trust her now, Cyrus. She trusts him. And if you cannot, then trust me." She took a shaky breath and stepped away from Cyrus in unspoken apology. "I love him."

She loved Bodhan. She stood before him, a strength inside of her that he'd always sensed, but never seen, and declared her love for a criminal whose existence went against every Theorrean law in the books. She had changed. He could not help but see that it looked good on her.

Cyrus nodded. "I assume you know exactly how he feels in return?"

Dare blushed and Cyrus stood up straight, ready to end this uncomfortable conversation. "Good. I reserve the right to dislike him, treat him rudely, and cut off any of his protruding limbs should he step out of line with you or treat you without the respect you deserve. That being said, we should no doubt take the captain up on her invitation to talk."

He watched the smaller Wode lead the way with confident strides. She chuckled. "That was no invitation. And consider yourself warned. If you argue with Captain Amaranthe . . . make sure you aren't anywhere near the railing. Or her blades."

Chapter Two

He rolled onto his back with a sigh and pushed off the blankets. The bed was comfortable, the sheets were soft, and he was clean and cared for. Why was he awake?

He swung up to a sitting position, resting his arms on his knees and savoring the cool wood of the floor with his bare feet. He could see the sky out the window. No desert dunes. No mountains beckoning in the distance. Just dark sky and stars. It should perhaps be a disturbing idea, such a heavy ship hovering this high above the ground. However, he had more pressing worries than gravity or its lack at the moment.

Still. The first twitch of a smile formed on his lips. He wished he could have been there to see Dare's face when she had first seen this. Or when she'd discovered she was on a submersible beneath the sea.

It had been a frustrating and unproductive meeting with the captain, Freeman, and Bodhan. Having to tell them the dagger had disappeared after he'd been taken, having to admit to that shame aloud, had done nothing for his pounding head or his pride.

In an effort to comfort him, Dare had come to his room, Bodhan in tow, and told him in detail about her experiences before he arrived. She'd reminded him so much of the queen, he'd had to bite the inside of his cheek to maintain his composure. Queen Idony did love to tell stories.

Dare's tale emphasized the loyalty of the people around her: Bodhan's tender protection, Freeman and the captain's concentration on protecting the queen, her unusual friendship with Seraphina and even the incredible message from the queen sent on the wings of what Dare described as a tiny metal hummingbird.

He had known that despite the Theorrean Raj's attempts to isolate her, the queen had a sweeping reach they could not touch. He had been sent on enough "training exercises" over the years to know that she was as beloved as she was wise.

Yet he had not imagined this. According to Dare, the queen knew Seraphina personally and believed her loyal. In his life, he had never known his sovereign to be wrong, but he could not believe the queen would countenance what the Felidae did while her back was turned.

Dare told him she had felt true regret in Seraphina when he'd attacked her on the deck. That she did not believe Seraphina could be responsible for his abduction—not knowingly.

While he was not so sure about that, he had regrets as well. Now that his mind was truly beginning to clear, he knew his lack of control was inexcusable. The yearning for the vayun that still lingered in his body, his slow recovery and her betrayal; none of those reasons gave him permission to forget himself.

He was the Queen's Sword. He was no abuser of women, no oafish brute that enjoyed inflicting pain. No matter what they had tried to turn him into, he had never forgotten that he was Wode.

His stomach rumbled and he got to his feet, grabbing his threadbare pants and tugging them up over his hips. Perhaps there was something in their galley's pantry for him to eat, now that he was finally regaining his appetite.

He slipped out of his bedroom and walked quietly down the hall, hoping he would not be interrupted. The captain wanted information, and his mind was finally clearing, but for the moment, he would rather work out his answers on his own.

He could recall his last meeting with the queen, when she had given him the dagger along with her cryptic instructions. She had been concerned, even then. Worried, and not just for him.

Cyrus should have known something was wrong. In that moment he'd wished he had Dare's gift of empathy, so he could understand her pain and ease it. Perhaps she'd known of the dangers that were coming for her, that he would disobey her to stay at her side if she'd told him. It made no sense, and yet Queen Idony's nature would cause her to make that sacrifice.

He walked past the floor hatch that he assumed led to the engines. Dare had told him about the Deviant, that it ran on both theorrite and steam power, depending on the need. He'd heard rumors of its existence, but he hadn't been aware it was this advanced. That it had discovered a way of hiding in plain sight.

He'd also heard stories of another, more frightening ship that only traveled the skies at night. No one had said exactly what it might be able to do. Only that no one was ever left behind to reveal its secrets.

His hunger gnawed at him once more and he sleepily scratched his chest. There was a door without a lock ahead and the smell of cooking meat coming from its direction. He had to assume it led to the galley. He pushed it open with the flat of his hand and froze.

Seraphina sat cross-legged on the thick wooden table in the center of the room, surrounded by dirty pots and empty jugs. James Stacy, the man Cyrus recalled from his short time on the Siren, seemed to be leaning toward her in an intimate fashion as she laughed.

His desire for food vanished.

The guard with the mussed brown hair and the ever-affable expression noticed him first. "Cyrus the Sword, I was hopin' to see you again." He chuckled. "Not sure you knew this, but when you first talked about bein' a sword, the boys and I thought you were talkin' about—"

James Stacy caught Seraphina's gaze and they both began laughing again, as though sharing a secret jest that did not cast him in a favorable light. Cyrus felt a tic pulsing near his eye but stayed silent. He could care less who she had moved on to. For all he knew, she had bedded the entire ship's contingent. If memory served, she certainly had the sexual energy required for such a feat.

When he did not respond, the laughter died out and James Stacy shifted awkwardly. Cyrus stepped inside the room and headed toward what he hoped was the pantry. Pulling back the curtain that hid the food from view, he studied the nearly empty shelves and the windup icebox that, when opened, revealed a paltry amount of shriveled produce and a single mauve-shelled egg swimming in a puddle of melting ice. The reason for tomorrow's descent made sense now. The ship desperately needed to resupply. It was not as if they could drop a fishing net off the port bow for sustenance.

Her voice surrounded him like a lover's embrace. "A bit of three-horn shank is warming on the stove. James and I were scrounging up a late-night treat, and we have already laid waste to the last of Freeman's stew, so you can have it."

Cyrus grit his teeth. "Generous of you."

She chuckled. "Not particularly. We discovered we would both rather drink than stuff our bellies tonight. Food makes somber sober men of happy drunkards, as they say. Isn't that right, sweet Jamie?"

James stood up politely to move out of the way as Cyrus grabbed a plate and headed toward the small stove. Meat. He had come here to eat, not wallow, and he would prove it. It no longer mattered that it was the last thing he wanted to do. He would chew down every last bite of the threehorn shank, imagining he was beating James Stacy bloody. Or carrying Seraphina over his shoulder to his bedroom.

Once he'd made himself a plate and turned away, the silence had become distinctly uncomfortable. He picked up the greasy meat with his fingers, gnawed a bite off, and chewed slowly. Seraphina watched him before taking a drink from her large opened jug. It was so quiet they could hear the wind rustling the side sails, and a male snore sawing through the wall from one of the bedrooms.

James Stacy was the first to blink. "Seraphina, I do believe I have sufficiently drowned my sorrows for the evenin'. I thank you for the company."

He nodded to Cyrus without meeting his gaze and headed for the galley door.

"Jamie?"

The man looked back at Seraphina. She lifted her half-empty jug and smiled. "Trust me. For you? She *is* the waiting kind."

The guard-cum-deckhand nodded shyly, his shoulders hunched as the door swung shut behind him. Cyrus felt his eyebrows lift. "Who is *she?*"

Seraphina tilted her neck in a stretch designed to drive him insane before answering. "You may remember a girl in a coral dress from your time on the Siren?" She shrugged, not waiting for his reply. "He believes himself in love with her, but his duty to Bodhan comes first. With the Siren closed for business indefinitely, he worries she will be in search of another job or another protector. Away from the security of the Siren, bad things can happen to a girl like Coral without a man to protect her. Despite that undeniable truth, he asked her to wait for him until his return."

Cyrus heard the touch of cynicism in her tone. "You lied to him."

Her lips pursed. "As my captain would say, men often believe their pricks are so unique as to change a woman's destiny. Coral found a way to survive before she met him, she will find a way without him." She sighed, swirling her jug of liquid and grimacing at the sediment that whirled up from its base. "James Stacy is a sweet man, and he would be no good to us in our search for the queen if he was pining over a broken heart. I said what he needed to hear."

Cyrus set down his plate and crossed his arms. "Is this your new calling on the Deviant? You don't exactly look the maternal part. Though I know you have ways other than kind lies and bad drink to comfort a man."

He felt like a bastard for his words, particularly after his earlier actions. Something about her brought out the worst in him.

She set down her jug with enough force to rattle the pots beside her. "I gave you leave to attack me once because I truly regret what happened and what you've been through." She lifted her hand to caress the base of her neck, drawing his attention to her throat and making him flinch. "You have used up the little pity I had. Go back to your room before I forget you are recovering, and that I enjoy Dare's company too much to watch her cry over your death."

Adrenaline and heat blazed through him in a way he'd not felt since . . . since the Siren. He lowered his arms and took a step closer. "For some strange reason I cannot sleep. Why do you think that is, Seraphina? Am I airsick? Still overcoming the remnants of vayun inside me? Or do I simply fear that the moment I let my guard down . . ." He reached out to touch her wrist gently, letting his thumb glide over the weaponized bracelet. "The moment I relax, I will discover I've been betrayed. Again. Sold into servitude and chained against my will by lunatics as fond of torture as you seem to be. As possessive of their whips."

She jerked her arm away from his touch, moving to her knees so he wasn't towering above her. "I do not sell people. And you are not the only soul to have been abducted in recent months."

"I know." His fingers curled into fists at the memory. "Believe me, I know."

Seraphina frowned. "I owed a man named Muller a debt. He said you had something he wanted, he refused to tell me what, but that my debt would be considered paid if I made it easier for him to retrieve it from you. I thought he was just going to steal something. I did *not* know—I would never have left if I'd known what he planned."

Cyrus pressed his fingers to her lips, unable to stop himself from caressing her there. From remembering her taste. "So no more lying. Good. I need no pity and I have no illusions that my prick was particularly unique." His smile was bitter. "Not even the best 'sword' on your trophy case, I am sure. We are both aware that you knew precisely what you were doing. Precisely why you gave me *comfort*. It was not true desire. The outcome was the same, regardless. You got what you wanted, and I had something precious stolen from me. What do you think we should do about that?"

Her eyes were green flames burning him with their heat. She opened her lips, sucking the remnants of the meat's juices from his fingers in answer.

She licked his flesh and he moaned. "What are you doing?"

She gripped his wrist in her hand and pulled his fingers away from her mouth with a low growl. "I don't know. Why don't you . . . fight me?"

Her lips were on his before he could respond. The same ones he had memorized in his dreams, searching for the lie within them. The pretense.

He tried to think, tried to reason. What was she after now? What could she gain? But after her tongue began to battle with his, he knew there was no hope. He simply did not care.

She tasted of life and freedom. The rare, wild rains that had brought the Avici desert to life during his stay there. Her teeth bit at his lips and he bit back, his passion as consuming as hers. His blood as raging.

Cyrus felt her legs wrap around his waist, clinging tight enough to knock the breath from his lungs. He repaid her in kind, tightening his embrace even as he cursed the rigid corset that dug sharply into his bare chest. He wanted to feel her breasts against him. Wanted to know she was real. That *this* was real, and not just another fantasy haunting his nights with images of freedom.

He tore his mouth from hers. "Claws."

She gasped and smiled in wicked delight. "So you want a little pain this time? My specialty."

Cyrus gripped her forearm to stop her from swiping his chest. Her nails had extended into long, razor-like points. Felidae claws were lethally sharp. Sharp enough to cut through skin . . . and clothing.

He shook his head, licking the small trace of blood from his lips. Her bite was sharp as well. "Claws or a galley knife, Seraphina. Your choice. I have to feel your skin on mine. I'm too impatient for laces and leather."

There was no hesitation in her movements. If she was disappointed in his commanding ways she hid it well, bending her wrist and slicing down the center of her corset with an accuracy and skill that should have given him pause.

"All of it?" Her corset had burst open at her action, her voluptuous breasts no longer confined or contained. It made it difficult to focus on her words.

Cyrus forced himself to nod, his attention riveted to her pale flesh as she loosened her legs' grip on his waist and used her nails to cut a slit down her leather shorts.

She sheathed her claws and reached for the panel of his pants. The buttons scattered, bursting through the silence around them.

Cyrus slid his fingers through her richly red hair and tugged so hard her neck was forced to arch. Lowering his head, he closed his teeth around the lobe of her tipped ear.

Her sensitive, Felidae ear.

She cried out and he lifted his head to quiet her. "You may enjoy being watched, Seraphina, but I prefer privacy for *this*."

He gripped her thigh with his other hand and dragged her to the edge of the counter. Heedless of the clattering glass and iron beside her, he guided himself into her heat.

They both groaned low and long as her tight sheath soaked him, clinging to his cock. She fell back on her elbows and he followed, tracing a path along the curve of her breast with his open mouth.

Seraphina cupped her breast high and pressed it against his lips, demanding his kiss. He felt her tail curling around his hip, along the seam of his ass, and he thrust deeper inside her in reaction.

She sent him to the brink of insanity and pushed him over without a thought. Her scent. Her body's reactions. The way she lifted her hips off the wood, taking him despite her submissive position . . . she was carnality in living flesh.

"Harder," she growled. "I *need* it. Or did you forget I am not as weak as your human lovers?"

He sucked her nipple deep until the hard peak scraped against the roof of his mouth. He felt the whip coiled at her hip and released its clasp.

He lifted his head and slowed his thrusts. He didn't want this to be over to quickly. "I have forgotten nothing."

Her muscles flexed. Alert. Good. He felt the leather-bound handle against his palm and let the long, braided whip glide up her ribs to the underside of her breasts.

His voice was rough. "How many men have felt the sting of this since our night together? How many have begged for your lash, for your brand of punishment?"

She tightened her legs around him, hesitating for a moment before tilting her chin. "I've lost count."

He thrust deep and smiled as she bared her teeth. "How many of them knew it was a lie? Knew that this was what you wanted, what you really fantasized about?"

She arched her neck as he scraped the whip across her sensitive nipples. "I'm betting none. You're a good liar, Seraphina. But you cannot lie about this. Not when I can feel how wet you are. How much you love—"

She grabbed the whip out of his hands and wrapped it around his back, pulling him forward until he was pressed against her. Her teeth bit into his chin and she growled.

He was lost.

There were no more words, only sounds of almost painful pleasure as his hips pounded out a powerful rhythm that made the heavy table shake, despite the bolts holding it firmly to the floor.

Cyrus felt her drop the whip to the ground and her palms slide along his back in restless agitation, over the rough ridging of scars he knew were there. Frustration and anger mingled with lust and need. Her touch tore him open. Her heat soothed him. Her name was a curse and a prayer repeatedly whispered in his mind.

Seraphina.

She consumed him from the inside out. He was breaking apart. Burning to ashes just as her high keening cry echoed off the galley walls. *Yes.*

He jerked his hips back, every fiber of his being rejecting the separation as he gripped his cock and ensured he did not find his release inside her. He cursed himself for not thinking of protecting himself before he'd taken her. Not thinking at all.

He lifted his mouth from her breast reluctantly, his mouth already empty, hungry for more of her. It was a feeling he had to resist.

Despite the weakness in his limbs, the pounding of his heart, he resisted the urge to collapse against her. To let her sensual phero-mones wash over him. Arouse him again.

He could use that as an excuse, but he needed nothing more than the sight of her, the thought of her, to seduce him. To destroy him.

He stood and adjusted the panel of his pants, grimacing as he searched for a galley rag. He would not look at her. Could not stand to see her perfect body opened and flush with pleasure. To meet eyes that would be warm, or cool with calculation. It was that thought that had dragged him from her initially—that she was not as lost as he was, just very good at what she did.

He caught the scrap of leather that had been her shorts as it bounced off his chest. "Use this to clean up, Wode," she said snidely as he clenched them in his fist. "And keep it. You may need to polish your sword when a warm body is not available. You can think of me."

Cyrus did not enjoy the accusation in her tone. Or the feeling of self-disgust weighing on his chest like a stone. Was this what he was now? Passion and anger, reaction with no control? Was this what he had become?

He should apologize, but instead he slid his hand into his pants pocket, watching her expression turn from smug to shocked as he dangled her bracelet between his fingers. "I would rather keep this instead, if only for the duration of our flight. I would sleep easier knowing this was not in your possession."

Her exotically sharp features took on a feral look, up-tilted green eyes slitted, high cheekbones taut, and full lips stretching, revealing just a hint of incisor. Her body shimmered with the aftereffects of heated sex.

Wild.

She slid off the galley counter with one smooth, agile motion, which took her not toward him, but farther away. Her breasts were unselfconsciously displayed when she stood on the other side.

Proud and wild.

Cyrus tensed, knowing a predator when he saw one. His willing partner of moments before had become a dangerous stranger. If he did not know what she was, he would believe he'd hurt her. Made her feel threatened and anxious. As if he had that power.

She curled her lips in a semblance of a smile. "You think I need that? I like the way it glimmers, nothing more. In all your Wode training, did you learn anything about Felidae? Not the trained, drugged, helpless ones. Not the mindless, lifeless miners that spend their lifespans in a cave or surrounded by a stormfence. *My* kind. My guess is no."

He knew more about Felidae than she realized. He had been born at Faro Outpost, a steamferry's ride away from the island designated for Felidae who could not abide civilization. He was chosen to be Arendal, privy to all the articles and history of the Felidae and the laws pertaining to them. Laws written by the Raj and enacted by the Wode. *His* kind.

With all of his knowledge, however, he would admit Seraphina was singular. She was unlike any Felidae, or any woman, he had ever known. It was what drew him to her. What made her dangerous.

"I know enough." He kept his voice low, his gaze steady on hers. "Enough to heed the Queen's Chalice when she speaks for her loyal friend. I trust her."

Seraphina's shoulders curled inward, as though he had dealt a blow to her chest. He slipped the bracelet back into his pocket, his chest heavy with regret. "Enough to keep this somewhere safe on the chance our compassionate shield guard is wrong."

"Phina, are you listening?"

She gripped her head to hold it steady as she leaned on the railing of the main deck. The sun was too bright, the side sails rustling obnoxiously in the wind. She dare not even look through the dodge, else she would disgrace herself. Perhaps a drink would set her right.

She cringed. "How can I help it, Captain, when you are shouting so loudly?"

Captain Amaranthe's sigh was a violent wind that seemed to shake the Deviant to its beams. "We need you present, Phina. I know you've been upset by Gebby's loss and our new crew. In any other situation, I would be tossing one an hour over the rail myself. Or sharpening my swords on their ever-wagging tongues."

The captain's hand patted her shoulder awkwardly. Her attempt to console was almost amusing enough to make Phina smile—if she were not afraid of the pain that would cause.

"Dare has finally offered us some positive news. She knows where we need to go. We are one short resupply away from finding our queen. Or another clue as to her whereabouts. I wanted the three of us to talk before the men arrived."

Phina's lips tilted at the way the captain said the word "men." It was worth the pain, and was precisely the way she felt this morning. The way she'd felt since Cyrus had walked out of the galley, regret and mistrust in his eyes.

She *wanted* his regret. Wanted to wear it like armor to protect her from this new, unfamiliar emotion. Guilt.

Seraphina Felidae, Lightfoot, Phina Fleet. No name she went by knew the meaning of that word. She had left it behind long ago. She did what she had to do to survive, to protect the people she loved and get what she came for. Whatever she came for.

Now every thought she had was laced with the emotion. What she had done to the Queen's Sword, what she had let happen to the queen. The fact that she had not thought of the fate of her elder sister since the moment Cyrus Arendal had come, stumbling and wounded, into view.

Perhaps she was as hopeless as her brothers always claimed. Born wrong. Unwilling to accept her destiny. Her path.

She opened her eyes when Dare pushed her tangled hair back and found the petite shield guard's indigo eyes welling with tears.

Damn. She'd forgotten.

"It's true, then? You can feel people's emotions?"

When Dare nodded, Phina made a face. "That might be the worst inheritance for a human I can imagine. Felidae have a similar talent. I'm told it's a defense mechanism to sense threats. Weakness. But it is just about heat and body language. I would loathe sensing every emotion the people around me were experiencing. I imagine I would learn I had no friends at all, or none whose thoughts I cared to be within shouting distance of."

Dare's expression was still somber. Knowing. It made Phina's hair stand on end. Did she know what she and Cyrus had done last night? That was a stupid question. Everyone knew. She had seen it in the men's eyes when she'd come up from belowdeck this morning.

She had never been good at being quiet.

"It can be difficult," Dare agreed. "It can also be insightful. It helped me make it to this point alive. Along with my friends, of course, whose emotions never bother me."

She needed to change the subject. "What is this news that I was dragged out of my bed for? I warn you now, I had too much to drink last night. Keep your voice down while you amaze me."

Dare's expression radiated excitement. It hurt Phina's eyes as the sun had moments before. "It was Cyrus, in a way. I was telling him about my time aboard the Siren, and he said I reminded him of the queen and the way she loved to spin stories." She let go of Phina to gesture adamantly with her hands. "*That* is where the clues lie. I've just had to work on recalling them. It was a daily ritual we had, you see. Queen Idony told me amazing tales, unbelievable stories about submersibles the size of cities beneath the sea, ships that flew like birds through the air. A tower in the shape of a white flower beside a lake of northern stars."

Phina rubbed her temple. "I definitely had an overabundance of drink. How are children's stories the answer?"

Bodhan came up behind her, clapping her heartily on the back. "Rough night, Seraphina? I would suggest a trip to the galley for something to settle your stomach, but I've been there. Looks like some of the men had a fight over the last of the supplies last night. Or whatever sort of stowaway pests airships carry, the kind who screech loud enough to wake the ship with their screaming."

She glared at his cheerful, knowing leer. "Fair Dare, is he still giving you pleasure? We can chain him up again if you'd like."

Dare blushed, giving Phina her answer. Bodhan went to stand beside her, his light eyes studying her face. "Dare barely slept last night, desperate to recall the details of that particular story. She thinks that since the queen's games taught her about the hidden qualities of the seal, her stories might have been intended to be helpful as well."

That no one hesitated to believe Queen Idony the Ever Young had the foresight to see this day was a testament to her wisdom. To Phina, it was an obvious assumption. The queen was more than royal—she was divine. But why then had she allowed herself to be taken?

The last voice she wanted to hear joined the others, making Phina whirl around. An action she instantly regretted. Damn the man.

"She's right." Cyrus stopped when she saw him, shifting as though he were as uncomfortable with her presence as she was with his. A fact that instantly elevated her mood.

He looked away from her, toward the others. "I know the story she speaks of. It was one of her favorites. The tower was a lotus, and the lotus held the universe inside its petals."

Dare nodded. "Yes, that's it. Captain Amaranthe thinks the lake in the story may be the key to our direction."

The captain's hazel eyes were surprisingly warm as she spoke. "Dare told me the tale and it jostled my memory. In the North, where the Yazata Range meets the Pearl Mountains, I saw from the air a lake that has similar properties to the one in Dare's story. Whatever plant life grows within it makes it glow." She met Phina's stare with a pointed one of her own. "Like northern stars."

Bodhan pulled Dare closer, the excitement apparently contagious. "Did you see a tower?"

Captain Amaranthe shook her head. "No. The area appeared untouched. Unpopulated. But I know of no other lake with those qualities in Northern Theorrey."

Phina was disbelieving. "When did this become a treasure hunt? The queen said herself that her time was winding down. Was I the only one who heard that? Are human ears that inferior?"

The captain stepped toward her, lowering her voice so the crew could not hear. "Seraphina, no one has forgotten the queen's message. Or our time constraints. She is the one who told us of Tower Orr. Her Chalice and her Sword, much as it pains me to admit it, know her better than we do. We have to take the chance. Unless you have another option, another direction for us to go."

They were all looking at her expectantly, but it was difficult not to argue. She wanted to head into Centre City, to break into the tight security of the Theorrean Raj's domain and demand answers. But the captain was right. Dare had known, when she hadn't, that the queen had been replaced. She had to trust in the gentle Chalice. Queen Idony certainly did.

Why did she still have such a terrible knot in her chest? Cyrus Arendal? Or the guilt that was growing inside her for her only real family, left behind in the Copper Palace?

Phina swallowed past the tightness in her throat. "I believe I need some of Freeman's strongest tea yet. I will have to be in top form if I'm to help you find this lotus tower."

The obvious relief of the group around her eased her mind. The last thing she needed was more scrutiny. More judgment from the blue eyes of the Arendal.

He had no idea how much she wanted to find the queen. No idea what she was willing to do to ensure Idony's safety. And no inkling of the personal stake she had in discovering exactly what had happened.

But despite her determination, the small voice inside her head could not stop wondering what had become of the queen's maid. What had become of Nephi?

Chapter Three

"Wulf. Hadiyah. How long has it been?" Bodhan called out in welcome to the strangely dressed men waiting under a copse of trees near the clearing where the Deviant had found its port. This was a favorite spot for the captain to resupply. Just outside of Newgarren. The small town on the western edge of the Avici desert drew many traders, and few Wode.

Phina sprang easily off the cargo platform as it lowered slowly, its mechanical arms on either side of her whirring loudly in her still sensitive ears. She landed gently on the ground beside Dare, watching the newcomers with an alert and wary gaze. Bodhan's mysterious friends.

She had gone back to her room to splash water on her face and get herself together. Freeman, her savior, had left his special blend of tea outside her door. The queen needed her to be Seraphina. Fearless and bold. That was exactly what she would be.

What she found on her dressing table had been a step in that direction. Cyrus had gotten into her room, leaving a memento behind.

Her brass and copper bracelet. He'd even left the darts intact. It was a gesture of truce she could not quite ignore.

That a Wode had managed to disarm her without her awareness was unacceptable. It was a move *she* had perfected over the years. Seduction and misdirection. Until now, no one had gotten the drop on her. Since adulthood, no human male had been able to catch her in the act of pinching any object she desired. And no one had ever taken anything from her without her permission.

How had *he?*

Still, he had kept his word. He had returned it to her possession for their landing, in time for her to meet Bodhan's friends. She had to admit, the jangling of her pretty wrist piece was comforting.

Now that her mind had cleared, she catalogued the features of the two men carefully. Bodhan had contacted them the same way he had his Siren guards. That wonder of a wrist cuff. She needed to get her hands on one.

They had been waiting patiently in the sparse shade granted by the wispy trees when the Deviant began to descend. She'd noticed their broad smiles as the ship moored and the landing dodge was unfurled, needing no monocular to see them clearly, even from a distance. Though both had their eyes hidden behind strange lenses similar to Bodhan's, which were tinted with varying hues of rose and violet, she could tell from their expressions that they were taking in every detail of the Deviant's design until it disappeared from view. Admiring.

They'd come bearing gifts, sacks of food and several large trunks laden, she imagined, with other necessities. She inhaled deeply, scenting nothing combustive or dangerous in their effects.

Neither man was close to Freeman in size, and they had brought no pack animals. She would ask how they had carried their load, but it was instantly apparent when they came closer. The dark-haired man took a rectangular metal box out of his pants pocket, causing Phina to tense, ready for weapons fire.

He did not aim, but shook the object, smacking it against his palm with a curse while the fairer man chuckled. Then small jets of steam puffed up into the still air behind the large wooden cart that had been stationary beside them. It juddered to life and the brass wheels of the wooden wagon started to roll between the two of them, seemingly guiding itself to where Bodhan stood.

She had seen carts move on a charged rail in the Theorrean mines, where her family had worked for generations, but never on rocky terrain. Never without a pre-laid track. She could see the value in it, the cleverness.

She wondered if they knew the Khepri.

Phina let her senses take over. There was no tension in these men. They had no fear of the ship or its crew. Their confidence was undeniably attractive, as was their unusual appearance.

One of them had a scent and look similar to Bodhan's. He wore a tunic shirt with a belt of leather pouches at his hip instead of a sword or pistol. His dark hair was contained in a long braid that came down over his shoulder to his waist, lending to his exotic appeal and darker coloring. He removed his rose-tinted spectacles and squinted against the daylight. Once revealed, his eyes were the same nearly colorless blue of Bodhan's. Like seeing the sky through ice, or a river that had frozen over in winter. Seraphina could not deny he was a beautiful specimen.

The paler man with silky yellow hair was even more startling. If it weren't for his brilliant red shirt and black vest and pants, he would seem nearly transparent he was that pale. Had he never left his home? Never gone out into the sun? And what was on his eyes?

He had placed what looked to be a smaller, trimmed-down version of an ocularia device on his spectacles, all wires and multiple lenses. He moved them up and down as he studied the area of the ship covered by the dodge. His friend nudged him and he removed the device and his violet lenses, reacting as the other had, reaching up to pinch the bridge of his nose at the brightness of the day. After her night of revelry, it was a reaction Phina understood.

Bodhan gestured to them, guiding them to the shadow the ship threw, even in its apparent absence. When he did, the blond man opened his eyes in gratitude, showing a color similar to the moss green of her favorite drink but much lighter. So light she had to squint herself to see the color within. Despite his pallor, he, too, was magnetically attractive. His smile was knowing and playful. Cocky.

She had always believed Bodhan unique. Now, however, she felt as she imagined Dare must have when she'd first seen the Deviant. Speechless.

The pale man spoke first, in a subtle accent that was also similar to Bodhan's. "It has been too long, Bodhan. I was sorry to miss you on your last visit home. We've been refitting the Slide."

The man next to him smiled sheepishly at the brothel owner. "I, on the other hand, was not expecting to see you again so soon. At least it is under better circumstances this time."

Bodhan chuckled. "As long as you've learned your lesson about bragging in alehouses, this trip should be simple in comparison."

Phina's brow furrowed but Bodhan's smile merely widened without further explanation. He turned to gesture toward her. "Captain Amaranthe is no doubt giving my men what for about how to properly lock down the concealment cloak—"

Phina snorted. "The landing dodge."

Bodhan shrugged, sending her a long, suffering look. "Yes. The dodge. Speaking of dodgy, this is Seraphina Felidae. Occasional employee on the Siren, and full-time mischief-maker. Keep your trunks locked, men." He winked at her to show he was teasing, but she was not particularly amused.

Then he did something that made up for it. He held out his arm to Dare, an expression of such devotion and passion on his face that she could not help the small sting of envy that it caused. She could not recall anyone looking at her that way. It was an emotion no pheromone could induce.

"This is Dare, gentlemen. The woman who unwittingly captured my heart. Love, meet two of my oldest friends. My cousin Hadiyah, Hadi to his friends, I've already told you about. The ghostly gentleman beside him is Wulfric the Great."

Wulfric's look was self-deprecating as he held out his hand. "I am pleased to meet you, Dare. I thought Bodhan was too focused on the family business to ever get to the business of starting his own family." He turned to Phina and studied her outfit with interest. "Wulfric the Great is my father. I am still but a shadow of that mad old inventor. Or a ghost, as Bodhan says. You may call me Wulf the Modest Yet Irresistible to Women."

Phina's smile tilted at the ease of his sensuality. She allowed his hand to engulf hers. He studied her in open appreciation, but he was not put off balance by her pheromones. Odd. But then, Bodhan had never been affected, either.

Who were these men and where did they come from? Wherever it was, she reminded herself to stay away. It was hard to trust a man she could not seduce.

Wulf caught her puzzled expression. "I may be immune to your scent, my dear, but the view has no need for enhancement. You are stunning."

When the men turned to Bodhan once more, speaking in hushed, enthusiastic tones about their journey, Dare leaned close to her ear. Her breath made Phina shiver.

"They are from Aaru. Queen Idony spoke of a secret Bodhan must share with the captain? They are it. That is to say, where they come from is. They are here to help, and meet with the captain. Can you imagine it, Phina? A hidden city not bound by Theorrean reproductive laws or castes. They are loyal to the queen, but not the Theorrean Raj." Dare's soft voice held a hint of awe. "Bodhan was born there. And Hadi? He is the reason Bodhan was missing from the Siren."

A hidden human city without laws? It sounded like paradise to Phina. Why on Theorrey would any of them leave that kind of bliss to come here?

And why had the captain forgotten to tell her about it? She did not enjoy being left out of things. She and Nerida Amaranthe had been through too much together. Was she so useless now? Perhaps she *should* stop drinking for a while, just to keep up.

She feigned cynicism. "Bodhan is the owner of a brothel. Not exactly the lowest of profiles if he is from this secret city. Especially considering his clientele."

Bodhan heard her. He turned, his light eyes narrowing. "You, of all people, should understand the thrill of hiding in plain sight. And the value. The Siren has given me greater access to funds and secrets than a noble's servant. Funds and secrets that have proved helpful in keeping my people, the queen's people, safe. They've helped you on more than one occasion. Not that you would show gratitude for that."

She was distracted from the barb in his tone by the man he'd introduced as Hadiyah. He was studying her closely. "Bodhan, wait. *This* is the infamous Phina Fleet?" He laughed in delight. "You did not tell me she was the Siren's Felidae. It was Phina Fleet who stole an entire cargo container right from under the noses of the Maithuna procurers, am I correct?"

Phina noticed Dare's confused expression at the same time Hadiyah did. He was quick to clarify. "There was a container full of children who had been sold or taken against their will from all across Theorrey. Being harvested like *dravya*, like nothing but a damned shipment of goods." He grimaced at his own words, obviously disgusted by the idea. "Sometime between the arrival of the elevated rail at Centre City, and the transfer to the Maithuna cargo ship, the entire container disappeared. Months later children were still arriving home, spreading the tale of Phina Fleet and her daring rescue." He took Phina's hand in both of his and squeezed. "The Aaruan Felidae spin the story often. I suppose you could say you are their hero. And mine."

Captain Amaranthe's voice behind her made Phina's shoulders relax. "I remember that. It was, I believe, the first time Phina and I met."

The first time the captain had met her, Phina amended, but not the first time *she* had seen the captain or the Deviant. Until that episode with the children, she had, in fact, been following the ship for weeks. Tracking their heat signatures, and studying them when they resupplied. It had taken that long to decide whether, despite the queen's instructions, she could trust the good Captain Amaranthe. Her pursuit to free the innocents from slavery had made up Phina's mind in her favor.

She waved off the praise, uncomfortable with the admiration. "Do they also tell the story of how I left a corpulent noble who enjoyed wearing corsets dangling from his balcony sans underthings while I robbed him of his art and jewelry collections?"

"That sounds more like the Seraphina I know."

Phina's jaw tightened at Cyrus' smug comment as he joined the rest of them. Why did he have to be everywhere she was? Surely the ship was big enough, and Theorrey vast enough, that they could spend the rest of their lives never bumping into each other again.

Even as she thought it, she knew there was less fire behind it. When had that happened? It was a dangerous turn of events. Letting her guard down would only make her more vulnerable to the still-bitter Wode.

Hadi shook his head with a chuckle. "Say what you will, but all of us have heard of your exploits. Most of them courageous and bold. As are those of the illustrious Captain Amaranthe."

The captain ignored the praise as well. "Bodhan, I was told you were bringing me good, sturdy crew. These men have the look of highborn traders. Are you sure they know how to hold their swords?"

Was Hadiyah blushing? He coughed, looking down at the wagonload of supplies, its engine still belching small clouds of steam. Bodhan patted him on the shoulder and laughed, though Phina noticed he sent a pointed look toward the captain. "They can hold their swords just fine. Did you bring everything you own, Hadi? I said we needed some food and medicine for a few men, not a town."

Wulf had sobered, his gaze on the captain as he answered for his friend. "We did as the Khepri instructed. We came prepared. I believe you will find what we bring to the crew to be more than sufficient. Speaking of which . . ." He leaned down and pulled the blanket off the top of the wagon.

Phina heard Dare gasp as four of the Khepri's bluish-green bugs came to life, fluttering their translucent wings, their brass bodies rising to hover with a familiar hum.

She grinned. How often had one of those adorable automatons come to her, helping to guide her out of some corner she had gotten herself trapped into? The Khepri always seemed to know exactly when they would be needed.

Wulf's voice held an answering smile. "Much as I wish we could make our own, and believe me I have tried, these aren't ours. They started following us a few hours before you arrived. It was the first time I had seen scarabs this small carrying a load themselves, so we offered them the wagon to rest in."

"Scarabs?" Dare spoke the question in Phina's mind. She had never heard that word before.

Bodhan reached out to touch a loose strand of Dare's indigo hair tenderly. "It is the Khepri's own name for his spies. They are his symbol. His eyes around Theorrey, as well as his less obvious messengers." He kissed her forehead. "The dragonfly is only used when he truly wishes to gain someone's attention."

How did these men know so much about the Khepri? Phina's tail twitched restlessly. Was Bodhan sure he could trust them?

The captain obviously felt her tension. "You have proven you know our ally, and Bodhan has spoken for you, but I have no patience for evasion. You said they carried a load. That is usually a job for a different machine. What was it?"

Wulf's strange eyes darkened with true interest. She could see his skin heat before her eyes, causing a lovely flush to his pale cheeks. Interesting.

He lowered his head respectfully. "I meant no disrespect, Captain Amaranthe. However, I would be remiss if I did not take a moment first to tell you that the descriptions of your beauty hardly do you justice. You take my breath away."

Phina sucked in her lower lip and bit down in an attempt to contain her mirth. This man was *flirting*? Now? With the captain? He may have heard of her beauty but apparently not her temper.

She turned to study Captain Amaranthe's expression and caught Cyrus watching her instead. His blue eyes were dark as they studied her lips. She turned away before he could see how that affected her.

"Wulf, was it?" The captain moved closer to the newcomer. Her signature coat had been removed so Phina could see the lithe, graceful movements of her body. Her bare arms slender but strong at her side, her dark hair flying like a silken banner down her shoulders as she strode toward him.

The man may be immune to Phina's pheromones, but he certainly was impressed with the captain. His lips parted, his tongue slipping out to moisten his mouth in unconscious preparation. Phina inhaled, taking in his scent. Yes, he was definitely aroused.

Captain Amaranthe drew close enough that Wulf leaned toward her, as though pulled by an unseen force. She used the opportunity to strike.

Before the other men could react, she had grabbed Wulf's arm, flipping him over her body and onto his back. She straddled his waist where he lay on the ground and Phina could see the curved, claw-like dagger the captain usually kept in a slender holster beneath her vest pressed against Wulf's neck.

Her smile was hard as she pressed her body against his. "This is how I take a man's breath away. Still impressed?"

Phina sensed Cyrus stepping closer and held up her hand. The man was in no danger. Not at the moment.

Wulf was breathing faster, but he showed no fear. "Impressed. In love. I cannot decide."

Captain Amaranthe studied him for a moment, then rubbed her hips against him and dug the dagger deeper into his flesh. "I could help you with your decision. If you would risk it."

"Nerida."

Phina stopped smiling. How did Freeman move so quietly? The other men reacted to the sound of his voice with varying degrees of shock and respect.

He had used her name. In front of strangers. It was low enough, tempered and even enough, that it did not sound like a rebuke. Yet the way Captain Amaranthe reacted, Freeman may as well have shouted, or prodded her with a loose stormwire.

She was off the pale Wulf, hands on her hips and wearing an expression of stone before another word was spoken. Freeman stepped back, keeping a respectful distance but remaining a silent sentinel that seemed to remind all of them of why they were here.

Bodhan helped his friend up and Dare went to stand beside him. "What were they carrying?"

Hadi reached into the odd wagon and pulled out another metal box, this one much bigger than the one he'd held before. It was made of a dark gray metal, exquisitely detailed with images of the Khepri's bugs—the scarabs—decorating each corner of the lid. It looked old. Valuable. The images etched with decades of patina. Being the Khepri's, sadly, made it off limits for Phina to pinch.

Hadiyah handed off the box to Bodhan. "Along with the need to be prepared, the Khepri informed us that he would be sending an important package along with us. When we saw the scarabs, we knew this was it."

He held it up in his hands and the flying automatons buzzed around it, each landing on one of the four corners of the box and attaching to it with a definitive click. Their wings folded and they began to turn in place. The noises from within the heavy mechanized box created a sweet sound to Phina's ears—that of a safe being unlocked.

After a full rotation, the scarabs' wings started to flutter once more, still attached to the lid of the box as they lifted it higher, into the air. They hovered impatiently above them, waiting.

Phina reached inside and began to gather up everything she could reach. She could never resist a present.

Cyrus was at her side in an instant. "Parchment? All that for letters?"

Phina forced herself to glare at him, grudgingly noting how much better he looked this morning. The hair on his head was growing fast, the indigo stubble swiftly becoming soft, touchable curls close to his head. Not that she wanted to touch his head. Or him.

Her tail twitched in frustration.

Bodhan was now beside them as well. "Letters to all of us." He took them out of her hand, rifling through them. She managed to stifle her possessive hiss.

"Cyrus. The captain. Seraphina and myself." He looked inside and his brows lifted. "Dare has a small box addressed to her. The Chalice."

The instant the box was empty the scarabs lowered the lid, relocking it to the container and lifting it into the air. Their little wings, it seemed to Phina, strained to carry the weight. "Poor bugs. Someone should tell the Khepri that birds make better messengers."

Wulf smirked, but his tone was full of admiration. "Don't think I haven't. He does enjoy his dramatic deliveries. I would forgive his flamboyance if I knew how he made those things so lifelike. Each time I've tried to trap one, they self-destruct before I can get a peek inside. Clever bastard."

The captain's distinctive boots paced behind them, drawing their attention away from the disappearing box. She slipped her note into the waistband of her pants. "This can wait. Between the supplies Freeman gathered and yours, we have what we need. We've been kissing ground too long and time is wasting."

She saw Wulf and Hadi share matching expressions of excitement and marveled at their utter lack of fear. They slipped on their shaded lenses once more, stepping back to watch as James Stacy and the others refurled the dodge.

Hadi used his small device once more and, now that she was closer, Phina could see it had four raised buttons with arrows carved on them that appeared to indicate direction, and two copper wires sticking out of the box's top. When Hadi pushed a button to send the wagon to the re-revealed cargo platform, a visible arc of energy danced between the wires. The wagon began to move and Phina came closer to Hadi's side.

"Did you make this?"

His expression was proud but wary as he nodded. She laid a hand on his arm, her eyes drawn to the box. "Have you ever considered making more for trade?"

Bodhan and Wulf answered for him at the same time. *"No."*

She joined them all, along with the cargo, on the lift. The machinery that carried them groaned with the strain. It was the longest ride to the deck in her memory.

She hated change. And men who refused to bargain.

Less than an hour later, Phina was still afraid to open her sealed letter. The one she had been so determined to grab when the box's lid had first been removed. Everyone else appeared to feel the same hesitation. Perhaps out of fear. Their messages were filled with dire news of late.

By silent consent they were allowing themselves a momentary distraction. Freeman had placed a table and chairs from the cargo hold onto the helm's deck, giving Hadi and Wulf a place to set one of their necessary supplies, an odd-looking game, on the table's surface.

She had never seen the like of it before, though Bodhan, Wulf, and Hadi were familiar with it. She supposed it was not surprising, since it had apparently been created in Aaru, the place they claimed to be from.

The captain and Dare watched in fascination along with Phina as the men played. Freeman pretended disinterest, fiddling with the buttons and knobs of the autobinnacle as he steered.

Phina stared intently at the oddly random configuration of brass tubes, bent joints, and copper coils set atop a thick leather-bound box. The men seemed to be taking turns attempting to create some sort of functional design. Or stop each other from doing so, she wasn't sure which. It looked like nothing more than a jumble of ill-fitting parts to her.

She noticed Dare was watching Wulf. Did she sense something from him? "Wulf, may I ask, have you ever met the Khepri?"

He shook his head without looking at her, placing a tube on the board before lifting a shimmering silver flask to his lips. "No one has. Not in my lifetime, or my father's."

Hadi took his turn on the board, his brow furrowed in concentration. "He has always been there. Encouraging our inventions, bringing us messages from our queen, and aiding those of us who choose to travel about in the world with help and guidance." He leaned back and patted the table with a smile. "Hah. Blocked you, Bodhan."

"Always?" Dare asked the table at large. She did not say it, but Phina knew what she was thinking.

Always. Like the queen? Like the Scarlet Lord who flew through the darkest night?

Cyrus's voice cut through their thoughts like a jagged knife. "No one but the queen is *always* there, regardless of their desire." He stood while the rest sat, his body projecting his impatience and discomfort as he watched the others play their game. He, too, had a problem with Hadi's choice of words. "That is, I would contend, the reason she has been taken. Queen Idony believed the Theorrean Raj was obsessed with longevity. Immortality. That they had tried, and would continue to try, anything to gain it for themselves. Including breaking into her rooms on a regular basis, to find something that contained her inheritance markers for testing. Perhaps this Khepri is similar."

Phina tensed in her chair, ready to protect him when the rumbling started around the table. To compare the Khepri with a member of the Raj was not the smartest action the Wode could have taken, but Phina would not let anyone, not even the captain, injure him for saying it. The protective feeling was just because she owed him. And she did not believe the queen would approve of them killing her Arendal.

Bodhan sighed and placed his piece on the board. "Wulf, it is your turn. Cyrus, tread carefully. The Khepri is the hand of the queen. He has proven his loyalty to her longer than you have been alive."

Dare agreed, her gaze sincere and calming as they looked at Cyrus. "From his actions alone I would say the Khepri is nothing like the science ministry or the Raj. But Cyrus, the queen does not believe that, surely? They have always wanted to keep their family lines in power, keep their inheritance pure, but going to those lengths? She would have told me. I've been to every meeting between the queen and the council members. I would have known."

Cyrus shook his head, regretful but still patronizing. "Dare, you have already discovered that she did not tell you everything. She protected you from many of her fears and feelings. *We* protected you. With your abilities, we did not want you to go rushing into danger. If they'd known what you could do, they could have used it against you. Against the queen."

His words were hard, but they made Phina think. The attack in the marsh—those men had wanted Dare. Wanted to capture her. Was that why? Did it have to do with the queen? Or Dare's abilities?

The hurt and anger in Dare's expression was plain for everyone to see. Her words were flat. Cold. "Aren't we lucky then that the Arendal Sword is here to protect the rest of us. We are saved."

She stood up with an impressive amount of dignity for such a little thing and headed down the stairs toward the rooms belowdecks. Her box was still pressed against her chest.

Bodhan, too, rose and excused himself. "I'm afraid you will have to finish this game without me." The look he sent Cyrus's way was lethal. "*I* am needed."

The captain's hazel eyes narrowed dangerously on Cyrus and Phina stilled. Thankfully, Wulf's frustrated swearing distracted them both. "Damn that Bodhan. There is no way to win. He has closed off every line."

The captain shook her head. "What *is* the point of this game?"

Freeman moved past Phina and leaned, casting a giant shadow over Wulf's shoulder. "I believe, if I am not mistaken in my rudimentary understanding of your little toy's complexities—" He took a piece of brass tubing from the pile in front of the pale Aaruan, and attached it to another in the center of the board. A small jet of steam shot out of the tube, emitting a high-pitched whistle. Phina started at the noise, but Hadi looked up at Freeman with a newfound admiration.

Freeman stepped back and crossed his arms. "Beginner's luck." His tone did not contain the same humility as his words.

Cyrus stalked away from them and down the stairs to the main deck, ignoring the laughter and male posturing around him. Phina followed, waiting until she was far enough away from the others to speak. "Are you that much of a cretin to everyone? Or just the people who care?"

Cyrus whirled on the deck to confront her, snarling, "Are you saying you care? Is that why you are following someone who obviously wants to be alone?"

Phina looked down at her message, her fingers tracing the lines of the parchment envelope. "Just trying to understand why Dare could admire a man like you. A man she mourned, and then nursed until he was healthy enough to treat her as if she were less than Wode. Less than *your* equal. She has been through a lot to get here, you know. And she did it without you. Without anyone."

"You think I don't know that?" He curled his hands into fists at his side. "I know what she's been through. I know no training I gave her prepared her for this. For what may come next." He shook his head. "She is special, Seraphina. To the queen. To me. She cannot be harmed. Yet we did not prepare for this. Did not prepare her for the world outside of the barracks and Queen's Hill that hates the Wode. For criminals who would use her naïveté against her. I was supposed to be there if trouble came. I was supposed to be *with* her."

Phina felt her heart freeze with that feeling again. That guilt. And not a little jealousy for his loyalty and obvious love for Dare. He hadn't been there because of her. Because she had been fool enough to believe he was just another mark. That Muller, her most reliable middleman when she needed something sold—the man she owed—had only wanted what he said he did from Cyrus's room. A trinket. And she had let him in, believing that when Cyrus woke he would be without his goods but still aboard the Siren. And *she* would be gone.

His endless blue eyes bored into hers. "No one, not even you, has asked what I've been through. Where I've been. Aren't you curious? Don't you want to know?"

She shook her head, a feeling of anxiety welling in her chest, but he hadn't been asking permission.

"I was stripped of all my possessions, drugged, and sent into the desert as a slave. They are building something in the Avici, Seraphina. Something horrifying. Those who are not indoctrinated into their cult are chained and whipped and forced to drink that numbing vayun day and night."

His cheeks were flushed and his eyes dark with remembered pain. "This is my fault. All of it, do you not see that? If I had been more careful, stayed focused on my mission, or escaped as soon as I'd been captured . . ."

He turned from her, burying his face in his hands, a moment of weakness she was sure he would hate for her to witness. Yet she could not make herself leave.

Phina lifted a hand slowly toward his back, wanting to comfort him. To touch his head, his shoulder and tell him he was wrong. That it wasn't his fault at all.

Her fingers curled, nails digging into her palms as she pulled back and dropped her hand at her side. Comfort was the last thing he wanted from her.

She looked down at the crumpled letter in her hand. "Perhaps we should open these."

She broke the seal and unfolded the parchment with trembling hands, seeing easily in the waning light. She breathed a sigh of relief when she heard him do the same.

The words were blurred, but she forced herself to focus. The message was for her from the Khepri. Her sister's name stood out as if it were etched in fire.

Nephi.

She had been like a mother to Seraphina, when there was no other to take on that role. Her champion when the rest of her family would have thrown her to the Wode for an extra room. It was for Nephi that Phina had made her initial vow to the queen. And for her that she needed to talk to the captain now.

Cyrus read his own message and turned to face her, crumpling the page in his fist. Phina looked into his eyes and knew that whatever he had seen had been just as bracing. And that he had no intention of sharing what the Khepri had told him. Not now. Not with her.

She could not blame him. Her family business had always been her own. Few people knew where she'd come from, how she'd grown up. Few people knew where her true loyalties dwelt. It was easier for her, and for all of those that believed Phina Fleet had no heart.

When this was over, she reassured herself, she and old man Khepri were going to have a serious talk. Face-to-face. Whips could be involved. But for the moment, there were other things to do.

Chapter Four

Cyrus washed his face and torso in the warm recirculating water of the copper basin, his mind in turmoil. He was thinking of the Chalice. His sister shield guard. His friend.

Dare had not come out of her room since the night before, allowing only the captain and Bodhan inside. Both of them had given him looks that could freeze the hottest natural spring, turning him away when he came to apologize.

And he could not get Seraphina's reprimand out of his head.

He was a bastard. Like his father and his father before him. An insensitive Wode bred for nothing but aggression. It was why his family line had been sent to the Faro Outpost in the first place. His inheritance deemed flawed. He had spent his life trying to earn his status as the Queen's Sword, to be worthy of regard. To be as true a protector as his mentor, Commander Iacchus.

All his effort had been for naught. The thin veneer of civilization he had formed around himself had been scraped away by his time in the desert. He found it hard to recall the lessons of his youth. The tools the queen and his commander had given him.

He was also beginning to wonder *why* Dare hadn't been as prepared as he. Why she was told stories and protected from the machinations of the nobles and Raj members who wanted more power. More power. More life. Always more life.

Why had the two people he respected most in the world not seen the strength in her? She had been chosen, despite her size, to be Chalice. Yet she had been treated as more of a sibling to Queen Idony than her shield guard. Sheltered because of her ability to feel emotions. Perhaps, despite his deep and abiding love for his companion guard, he was jealous of her treatment. A ridiculous emotion for a Wode, for an Arendal, and one he had always striven to hide from Dare's gift.

But it existed inside him for a reason. While Dare had searched for hidden notes within the palace walls and been told stories of daring adventure, Cyrus had been tested. Long hours of physical training, long hours of studying Theorrean laws until he knew them by rote. Then there were those times he had been forced to listen to the rabid ravings of the science ministers. Once, he was allowed to observe a section of their massive laboratory complex beneath Queen's Hill after pushing forward the pretense that he was not as loyal to the queen as he appeared. He had only been allowed in one section, but he had hoped, eventually, to see more.

Under Her Majesty's orders, of course.

His only true joy had been the part of his day spent with Dare and his queen, making them laugh or simply enjoying their company. Dare had always given her friendship and loyalty without hesitation, making his current outburst and past jealousies all the more petty and cruel.

All of his training, all of his groundwork meant nothing, if his letter from the Khepri were to be believed. His last mission had been more than a mere test. It had been crucial. It had also been a failure.

He had done everything right at the start. He had allowed himself to get knocked around and bloodied during training and, once outside the Copper Palace, he had shaved his head and donned the clothing of a lowborn.

Cyrus followed the instructions of the queen, the ones Commander Iacchus had sent to him, to the letter. He'd arrived on the deserted beach and, when he was sure he had not been followed, turned on the small pocket watch he'd been given. It had no markings of time, only hands, which he moved to their correct direction. He wound the watch, hearing the gears buzz before holding on to the chain and dropping the body of it into the sea.

He recalled how hard it was to hide his surprise when the watch began to emit a brightly glowing pulse that seemed to travel farther than it should have. He could feel the vibrations that went with it as his fingers kept a grip on the chain. When it stopped, he'd turned it off, slipped it into his pocket, and hid behind the rocks nearby to wait.

Others came. Young nobles and old Raj members he recognized. All dropping their watches in the water, some joking softly with each other as a submersible began to surface once the sun went down.

The commander had told him of the Siren. Had warned him. But Cyrus had been unprepared. This was no random case of rogue Wode he had been sent to mingle with. No one attempting to sell replicated elixirs for strength to the lowborn. This was political corruption. Men speaking and dealing in secret without recording it for posterity. Highborn men making plans as they paid for women not of their caste to bed them. Or spank them.

Cyrus shuddered as he thought of some of the strange requests he'd seen fulfilled in the few days he spent there, splashing more water on his face to erase the images.

He had sought pleasure before. In truth, pleasure had been forced upon him in his thirteenth year. It was his father's gift to him for being the first in their line to ever make good, the first of his inheritance to be chosen as an Arendal Sword—though the old man could not resist mocking his future career even as he bragged to his peers.

Laughing that his son's future of blood and justice was to be replaced with adjusting the eternal queen's cushions.

It had not been an unpleasant experience, once his father and the other men had left him with his new companion. She was a favorite of the outpost Wode, a Felidae who, for whatever reason, had been banned from her tribe.

She told him not to be nervous. That her pheromones would ease his tension. Take away his hesitation. They had. She had been gentle. Instructive. And when she left the next morning, he had felt more an unready boy than he had been before.

She had been his first, but by no means his last.

For some reason it was a fact the guards of the Siren, many of whom had decided to take him under their wing, chose not to believe. They thought him an innocent half-breed who'd saved up to escape and hoped to be fucked. It was a belief that had served Cyrus well, other than their constant attempts to fill him with drink and offer him women.

He meant to resist, to keep up his shy pretense until they arrived at the port Commander Iacchus had specified. Once the older man boarded the Siren, Cyrus would complete his mission and return home.

He had not counted on Seraphina.

The instant he saw her, he had known she would bedevil him. She strutted about in her revealing costume, her red hair tousled and her Felidae markings uncovered for all to see. She'd slipped into a nobleman's lap long enough to steal his drink and kiss the woman who had been given to him for the night. Titillating and dangerous.

She'd caught his stare and he saw the interest flicker in her brilliant green eyes. That interest had turned to disbelief the first time he had turned her down, determination the second. The third time . . . the third time he had given in—on *his* terms.

Seraphina had allowed him to take her over that night. Everyone on this boat but Wulf and Hadi knew how she had repaid her temporary capitulation.

It was odd that the memory no longer filled him with the rage it had only days before. Not for her.

Not only did he not make his rendezvous, but the dagger he was to deliver—the safety of which meant so much to the queen—had disappeared with his other belongings.

The Khepri had told him the dagger now lay in the private rooms of the false queen. That the one who had taken Queen Idony had also attempted to remove Cyrus as a threat. It was *he* who had charged the cult with building the monstrosity in the Avici desert, he who had stolen the dagger.

Seraphina had nothing to do with it, and no knowledge of the plot.

The Khepri emphasized the dagger's importance. If the queen were to be saved and restored to power, he'd insisted in the florid missive, Cyrus needed to get the dagger back into the right hands. His hands.

More than Idony's life was in danger, it seemed. Though that was enough. Theorrey and its rule were being challenged at the core. Something dark was looming.

He had told Captain Amaranthe, who was either disturbed by her own letter or still nursing antagonistic feelings over his treatment of Dare. Whatever the Khepri said to her, it must have coincided with his command, because he had met her as she was on her way to helm's deck to have Freeman change the Deviant's course.

They were pausing in their search for Tower Orr and turning back to Centre City.

Now, so close to returning to the palace that had been his home for most of his life, he found he needed Dare. He needed the Chalice to accept his apology. To feel the sincerity of it inside him.

She had proven herself to the Wode in him, loved the man in

him, and had never wavered in her loyalty, despite the truths she had been stunned by since this began.

They had all underestimated her. Even, may she forgive him for thinking it, Queen Idony.

The knock at his bedroom door made him wince in surprise and the basin tipped to fall on the floor. Water splashed on his boots. "Damn. Come in."

The wooden door creaked open and he saw the small, feminine figure silhouetted in the hallway. "Cyrus?"

That she hesitated, said his name with that much doubt in her voice, made him ache with regret. "Dare, I'm glad you came. I have wanted to talk to you. To say—"

"I know." Dare came in and closed the door behind her. "You've not been suppressing your feelings the way you did inside the palace. In fact, on occasion, I would prefer it if you did not think so loudly, but I do understand. You are forgiven."

She wrapped her arms around herself protectively and gazed about the room, a forlorn expression on her face. "I just . . . I truly thought I knew her. Knew you. All this is a surprise to me. Each day, each fresh revelation has left me feeling—"

"Lost?" Cyrus stepped toward her, heedless of his damp, bare torso, and pulled her into his arms. "As am I. Dare, we are soaring through the air with the birds, with a crew that already shows and owes its loyalty to you. You have, without any help from me, brought us all together. It's who you are on an elemental level. Who you've always been. I am the odd man out. The cog that serves no purpose."

She shook her head. "It was all chance. Circumstance."

He laughed, but there was little humor in it. "Was it? I am beginning to wonder if there is such a thing. The island Felidae believe that there is a destiny, a path to which you are drawn. One that supersedes the caste you are born to, or the family. Maybe this is your special path. Where your gifts have brought you."

She pulled back and looked up into his eyes, her own wide and unsure. "Brought *us*, Cyrus. This is your path as well as mine. I thought you dead. When you wandered into our camp whistling that ridiculous tune—" Her lower lip trembled. "I was so thankful."

He cupped her chin with his fingertips. "Have I ruined our friendship, then? No one could or should forgive me for letting this happen. For failing my post. But I fear I would be unsalvageable if I were unable to redeem myself in your eyes."

She narrowed her gaze. "Are you still keeping things from me? Protecting me?"

He refused to look away. "Yes. But only at the queen's command. Until you are ready. Until it's time."

"I can feel her now." Dare's voice was soft. Far away. "She is safe for the moment, but worried for us."

"You can *feel* her?" Cyrus studied her in surprise, then smiled. Her abilities must be growing. "I am glad. That means I still have time."

Dare pulled herself from his embrace and clenched her fists. "*We* have time. We. I have killed now, Cyrus. Shed blood. What more should I do to prove to you I am Wode? That I am just as capable as the captain or Phina or you. Better, it has been said, than many who are twice my size. And I feel her because—"

"I have no doubt in your abilities," he interrupted her. "I also know you did not enjoy it, even when it was necessary. That you felt no small jolt of pleasure when justice was served to your enemy. That you grieved instead for the loss of life. Grief is dangerous. Makes you hesitate."

"What shield guard *would* find pleasure in that way?"

The door opened again and Cyrus sighed, seeing Bodhan standing there with a grim expression. He'd been listening through the door. "Every Wode I have ever met but you, princess."

Dare grimaced apologetically before turning to face Bodhan, but

Cyrus saw the burst of relief and pleasure that lit her gaze at his arrival. He was glad she had someone who did that for her. Brought her joy. She had more than earned it. It did make him envious. He was no longer needed.

"I told you I wanted to talk to him alone."

Bodhan shrugged, leaning against the doorjamb lazily, the clasp for his holster purposefully undone. "And I told you that I respected your wants, my love. However, I am still not sure the Sword is over his bout of . . . shall we call it melancholy? I know he will respect my desire to protect you. It is, as you have assured me, his nature as well."

Cyrus noticed Bodhan's eerily colored gaze light on the damp spots on her jacket. Then on *his* bare chest. He shook his head, reaching for the clean shirt that Freeman had brought with the other supplies. "By all means, enter before I lose control and grovel her into the pyre."

Bodhan smirked and walked toward them, closing the door solidly with his boot heel. "Was he groveling, Dare? I am sorry I missed that."

Dare crossed her arms again in agitation. "I'm beginning to understand the captain's antipathy toward men. That is, if all of you cause this much aggravation."

Cyrus watched as Bodhan pulled her into his arms and nuzzled her neck. "We have talents that make up for it. You know we do."

He looked away when his lifetime companion melted into the cocky man's embrace, gazing instead out the window. He caught a glint of light in the distance. "We are getting close. The copper domes are coming into view."

Dare's tone was concerned behind him. "Captain Amaranthe told me about your message. Your's and Phina's. I know it has to be done but I am worried. Queen's Hill is no longer safe for any of us."

Seraphina. The captain had informed him this morning that they would have to work together. Apparently they both had instructions that required reconnaissance and retrieval inside the palace. Despite her obvious abilities, he hated the idea of her diving into danger. He chose not to consider why. However, it was clear arguing the point would be unwise and fruitless. Captain Amaranthe was a woman bound to have her way. He respected that. Respected her. It was, after all, her ship. And no one could stop Seraphina.

He turned back to them and smiled. "Don't worry about me, Dare. I am the Queen's Sword. The men at the gate know me well. Seraphina may have a harder time of it."

Dare bit her lip. "She told me she's done it a dozen times over the years. But neither of you have had to face a woman who wears the queen's face but is not the queen. You will have to craft your words and reactions with care."

His smile hardened. "I know exactly what to do. You will see me when I return, with the dagger, long before our Felidae."

Bodhan lifted one dark brow in interest. "Care to wager on that, Arendal?"

Dare sent him a telling look. "Are you sure you want to do that? Until a few hours ago, you thought Phina had taken the dagger, even when I told you she hadn't. And last night Freeman beat your move at a game he has never played. Luck has not been on your side of late."

Bodhan's expression was confident. "My love, with you, luck is always on my side. Besides, we are discussing Seraphina Felidae and her talent for escape. My odds have never been better."

Cyrus refused to admit that he agreed with the man. He also refused to make the wager. He had not lost all his faculties. Yet.

This was a disguise. It did not define her. She was not this person anymore.

Phina studied herself in the beveled mirror in her room, her shiny bracelet off once more, lying on the table beside her. The knot in her stomach made her want to howl. To scratch someone's eyes out. To do something wild, anything wild, to make the feelings disappear. To make this old identity disappear.

Seri the slave. Younger sister to Nephi, Jobi, Eli, and Nob. All born to work in the mines. Lower in stature than the factory Felidae who lived among them in the settlement.

Nephi once told her that they were named for the old angels and the great chosen in human myth, though everyone used a shortened version. Phina had never been able to ask their mother why they had been given such big names for such small lives, since the woman died a few days after she was born.

Her brothers had blamed her, but Phina had long since deduced that it had to do with her mother being put back to work the day after her new baby was born.

Born wrong. Phina sucked in her cheeks and glared at her reflection. Her life certainly hadn't started out well. But she had more than made up for her lack these past years. She had *lived.* She had thrived knowing her eldest sister, the unconditionally patient and loving Nephi, was safe with the queen.

The Khepri's message was simple and clear. Nephi was no longer safe.

Phina smeared the black soot more artistically across her cheek, her chin as defiant as the wild shoots of bright red hair framing her face.

A dingy gray woven shirt with long sleeves and a pair of shapeless pants, their hem tucked into black buckle-less boots, covered her body. Concealed her figure from view.

It was a Felidae's nature to stand out. Their colorful eyes and hair, the unique patterns of their markings, were all indicators that their bodies were meant to be seen. But for miners, attracting attention was not a priority. In fact, with the type of Wode they sent to guard the entrances to the settlement and the factory, it was better to go unnoticed.

Safer.

She picked up the *ton* sticks Freeman had made for her the first time she had done this, and twirled their short handles in her hands. She may not be bringing her attention-drawing weapons with her, but she would never go completely unarmed. She swung them a few times, loving the balance and flow of the smooth wood, before tucking them in the empty belt loops of her pants. Their weight brought her comfort.

The sounds of the engines had changed. She could easily hear the ugly churning growl of the steam power making the transition to the near-silent hum of theorrite as they moved closer to civilization. Almost time.

She grabbed the knit cap that would conceal her hair until she was as indistinguishable as any of the others who lived in their drab community. Only her claws had grown back, and she meant for them to stay sharp.

He was in the hall. Cyrus. He'd obviously just come from his own room. Phina heard Dare and Bodhan climbing the stairs that led to the deck above and knew they were talking about her and Cyrus. What they had to do.

Cyrus wore a pristine white shirt, well fitted across his broad shoulders, dark brown pants that clung to his lean hips and muscular thighs, and military boots. Draped over his forearm was a worn-looking hooded cape. To indicate a long journey spent in hiding, she assumed.

The Sword planned to walk right through the front gates and into the Copper Palace. Phina had a more roundabout way inside, but his way held more peril. Each step could be blocked. Wode could have been instructed to imprison him. The members of the Raj, or whoever was behind this treason, could easily lay a trap for him to fall into.

He stopped at the sight of her and she stared into his blue eyes, noticing not for the first time that his long lashes appeared more black than blue. He studied her in return.

When Cyrus smiled, she felt a snarl ready to curl her lips, her tail go taut as a wire. If he teased or insulted her, he would trail a bloody path behind him to the palace. She was on the edge. Eager for a fight. For blood.

"Your disguise isn't working, Seraphina." He tilted his head, shaking it a bit as if in bewilderment. "As if your firelight could be dimmed so easily."

He turned his back on her and walked away, leaving her stunned. Had that been a compliment? She replayed his words in her head, certain there was a barb, a tone that she would find that would prove her wrong. But no.

Had Cyrus Arendal seen her covered in muck and dressed in shapeless rags and called her . . . attractive? More than that. Firelight.

Her claws came out and she cursed under her breath. Damn the man. Now she wanted to scratch another type of itch. He was a bastard for throwing her off by not playing their game. By not hating her and wanting her. And then hating himself for wanting her. She deserved it. She wanted his scorn. It made it easy for her to stay away from him. To not care whether or not he was hurting, or how he had suffered.

Damn him.

On deck the crew had grown quiet. Many had their guns drawn and wore expressions of disbelief. Most had never flagrantly sailed a giant airship over a populated city in the full light of late afternoon, unseen. They would learn. She corrected herself—they would learn if the captain let them live long enough.

It was a bit like tiptoeing past your own pyre. As long as they never hung from the aether cocoon announcing their arrival, the dodge and the silent running engine would work their marvelous magic and keep them hidden.

No one would ever know they were there.

Captain Amaranthe headed in her direction. "There is no way I am landing in Centre City. I don't care if he is the Queen's Sword, her gun, or her entire bloody arsenal." Her voice lowered when she noticed Phina's new look. "Are you sure you want to do this?"

Phina smiled, knowing that her sharp incisors showed brilliantly white against her dirty face. "I have to. The commands come from the right hand of the queen. More than that, I need to. The cargo I'm returning with is more precious than any weapon."

The captain nodded, slipping a hand beneath her long dark hair to rub her neck. "Then it is settled. The usual location for the drop, but this time you will have an irritating man who, no doubt, has not the first idea how to get down from an ironwood tree."

The idea lightened Phina's mood considerably. She would finally have the upper hand. "Have you told him yet?"

Aramanthe could not contain the obvious sparkle in her hazel gaze. "Why would I want to do that?" She sobered swiftly. "I trust you to keep him safe on the way down. He is the Queen's Sword, after all. Just remember you'll need to hurry. We should get you in with not much time to spare for shift change. You mustn't allow yourself to be sidetracked or you will have to spend the evening inside. And you and I both recall how well that turned out the last time it happened."

Phina shuddered, her markings tingling in a decidedly unhappy way. She remembered. "I know what I'm doing. I can only hope the Arendal won't get lost between the settlement and Queen's Hill. It is farther away than his feet will tell him."

A world away, despite its proximity. The sun did not shine at the same angle where the settlement stood. The moons were always shadowed by factory steam and ash. The line of windwinders, with their massive turbines that dotted the grassland before Centre City appeared ensured that the wind always blew from the west. Keeping the smell of Felidae and heated metalworks far away from the Hill and blowing it toward the settlement and the dour, simple fishing village on the coast. A village populated more with retired and posted Wode than fishermen. It had been settled in that location, with that unpleasant aroma, for the singular purpose of bordering the settlement, ensuring Felidae land did not reach to the eastern sea. Penning them in.

She shook herself visibly. She was thinking dark thoughts again. Thoughts she usually killed with drink or intimate pleasures. But there was no drinking for her today, and no one she had the time or inclination to take her grief out on. Almost no one. She had a purpose. She had to keep her head.

There was thieving to be done.

She glanced up over her shoulder at Freeman as he stood at the wheel on the helm's deck. The three men from Aaru sat once more at the table behind him. A handsome trio, they were. Bodhan, Wulf, and Hadi. She wondered if all Aaruan men looked as they did. If so, the city was blessed with a fortunate inheritance indeed.

The two men were still fussing over that damned game. If only Cyrus hadn't come aboard, she would have played any game that Wulf or Hadi had in mind.

Hadi snared her gaze and winked. Phina's smile grew wide. The Khepri must have told him the same thing he'd told her. Even in captivity, the queen would keep her vow to Phina. If she could get Nephi to safety, Hadiyah of the long braid would bring her the rest of the way. To a place that Phina had not believed existed. A place where families of Felidae and humans lived together as equals, and even mingled inheritance. A place called Aaru.

It was a thing Phina had not been entirely sure was possible. But she *was* sure of one thing. Nephi would be fascinated by those babies. By a life where she no longer had to hide her beauty for fear of abuse or work herself to an early pyre for fear of starvation and scorn. All Phina had to do was get into the palace and out again undetected.

Simple enough.

The low argument Cyrus was having with the captain drew her attention, their words sounding like shouts in her ears.

"You have sailed past the city, Captain."

"Thank you for keeping me apprised, Arendal."

He swore. "Any idea when we will be landing? Where?"

The captain pulled her dagger out from the low collar of her vest and studied it, polishing it before displaying it against the black of her long jacket. "*We* will not be landing," she said without looking at him. "You will. As to where . . . I suppose that all depends on how gracefully you fall."

As delicious as this was to Phina's taste for torture, she felt compelled to join the conversation. Protecting him again. A few long strides took her to their side. "My lovely Captain, if you scare him too badly he won't be any use to us."

Cyrus glared at her. "There has been no *scaring*. Frustrating, yes. Bone-grinding irrationality, yes. But no scaring."

"Shame," the captain muttered, sheathing her dagger and walking to the center of the deck. "I thought I was doing a fair job of scaring."

Phina knew what was coming. She looked back at the helm's deck and watched as Freeman shook his head in subtle exasperation. So did her first mate.

Captain Amaranthe drew her sword and pushed down the false gem on the weapon's hilt. Its vibration made a sound that always seemed to Phina like a man dying, or a woman finding her pleasure. In the captain's hands, both analogies could be true.

Most on board had never heard that sound, or had seen the silver steel of a sword blur unless it was swinging toward them. Phina could see more than the blur. She saw turbulent waves like heat rolling across the desert. A storm of motion in one slender, beautifully efficient weapon.

The first time she saw the captain's sword she'd wanted to steal it. For Phina, considering the danger she had already known would be involved in such an undertaking, it was the highest compliment she could pay.

The captain turned to Cyrus. "You'll need to take some rope with you." She raised her voice without looking up. "Freeman, if you could spare a moment."

Freeman leaned his big frame forward, grabbing a heavy coil of rope easily with one hand and tossing it over the railing toward the main deck.

It soared with his strength, heading directly for the captain. She bent her knees a moment before springing into the air in a way that the Felidae in Phina could only admire seeing in a human.

She made two swift slashes with her sword, the sound a bright song as the steel connected and passed through the thick fibers.

Phina knew to the rest of the crew this would mimic flight. The sword moving so fast it seemed the captain had sprouted steel wings for a glorious instant.

Before anyone could release the surprised breath they had gathered in their lungs, it was over. The captain had landed lightly on the deck in a stance Phina had taught her long ago, her sword tip inches from Cyrus's left eye.

She stayed perfectly still. They all did. The only things that seemed to move were the four even lengths of rope that fell haphazardly to the deck in front of her.

Captain Amaranthe straightened and stepped away from him, turning off her sword, sliding it back into position on her hip. She scooped up the rope with her boot and caught it in her hands, handing them to Cyrus. "Here you are."

Phina watched Cyrus accept her offering, his white-knuckled grip on the lengths of rope the only indication of his reaction to her maneuver.

The rest of the men were not so closed off. Phina heard their gasps, felt their fear. Their awe. Her hearing picked out Wulf's admiring, "Stunning sword for a stunning woman."

But it took no special abilities or senses to hear James Stacy. He stood in the middle of the deck, the men behind him wearing identical expressions of shock and pallor when he said, "You do more than a fair job at scaring, Captain. Don't let anyone tell you different."

The chorus of hearty agreements did something that surprised Phina. It made the captain smile. She had a feeling the crew was as astonished by the change in her appearance as they had been by her sword.

"Why, Mr. Stacy." The captain ducked her chin in acknowledgment. "I believe that is the nicest thing you could have said to me." She started to turn away but stopped herself and forced a frown. "Flattery, as a rule, is not tolerated on the Deviant. I've shot men for less."

Phina lifted her hands and bit into the hat she'd been holding to stifle her laughter. It was true. She had shot men for less. But somehow, Phina had a feeling James Stacy would still be here alive and well when she got back.

Cyrus sent her a confused expression and followed her as she walked to the bow of the ship. "Why did she give me rope? Why are we not landing?" When she failed to answer he sighed heavily. "I suppose I shouldn't have to ask why you're eating your hat, either. The answers will just come to me."

She snorted and her face flushed a little at the unexpected sound. She took the partially bitten hat and placed it on her head, tucking every last strand of hair beneath it as she leaned over the railing, studying the line of tall trees. "Do you enjoy surprises?"

"No."

She smiled and took some of the rope from his hands, coiling it deftly over her shoulder. "I am torn on the issue myself. I enjoy the giving but not receiving of surprises. That sounded a bit naughty. True in more ways than one."

She turned her body toward him, meeting his gaze while she gathered the extra fabric of her shirt and formed a knot, which bared her stomach, but it was necessary. "Do not worry, I have done this many times. Tie that cape around your waist. The rope as well."

He made a move as if to step away from her. "What?"

She blew a frustrated breath upward, wishing she had more time to explain. "She is not landing. Too many chances of being caught, even with the dodge."

His eyebrows lowered. "She's not landing."

"That's right. We are jumping."

"Fuck."

She watched him make quick, sloppy knots as she hopped up and easily balanced on the rail. She reached her hands out toward him. "Not now. Now we jump. If you still want to afterwards we can discuss it."

When he jumped up beside her, Phina used her strength to stabilize his larger body on the railing's edge. She leaned in close so he would hear her. "You have to jump out, not down, or you'll fall into the dodge and take me with you. Do not fall in the dodge."

He was afraid, but not frozen with it. She could appreciate that kind of fortitude. She could also tell he was listening to everything she said. She appreciated that as well.

He glanced down quickly. "Trees don't look *that* far. We can do that. Right?"

She fought her smile. Men. "*I* can do that. I am Felidae. We have to see what you can do. Just keep hold of my hand and when you hit the tree do not let go. Ironwoods only have branches up top. If you fell . . . Just don't. Do not fall."

"Good advice."

Phina looked down. Perfect alignment. "Jump. Now."

She launched herself into the air, her hand caught in his bruising grip. Flying. She loved this feeling.

Her laughter drowned out the stream of male cursing she could hear on the wind.

Chapter Five

"Are you broken?" Phina used her legs and tail to cling to the sturdy branch, the top half of her body dangling upside down in order to check on him. He was tightly gripping the trunk of the ironwood, balancing on a heavy limb several feet below her. The last limb before a straight, long drop to the ground.

Phina had to admit, she was impressed with how well he had handled himself. She'd known his legs were strong enough to take him past the dodge, but he'd stopped himself from tumbling to his death as well. He had decent survival instincts for a palace Wode. She'd had a feeling he would.

She catalogued him from her unusual angle, hearing his racing heartbeat, seeing the heat that radiated off his body. She assumed it was fear until he looked up at her. He was *not* afraid.

He was angry.

Cyrus moved until he was straddling the thick lower branch, one of his arms grasping a thinner limb just above his head.

"Did you think?" His words came out like shots from a pistol. Short bursts of angry sound. "Did it occur to you even for a moment that I should have been told? Prepared?"

She *had* told him. Within moments of discovering he would join her on her jump. The captain had, in fact, descended more than usual to compensate for his human disabilities.

There was no doubt in her mind that he would respond badly were she to defend herself with *that* bit of information.

She swung back up, away from his reach and judgmental gaze. "The captain is the way she is for a reason. She knew I wouldn't let anything happen to you. Dare knew I wouldn't let anything happen to you. And nothing has. You are alive and unbroken, with a lovely view of the Felidae settlement and Queen's Hill beyond. Are all Wode as ungrateful as you?"

"Ungrateful?" She could hear his teeth gnash. "What reason do I have for that? I am merely trapped ninety or more feet off the ground without the human trappings of wood grips or sawboots to get down." His laugh was more a groan as he looked down. "I am also lacking Felidae claws and equilibrium. No. Nothing to be ungrateful for."

Phina rolled her eyes. "The rope is all you will need. Let me see it. And keep your voice down, if you would. We are not that far from the stormfence."

Cyrus handed her his two strands of rope and her fingers began to weave a harness as she had done so many times. There were occasions when simple stealth was more necessary than gadgetry.

"May I ask how you plan to get inside the palace, from here, of all places?" Cyrus stilled when the wind made the ironwood creak and sway. "It seems a backward sort of route."

She would not share her secrets with him. Not all of them. She finished the last knot and grinned. "That should do the job. Did you know I once gave a tree feller an enormous amount of pleasure in one of these contraptions? I was distracting him at the time, of course—"

"Seraphina."

She bit her lip at his warning tone. "I was trying to reassure you that it works." She slipped backward into a hanging position once more. "Come on, stand up on the branch."

Cyrus grumbled, but did as she asked, if a bit unsteadily. He had a crushing grip on the limb above him when he finally muttered, "Why am I standing?"

She watched his struggle for balance without a tail, and decided not to tease him. For the moment. "You're going to put this on like a pair of pants. One leg at a time and pull it up."

"Now is not the time for fun at the gullible human male's expense, Seraphina." His teeth were clenched and she quickly readjusted her strategy.

She shrugged, though she knew it would be hard to see from their current positioning. "It makes no difference to me. You can build a nest and live here until you sprout wings if you'd like. I was just attempting to give you an alternative other than that. Or death."

The look he sent down to her was withering, but she knew he understood her meaning. He was still listening. Good. The last thing she needed was another person to worry about. What was waiting for her down below would be bad enough.

With a stream of curses that surprised even her bawdy sensibilities, Cyrus took the harness she was holding out to him and did as she asked.

While he did, she uncoiled the rope she had wrapped around her shoulder and, with some creative knotting, let one end fall toward the ground.

She swung forward and grabbed the middle of the harness where it met between his thighs. She licked her lips, studying the buttons that held his pants closed. "This is something I've never tried before. Interested, Cyrus?"

He made a sound she could not decipher and she laughed. "Perhaps another time." Her free hand reached around to slap his rear end playfully, then finished attaching her rope to his. "Now all you have to do is grab the rope and lower yourself down. Then you can control the rate of your descent and you won't break anything when you land. Although the rope isn't as long as I'd imagined. You may fall the last bit."

"You want me to slide down the tree, and I may fall the last bit." His voice was emotionless, but she knew he was still perturbed.

She pulled herself upright once more, tilting her head so he didn't notice her looking at his lips. He had lovely lips . . . unless they were pinched and frowning. "I believe that is what I said, yes."

His sigh was like a caress. "You've given me all the rope, Seraphina. How do you intend to get down?"

She got to her feet to stand on her branch without aid, causing him to call out to her in warning. In worry. There was no need.

She smiled coyly. "You keep forgetting I am Felidae, Sword. These boots may stop me from climbing as, I'm told, the old tribes of my people could." She reached for handles of the *ton* sticks, pulling them out and spinning them in her hands. "But I am a master at the art of leaping."

"So I've seen." He still sounded concerned.

Phina sighed. "Slide down and take the southern route around the settlement. The Wode assigned here are lazy, and since there is no opening on that side, they rarely guard it. With a swift pace you can reach Queen's Hill by nightfall. I will be close behind."

She had not allayed his concerns. "There is no place for you to land. If you jump too far you will hit the fence. You know what happens to any flesh it touches."

She met his indigo gaze, her feelings a jumble. She was irritated with his disbelief in her abilities but gratified at the protectiveness in his tone. There was no time for that kind of distraction. The kind that would revel in someone caring whether she lived or died. She decided the irritation was safer. For the moment. "Let me ease your mind. If I do not see you in the palace, I will do your job as well. Once I have the dagger and return to the Deviant, we will come back to gather any pieces of you that might be left."

She smiled, though her tone was determined when he opened his mouth to argue. "I refuse to listen to another word. Perhaps a demonstration of what I can do will help you focus on your own task."

She would not stay and watch over him to ensure his safety. He could handle himself. And now he had to. If only to prove her wrong.

She took off at a run toward the edge of the long branch, leaping out with her arms outstretched, the *ton* in her hands. Her tail swinging instinctively to direct her flight, she aimed for the top of the stormfence, keeping her eye on the whitish-blue light that arced over the charged wire, a clear indicator of the potential danger.

It was thrilling.

She slipped the *ton* sticks long end down and directed their tips toward the wires. These weapons of wood were good for more than protection. They were also nonconductive.

When the wood touched wire, she used her momentum to flip midair, pushing off the flexible fence and pointing her body toward the nearest earthen roof.

Her boots touched down and she rolled on the curved surface, landing with a soft bounce on the ground behind what she knew was the mound home of an elder Felidae.

She glanced up at Cyrus, seeing him clearly through the branches of the tree, and lifted her arm. He may not see her expression, but the relief in his told her he had watched her flight. Knew she had been successful.

Now she was back where she had started. Trapped.

As she untied the knot in her shirt to let it hang, she wondered if Cyrus believed, as Dare had told her *she* had, that the Felidae had chosen this life. That they preferred solitude to intermingling and had asked for protection from human invaders.

It was not a belief unique to nobles and Wode. The ignorance stunned her. What sentient being would choose this? She had comforted Dare with a partial truth—most Felidae here accepted their lot and did not suffer for lack of food or excessive violence. Certainly not from lack of drink.

Most were docile, tamed after generations, despite the stories the elders would spin for them. Stories of a time when the Felidae were wild. When they outnumbered humans and lived freely, honoring their abundant world and soaring through the trees. Soaring on the wind.

Now they watched the gears of the giant shift clock at the settlement's gate, living and dying by its chime. Those who chose to disobey its call led a different life. Scorned and spied on by their own kind, learning to steal or starve. To pleasure Wode instead of being forcibly taken. For Phina all of it had been untenable.

She slid along the back walls of the mound homes, breathing harder through the heavy air around her. She already missed the Deviant.

Felidae milled about, most preparing for their shift, finishing their meals or refreshing the fires of the outdoor ovens that would soon be used by their returning family members.

"Seri, I thought you had learned. Eli may kill you if he finds you've snuck in again."

Phina lifted her *ton* defensively out of instinct before she realized who the voice belonged to. "Nob, how are you, my brother? Have you bedded that luscious girl with the facial markings yet? I remember she had her eye on you."

Nob looked around, his body's movements a strong indication of his disapproval. Phina used the time to slip her weapons back into her belt loops. "Shift is about to change and he'll be heading back. We cannot let him see you, though I suppose you timed it this way. Why do you play these games with our lives, Seri? And why are you back?"

She would not admit how the words made her heart ache. Eli was the eldest. The strongest. Out of all of her relatives, he most despised her. But Nob had helped her get into the mines many times, as had Jobi, despite their displeasure with her. It seemed their patience was running out. "Is Jobi with him?"

Nob narrowed his gaze, as piercing green as hers. "You did not come back to see him, then? Neither has Nephi. We sent word to her weeks ago. Eli believes the palace life has corrupted her. Made her forget her family the way you chose to."

"What happened to Jobi?" The hair on the back of her neck stood on end and the pain in her nerve endings made her flinch. If anyone had hurt him—a Wode or another Felidae—they would suffer before they died.

Nob shook his head. "An accident in the mines. A stupid accident. We lost control of one of the ore carts. It slammed him against solid rock, pinning him for hours until we could reverse the magnetism." Nob paled at the memory. "His arm is crushed beyond healing. His tail . . . it had to be removed. The settlement elders have helped us hide his infirmity, but he will be seen. And when he is, he may be taken by the Raj."

Or their science ministers. How many Felidae had disappeared after they were too injured to work? Told they would be cared for and given the best Theorrean medicine they had to offer for their sacrifice. Phina knew there was more to it than that. She could not let that happen to Jobi.

She gripped the woven shirt Nob wore, which was identical to her own. "Listen to me. I must get into the mines. Nephi is in danger again."

She had his attention now. "Raj Ellsworth?"

Phina nodded. "The queen cannot protect her. I can. There is a place for her where she will be free. Where he can never hurt her with his obsession again. I can take Jobi as well, but I need your help."

Nob pulled away from her. "You would take everyone from me. Kill or steal every person I love."

She felt her claws extend and forced herself to close her fingers into fists. The pain would keep her on task. "You could come with us. It never occurred to you, did it? To leave. There is so much out there, Nobel. So much life and sunlight."

He shook his head. "I will help you one last time, Seri. For my brother's sake. And for Nephi. After this I want your true oath—in moon's blood—that you will never put our family in jeopardy like this again. Never come back to our home."

Moon's blood. It was a Felidae oath that was unbreakable. She freed one hand and reached down to take a slender blade from the lining of her boot, the only weapon other than the *ton* she'd dared carry into this place.

She opened her palm, which was already bleeding from her sharp nails, and sliced into it with the blade. Nob held out his hand and she did the same to him. With the moonlike silver of the blade pressed between their palms, she swore, "Help me, and I will save our family. I will never return."

Phina wanted to believe she saw pain or regret in his expression, but she knew it was a lie. She had caused her brothers too much suffering for them to forgive. Jobi as well as Eli and Nob, may hate her for what she was about to do, but Nephi would understand. And they would be safe.

Her brother nodded his agreement with the sound of the clock's chime. He tugged her hat lower on her forehead and took away his hand, licking the blood off with his tongue.

Phina did the same.

He took her blade and stuck it in his own boot. "Wode haven't searched me in over a year. Since the last time you paid us a visit. Keep your head down and follow me."

They merged into the thick queue already forming in the settlement. Factory and mine workers together in a single line that would only diverge once they reached the pipeline of the large metalworks that surrounded the factories.

She'd snuck inside once. Despite their haughty demeanor the factory Felidae had the harder job. The heat, the mechanisms that had to be maintained, the danger . . . Mining was simple in comparison.

None of the other Felidae—who Phina knew could easily sniff her out—said a word to alert the Wode to her presence. Perhaps they knew she had come to save Jobi from his mysterious fate. She knew how well loved he had always been by his peers.

They seemed to understand her purpose. As they passed her old mound home, two Felidae ducked out from the open door, keeping the injured man between them.

He looked terrible, his skin pale and sweating, one sleeve of his shirt dangling past his hand to hide it from view. The handsome face she had looked to throughout her childhood was bitter. Twisted. He saw her and curled his lip in disgust, but did not speak.

They moved into position ahead of Nob and Phina, and she watched her brother lay his palm on Jobi's back in support. How hard would it be for them to say goodbye to each other? They were each other's only consolation. The one left behind would have only Eli, who had no love in his heart to give. Nob may as well be alone.

The Wode asked why the men weren't in single file and one of the Felidae holding Jobi's weight mentioned something about too much Spotted Ale. It was a plausible excuse. It was the most plentiful resource in the settlement and, Phina imagined, the reason for most Felidae offspring.

They were allowed to pass and none of the guards glanced her way. But she was not out of danger yet. Her only hope was that Eli was in the first batch of the return shift. That he would not seek out his brothers in the line. That he would not catch her scent. It was a slim hope, at best, one she knew Nob was clinging to . . . for Jobi's sake if not hers.

Half of the crowd headed to the right, including one of the men who had been keeping Jobi upright. Nob quickly replaced him, leaving Phina to keep up behind them.

Jobi's low mumble was meant for his brother, but Phina heard him. "Do *I* get to go be the queen's pet Felidae now? Will I be fed queensfruit tarts and ale? Or does Seri plan to sell me to a passing noble?"

Moons, how they saw her. She knew. Of course she knew. She was reminded each time she returned that she was unwelcome. She had never allowed herself to care. Perhaps she had grown soft. Fair Dare, who cared about what she was feeling, had softened her. Or perhaps it was the guilt that Cyrus had awoken within her.

She straightened her spine, stilling the restless motion of her tail. Nephi mattered. No one else. Let them think what they would, she knew who and what she was. She had never needed their approval before. She did not need it now.

Phina looked up and saw the entrance to the mine with fresh eyes. Dare would no doubt see the large opening to the underground as another marvel she had yet to witness, large enough for the Deviant to sail into and framed by carvings on either side. The images were of the same female. Not Queen Idony, but an elder Felidae whose name meant Peacemaker.

She was beautiful, her hair wild and decorated with feathers and flowers from the marsh as well as the desert. An open floor-length robe revealed a body covered in sensual markings. Not merely along her spine or arms but along her belly. The markings lined her collarbone instead of jewels. The image, it seemed, welcomed her children into the deep, secret places of the world. Into her womb.

Phina recalled the stories from childhood. The Peacemaker was the leader of all Felidae. Under her they had been one tribe united. Her mere presence inspired peace and harmony. She'd ruled at Queen Idony's side for an age, ensuring her people were kept safe. Protected.

Phina was never sure if the stories were true. She had been tempted to ask the queen many times over the years but hadn't wanted to seem ignorant. She also hadn't wanted to be disappointed with the truth. To know that those stories, just like the ale they were eternally supplied with, were meant to distract them. To soothe them. To keep Phina's people compliant.

The sun was low in the sky when she took her first step into the mine. She would have to move swiftly—Jobi's injuries would no doubt slow them down.

No one spoke but went to their posts or picked up the tools left for them by the last Felidae workers. Phina moved to the other side of Jobi, glaring when he momentarily resisted. He was going to make this as difficult as possible.

Nob was grunting with exertion. "Your luck holds out as usual, Seri. The ore's veins take us in the opposite direction of your special tunnels."

"They are not *my* tunnels."

"You are the only one fool enough to use them." The voice Phina had always associated with pain froze the three of them in place as they turned the corner that would lead them to their destination.

Eli.

"You're the only one who crawls like a Theorrean worm in the dirt to find someone to spread your legs for," he growled. "Someone who doesn't know what you are."

She helped Nob sit Jobi down on a flattened area of rock and turned to face her brother. Still just as big as she remembered. So much larger than his life. One eye closed with scars made by a Wode dagger, the rest of his face a continued study in hate and violence. In another world he could have been a warrior. In this one he had long since given up. Long since sold his soul to survive.

Jobi chuckled morbidly. "I love these family gatherings. All singing and nestling. When do we toast with ale?"

Eli turned to Nob. "He got past the Wode? What have you let her talk you into this time? When will you learn what she is? The curse you call on yourself by listening to her?"

Phina stepped between them. "I am here to—"

Her words were cut off by the back of Eli's hand.

She spat out dirt and blood and lifted herself off the ground where she'd fallen. She snarled, claws out. "Thank you for the kiss, brother. I only wish I'd brought my pretty bracelet. Then I'd have something as special to give you in return."

He came toward her but Nob grabbed his arm in challenge. "Nephi is in danger. Jobi is ill. She can help them both."

Eli's frustrated roar echoed through the mines. "She cannot help. She is a fiend." He pointed to his face. "Look at me. I spent my life accepting her punishment. As the eldest it is my duty. A duty that has left me childless. Mateless. No chance of gaining respect as an elder. Nephi suffers without us, unable to be with her family. And Jobi? Nobel, *look* at us. You are the only one of us who stands whole. Undamaged by her. If I killed her now I could spare you before she destroys everything we love."

The fight spilled out of her like blood onto the ground. Was he right? Did she destroy everything she cared about? Everything she touched? She thought about what her family had suffered—what Cyrus had suffered—because of her.

A few steps took her to Eli's side. She gripped his wrists and lifted his hands to her throat while he looked on in bewildered rage.

She smiled sadly, thinking of what he might have been if not for her. "Kill me then, Eli. You go save Nephi from Ellsworth. From being hunted and watched in every private moment. From being raped or beaten each time she feels safe enough to let down her guard. Save her, brother. But kill me."

The salty dampness leaking down her cheeks went unheeded as she forced him to apply pressure to her neck. "There is still time to save them all," she gasped. "Stop them from taking Jobi to sell as a slave or to experiment on for medicine meant to heal the nobles. Kill me and this nightmare will be over. For both of us."

He had hesitated before starting to squeeze her windpipe. She could take comfort in that. Only a moment, but he had tried.

Phina closed her eyes, hearing him weep in self-pity, and sent a silent apology to the queen. She had tried, through service, to make right what was wrong, but perhaps a true sacrifice was required. The captain and fair Dare, strange smelling and special, would save the queen without her.

When the pressure was suddenly removed from her windpipe, she began to choke, her body desperate for air despite her willingness to die.

She saw Eli lying unconscious on the ground and Nob standing over him, a shovel in his hand. Phina knelt to see if her prone brother was still breathing.

"He'll live." Nob was quiet. "He will be sorry he did, as he is each time he wakes, but he'll live. You and Jobi need to go now."

Jobi's expression was as somber as his brother's. "He won't thank you when he wakes up. Sure you want to stay?"

Nob shrugged. "I am all he has left. Eli could never survive on his own. You know that."

It was a surprise to Phina. "Nob?"

"Go." His tone was adamant. "Save the ones who must be saved. My life is in no danger." He tried to smile. "I may finally bed that girl with the pretty face. Who knows? Just remember your oath."

She would never see him again. She had sworn it. She embraced him and whispered a soft "Thank you" before hefting Jobi up the rise to the tunnel's entrance a few feet off the ground.

"Crawling one-handed without a tail." Jobi's voice was cynical. "I will take my chances with the scientists."

Phina pushed him inside. "*You* will move faster than you have in years and do it with a smile." She gazed at Nob one last time. "We have a sister and possibly an Arendal Sword to save. Then we have a ship to fly."

"Fly? Seri, did you say fly?"

Chapter Six

He was being led into a trap.

Cyrus sighed, aggravated beyond all measure that they had barely made an effort to conceal their intentions.

The Wode at the stormgate had real enough reactions. He'd lowered his hood and they had beamed, slapping him on the back and saying they had known he was alive, despite the rumors.

He'd watched one young Wode pull the lever that opened the circuit of the gate, breaking the connection to the protective charge around the wall to Queen's Hill. He then began to turn the crank on the gate's wheel to raise it up for Cyrus to pass.

He'd strode swiftly up the three ridges of Queen's Hill, nightfall making his journey less eventful. Few people wandered about at night. The artisans and scholars were tucked into their houses, raucous laughter and music drifting through the nobles' open windows. It was always best to leave what *they* were doing to the imagination.

Heading up the steps of the Copper Palace for the first time in what seemed like ages, he realized he did not feel as if he had come home. The Wode at the door were strangers to him, which was suspicious in itself, though he refused to show surprise. They knew the name Arendal. After a slight hesitation, they, too, let him inside.

It was Behrnard, the palace steward, who had given it away. He had gone white as snow on the mountain when he saw Cyrus's face. After a momentary hesitation, his shock had transformed into effusive welcome. Too effusive. Too welcoming.

He took Cyrus through the grand hall and up the wide staircase, his words seeming to tumble out faster than he could breathe. He assured Cyrus that both the queen and the Chalice would be overjoyed to see him alive. That they had been beside themselves with grief.

Queen Idony and Dare, he'd added, were visiting informally with a few members of the Raj in her rooms. He could join them as soon as he cleaned up and changed into his Arendal uniform.

Cyrus looked around his room and shook his head. Berhnard had lied. Repeatedly. Dare was on the Deviant, hovering in secret somewhere nearby, and the true queen had never allowed any member of the Raj into her personal sanctuary.

At least his suite had not been invaded. The Wode-sized bed was as neatly made as when he had left it. His personal items, including the tribal hide painting he had been given to remember his origins from the Faro Outpost, still hung on the wall.

The gesture did not comfort him. The rooms of the Queen's Sword were not meant to be a shrine. It was meant to be the dwelling for a Wode who swore his fealty to the queen. Someone who would protect her with his life. If they'd believed him dead another should have been chosen immediately.

The scope of the situation momentarily overwhelmed him and a red haze blinded his vision. The villains who had perpetrated the crime may still be unknown, but everyone in this palace was complicit. Even Berhnard, whose only crime in the past had been that of being an irritant.

He noticed his sword, the true Arendal broadsword, leaning against the wall beside the open doors of his balcony. As though it deserved no better treatment than to be left to the elements when the servants let the air in each day. He would be taking that, along with the dagger.

His fingers reached out to trace the familiar design on the white gold of the hilt when his heart began to pound tellingly. He would recognize her scent anywhere. The Felidae and her damn pheromones.

"What are you doing on my balcony, Seraphina?"

From the corner of his eye, he saw her tail curling around the door. "Wondering what is taking you so long, Sword of the Queen. I left someone waiting and you are too busy strolling down memory lane to accomplish your mission. Also, you have a lovely view from here. The Twin Mountains are so close you could almost touch them."

Relief at seeing her relaxed his shoulders. He did not want to think about how worried he had been when he saw her leap into the air, aiming for that damn shock fence. She could have died. Could have been caught by the Wode who guarded the settlement.

He took a calming breath. "Are you ever going to tell me how you got from a fenced-in settlement to the palace? And who is waiting for you? If someone else followed you, it could be a security issue when the true queen returns."

She entered his room and he saw the streaks in the soot that had covered her face. He reached for her instinctively. "Seraphina? Have you been crying?" A clinking sound made him look at what she was holding. "Where did you get the absencea?"

She stepped back, placing one hand on her hip and lifting the crystal container full of light green liquid to her lips before answering. "Yes, I have been crying. That is my secret. You have found me out. I have no actual skills at escape or theft. I simply find a big, strong Wode and cry on his shoulder until he offers me a tour of the Copper Palace. He even got me into the library where I know the steward hides the absencea while I was waiting for you. Works every time."

Cyrus sighed. "Do not tell me then. I cannot play guessing games. I am to bathe and change before I meet Queen Idony in her rooms. *Dare* is with her, I'm told."

She raised her eyebrows, and when she pushed her wild red hair behind her ears, he had a sudden urge to nibble on them.

"They don't expect you to leave or they would not be lying to you."

He nodded grimly. "My thoughts exactly. I was planning on keeping the pretense until I discovered and removed the dagger from her possession. However, no one is giving me that option. Berhnard had to know that when he informed me that she is entertaining members of the Raj in her suite. Unless he was simply too panicked to think straight."

He heard Seraphina hiss, saw her tail stiffen and her nostrils flare. "Bastard," she whispered angrily.

Cyrus could see her rage was not aimed at him. "What is it, Phina? Tell me."

She turned back to him in surprise when he used the shortened version of her name, sloshing liquid out of the container. "Raj Ellsworth. He is here, in the palace. His stink is everywhere." She started to pace. "There's no time to tell you everything, but you should know. A member of the Raj covets the queen's maid, Nephi. He enjoys hurting her. Torturing her. Without Queen Idony's or my protection, she will not survive him. She has always been too gentle to fight."

"Nephi?" Cyrus had always been fond of the quiet Felidae. She was shy, but utterly loyal to the queen. "I take it you know her."

Seraphina nodded jerkily, setting the absencea down. Her clawed hands flexed. "She is my sister. Our queen has kept her safe, out of the mines and out of the hands of Ellsworth. Now everything has changed."

It made sense now. "The Khepri . . . *She* is why he sent you to the palace?"

She'd stopped pacing to stare intently at the door. "The queen protects all those under her care. Even in her absence she and the Khepri mean to honor that promise. Nephi will be safe if I can get her back to the ship. To Hadi."

Her mission had not been for any trinket or possession. She was here to steal back her sister. Seraphina's connection to the queen was finally beginning to make more sense. Of course Queen Idony would protect an innocent Felidae if it were in her power. "How did the queen find out?"

Her reply was so low Cyrus had to lean in to hear her. "Ellsworth tours the settlement once a year to ensure we are all being treated well, to count those with child among us for the census. He brings a science minister who bears a device to trim our claws to the nub. It is more humane, he insists, than the permanent removal forced on our kind on Maithuna." He placed his hand on her arm in comfort and she allowed it, showing him the depth of her distraction.

"When my elder sister, Nephi, came of age, Ellsworth noticed. That year we were given more food and ale than the other miners. Our bedding was restuffed and the roof of our mound home repaired. The next year he attempted to rape her inside our home, but she resisted. I was too inexperienced then to fight so I called for help. A few weeks later a noblewoman requested Nephi specifically as a caretaker and servant for her child. It meant more rations for the rest of us so she agreed." Her lips curled back in a silent snarl at her memories. "Her visits home grew shorter. We could smell the blood on her. The injuries. I learned that while members of the Raj are forbidden from taking Felidae into their homes by Theorrean Law, he could bribe another to do it for him. He had been tormenting her with the noble's permission. Forcing his attentions on her. The only way I could get out to help her was to find a bribe the noblewoman could not resist. It was known she was rather fond of the queen's emerald lotus ring."

Cyrus caressed her arm almost absently, studying her face, his heart wrenching at the story she was laying out before him. "You meant to steal from the queen to bribe a noble? But how, if you could not get into Queen's Hill?"

Seraphina shrugged. "I was young, I could do anything. And there were tunnels. Tunnels no Felidae had ever made, small but perfect, and leading out to several openings in the Twin Mountains. One extended down nearly half the Yazata range. There is also one that leads directly to the outcropping facing the Copper Palace."

Her voice had softened with remembered wonder and disbelief. "I did not see the queen sitting in the shadows when I entered her room and began to search for the ring. When I finally saw her, she did not call out for help. She simply smiled. She was so beautiful, her eyes so wise. She asked me why I had gone to so much trouble, so I told her, not believing it would change anything. Nephi became her personal maid that very night. Under the queen's protection."

Seraphina stepped away from his touch and wiped her face. "We have no time for this. I'm not sure why I told you but—"

"I'm glad, Phina. I am *honored* that you told me. That you trusted me. The queen chooses her friends wisely." And he had, perhaps, judged Seraphina too harshly.

"How big is your wardrobe, Sword?"

Her question brought him up short. "The armoire? Too excessive in my opinion. My clothing hardly fills one sec—"

She covered his mouth and walked him backward in its direction. "Someone is coming. We need to hide."

He reacted in an instant, reaching behind him to open the wardrobe door. His arm curled around her to pull her inside and he saw her tail lash out to tug the door closed behind them. In that same moment, he heard loud voices arguing outside his door.

"You left the Queen's Sword alone to *wash up*? Are you insane, man?" Cyrus did not recognize the voice, but Berhnard certainly did. So did Seraphina, if the tension in her body was any indication.

"Sir, did you want him to suspect something was amiss? The Raj, he may accept, but the absence of the Chalice? Besides, it was diffi-cult to concentrate, what with that lowborn and wretched looking-urchin who has come today with her hand out. I had only thought to inform the queen that Her Majesty might prepare to greet him. She has already suffered so from their betrayal."

Betrayal? Cyrus stiffened but Seraphina kept her hand over his mouth and leaned into him, telling him without words to take care. To keep silent.

Was this what Berhnard had been led to believe? That Cyrus and Dare had betrayed Queen Idony? That it was the reason she seemed so changed?

"He is not here, lackwit. He could be, even now, on his way to make an attempt on your queen's life. I will ask her to dispose of you when this is done, Berhnard. You have been nothing but a thorn under my skin since this started. I would pluck you out."

Berhnard's voice was high and panicked. "I'll find him. I will have the Wode in the palace search every room. I will not let you down, sir."

Phina's gaze had narrowed to brilliant green slits as she listened to the men. She definitely recognized the other man's voice. He was amazed he could see the color of her eyes, even in the shadows of the armoire. She was so damn beautiful, whether she was covered in soot and grime or naked as sin on the Siren. He could hardly breathe from the need that hit him like a booted heel in his chest.

Her gaze focused on him and her lips parted. "Close quarters," she whispered in explanation. "You're more affected by my scent.

They are gone now. I just want to make sure they don't come back before we find another way out of here."

It wasn't Felidae pheromones. It was *her* pheromones. *Her* scent. Her eyes. She could have died. There could be no escape from this palace alive and all he could think about was being inside her again. Her breasts against his chest. Her hands on his skin.

"Seraphina."

Her arousal could not have come at a worse time. Her family was in jeopardy, as were Cyrus and the queen. She was here to save her sister from unthinkable abuse. That knowledge should cause her to hate every creature with a prick. She was trapped in a closet with a man who had every right to despise her. A man she still desired more than any other. More each day. Beyond reason.

And the one responsible for his mysterious disappearance from the Siren and subsequent hardship in the Avici was here, reprimanding a member of the palace staff. Muller was here.

It made no sense. He had money, yes, but all of it was ill gotten. His influence was over the criminal element, not the nobility, but even that influence was not impressive. He was a middleman. Petty. This could not be *his* plan. Someone else was winding his gears.

Her need was winding hers. Even as she thought to push away, she rubbed herself against Cyrus. The few uniforms that hung around them smelled of him. She was drowning in his scent. And it was getting stronger with his heat. His arousal.

She felt his tongue caress the palm she'd forgotten was covering his mouth. Her other hand slipped between their bodies to grip his hard cock.

He groaned and Phina smiled. "Shh, Sword. You do earn your name, don't you? I wish we had time for a demonstration."

There were Wode walking up and down the halls outside the

room, opening each door they came across. She could hear them. Damn it. Without the right equipment, Cyrus would never be able to leave the way she had come in. She wished she had told him to keep the rope.

They would have to wait for the guards to move to another wing. Wait with him this close. Touching her. Wanting her. "Maybe we do have time after all."

She lifted her hand and replaced it with her lips on his. Her body tingled at the contact. His taste. She'd been unsure if she would ever feel this again. After their encounter in the galley—as much a release for their anger as their passion—she had believed he was done with her.

When he became the aggressor, his kiss eating at her mouth, his own hands seeking beneath her loose clothing, she knew he wasn't done. He still wanted her.

She loosened her grip enough to unhook a few of his pants buttons. The fabric opened and she slid her hand inside, the heat and hardness branding the sensitive skin of her palms.

Phina recalled that first night on the Siren. How easily she'd submitted to him. How powerful his effect on her had been that she'd given him what she took from so many—she'd knelt at his feet and taken him deep into her mouth.

He had gripped her hair, not to force her, but to touch her, and she had given him everything. Wanted to please him. *His* pleasure, not hers. It was the kind of feeling she had been told signaled to female Felidae that they had found their heart's mate. It had terrified her then.

It still did.

Phina came back to the moment with a moan when he tore his mouth away from hers and covered the dark rose nipple he'd revealed by pushing up her overlarge shirt.

She bit her lips, knowing she had to stay silent. Had to not shout at the violent need that was clawing through her, burning her from the inside out as she stroked his thick shaft. She wanted him inside her. Needed him.

He slid his thick-fingered hand inside her pants, past the belt that held the *ton*, until they rested on the damp patch of fur between her thighs. He hummed at the softness of it, curling his fingers in it and tugging while his teeth tugged her hard nipple.

Ecstasy. Phina's eyes felt as though they'd rolled back into her head, her body arching, thrusting into his hand. Begging him for more.

Her heartbeat filled her ears, drowning out the world outside. All her attention was focused on his touch. His fingers slipped through her arousal, circling and teasing until she was sure she would scream loud enough that Queen's Hill would echo with her cries.

She squeezed him tighter. Warning. Begging. Cyrus growled and slid his fingers inside her. Not enough. It was not enough.

He lifted his head from her breast, taking her mouth to muffle her needy whimpers when he pumped two, then three fingers deep inside her sex. His rhythm mimicked her sliding grip on his erection and she keened softly against his lips, biting at them, letting his tongue distract her.

She sucked it deep and hard into her mouth, knowing he was remembering, too. Wanting her mouth on him. Wanting to feel her clinging to him as he took her without worry that anyone could hear.

His touch was as desperate as hers. No anger. No resentment. Just passion. Phina reveled in the change. She rocked her body against his, scraped her nipples across the rough fabric of his shirt and increased the speed of her strokes. Pleasuring him the only way she could in this confined space. Every way she could.

Yes. Moons, yes. She could feel it from the tips of her ears to the balls of her feet. Lava-like heat coiled in her belly and her tail quivered with excitement. Just from his touch. Just from—

"Cyrus." She muttered his name when she wanted to shriek. But she knew he felt her restrained passion. Felt her drench his hand, her muscles grip his fingers tight enough to bruise as his touch singed her. Sent her into the flames.

She was still quaking with it when she dropped to her knees in the wardrobe, dragging herself away from his fingers and mouth to wrap her lips around the head of his cock.

She craved him. Craved the taste of him in a way she could not explain. She wanted him to find his release this way, wanted to take his essence inside her.

"Phina. Damn, Phina—*love.*" His hands were in her hair again and his whisper was harsh with pleasure and surprise.

He was close. His scent was strong. Male and Wode and Cyrus. Hers. He smelled like hers. She could smell herself on the fingers he'd slid into her hair and it mingled with his taste.

She breathed out slowly and lowered her mouth, mindful of her sharp teeth, until her lips were nestled against the base of his shaft. Her tongue traced a veined line and his hips jerked in reaction.

Yes. Let me taste you. Please.

He answered her wordless request with a sharp breath of pleasured pain. His hips thrust helplessly against her mouth once. Twice.

There it was. His taste. She swallowed it greedily, her tongue desperate to capture every lingering drop as his big body shook against her.

Phina was still nuzzling the heated skin of his inner thigh when he lightly tugged her hair, reaching down to cup her chin and raise her gaze to his.

His expression was regretful, but his voice was urging. "Seraphina, we have to hurry. I cannot hear them. I think we have a chance now."

A chance for what? Her mind was clouded. His scent was fogging her thoughts.

He bent over and gripped her shoulders, hauling her into an upright position. "Phina, you have no idea how much I would love to continue this, but you have a sister to save. And I have a dagger to get for the queen. Also, an escape should follow. I need your help for all of it."

He needed her. They needed her. She looked at him and shook her head. She did not regret this. How strange. But he was correct, it was time to complete their task.

She opened the door of the wardrobe and looked back at him with a grin. "Button up, you delicious man. Time to go." She studied his cheeks and chin and chuckled softly. "Sword, did you know you have soot all over your face?"

She turned without waiting for his answer, but she had seen the sparkle start in his indigo eyes and knew he was as energized as she by their encounter.

Phina padded swiftly to the balcony and gripped his sword, spinning to hand it to him while she slid the one he'd borrowed from the captain out of his sheath and gave it to her.

There was no choice. He may not be able to scale the outer walls of the palace, but she could see how they might make it to the queen's balcony from his.

He frowned at her calculating expression as she studied the drop. "Tell me we are not jumping off anything again."

She nodded obediently. "We are not jumping off anything again."

"Please say you are not just humoring me."

She wrinkled her nose in consternation. "I am not just humoring you."

He sighed and turned her chin toward him with his fingers. "Seraphina Felidae, you are planning something. What is it?"

She pointed to the curved copper piping that ran from his balcony to the adjacent turret. "That rain catcher will not hold your weight—it will disconnect and fall. I'll attach the whip and, if you can control yourself, you can run the wall with it as it falls and get to that ledge there. Keep your grip until we get around that corner and we can make it to the queen's balcony." She glanced at him and smiled. "Simple."

"The rain catch—Phina, you want me to fall *sideways*? In the dark?" He lowered his voice, glancing back at the door to his room. "I believe I would have better luck with those Wode."

He might think so, but he had not a clue what he was up against. "They aren't your type of Wode. Cyrus. Don't you know rogues when you see them? They don't play by the rules. If Nephi has a chance, if you and I want to get out of here intact, this is our only way."

"Son of a lowborn wretch," he swore, pushing up his sleeves and eyeing the distance between his balcony and the ledge. "I suppose you'll just leap onto the roof and walk across? You can see perfectly, can't you?"

She loved his petulant tone. "You made it out of the tree alive, yes?" She patted his shoulder, stroking it one second longer than she should have. "Trust me. You can do this as well."

He was still muttering as he clambered up onto the balcony railing. She uncoiled her whip, sending it out with perfect aim so it coiled around the pipe, handing it to him. He gripped the leather handle and took the small leap toward the water-filled drain attached beneath the roof.

As she'd predicted, the end closest to him groaned and creaked under the pressure, breaking away from the wall and dousing him with water as he swung the length of the smooth copper wall. She saw the whip begin to loosen and slip, but by that time he was low enough to reach out and grab the turret ledge, hanging on as though his life depended on it. Smart man.

"Damn," he gasped through gritted teeth.

Two small leaps and Phina was on the roof, her tail out for balance as she walked the ledge and hopped on the turret's rounded dome. "Don't swear. They may hear you. I can see the balcony from here, Cyrus. Hurry. And don't drop that. I fancy it."

She was talking about the whip, of course.

Long, grunting moments later she watched him reach a ledge wide enough for him to stand on. It was but a step away from the queen's balcony. She dropped down to join him, her smile wide, hand held out for her long leather toy.

He was glaring as he handed it to her. "You enjoyed that."

She could not deny the truth, but she was smart enough to know when to keep her mouth shut. On occasion. Besides, he had enjoyed it as well. She could smell it.

They moved as one to leap over the balcony and through the open doors to the well-lit rooms of the queen. Who they saw first made Phina's jaw drop.

"Lucy Thrice?"

The young woman turned around, the side of her face not scarred with old burns smiling in surprised delight. "Lightfoot? By the two moons, my luck is still with me. If anyone can get what's mine it is Lightfoot, sure enough."

Cyrus, still dripping wet, had already drawn his sword, but Phina stepped ahead of him, looking around the room suspiciously. "What business could you have in the palace, Lucy? Someone purchasing poisons?"

Lucy Thrice cackled, making Phina smile. "They don't need little Lucy Thrice to poison each other. You know that. I did a job for a lord, is all. A job I lost two men and got a lot of grief for. I deserve payment."

Cyrus's tone was disbelieving. "What kind of job?"

She shrugged carelessly. "Basic baggin' job. Little half-breed Wode from the Hill here intent on runnin' away. I was told to make sure she got somewhere she could earn her keep. Somewhere she would stay alive, but be confined." She turned around and raised her voice as if hoping someone would hear her. "Not Lucy Thrice's fault she wasn't put on display. I did my job, and I should get what's mine."

Dare. Lucy was talking about Dare. She sent Cyrus a warning look. She knew Lucy Thrice. She could handle her. "I heard about that. Saw her myself. I can be your witness. The Siren's owner took a personal fancy to her and kept her behind the curtain, so to speak. Why are they refusing to pay?"

Lucy looked relieved at Phina's understanding. "That is it all over, Lightfoot. Why blame Thrice?"

But Phina thought she understood. They'd wanted her whored out. Wanted Dare, who had been sheltered and protected and isolated her entire life, to break. The line of men who would want a turn with a beautiful, helpless Wode half-breed would have certainly done the trick.

She could sense Cyrus's anger. Knew he understood as well. They had known Dare would leave the palace and taken steps to ensure she would be snatched.

Just as they had discovered Cyrus would be on the Siren, and paid Phina to sedate him. Not to steal *from* him, but to steal *him.*

How did their enemy know so much? Phina had believed only the Khepri had eyes everywhere. Now she wasn't so sure.

Lucy Thrice went still. "I have a bad feelin'."

"So do I," Phina agreed, catching a familiar scent in the air. A scent that was growing stronger. Where was she?

"You are a tenacious Arendal, aren't you, Cyrus? And Seraphina? Did you come with Lucy for your reward? You should get more, I think, since you did catch him for us twice."

"Muller. Queen Idony has certainly lowered her standards if you've been invited for tea." Phina gripped the hilt of the sword more firmly, ready for anything, and sneered. "I notice Lennis was not invited. But then, I killed him, so I imagine he would not make very good company."

Muller chuckled delightedly. "So that's what became of my not so silent partner. I had wondered. I owe you this time, Seraphina. You saved me the trouble of ending him myself."

She had the strongest urge to claw his eyes out, but Muller was not alone. What's more, her sister's fear was a scent growing stronger with every passing moment. Drawing her attention.

"Is this the man, Seraphina? The one you let in my room?" His tone was expressionless, but Phina felt a needle pierce her heart at his words. He would never forget that betrayal.

"Yes. I am sorry. Cyrus? *Nephi*. She is nearby."

"Go," he muttered. "I can take care of him. He'll tell me where the dagger is before he dies."

She had no desire to leave him. Muller was tricky. But she could not ignore her sister's silent cry for help. Ellsworth could have an army of Wode between them. Finally, an excuse to shed some blood.

Chapter Seven

"I am Cyrus Arendal, the Queen's Sword." He kept his gaze and sword pointed at the short gray-haired man near the doorway, but addressed Lucy Thrice. "If you leave now, Ms. Thrice, you may escape punishment for abducting the Queen's Chalice. I will not offer you this boon should I see you again."

"The Chalice?" Lucy sputtered. "They never said she was the Chalice. Yes, sir. Of course, sir. Lucy Thrice knows when she's not wanted. We'll just call it even."

She pushed the older man out of her way as she scurried out the door, in too much of a hurry to look back.

Muller smiled, but Cyrus could see the weakness in it. The telling tremor. "I am a guest of your queen, Arendal. Is it your habit to greet guests with your sword?"

Cyrus quirked his lips. "It is if the guest is the same man who stuffed me in a trunk and sent me to the desert to die. Toss your pistol on the floor."

Muller held up his hands, one slowly reaching into the holster inside his jacket and pulling out his weapon. Cyrus was alert, but Muller dropped it on the floor without a sign of resistance. Damn it.

He was hoping for an excuse to gut the villain. Was he such a coward that he would not even try for one clean shot?

Apparently he was. Muller kicked the pistol toward Cyrus, who knelt to grip it with his free hand.

"I followed orders," Muller offered. "I plucked your dagger and handed you over. What happened to you after is not my responsibility."

Cyrus laughed, but there was no humor inside him. Just the memories of the pain he'd suffered. The others who were forced to work alongside him. The beatings. "You sound like that woman Thrice. I believe you. The both of you. You are cowards. Not to blame for what happened after you sold us. After you took all those people from their homes and sent them to death or servitude. You are not to blame for my scars or the danger you have put all of Theorrey in by following orders and taking your cut. I absolve you. That does not mean you won't die."

He stepped closer. "Still, I might spare you if you told me where the dagger is. And where is the queen? I should rephrase that. Where is the true queen?"

A high-pitch voice drew Cyrus's attention. "The queen has been taken to a safe place, away from you and the Felidae. I was left behind to relay a message."

Berhnard had staggered in, the blood staining his stomach spreading across the bright fabric of his tunic. "She was disturbed at your arrival. Claims you were not supposed to come back, sir. Odds against your survival were apparently rather high. The lord did not take enough precautions to protect her, she said."

Cyrus swore. The man had fallen to his knees beside Muller, gripping his side as his life's blood drained from him. "Berhnard. Damn it, man, could you not see she is not Idony? What lord? Did she have the dagger with her?"

"Dagger?" He seemed pale, confused. "No, sir. Only Wode and a contingent of oddly dressed men with strange claw-like gloves. I *am* sorry, sir. I do not know what lord she was referring to. Only that she mentions him often of late. If I can do one last thing for you . . ." Berhnard used his remaining strength to stab Muller between the ribs. He must have been hiding a blade of his own.

Cyrus looked on in astonishment and helpless rage, taking a pointless step forward as the two men collapsed on the floor of the queen's sitting room. One dead, the other soon to follow.

What the hell was going on?

He heard the sounds of shouts in the distance. Seraphina. He should help her. He started for the door but before he reached it, something stood in his way.

Hovered in his way.

One of those scarab bugs of the Khepri's design? Its brass body glowed a bluish green, its wings a blur in the air as it stared at him. A mechanical bug was staring at him.

Cyrus let out a frustrated breath. "I don't suppose you know where the dagger is, do you, bug?"

The scarab flew over his shoulder into the room, leaving the sitting area and flying toward the queen's bedroom.

Cyrus followed, a strong wave of sadness crushing his heart as he looked around at his queen's room. The Theorrean globe that spun eternally on its own. The shelves of books and journals, and the familiar paintings on the wall. She had done them all herself. Over the years the queen had become all things. Scholar, artisan, scientist. She always pushed his compliments aside, saying that with enough lifetimes, anyone could be thought wise or mad. She strove for wise.

He studied the images in her paintings. She had created dragonflies hovering over white lotus blossoms, mermaids rising from the sea. All her stories come to life.

She had also painted Felidae. He moved closer to a painting he had always been drawn to. A female Felidae with flowers and feathers in her hair, her smile breathtaking—it reminded him of Seraphina's. The woman looked powerful, serene. The queen had drawn a city in the trees around her. A city filled with Felidae. Was this another fairy-tale scene? He'd always thought so. The Felidae on the island lived in staggered huts on the ground, and there were no trees inside the settlement on the edge of Centre City.

Cyrus swore when he saw the gem the queen had painted around the Felidae's neck. "Impossible."

He knew that unique jewel. Two ruby circles merged together, one on top of the other. But this was no ordinary ruby. This interesting jewel had a flame inside it. Orange and gold with a hint of blue.

He had seen it. Held it. And he knew that it did not merely appear to be flame. A trick of the light. It was a true flame. Moonfire.

It was the only one of its kind, and currently embedded in the queen's missing dagger.

The scarab's hum drew his attention to the small bureau beside the bed. Cyrus shook his head. It was clear this particular automaton had no idea what he was looking for. The false queen had no doubt taken the dagger with her. He could not imagine she would have left it in an unlocked drawer.

The bug was insistent, bumping its miniature metallic body into the wood. Cyrus opened the top drawer, feeling guilty as he rifled through Idony's private letters and keepsakes.

Nothing.

The scarab had landed on top of the bureau, buzzing its wings rhythmically. "Why do I feel you are leading me on a merry chase for nothing, Khepri? Or distracting me long enough for the enemy to attack?"

As if in answer, he watched it walk back and forth on its tiny brass legs, its wings buzzing every few heartbeats, seemingly impatient for him to make a discovery. Cyrus looked closer.

He saw a slender drawer beneath the one he'd just opened. He wrapped his fingers around the pearlescent lotus-shaped knob and tugged. The drawer was empty. He looked closer. More than empty. It looked . . . incorrectly made.

He reached inside, running his fingers along the back seam of the drawer's bottom, and felt a cold latch or key of some kind. He gripped it, pulling blindly, and heard something click into place, like the catch on a large door.

The entire bureau started to slide from its position against the wall and he stood up, stepping back in shock. How had he not known this was here?

It had moved across the floor to reveal what appeared to be a steel strongbox built into the wall. The mechanism on it was complex and unique, with brass wheels and strange symbols he did not recognize. Cyrus hadn't the first clue how to get it open. "Any insight into unwinding *this* riddle?"

He sighed heavily in the silence of the room. "I am conversing with a bug."

It must have heard him. The Khepri's fascinating scarab buzzed over his shoulder and attached itself to the top of highest brass wheel, spinning one after another into its proper place before his eyes.

"You have my thanks." Cyrus shook his head at the insanity of the situation, looking over his shoulder cautiously as the automaton continued to work. He walked out to the sitting room and tilted his head. He heard nothing. No one. But that would not last long. Surely the shield guards on the Hill had been alerted by now. And if they'd been informed that the Queen's Sword had gone rogue . . . it would not be an easy task to get Seraphina and escape.

Who was behind this? What member of the Theorrean Raj or noble had this much reach? Had sway over desert cults and common city criminals? Dare had told him another was involved. This noble Berhnard had mentioned? This lord?

He had an overpowering desire to cause someone pain. But who? It was difficult to focus his rage when he did not know where it belonged. And he needed to focus it, use it to find his queen instead of letting it control him.

Though he had to admit, he had a much stronger handle on it since Dare and the Deviant had first stumbled across his path.

Since Seraphina.

When had her betrayal stopped stinging so intensely? Why did he, despite all personal evidence to the contrary, trust her? Why did he already desire her again?

The sound of the seal on the heavy iron door unbolting lured Cyrus back into the queen's bedroom. "You did it. Now let's see what we have found."

Cyrus opened it farther, unsure of what he would discover. When his eyes focused on the object in the vault, he was at a loss. The dagger was here. Somehow the false queen and her accomplice must have found Queen Idony's hiding place and used it to their own end.

Who would be fool enough to leave this behind after going to so much trouble to take it? Unless he had been the only true target, and the dagger merely a trophy.

The scarab hummed as it flew lazily nearby, no doubt drunk with victory. The flapping wings, however, did not conceal the new noise coming from the shadows of the steel box. A clicking sound. Or the hissing of steam. Perhaps it was a timer. Cyrus bent closer, lowering himself to see the flame of the dagger so close to his hand. He reached for it before the door could close again, in case there was a timing device attached.

Two greenish-blue points of light appeared beside his hand an instant before he felt the bite. Sharp needles like fangs sunk into his skin.

He dropped his sword and grabbed the dagger with his other

hand, cradling the wounded hand to his chest. The pain was excruciating, and his only distraction was the revelation of a strange snake unlike any he had ever seen.

It was not living. An automaton like the scarab, but nowhere near as innocent in appearance. It slithered out of the box, its segments pushing it forward on the floor, giving it the appearance of gliding. Of grace. The top of its head flattened like a crown or hood, its glowing eyes and brass fangs were hypnotic. Staring at him.

The scarab dove at its head, and Cyrus was their stunned audience of one as they fought. The snake made a move to bite the large bug, to strike it with its tail, but the flying machine eluded the attacks.

Finally, in an apparent act of self-sacrifice, the scarab attached its legs to the snaked head and clamped on, its wings beating faster, causing a static charge to fill the air. The light around it grew, the mechanical hum growing louder until Cyrus rolled away from the struggling pair, covering his face with his arm as their theorrite power sources overloaded.

Not fools after all then. Cyrus was grateful to the Khepri's now lifeless helper lying on the floor beside the equally powerless snake and shook his head, trying to clear it. "I am sorry, little bug. I will tell them you died with honor. Which will be more than I can say for myself."

Black spots were swimming in his eyes. Seraphina. He got to his feet and took a few staggering steps before looking down at his hand. The pain was gone. It was numb. The skin around the wound was raised and the veins turning dark with sickness, but he could not feel a thing.

This was no way for a Wode to end. Killed by fake snakebite. A toy of destruction made by someone too cowardly to face him man to man.

Phina. He had to get Seraphina out of here and safely aboard the ship with her sister and Dare.

Cyrus tucked the dagger into his belt, left the pistol on the bed where he'd set it, and lifted his sword. He had to find her. He tripped around the bodies of Muller and Berhnard and into the hallway.

He could hear the clash of swords down the hall and headed in that direction. She might need him to save Nephi. Nephi, the queen's lady maid. She'd always covered herself from head to toe, keeping her face lowered when he came in the room. Did she look like Phina? Beautiful Seraphina.

A frightened male voice cried out, "You won't take her away from me, demon. She is mine."

The words helped him focus.

He arrived in a guest room full of rogue Wode. They were surrounding a bed, protecting the man he assumed was Raj Ellsworth and a terrified Nephi.

Seraphina was hacking through them like a bloodthirsty warrior. "Need any help?"

She huffed out a breath as she slashed the closest guard with a dagger. "What took you so long?"

The poison was spreading quickly through his system. He had to push past it, make sure she was safe. Not even she could handle all of these men alone.

He held his sword in the hand that he could still control, using the flat of it to fell the Wode coming up behind Seraphina.

"I finished my mission and grew impatient waiting on you," he huffed heavily. "Thought you could use a hand."

A hand. He laughed raggedly at his private joke, knowing he had a perfectly useless hand to spare. One that was blackening with venom even as he killed two more of his fellow Wode. It seemed he only needed one hand for this.

He could see the Raj growing paler with each guard that fell. "Ellsworth? The Queen's Sword charges you with crimes against

Theorrey. Unspeakable crimes that can only be paid for in blood. Unless you release the Felidae into my custody at once."

The rogue Wode paused at his words, as did Seraphina. Some remnant of their inheritance, their training must have recognized his authority. He focused on standing tall, unwilling to allow the men to see him weave. "I am the Arendal. I am taking this man into my custody."

One of the men shook his head slowly. "We no longer follow your command. *We* are the queen's protectors. Her Arendal and Senedal are dead. If not, they are traitors to the throne."

Cyrus swung his sword outward so they could see the design on its hilt. "And you believe the queen would allow this injustice to stand in her palace? You are a fool, and no one calls me a traitor."

They rushed him, their figures blurring before his eyes, but he could still see. Could still fight. The moves were instinctive. Years upon years of training until fighting was as natural as breathing, as necessary.

These men were already dead; they simply had yet to reach his blade.

When he finally heard the voice calling his name, he realized the floor was covered in bodies. Luckily, none of them were his own.

"Cyrus? Cyrus, you're hurt."

Was that Seraphina? He could not tell for the pounding in his ears. He looked up and shook his head. No, it couldn't be her. This woman had black streaks and blood covering her face. Blood on her clothes. Red blood everywhere to match her hair. Red hair. Green eyes.

He lifted his arm, wondering where his sword had gone. "Phina?"

"You killed them. Ellsworth tried to get away but with no one to protect him he was no match for me. He's dead, Cyrus. He is dead and we need to get out of here now before more Wode arrive."

The bloody Felidae was speaking. He heard her words but he was having a difficult time comprehending what they meant. Leave? Yes, they needed to leave.

"Damn it, you *are* hurt." She'd grabbed his hand, the one he couldn't feel. The dark lines of poison had traveled halfway up his arm.

"But you are safe. And Nephi. And I've been bit by a cursed windup toy," he muttered.

He felt her drag him back toward the queen's sitting room and heard the phrase, "Nephi, we're going to need rope." Then he watched as she lifted his palm, biting into his wound with her sharp teeth, making him shout at the pain. He finally felt it.

There was nothing after that but blessed darkness.

A few days' journey from the palace he watched the sunlight glisten off the pristinely white peaks of the mountains as they moved by him on the starboard side of the Deviant. They were following the Yazata Range north, letting Centre City fall away behind them. If he crossed the deck, he knew he would see the shimmering black sand of the Avici to the west. Not far enough away for his liking, but then, it never would be again.

The captain was flying hard to make up time. The engine pumped at full steam, and he could hear the Deviant's propellers chopping at the thin air. They were moving so swiftly, the wind was wrestling with what Dare had called an aether cocoon, causing it to ripple in reaction.

He could get used to this mode of travel.

"Someone is looking out for you, my brother. And I think she has a tail."

Cyrus looked away from the scenery at Dare's words and over his shoulder, catching only a glint of brilliant red hair and corset lacings before she disappeared below decks. Again.

She had been avoiding him since he woke up. Seraphina had saved him, the dagger *and* her brother and sister while he had been bitten by some inventor's idea of fun.

The mighty Queen's Sword had a penchant for getting poked with needles and falling like an ironwood in a storm of late. A weakness that was unacceptable to him. A weakness she could no doubt smell with her keen Felidae senses.

At least he'd managed to kill a few of those Wode.

Dare pinched his arm and he looked down at her in shock. "What did you do that for?"

She glared up at him defiantly. "I never realized how idiotic men could be. You, Wulfric, even Freeman. Idiots."

Cyrus grunted and looked out at the scenery once more. "I notice you conveniently left Bodhan's name off that illustrious list."

Her voice was smug. "I did. Bodhan knows how to treat a woman. He admires and respects them for their abilities, even thanks them for saving his life." She lowered her voice to ensure none of the passing crew would hear. "He *understands* that a woman with a difficult past may need a different kind of protection. Particularly when that past comes back to bite them, then leave again at the first port."

She was talking about yesterday. The captain had descended and Bodhan's cousin Hadi had gotten off, taking Nephi and Jobi with him as they headed for the mysterious Aaru. They had both been offered sanctuary. Safety. And they'd taken it.

To be honest, Cyrus was glad Phina's brother Jobi was gone. That was one mean Felidae. Angry at the world, and crueler to his youngest sister than he should have been allowed to be. If he hadn't been wounded, Cyrus and Freeman had an unspoken agreement that they would have politely taken turns beating him bloody.

Nephi had been as sweet as he remembered. As shy. She had also been badly beaten, he assumed by Raj Ellsworth. The *late* Raj Ellsworth, according to Seraphina.

A member of the Theorrean Raj was dead. Justifiably murdered by Seraphina herself. If Cyrus had not been struggling against the poison, he would have killed the bastard himself when he'd gotten through with the treasonous guards.

He could not recall a time in history when that had occurred. A Raj killed. They usually held their own lives too sacred to risk them in any fashion. Ellsworth's obsession with Nephi had obviously been stronger than his obsession with life. He'd made a deal with the wrong side, supported the false queen, just to satisfy his twisted need for the innocent Felidae. He'd paid with his life.

"I would thank Seraphina if she would let me." He gazed down at Dare, noticing a few strands of gold were appearing in her indigo curls. "Dare, what's happened?"

She touched her hair self-consciously. "You are changing the topic so we don't have to talk about you and Phina ignoring each other."

Cyrus shook his head. "You can berate me all you like, so long as you tell me if you are ill or not."

She bit her lip and studied him, her hand going up to touch a button near the neckline of the fitted jacket that had become her new uniform. "I told you before that I could feel the queen. That I saw her and felt she was in danger, but it was not immediate."

He remembered. "I have always been in awe of your ability. I had no idea until you told me that it extended beyond sensing the feelings of people who were in your close, physical proximity."

"It doesn't." She hesitated. "That is, it never had before I got what the Khepri sent me."

She pulled a chain from beneath her jacket to reveal a necklace with a small charm. A theorrite charm. "What's that inside it?"

Cyrus could see a miniscule mechanism working within the

charm, but saw no way it had been placed there. No opening. What exactly had the Khepri given Dare?

His question must have been strong enough for her to hear it, because Dare answered him. "I believe it is somehow connected to her. A piece of her. A piece of the Nymphaea Infinitum. The workings inside seem to be of the same metal. And when I hold it, and think about the queen . . ." She paused, closing her eyes. "I can feel her. See the things she sees."

Cyrus rubbed his face with his good hand, trying to hide his emotions from her. Disbelief was the strongest. Concern followed closely behind. He had seen many things of late. Automaton creatures battling as though sentient, theorrite engines, weapons that were so far beyond what the Wode knew of, what the shield guards could fight against . . . it was almost like magic.

Dare smiled sadly. "I can sense the rest of you more than ever before as well. Queen Idony has been alive for hundreds of years, Cyrus. Never aging. Ever young. Why is this so hard for you to believe?" She tucked the charm back inside her clothing, hidden from view. "I think she can feel me as well. And she knows we are on our way to Tower Orr, still trying to find her. It has given her comfort."

"I am glad of that, at least. Though I will be keeping a closer eye on you now. I refuse to believe she would want you to wear it if it has adverse effects." He looked down at his bandaged hand.

He was training rigorously every day, with the help of James Stacy and, interestingly enough, Wulf. With no one to play his game, Wulf was a skilled sparring partner. The two men had very different styles of fighting, but the same amount of zeal.

He was not ready to take on Freeman yet. Not as ready to protect the women he cared about, this crew, as he wanted to be. He felt a vein at his temple throb. "I regret I have not been more help on this mission. I seem to be the weak link of the chain more often than not. I fear I am setting a low bar for the next Arendal Sword."

Dare touched his arm. "Even poisoned with something that would have killed a normal man in an instant, you still protected Nephi and Phina. You still retrieved the dagger. Phina knows how strong you are. How courageous. She told me how you survived the desert. How you escaped your fate all on your own. I, as usual, had help."

Cyrus glanced back toward the door that led to the cabins. He wanted to see Phina, talk to her about what they'd been through, what they had done in the wardrobe. But now was not the time.

He lowered his lids in thought. "Does the queen know who this is? What kind of mind planned abductions for us both that were designed not to kill us quickly, but to break us?"

"She knows. But she is not telling me. I haven't learned to control it yet, this new ability. But it comforts me, at least, knowing she is alive. Knowing she still has time." Dare stepped away from the railing. "What doesn't comfort me is the knowledge that while I have told you all of my secrets, you have shared none of yours. The dagger you nearly died to obtain, for instance. May I see it?"

He pulled it out of his belt. He had refused to let it out of his grasp, even when he was recovering from the mechanical serpent's venom. He handed it to Dare. "I would do more than have you see it. I want you to hold on to it. Keep it safely in your care until I am back to full capacity. The Khepri said it was important to restoring the queen to power." He tried to smile, knowing she could still feel his shame at his weakness. "I have seen you training with Seraphina. Between you, the captain, and our Felidae . . . I believe the men here feel there is no use for us."

Dare's grin was more knowing than he wanted to notice. "I am certain she could find a use for you. Were you brave enough Wode to tempt Seraphina Felidae."

Cyrus's blood heated in his veins at the thought. "Is that a dare, Chalice?"

She laughed. "Is that an acceptance of my challenge, Sword?"

He turned and strode across the wide expanse of deck, knowing the men were watching him from the corners of their eyes. Wulf was on the steps that led to the helm's deck, his shaded spectacles shielding his expression.

Perhaps it was time. He needed to tell her, show her what he wanted. He knew he was man enough to hold on to her. That he wanted her. He had to make sure she did as well.

"There it is! I see it. We're here, Freeman. By the two moons, it is just as Captain Amaranthe said it would be. The lake is lit up like a sky full of stars." James Stacy's voice came down from his watch in the lookout just below the bow of the aether cocoon. He had a monocular trained on the port side of the ship.

Cyrus moved with the others to the port side, and was staggered by its beauty. The lake was a massive bowl cradled in the mountain's grasp. Two ranges met here, and their inspiring sight alone would have been enough. But the water was full of clusters of violet and silver light so brilliant the overcast day could not disguise it.

"She was worth the getting here. Now we just have to find that tower," James crowed, and Cyrus winced at his words. He could not decide if he wanted to kill the man for poor timing or thank him for the salvation of a new mission. A new chance for him to make a contribution.

He knew the Felidae women from Faro Outpost demanded their suitors perform feats of bravery before they accepted them. Perhaps if he found the tower, found the answers to the queen's whereabouts, Seraphina would see him as a worthy mate.

He would not allow it to be any other way.

Chapter Eight

"I do believe Freeman is unhappy with you, my friend."

Phina's ear twitched in amusement as she listened to Wulf and Bodhan's hushed conversation behind her. They were scouting the area around the lake—Bodhan and Dare, Wulf, the captain and Freeman . . . Cyrus. The rest of the men had the good fortune to deploy the landing dodge and either stay inside or guard the perimeter.

Wulf had a smile in his lilting voice. "The burn of the sun is worth it, for that reason alone. Besides, you know me, Bodhan. I am an adventurer."

Bodhan covered his laugh with a cough. "You are a great inventor, Wulfric, son of Wulfric the Great. You are a humorous companion as well. But you cannot call yourself an adventurer when this is the first time you have left Aaru."

"If something is worth doing, it is worth pretending expertise in until you are as perfect as you appear to be." Wulf made a tsking sound. "The irresistible Captain Amaranthe's first mate has the opposite problem. He is *too* good at his jobs. All of them. So perfect, the appropriate people are not impressed by his prowess. A clock that needs no winding is never cleaned. His loss could be my gain."

She raised her eyebrows at that. She had seen the dance the captain and their latest passenger were doing. She knew the fearless Nerida Amaranthe had been impressed with Wulf's . . . *appreciation* for her type of foreplay.

But they did not smell right together. Wulf was correct, in his way. Freeman needed to stop being perfect at everything. To stop being everything the captain needed before she knew she needed it. It might be the only way to change the state of things.

As they wandered around the clearing near the lake, she noticed suddenly that her skin felt odd. Unusual. Something was here, just out of reach, but she could neither see it nor quite smell it. It was simply off.

She wanted to blame Cyrus. But then, she could not seem to blame him for anything these days. He had helped her to save her sister, though he'd nearly paid a fatal price for his actions. She'd sucked the poison out of his skin and strapped his unconscious form between herself and Nephi so they could cross the steep drop between the Palace and the tunnel's opening. She'd listened to her brother's endless stream of complaints and insults while she tried to assure Nephi that her demon was truly gone as they waited for the Deviant. But her thoughts had been with him. Cyrus. She'd prayed for the captain to hurry. For Freeman to know what to do to make him better. She could not lose him now.

Ellsworth was dead by her hand. She had reveled in his blood, and reveled in watching Cyrus end the lives of those who'd guarded him. It had been a primal need to protect her own. She had seen the insane light in Ellsworth's eyes as the Raj member had stroked Nephi, begging for her love even as he touched the bruises he had caused. Phina had lost control.

Killing a Raj was the highest offense in Theorrey. Despite his aid in the rescue, was that the reason Cyrus was not throwing her over his shoulder and holding her prisoner in his bedroom until neither of them could walk?

No. She knew it wasn't true. He no longer hated her. The way he looked at her now scared her more than his rage ever had. It made her crave things she wasn't sure she deserved.

After what happened in the palace, that the stalemate between them had changed. He was no longer angry. And she? She was no longer the same. She wanted something she'd never dared imagine before. Something she had scorned but secretly desired her whole life.

And she wanted it with him. She just needed to find the courage to tell him.

"Phina?" She turned to see Dare staring innocently in her direction. She was standing close the captain, and both the women watched her with knowing smiles.

She lifted her chin. "Yes, fair Dare?"

"Cyrus went to check the tree line at the forest's edge. Could you please find him and tell him it would be nice if he remained in view?" Even from this distance, Phina could easily see the mischievous sparkle in her eyes. "I am sure he would be grateful for the help."

Humans had no true subtlety. But then, Phina hated subtlety. She also hated the surge of excitement that heated her blood at the thought of speaking to him alone, knowing Dare could feel it. "I am always eager to serve. You know that. In some towns I am famous for it."

She winked her thanks with the pretense of playful ease and headed off in the direction of Cyrus's scent. She was, she had to admit, rather hopeless when it came to the Queen's Sword. She wanted to scratch and bite him, fight him almost as desperately as she wanted him to force her to stop. She wanted him to make her submit. To love her.

Phina would never admit that to the captain. To Captain Amaranthe, submission, sensual or otherwise, was a sign of absolute, unforgiveable weakness. It was a belief that they had always shared. Men were tools never to be trusted, and to be discarded when their usefulness was at an end.

What did you do when you felt you needed a particular man in order to breathe each day? To smile? To keep your heart from breaking?

Jobi had sensed her new weakness before he was taken off the ship and reveled in it. "I always thought you were cracked, believing you could live amongst humans and be treated as an equal. More than that—be treated better than an equal." He'd sneered, glancing at the battered Nephi. "We are lower than pets to them. Less important than the threehorn they feed and raise and keep confined until it's old enough for slaughter. At least they need it to survive. And you believe, what? That a Wode, the Queen's Sword himself, would want to claim you?"

Now she caught Cyrus's scent easily when she stepped into the wooded area at the edge of the lake, but she allowed him to think he retained the advantage. He was still, his heart racing. He knew she was coming.

Phina's tail seemed to have a mind of its own, lifting and swaying provocatively as she strode past the tree he skulked behind.

Letting him grab her around the waist and spin her until her back was against the tree was exhilarating. The hardness of his lower body pressing against hers was arousing her beyond thought.

A sound of pleasure escaped her throat and she rubbed herself against him. "We are supposed to be looking for the tower."

His jaw was clenched, the indigo of his eyes nearly black. "I heard you coming. Phina, we need to talk. I have something I want to tell you. Need to tell you."

The strange sensations along her spine had only increased with her elevated adrenaline. This place felt wild. Free. No factory stench, no aroma of civilization.

Cyrus. And something else. Both scents made her unable to crave anything but release. "The Sword wants to talk? What a shame." She leaned forward and licked his neck. His taste was more addictive than any drink, any herbal concoction. "I would rather play."

His grip on her tightened and he swore, lowering his forehead to hers. "This is not play for me, Seraphina."

No, it was not play for her, either. She reached for his wrist and lifted it up so she could see. It was still bandaged, but she could sense it was healing swiftly. It would hurt him for a while to come, but he could use it. She had never seen such a destructive, fast-acting poison. And she knew her poisons.

Her lips opened over the tips of his fingers. "A bit of play would be good for you, Sword. You are far too serious."

She lifted one of her legs up his thigh, using her strength to pull him closer, harder, against her. Cyrus huffed out a helpless breath. "*You* are far too dangerous for my peace of mind. Too—"

She slid her free hand through his hair and tugged him down for a kiss. She did not want to hear that he thought she was too dangerous, too anything for him. Did not want to hear the rejection his mind may tell him to give her, though his body was saying something else entirely.

She moved his bandaged hand to her breasts. He loved them, she knew. Loved touching them. Kissing them. Watching them bounce when she walked by, believing she did not know he was looking.

His fingers scraped the cream-like mounds that pushed up over her corset and curled instinctively into her skin. *Yes.* She knew him. Knew what he desired. What he loved.

He could take her here, in the wild, and forget what she had done. Forgive her again. The thought made part of her mind cringe, but she wanted him too much to care. Loved him.

"You will step away from her now. Should you call out to the others you will die."

The strange male voice interrupted her internal struggle, her rising passion.

Felidae.

Phina's reaction was instantaneous. She slid out of his embrace, under his arms, until she had her back to him, facing the newcomer with a glinting grin and extended claws. The meaning was clear. Cyrus belonged to her and no one was to hurt him.

There were eight Felidae males, all barely dressed. All carrying weapons equipped with long, deadly-looking darts. The men themselves were strong and lean, with interesting markings and varying shades of colorful hair, each more wild and tangled than the next, as though their locks had been combed by the wind. And they were laughing. Not at her.

At Cyrus.

He had turned to face them, his readiness to protect her, to fight them, crashing in waves against her back.

The leader stepped forward and mocked him over her shoulder. "You are tall for a newborn infant. Only the youngest cubs must be protected by the weaker sex."

Cyrus tried to move her out of the way but she resisted. She reached for the whip at her waist, and lashed out with skill, the braided leather deftly coiling around the nearest Felidae's weapon and wrenching it from his hands.

She smiled at their leader. "And you are foolish. Only a man who wishes to die would refer to a Felidae female as the weaker sex."

His burgundy eyes lit with respect as they studied her figure. Her fighting stance. He inhaled and his pupils dilated.

He lifted his hand to stop the angry man beside him from picking up his gun. "I caught your scent as soon as you landed, little warrior. I am Stet. Guardian and glider." He gestured toward Cyrus with a grimace. "You are too proud and beautiful to be wasted on this wounded human. To dwell amongst those wandering like lost, ignorant children at the Lake of Light. I will claim you and let you fly."

Phina saw the other men looking at her with newfound deference, as if she should be flattered this oddly speaking stranger wanted to drag her off to mate. She opened her mouth to speak, but Cyrus beat her to it.

He had also drawn his sword. "I am the Queen's Sword. And you will claim her over my rotting, human corpse. She is mine."

Mine. How she reveled in his words, despite the situation, which was ludicrous and dreamlike. She could hear the captain and the others. Surely they would glance toward the trees and see the men surrounding them. Felidae surrounding them. What were these Felidae doing this far north? Where were they from? They smelled different. Unique.

Stet smiled, noticing the deep breath she'd taken. "She is already mine, Queen's Sword. I am Felidae. I know your title, know you serve the false one, but it does not sway me. I accept your challenge."

Phina did *not* like the sound of that—the claiming or his insult to Queen Idony—but she rewound her whip, caressing it as she attempted her best expression of seduction on Stet. "I do love a good fight. Particularly when it is over the right to pleasure me. Would you mind if I waved my friends over so they could watch you in action?"

The other Felidae chuckled and Stet shook his head, his expression unconcerned. "You can wave if you like, they will not see you. We closed the spirit veil. I will kill the Queen's Sword, the treasonous Arendal. With his death and my vow to serve the true lord, I will become the leader of my people and mate with you before they notice you are gone. Humans are many things. Perceptive is not one of them."

For disliking humans so much, he certainly spoke like her least favorite among them. A vain, superior brute. It should not surprise her that other Felidae men were like her brothers. Condescending to women. Domineering.

Frankly, she wanted to snatch Stet the Guardian's eyes out of his head and chew on them for sport. "*I* choose who I mate with. Usually I am extremely open-minded about it. I do love a good fuck. However, I'd kill the man who'd try and force me."

Stet appeared insulted at the idea. "You would never be forced. And our females are respected and hold the highest positions of authority in all things. In this, however, instinct abides. I will explain and introduce you to our Peacemaker, if you give my men your sword . . . and that interesting jewelry on your wrist. It has a dangerous aroma."

Peacemaker? Could the woman on the carving in the mines still be alive? Phina could not deny her curiosity. She loosened her bracelet and glanced over her shoulder at the stewing Cyrus. He was itching for a fight, but she knew he had recognized the title Stet had used as well.

He snared her gaze, his expression alert, but thoughtful. "Give them your sword, Seraphina. I think we should go with them. Just remember what we are looking for."

The tower? Did he think these men might lead them to Tower Orr?

"Seraphina?" Stet sighed lustily. "What an unusual name for a Felidae. My future mate is unique in all ways. Worthy of me. Surely sent to me as a gift for my loyalty."

She noticed Cyrus's eye twitch with animosity and she nearly laughed out loud in delight. There was no denying she was enjoying his discomfort, his possessiveness. She was wicked, but it made her feel special. Made her feel as if she were truly his, as she wanted to be. She could have told him there was no danger of her falling for Stet's insulting arrogance. That he was a child compared to Cyrus.

"Perhaps I am a gift too good for you. Let your Peacemaker decide."

The men surrounded them and Phina could not resist looking back at the captain and the others. Freeman appeared to be looking in their direction, scanning the area as though he could not see them. He also, she noticed, appeared fuzzy. Blurred. She studied the trees, searching for the source before turning in curiosity to a Felidae walking beside her. "You use the dodge?"

Phina was taught that the Felidae respected the great, illusive monster of the deep. Honored it. When she'd first realized what was hiding the Deviant, she'd had difficulty coming to terms with that—because of the elders' stories.

The man wrinkled his nose. "Dodge?"

"Your *veil* that no one can see through? I thought the Felidae held the beast sacred. And how do you charge it?"

Understanding lit his gaze. "We do. It creates our spirit veil. It has been in place for longer than any can remember. Each generation of silent warriors are sent to the coast on the west to battle. They always return with more of the veil. We celebrate its spirit with ritual and honor, giving it new life with our people in gratitude for its protection."

Phina's tail reached back to brush against Cyrus's leg, reassuring her that he was still there. She needed reassurance now, because she was at a loss to explain what she saw when she glanced up to ask the man another question.

Gliders. Trader's stalls had reproductions of the transport. The mechanics of those facsimiles rarely worked in practice. She had never seen Felidae equipped with wings, soaring over the treetops, until now.

Stet must have noticed her bemusement. "The others are curious. They will lift the inner veil so we may pass."

Cyrus looked up as well. "I'll be damned. I wish we'd had a pair
of those in that ironwood tree."

Phina noticed Stet's tail stiffen at the words. Interesting. "The
rope worked well enough for us, my Sword. After I made certain the
knots were . . . tight enough."

In her experience, it was the way in which a thing was said more
than the actual words themselves that mattered to a male. Said in a
particular tone, and everything could be considered intimate. Scandalous.

Stet hissed but refused to look back. He deserved it, the oafish
forest dweller. She studied the landscape and saw no tower. But she
was curious. She knew of only three types of Felidae. The ones who
lived in one of the two settlements in Theorrey, the servants or sexual slaves whose tails were bobbed and claws removed at the root,
and now, the ones whom Nephi and Jobi were soon to join in Bodhan's mythical Aaru. She could only hope it was as free and inclusive
a society as he'd claimed.

Four. The number echoed through her head as the scenery
changed. The endless forest became a colorful, busy place full of
male and female Felidae of all ages and markings.

No earthen mounds dotted the landscape as they passed through
the second layer of dodge. She saw brightly painted houses like birds'
nests circling the trees above. The trees themselves were as thick as
rail cars—not ironwood. It was a hardy, rough tree that must be na-
tive to this area. Wooden steps and lifts of rope and beam took Felidae to the different levels with weights and winches. She could even
see Felidae children peering between the railings high above while
adults gathered on the ground, talking and trading.

All stopped to stare openly at the newcomers.

Stet raised his voice. "Summon our Peacemaker. I have accepted a mate challenge for the vibrant warrior Seraphina. I ask for all to witness my claim."

"When can I kill him?" Cyrus spoke softly in Phina's ear, but it was Stet who answered.

"You can attempt to kill me shortly, Queen's Sword. Seraphina will soon see who she must choose."

An older man's voice cut through the excited chatter of the crowd of Felidae females closing in around Phina. They were making her nervous, touching the buckles on her corset and murmuring to themselves. She sent them a wink and they all started giggling.

"Cyrus? I had to see for myself when I heard they were bringing you in. How did you know where to find me?"

Phina saw the man leaning heavily on several Felidae females, his right shoulder and chest bandaged. The smell of death and decay hovered over him like a shroud.

His hair was a faded shade of indigo.

"Commander Iacchus?" Cyrus pushed past his guard who, with a nod from Stet, let him pass. "What happened, sir? Did *they* do this to you?"

Phina nodded politely to the women but broke their grip, following Cyrus to the older man's side. He seemed familiar, but Phina wasn't sure why.

He laughed. "No, Cyrus, no. They had no part in this. Though some of them, I admit, would rather I pass more quickly." He noticed Phina standing there and tried to stand up taller. "Seraphina Felidae, I presume." He lifted his arm to salute and flinched. "I am, as you are, the queen's loyal servant. Though that, too, may not last much longer."

"You know her?" Cyrus sounded surprised. "Sir, I must tell you, I missed our rendezvous because I was—"

The old man coughed. "Snatched? Yes, I know. Had my own run-in before I could get to the Siren. Still recovering to be honest."

He wasn't being honest, Phina knew. He was dying. Slowly, and for a while. But from the scent of his injuries, it wouldn't be long before his suffering was at an end. He and Cyrus had planned a meeting on the Siren? Was that how this man knew her? Somehow she didn't think so.

"It wasn't your fault, Arendal. He was one step ahead of us. Maybe two. But you got away unharmed, yes? That is what matters to the queen. We will get the dagger back soon enough." She and Cyrus followed as the women supporting Iacchus led him carefully to a burnt orange hammock that would give him a view of Felidae life as he rested. He sat down heavily and took a few deep breaths from the exertion.

Cyrus knelt respectfully at the older man's feet and bowed his head in regret. "Commander, we have the dagger. We do not have Queen Idony. She was taken after *my* abduction."

The older man nodded, his expression one of sorrow. "They thought that might happen from the start." At Phina's look of confusion he clarified. "Queen Idony and the Khepri. They saw it on the wind, as they say around here. They prepared. I have been ready for it most of my life, but now that it has happened, I am no longer the Wode I was. No longer ready."

He laid his hand on Cyrus's shoulder and squeezed. "Perhaps that is best. I have lived too long with my secrets. I was told once that long life is a curse. If you live long enough to see your friends become your enemies, and the people you love disappear, you will lose your heart. And what is life without that?" He took another labored breath. "You brought the dagger?"

Cyrus nodded. "It's with the Chalice, at the lake beyond their veil. Commander, you mentioned someone? A 'he'?"

Phina inhaled sharply at the hopeful expression that transformed the Wode's pain-lined face. "She's here? Demeter is here? She still lives?"

Phina came closer, drawn to him, to ease his mind. "Dare lives. She is under the protection of Captain Amaranthe of the Deviant and Bodhan of the Siren. Though she handles herself well enough on her own."

His eyebrows disappeared into his hairline. "Astonishing. She does bring out a man's protective side, it's true. Always such a gentle little thing. Too gentle for our times."

Something in his tone sounded possessive. Familiar. She cocked her head in surprise. "You are her father."

Commander Iacchus nodded. "I helped bring her into this world."

She moved closer, her gaze narrowing. It was an interesting choice of words considering what she had seen when they'd first taken Dare off the Siren. "You helped? Then you must know why she has a birthmark shaped in the image of the Khepri's scarab symbol?"

The man's pleasant features hardened. "What I know I'll tell *her*, as soon as the Arendal Sword defends your honor and saves you from Stet so we can get that dagger." He gestured behind her with his chin. "Unless you would *like* to belong to him. To be honest, I always thought he was a bit of an arrogant pissbucket myself. Easy pickings for the queen's enemies."

"Defends my—" Phina whirled around and noticed Stet, his wild mane of reddish-blond hair flying as he gestured to the crowd. He pointed at her breasts and showed off her bracelet as though it were a trophy he had already won. And he slandered her queen as well. "He *is* a pissbucket. Can I accept his challenge instead? I think I could take him on."

The commander chortled. "You think you can, but he is stronger than he looks. Damn fast, as well. I have seen that boy run straight up a tree; he nearly reached the top before he turned and glided down like a feather on the breeze." He studied Cyrus. "You have our training, but that won't help much here. You've learned how to fight dirty over the years? I suggest you use that."

Phina's stomach knotted. "He does *not* have to fight for me. *No one* is going to fight over me."

Cyrus stood up and took her hand in his, squeezing until she looked in his direction. His gaze was almost tender. And utterly determined. "Yes, Seraphina. I am."

Cyrus felt like he'd walked into the queen's painting of the Peacemaker. That was what she'd called it. When he heard Stet mention that moniker, he'd known. Somehow this place was connected with the dagger. Connected with his mission, the commander . . . and now Phina as well.

He felt his muscles ripple, already eager to pummel Stet into the rich soil beneath his boots. He had been drugged, chained, beaten, and poisoned. He had watched his lover slay enemies he should have protected her from, and his companion guard who he'd been bound to protect shield him instead. He had wanted to tell Seraphina how he felt, but this was better.

He needed this. Needed to fight to find his strength again, to prove to by his actions Phina how completely he could protect and defend her. Could satisfy all her needs and desires. Be her mate. Her match. Whether she wanted him to or not.

He was Wode. He was the Sword. The preening male Felidae would know to whom Seraphina belonged before the day was done.

"Stet," he called out before Seraphina could stay him. "When you are done claiming victory before the battle has begun, I am here."

An older woman's gentle voice parted and silenced the crowd with surprising ease. "Wode are ever eager to fight, regardless of the reason. It is how they are made, I understand. Put into their inheritance long ago. The Felidae inheritance is one of peace. Only when one is compelled enough, by belief or emotion, is action taken. Stet, what compels you to accept this challenge?"

Stet bowed his head respectfully. "I am a Guardian. One of the best Gliders of the Felidae, sought after for my distinctive coloring and prowess by every female still unclaimed. Seraphina is not from our people, but she is *of* our people. Her scent compels me. Her strength compels me. She is worthy of me and I am compelled to claim her."

The old woman came closer and Cyrus noticed the flowers woven through hair of red streaked with silver. Her robe was closed, covering her markings, but she was still a stunning presence.

She was also not the same Felidae Queen Idony had painted. This was a different Peacemaker. He glanced down at her robe's neckline. She wore a similarly designed stone around her neck, but it wasn't moonfire. That stone was inside the dagger.

She looked up at him and raised her eyebrows in silence. Cyrus glanced over his shoulder at Commander Iacchus, who smiled supportively and gestured for him to speak. He assumed he was to say what had compelled him.

He shifted, wishing to fight. To show them how he felt with his fists, not his words. He was not good with words. He met the woman's gray-green eyes, their exotic tilt no distraction from their kindness.

"I am compelled," he started loudly, stopping to lower his voice when he noticed the old woman's ears twitch. "I am Cyrus Arendal, the Queen's Sword. I am not Felidae, I am Wode. Born in the Faro Outpost." He heard the murmurings that let him know they knew that name. Knew that it was the outpost that guarded the island settlement of Felidae.

He shifted so he could speak to the elder while catching Phina's gaze as well. "Since being in Seraphina's company I have been in danger more often than not. I have leapt from ships and dangled from trees. I have been accosted and aided by automatons and injured more than I have been since I first started training to be Wode."

Her tail was swishing back and forth and her arms were crossed. He would think her angry but for the vulnerability, the hurt in her emerald eyes.

His lips lifted helplessly. "I am compelled because I have never been more alive than when I am with her. Never been able to be more myself. The man behind my duty and title. Never worked harder to be better than my inheritance. To earn her loyalty. Because I have seen that when Seraphina gives you her loyalty, her trust, you never need doubt it. I am compelled to be worthy of *her.*"

As he spoke he realized it was all true. Every word. He saw the stunned expressions around him and his smile grew. Old gray-green eyes that were decidedly moist caught his and he shrugged. "Now we fight?"

The old woman laughed, surprising herself before catching Commander Iacchus's eye. "Yes. Now you fight." She lifted her voice and to Cyrus it was like music rustling the leaves. "No claws and no sword, but whatever else nature provides are yours to fight with. Until you cry halt or one of you stands alone. Wode?" She studied him closely. "Should you win, you must claim her immediately, or face another challenger. She will need you. It is our way. Do you understand?"

Cyrus wasn't sure he did, but he nodded. Whatever was needed to ensure this libidinous Felidae did not get a chance to touch his woman, he would do. *His woman.* Why did those words bring him ease?

The small community of Felidae backed away, gathering baskets of food and woven blankets, creating an impromptu arena.

Cyrus watched Stet's friends pound his back for luck, to energize him and prepare him for what was to come. He nodded, smiling and strutting.

Cyrus did not need reinforcements. He had his memories. At last he had a focus. The shot of excitement and adrenaline his Wode inheritance had given him when he killed his guard in the desert, the one who had beaten him one too many times, was nothing compared to this. Then he was fighting for survival. Weakened by the vayun.

He was no longer weak.

He watched Stet walk a wide, wary circle as he unwrapped his bandaged hand. He flexed his fingers and reached for his sword belt, unbuckling it and letting it drop where he stood.

Cyrus stepped into the circle of soil beneath the canopy of trees, shafts of sunlight breaking through the foliage, lighting his way. He knew they were all watching him. She was watching him.

He was watching Stet, his rage giving him focus. The gift of the Wode.

Stet showed his claws before retracting them, playing for the crowd as they cheered him. He was lean and young and Felidae. The commander was right; he would be fast. And Cyrus would have to bide his time. To wait for the weakness he knew Felidae were prone to possess: impatience.

Stet was keeping his distance, and Cyrus sighed loudly. "Whatever nature provides, she said. Is this your nature, Stet the Glider? Without wings do you merely lurk and wait for your prey to tire and fall asleep?"

Stet's skin flushed as soft laughter lingered on the breeze but he merely sneered, unwilling to take the bait. "You have an odor, Queen's Sword. Did Seraphina never tell you? It is foul and filthy and human. I prefer to keep my distance."

Cyrus just nodded mockingly, as if in understanding. "I see. You disapprove of my scent. You should just call this off then. Cry halt. Or better yet, come closer and I will fix it so you never smell anything the same again."

As they moved, Cyrus kept his back to the circle of trees and Felidae that framed them. He saw Phina kneeling near Commander

Iacchus, his mentor's hand on her shoulder as he spoke words of comfort. Was she shaking? Did she doubt his abilities?

"Do not look at her!" Stet growled. Good. He would attack soon.

He said the words that would guarantee it. "Why shouldn't I? She is already mine. You say you smell me. Can you not smell her on me?"

He saw the telltale bunching of Stet's powerful Felidae leg muscles before he launched himself across the small space, arms outstretched, toward Cyrus.

A twist of his body away from the move made it a glancing blow, but a strong one. Still, Stet was close now. Cyrus grabbed his shoulders as his feet touched the ground and turned, ramming his knee into Stet's stomach.

As the Felidae doubled over and rolled away, his strong, dexterous tail wrapped around Cyrus's ankle and tugged him off his feet and into the dirt.

Stet let out a shout of triumph and dived for his prone body, but Cyrus rolled away, leaving Stet with a face full of dirt.

The look in his nearly red eyes when he lifted his head was one Cyrus recognized. Stet had forgotten the reason for the fight. He only knew he wanted to cause pain. To kill.

Cyrus got to his feet in time to meet his attacker. Stet was keeping his claws retracted but his fists were powerful enough. He felt the blows to his jaw, his ribs, the center of his chest knocking the wind out of him before he could lift his arms.

Cyrus gripped Stet around his middle, squeezing until Stet yowled as he lifted the Felidae high in the air and tossed him against the rough bark of the nearest tree.

He brought a hand up to wipe the blood off his mouth as Stet got to his feet, shaking his head, momentarily stunned. Or so he wanted Cyrus to believe.

The Felidae's tail whipped up and he kicked out high behind him, catching Cyrus in the throat with his foot. For a moment, it was impossible to breathe, and he instinctively reached for his throat as he fell to his knees.

Stet pounced on him, gripping his hair and bringing his knee up into Cyrus's face, breaking and bloodying his nose. He raised his arms and a small group of his friends cheered Stet on, praising him.

There it was. Impatience. Bastard believed he'd already won.

Cyrus grabbed for one of Stet's upraised arms and his tail and pressed him down onto the ground. The arm he twisted down and behind Stet's back until Cyrus heard the crack of bone. "This is what we do to people who try to take what doesn't belong to them." The tail he yanked hard in a bruising grip, knowing it was more humiliating than painful. "This is what *I* do to Felidae who cheat with their extra appendage."

Stet shouted in pain and surprise. "Halt! Halt!"

A gasp of surprise washed over the gathered Felidae. Cyrus, too, had not thought he would capitulate so easily. A broken arm was a child's injury, and easily mended. As was his pride, since he had gotten his own decent jabs in during the short fight.

He got up, stepping away from Stet, indicating the Felidae was free to go. He put a hand to his nose and took a few steps forward. "I assume this means I have claim?"

He heard a hiss and turned back in time to see Stet leap from his previously prone position into the air, his feet aiming for Cyrus's collarbone. He could not have moved fast enough; he knew that before the foot made contact. The force threw him backward into a nearby uninhabited tree. The power of it stunned him for a moment, the pain making him look down.

He was held less than an inch off the ground by a low, thick branch. It had pushed through his flesh from back to front, growing out of his shoulder like an extra arm, and coated in his blood.

No one made a sound or moved as Stet stalked closer. "The Queen's Sword impaled by Stet the Guardian. It is a story my people will tell. That I was the one to destroy our lord's enemies. I was the one who helped him bring my people back to their rightful place. Back to power." He leaned in until his face was inches from Cyrus's wound, his grin pained as he cradled his arm. "Your arm for mine. Your woman will be mine as well. Seraphina will be at my side. She will give me sons or die trying beneath me."

Cyrus took slow deep breaths, stretching his legs until his feet touched the ground despite the tearing flesh, and pushed his body forward. He grit his teeth with a feral snarl, the blindness of his rage making it easy for him to slide off the branch. To turn and rip it, crackling and snapping, from the tree and aim it at Stet, heedless of the pain streaking through his body. Pain was temporary. It made him stronger.

He was Wode.

The cocky prick was too filled with disbelief to move, which suited Cyrus well. He knocked Stet to the ground with the first blow, breaking several ribs and rendering Stet unconscious with the next. He raised his arm to land the third and final blow but was stopped by the one voice he would listen to.

Seraphina.

"Cyrus!"

At the sound of his name, he dropped the heavy branch and walked around Stet's prone body, adrenaline racing through his veins as he kept his eyes fixed on her.

His. She was his. It was time to claim her.

Chapter Nine

The two Felidae females who had held Phina back when Stet sent Cyrus slamming into the tree released her, taking several cautious steps back. No one came near her. None of them wanted to be in the path of the tall, blue-haired Wode who was covered in blood.

Coming to claim his mate.

She was not sure what was happening to her. What had been happening since he declared himself and Stet began to stalk him.

He'd fought for her. Had any male in her lifetime done the same? She had been wanted and desired. She had been hated. Chased down as a thief and coveted as a mistress.

Cyrus had claimed her for all to hear with his words. Claimed her long before he landed the first blow. But seeing him fight had lit something inside her. Ignited something that grew hotter, more powerful, with each passing moment.

The Felidae he passed reacted to him as well, the men lowering their tails in respect, the women subtly panting. She understood their reactions.

Phina felt like she could shatter apart at any moment. Sharp, burning shards of sensation that aroused her with their sting. The smell of his blood only increased her desire, made her ache to taste him. To feel that strength, that power, inside her. He was hers.

She shook her head and took several steps back, scared of her own thoughts. She jumped, startled when the elder Peacemaker came to her side. She knew it was her from the soothing scent and soft voice, though her attention could not be removed from the oncoming Cyrus.

"This is as it should be, Seraphina." Her voice was soft. "It's instinct. You belong to him now, and everything inside you is showing him. Your scent is in the air, calling to him. You have chosen and he will ease your fire."

Her scent . . .

Phina tore her gaze away from Cyrus and looked around at the male Felidae closest to her. Their lips were stretched over their teeth, curled in snarls of need as they took in the scent of her heightened arousal. They respected Cyrus for the moment, but she knew they would challenge him if they saw him stagger. If they saw weakness.

She had seen nothing like this in the settlement. She'd seen occasional fights, most of them drunken, but nothing came close to this. Their reactions were nowhere near as intense as her own. As volatile.

When Cyrus reached her he did not hesitate, lifting her up with his good arm and carrying her past the others without a word, back down the path they had come.

When they passed a copse of trees he hesitated, as if unsure where to take her. Phina slid down his body, taking his hand and walking with him in silence to the edge of the dodge. The spirit veil. There was a small clearing with trees and ground foliage to hide them from the view of the others. She led him there.

He leaned against the tree and she could see waves of arousal and tension rolling off his body. He was vibrating with it, reminding her of the captain's sword. But he was hers. Her Sword. Injured. She would take care of him.

Phina unsheathed her claws and slid them inside his shirt as he watched her, his beautiful eyes dilated and dark with need for her. She slit his shirt into shreds, kissing his chest around his wound gently as she turned the fabric into a makeshift tourniquet for his wound.

He hissed through his teeth at the pain, but instead of merely sympathizing, the sound caused her tail to tremble, her thighs to clench. He met her gaze with a fire that matched her own. He knew.

"Are you mine?" His words were harsh through gritted teeth that were attempting to form a smile.

"Yes." She did not hesitate. Later she might hate herself for being so abnormally submissive, despite her feelings for him. Now it was the only truth she knew.

"As I am yours." The smile disappeared. "Show me, Phina."

She shuddered at his command. It was that feeling again. That she would offer everything, open herself completely for his pleasure. Only it was a thousand times stronger, feeling more a necessity than a desire.

Had this been what the Peacemaker meant? Her instinct to belong to him in all ways? She retracted her sharp nails and removed her boots and the long pants she had worn for Nephi and Jobi's modesty since they'd come aboard the Deviant. She unclasped the front of her corset, her trembling fingers making it more difficult.

"Phina."

She knew. But this was more than a quick thrill in the galley. It felt sacred. She knelt in front of him on the soft loam at his feet. Her knees spread and she watched his gaze lower to the small triangle of hair between her damp thighs.

Her hips were swaying, gently rocking toward him, an ancient dance every woman knew. He licked his lips and kicked off his boots when she finally removed her corset.

She saw him cringe in pain. It felt like her pain. "Let me."

She reached for his pants and unbuttoned the panel that concealed him, tugging the thick brown fabric down his muscular legs until he was as naked as she was. She opened her mouth to speak, to tell him how much she wanted him. How thankful she was that he was alive.

No words would come.

He knelt in front of her, looking into her eyes with the same kind of awe. With tenderness. He kissed her lips but they were too sensitive. It was too much.

What was wrong with her?

She pulled back and his brow furrowed. How could he not know? She needed something. Needed him to . . . "You claimed me."

He stilled, looking much like a Felidae catching a scent on the wind. "Yes."

Instinct and desire had her turning her back to him, lowering her arms to the dark, richly scented ground and lifting her hips in the air.

He groaned. "Damn it, Phina. You *are* trying to kill me."

She wanted to laugh, to tease him with bawdy wit, but her skin was too tight. Her body too shaken. She lifted her tail to caress his good shoulder. His hair.

Cyrus swore again, reaching for her hips. "You want to be claimed, Phina? I can do that. But I will not rush this. Your arousal is so sweet I can almost taste it. I have to taste it. Lift up for me, love. I need . . . Yes, like that."

She'd straightened her legs, spreading them wide until her sex was even with his mouth. Her heavy breasts rocked with the motion of his mouth on her most sensitive flesh. His tongue filled her, his grip lifting her up on her toes, pulling her closer so that he could give her a deeper kiss. Drink her in.

He hummed his enjoyment and the vibration sent small shocks through her body. Her fingers dug into the ground and she bit her lip, every thrust of his tongue causing fire to lick her spine.

She had never felt desire like this. Phina had lusted, she had craved and she had taken. She had never ached until Cyrus. She needed more.

She pressed her sex against his mouth, small whimpers escaping her throat that he understood. He lifted his mouth and her trembling knees collapsed to the ground once more.

"You don't know how hard it was to stop, Phina. You are addicting. Your taste. But I know what you need." He moved until his hips were pressed against hers. "I am yours, Phina. I won you today, but you won me long before. Good or ill, we belong to each other."

Phina could not hold back her cry of delight as he filled her with his thick erection. That was what she needed. Her body instinctively opened to his, recognizing him. Welcoming him. Her forehead pressed into the ground as his hips rocked against her with long powerful strokes.

"Cyrus. Yes, please."

He pressed one hand into her back, his thrusts more forceful. "Phina says please," he rasped. "No one would believe it. Say it again."

She shook her head, moaning in ecstasy as he continued to fill her. Deep. Moons, so deeply.

His thumbs spread the skin of her bottom, slipping down between her folds to soak them in her arousal before pressing them in that spot, so sensitive, beneath her tail. "I have claimed your mouth. I have your 'please.' Your beautiful succulent breasts are mine to claim. Is this as well, Seraphina? Do I have all of you?"

"Yes." She wanted that. Wanted him inside her everywhere. His thumbs pushed through the tight ring of muscles while his cock continued to thrust deep inside her. *"Yes.* Please, Cyrus. I feel . . . It feels . . ."

"I know." His words were guttural, closer to a growl than he knew.

Phina felt the fire begin to consume her, every inch of flesh attuned to him. Knowing he was close, so close. Knowing she would erupt with him. Her thighs were shaking so hard he had to tighten his grip to keep her steady for his claiming. Her tail wound around him, holding him close.

It reached for her out of nowhere. A streak of lightning that blazed through every limb and made her scream. The sound echoed as her back arched in an almost painful manner, the muscles of her sex gripping him tightly as though they would refuse to let him leave.

"Seraphina!" His release came with hers. In her. She felt him pumping into her. All of him. A piece of him inside her.

Her upper body collapsed onto the ground and he followed, his teeth closing over her shoulder. She shuddered and smiled, weak and spent. More satisfied than she had ever been. Safer.

She belonged to someone. She loved someone. Cyrus.

He drew back and kissed the spots on her spine, his tongue caressing the sensitive markings soothingly. Lovingly. Then he groaned, dragging himself up to lean back against the rough bark of the tree. He pulled her up with him, rocking her in his arms.

"Phina?"

"Hmmm?"

"I am hallucinating. Perhaps it is from loss of blood and the most pleasurable after-combat claiming I have ever had."

She chuckled softly, nuzzling his chest contentedly. "It better be the *only* claiming you have ever had. What are you hallucinating?"

"Freeman appears to be glaring at me. Wulf is playing with those strange spectacles as if he can actually see us. And Bodhan is laughing." He paused. "Freeman is definitely glaring. And I thought he was such a nice giant."

Phina jumped off his lap and whirled to face the dodge, her body still trembling. How did they all get here? She could see their distorted images through the dodge. They were all being held back by armed Felidae, but if she knew the captain, that would not hold them long.

Captain Amaranthe appeared as if Phina had called her name, peering around Freeman's large form to scowl sternly. "You can try to stay quiet, but they haven't invented soundproof dodge yet. We heard your screaming as soon as we entered these booby-trapped woods."

Wulf waggled his pale eyebrows above his shaded spectacles. "We were told we were invited, however, we can come back later if you wish to continue. Or I can keep watching. I know it's giving me ideas."

Watching? Could he actually see through the dodge with those strange spectacles?

Phina saw Dare pressing her face against Bodhan's chest, her shoulders shaking. Was she crying? Disappointed? "Is Dare unwell?"

Cyrus groaned in pain as he dragged himself to his feet. "She is laughing, too, Phina. She's just too polite to do it to my face."

She turned to him and he cupped her cheek. "It changes nothing, Seraphina Lightfoot Fleet Felidae. You still belong to me. I still love you. Please remember that and tell them all how manly and Sword-like I finally was in battle, since I fear I will be passing out at your feet once more."

She caught him as he sagged heavily against her and kissed his forehead. "I promise I will."

*   *   *

"This is the secret you've been keeping from me? That you have been working with the commander for the queen?"

Dare's voice was expressionless. Too much so. But it was time to face her. Time for honesty for all of them. Cyrus looked around at the motley crew who had gathered around Commander Iacchus and his hammock. They were drawing excessive interest and curiosity from the Felidae. Captain Amaranthe, Wulf, Bodhan, and Dare. Freeman was causing the greatest stir. He was, no doubt, more gigantic than any human male they had ever seen. The females, in particular, were showing flagrant interest. Unfortunately, there was no time to tease the poor, uncomfortable fellow.

Cyrus sat up straighter, adjusting his shoulder. It was currently covered in some sort of Felidae poultice. It took away the pain, but he grimaced at the smell as he answered Dare's question. "I am a few years older than you, as is the Arendal custom. Even though I was just a small child, I remember when the commander announced he had joined with a female Wode and she was with child. You were born near Faro Outpost, outside of the barracks, and the commander was transferred to Centre City shortly after."

He studied the man resting in the hammock not far from them, knowing he was listening to every word. "He came back to visit me often. Helped to train me. Said what my father never had. That I was different. Special. Arendal material. He was a mentor to me and, I believe, the reason I was chosen to be your companion shield guard."

Dare slipped her fingers beneath the buttons of her jacket, and he knew she was touching the charm the Khepri had given to her. The connection to the queen. "And you saw him after he brought me?" she asked. "More than just his official visits, and after he left the main barracks?"

Cyrus nodded, knowing it would cause her pain. How many times had she shared her insecurities about her father's distance, wondering if he was proud of his unusual daughter? "He wanted you to have an easier transition. Wanted to give you a chance to truly bond with the queen, as the Chalice must, to be a true companion to her, instead of longing for family. Yes, I worked with your father to keep the queen safe. He was my teacher, and I was lucky to have him." Hurt sparked in her eyes and he felt his own heart ache for hers. "We were wrong to keep you so isolated, but I do not believe it was ever done out of malice. Only love."

Phina got up from his side and started to pace. The captain looked disdainful as well. Angry. "What is it?"

Captain Amaranthe's jaw was clenched. "I do not believe the queen would so distrust her Chalice. Dare is one of the strongest women I know."

Dare sniffed and turned her head to rub her eyes discreetly. "Thank you for that, Captain. However, I cannot deny the truths I have seen for myself. Perhaps she felt sorry for me, malformed as I was. There is no wisdom in entrusting dangerous political secrets to someone physically and emotionally unprepared to deal with them."

Commander Iacchus cursed loud and long from his prone position, coughing wetly as he struggled to come to a sitting position. "Demeter Senedal, you are the Queen's Chalice as you were born to be. Wode do not feel sorry for themselves and they do not cry." He softened, his tone becoming less militant as he continued to study every curve of his daughter's face. "You were not malformed. You were made perfectly. You are as precious to me as Queen Idony herself, and I believe she would not fault me for saying that."

Cyrus sighed when Phina's green eyes narrowed. He was in love with a woman who did not know when to stop fighting. She tilted her head. "Interesting choice of words again, Commander. You said you were going to tell her about her birthmark. Would now be the right time?"

Dare huffed. "Why is it everyone is so fascinated by that particular mark? I am surrounded by Felidae with unique markings. Why is mine so strange?"

Bodhan came to stand behind her, his hand caressing her hair. "You told me your father warned you to keep it hidden?"

The older man glared at him. "Advice she respected until recently."

Cyrus leaned forward, sending a stern look to his mentor. "Advice that no longer applies with the palace overrun and our queen in danger."

Iacchus nodded, properly chastened. "True enough. I had planned to tell her. In my time." His eyes grew distant, lost in memory. "I was young when I first came to duty at Faro. I spent most of my time stationed island-side, and it was eye-opening. The cruelty of the other Wode in my regiment. The kindness and serenity, the open friendship I was given by the Felidae on the island. By the Peace-maker who leads them there." He shrugged. "I learned some of their ancient words and rituals. I fell in love with a beautiful creature who was too polite to tell me she belonged to another, but we remained friends in spite of my ignorance.

"Then I began to receive messages from strange little insects. It was the Khepri. He said the queen wanted to see me. I thought I was to be demoted or punished for my inappropriate attitude, but no. She asked me to tell her all about my time with the Felidae. To ask if I had heard the stories of the first Peacemaker or the myth of moon-fire. She told me to trust the man who sent me messages and to go back and continue to learn from the Felidae. To protect them until I was called again. So I did."

He coughed. Cyrus cringed at the painful sound, but Iacchus could not seem to stop now that he had begun to speak. "I did, and I heard the stories of a hidden tribe that kept the old ways and waited for the return of the moonfire oath. I also heard about the rumors against the queen. False tales of a god king who had been banished for his love of the Felidae. I reported to the Khepri and we became friends."

Wulf, who had been studying the small treetop village in silent fascination, focused on that. "Friends? Have you met him then?"

The old man started to nod, but hesitated. "In a way. Never got a look at him. But we talked. He offered me the opportunity to aid my queen for a generation. To protect her from something we could both feel coming. Though he knew far more about the specifics than I." He turned his gaze once more to Dare, and Cyrus could see how difficult it was for him to say. "He took samples of my inheritance markers. Not long after I held you in my arms for the first time."

Dare had gasped, covering her mouth and shaking her head in confusion and disbelief. Commander Iacchus held out his hand toward her, as if he could stop the pain not even Cyrus had known of. Samples of inheritance markers. He'd believed Dare conceived naturally.

"Demeter, my inheritance, my blood, is still a part of what you are, though you are not mine alone. He said you would be a special child belonging to all of Theorrey, and he was right. You have the best qualities of all of us inside you. Your gifts, the queen's love for you—" His voice cracked. "I have always been proud of the part I played."

Cyrus watched the captain move closer to Dare, hand on the hilt of her sword. Phina, as well, knelt at Dare's feet, her tail brushing against Cyrus where he sat beside them.

Phina nuzzled Dare's knee. "*That* is why her birthmark is shaped as a Khepri scarab. He, in a way, is more her father than the Wode commander."

He, too, felt the sting of betrayal by his mentor. For the sake of the Chalice. He had a feeling that Phina and the captain had been suspicious before now. But he could only imagine what Dare must be going through.

Her laugh held a tinge of hysteria. "Everyone's been right all along. Phina's instincts weren't off. I was fooling no one. I am not Wode. I *am* a half-breed. Worse than that, an experiment of some kind made, not in love, but by invention. And the Khepri, the queen's Khepri did this? Made me . . . what?"

He watched the women allow Bodhan to drag her up and turn her until she was in his arms. "Mine, Dare. He made you mine. My princess. My heart. Your inheritance, despite what the damn scientists or the Theorrean Raj want you to believe, means nothing. They can change your hair or your height, *not* your soul. Not who you are."

Freeman spoke beside them. Cyrus was surprised at the smoothness of his voice. And the sadness in it. "I do not believe the Khepri meant Dare harm. The commander is right to call her special. She is. Perhaps more than we realize. She is the only one who could not be fooled. She knew the true queen was gone and can feel her even now. I, for one, am thankful to have her on the Deviant. Proud to fight beside her."

Cyrus lifted his eyebrows high in surprise when the captain walked over to Freeman and placed a hand, only for a moment, on his arm in gratitude. She lifted her chin. "Well said, Freeman. I am inclined to agree."

The Peacemaker, carrying an empty greenwood bowl intricately carved with Felidae symbols, joined their small somber group. The others moved awkwardly out of the way until she could reach Dare. "Iacchus said he would return the moonfire and restore the oath the queen made, not that he would bring us the true child of Theorrey. A story on the wind come to life. You will forgive me, I could not help but overhear . . . You have the mark of the blue beetle?"

Phina had backed up onto Cyrus's lap, watching the exchange with fascination while absently stroking his shoulders and arm. He felt his body heat and his heart begin to heal at her unconscious show of affection.

"It is on my back. I have never seen it clearly." Dare drew his attention once more.

The captain, Freeman, Phina, and Bodhan all spoke in unison. "I have."

Cyrus sighed. He did not want to know how so many people had seen the bare back of his companion shield. Neither, it seemed, did Commander Iacchus, whose face had turned purplish and swollen with discomfort.

The old woman nodded. "If you would grant me the honor please."

Dare looked around and blushed, and Bodhan's glare touched every male, including her father, until they looked away. His voice was tender when he spoke to her. "Face me, princess. We can just lift your jacket and show her together."

Cyrus heard fabric rustling, Dare's muttered, "Beneath my binding," and then a gasp.

"So it is true." The Peacemaker's voice had a strange tinge to it. Cyrus was not sure if the fact troubled her or eased her mind.

They all turned when Dare's fabric ceased its rustling and Dare looked down as the elderly Felidae pointed at the center of the bowl. "This is the symbol that dwells beneath your skin. Theorrey dwells in your blood."

He wanted to stand, as curious as everyone else, but decided he would rather keep Phina where she was. Safe beside him.

Iacchus spoke, his voice solemn as he addressed the matriarch. "In her *blood*? Does that mean . . . Peacemaker, will you accept hers in place of the queen's for the oath?"

The Peacemaker dipped her head in acknowledgment, never turning from Dare. "She carries the mark of the blue beetle. She is the Chalice, the element of empathy that carries the heart of the queen. It will suffice. Do you have the dagger?"

Phina's body tensed on his and Cyrus whispered in her ear, "What is it?"

"Moon's blood oath. In the settlement it's unbreakable." She pulled from his shoulder and showed him the small healing mark on her palm.

"Have you made one?" he asked.

She nodded. "Not one as important as this one I think."

Dare reached into her belt, catching Cyrus's gaze as she did. He nodded. This had been his mentor's goal all along. To bring the queen's dagger to these people.

"The first Peacemaker held our people together. She befriended the eternally youthful queen, recognizing her as a bringer of light and knowing her people would prosper as long as the queen dwelt among them."

The woman swayed in front of Dare, speaking as though reciting an old story she had spun a hundred times. "To honor her ways, the Peacemaker carved out a cavern in the mountainside, gathering drops of its silver blood to create a blade."

Dare handed the dagger to the Peacemaker and Cyrus studied it with new eyes. Its symbols he had believed decorative were Felidae, matching many on the bowl she still held with one hand.

"To honor our ways, she sacrificed her most valued possession." The woman lifted the dagger to her chest, showing the similarity between her own necklace and the jewel embedded in the hilt of the silver dagger. "The symbol of the fire in her heart that had dropped from the sky into her hands. The moonfire stone. The only one of its kind, containing the true fire of the universe. She placed that inside the dagger."

Dare leaned in to study the dual-bodied stone and she knew she would see it. Knew she had not seen it before. Only when you are looking could you see the fire flickering inside the stone. "I can see it. So this Peacemaker, she gave the dagger to the queen?"

The Felidae nodded. "They made an oath with their blood. The queen promised to bring no war to the people. My people. And the

Peacemaker vowed to stand by the queen and her own people in battle, as she had before, should the need arise."

Cyrus glanced at Iacchus and saw him wiping the sweat off his brow, his attention riveted on the scene despite his illness. Had this been his life's work? His mission?

Dare tilted her head, sensing something only she could. "You do not believe the queen kept her oath."

The Peacemaker appeared startled, but she nodded faintly. "Having no war is far different from living in peace. Many who travel hidden by the veil have returned with claims that war can be bloodless. War can be captivity with the excuse of protection. War can be isolation wrapped in the lie of freedom. The men who followed Stet, who has been banished for his cowardice, believe the queen's immortality is her weapon. That she would live to see us all die a slow death. They are not alone in their beliefs."

Dare reached out, holding one edge of the bowl with one hand and cradling the edge of the dagger with the other, connected now to the Peacemaker. "She is not responsible for the treatment you have seen. I did not realize it, but I know now she was imprisoned long before she was taken from us. I'm not sure how or why, but it is true. I have felt her sorrow for the Felidae. Her anger at those who would harm them all of my life."

Phina spoke quietly, but with vehemence from her perch on Cyrus's lap. "I am Felidae and I have lived in the settlements. Those atrocities are not hers. She saved me from them. She would save all of us if she could."

The Peacemaker beamed at them, tears filling her eyes. "Then my hope is restored. It will be difficult, but if you make the blood oath with me, with this dagger that holds the true moonfire, I and all who follow me will stand at your side, at the queen's side, should you have need."

The matriarch bent and set the bowl at their feet between them, held the dagger in her hand, and cut her palm. Cyrus watched as the innocent girl he had grown up with stood proudly, following the actions of the Felidae leader. Dare held her hand out, not flinching when the blade sliced open her flesh.

Her blood must not be spilled. She is precious, not to be harmed.

How often had that mantra been beaten into his skull? He had believed he protected her because of her weakness, soft heart, and vulnerable size. He'd had no idea.

Bodhan, as well, did not seem pleased with seeing Dare's blood. His expression was protective. Watchful. Suspicious. A man after his own paranoid heart. He knew no harm would come to her if Bodhan had his way.

The two women pressed their bleeding hands together, the blade and stone between them. Blood dripped into the green bowl, onto the image of the blue scarab Cyrus could now see sitting at the center, at the heart of it all.

The hair on the back of his neck began to rise and he could feel it—a strange static charge building around them. The forest and the Felidae went eerily quiet. They felt what he did.

Dare gasped softly, "It is hot."

The Peacemaker lifted her other hand, covering Dare's firmly. "It will get hotter. The oath will burn into our blood, that we will never forget."

Cyrus watched the dagger begin to emit a silvery blue glow. Dare was shaking but shrugged off Bodhan's hands when he tried to touch her.

They all stood. Even Iacchus had gotten to his feet in concern. This was more than a bloodletting ritual. Much more.

He could have sworn he saw a flash of the moonfire flame spark between their fingers, and then it was over.

The Peacemaker wrapped her arms around Dare for a moment and murmured, "The blood of the Chalice. Truly you represent the eternal queen. The oath is restored."

She slipped the dagger into her belt and picked up the bowl. Walking past them, out into the middle of the milling crowd, she held the bowl above her head.

Silence.

Her voice, when it came, seemed to tremble with power and authority. "The heart of the blue beetle sings and the truth is revealed to us. The moonfire has been restored and the blood oath of old renewed. Those who would have faith in me, prepare for what is to come. Those who follow another path, the path that leads to the Lord of Blood, can dwell with us no more." The murmur of the voices grew louder, drifting down from the houses above. "Spread the word. Lift the spirit veils throughout the mountainside and tell them what you have heard here. Revenge has no refuge amongst our people. Malice no home. The first Peacemaker unites us all once more."

A cheer broke out and traveled, causing Cyrus and the others to watch in awe. He had seen this in the painting. How had the queen known?

Cyrus watched the Felidae men who headed deeper into the forest, past the village. What appeared to be vines gave way to ropes and pulleys that they began to work, revealing more dodge. More illusion. This small community was not small. He could see dozens of dwellings spiraling up massive trees far in the distance. Gliders drifted in the distant skyline, from one tree to another.

This part of the journey had brought more questions than answers. He had believed he understood what was at stake. Now he was not so sure.

The Khepri had a few things to answer for. He needed to speak to the commander. Perhaps he knew where the mysterious hand of the queen could be found.

The Peacemaker came toward them quickly, gently cradling her palm. Cyrus could see the cut had been sealed closed by the heat the ritual had created. "The gliders told me you were searching for a tower beside the lake," she said. "Is that true?"

The captain came forward, nodding. "The queen left us a message, telling us to find it."

"It is not a place easily seen. I will send you with one who will show you, but you should go now. My people need to adjust to this news without interference from outsiders."

Cyrus cringed a bit with his first few steps but shook his head when the others looked on in concern. "I've survived worse." He glanced at Dare and offered her a playful, apologetic smile. "Perhaps I was chosen because I can take a beating?"

"No." Commander Iacchus was lying down in his hammock once more, clutching his chest.

Cyrus moved toward him as the others gathered themselves together. "Then why? What in the name of the queen did you see in me that made you think I was meant to be the Queen's Sword? At this time? With this Chalice?"

Iacchus tried to smile. "Honor. It is, sadly, a trait many Wode seem to lack in their inheritance. I do not believe we started out that way, but that is where we have ended up. You were so determined to prove your honor, to prove your worth, never knowing that desire alone made you the only choice. I am as proud as a father could be of you both."

His expression grew regretful, painful in its intensity. "Tell Demeter . . . she will not look at me. Go to her. Make her understand that I was proud. That she *is* my daughter in my heart. Even if she was never really mine."

Cyrus reached for the older man's hand and looked over his shoulder. Bodhan held Dare's hand in his own, studying the wound, but she was looking toward her father with sorrow and regret. With confusion. "You know what she can do. What she can feel. She knows, Commander. If you feel it, she knows." He looked down at his mentor for a long, silent moment. "You are staying here?"

"Iacchus is one of us." The Peacemaker came to stand beside the hammock, stroking his faded blue hair fondly. "He honors our ways and wishes to die as he lived, connected."

Cyrus nodded and sent the man the salute of the Wode, knowing it was, perhaps, the last time he would see his face.

Phina was waiting for him, lagging behind as the others followed their Felidae guide. He was drawn once more to the brightly colored fabric she'd replaced her corset with. She had wrapped the soft, brilliantly patterned sarong around her breasts and tied the strands jauntily on one side, drawing his attention to the bare skin between it and her leather pants.

She was breathtaking.

"Are you sad to leave?" He had to know. These Felidae were free, honoring ways that were ancient to her kind. Even he would be tempted.

"Are you *mad*?" Her disbelieving expression made him smile and she made a face. "They are fascinating and wonderful and I will make great use of the glider I slipped in Freeman's pack before we left—but I have no desire to live in a tree and sing songs about how everything is connected. I would much rather stay with you and save the queen." She shrugged her bare shoulders, distracting him. "The Deviant is my home now."

He stopped and tugged her arm until she faced him. "You stole a glider?"

She grinned. "It should not be called stealing. I am Felidae. It is my birthright. And I cannot wait to try it."

He wanted to explain why stealing was wrong, but he couldn't seem to work himself up into a good bout of righteous anger.

She'd said she would rather stay with him.

Chapter Ten

It was disturbing, how alive she felt. How happy. Phina knew the situation was dire and her new friend Dare was suffering with the shock of their strange discovery, her mysterious inheritance. With each passing day it seemed, the conspiracy against their missing queen grew and twisted and bound them in further confusion.

Yet what occupied her thoughts above all of these worries, was Cyrus. Her Wode had just claimed her and—the elder had been correct—his claiming had eased her fire.

She still wanted him even now. But what she had felt before? She never knew that existed. It was wild and untamed, an old instinct from a long-forgotten heritage.

She glanced back at the trees, wondering if anyone was watching them leave behind their spirit veil. Not completely forgotten, it seemed.

Nephi would love to hear this story. Would want to know all about her encounter with the hidden tribe, the claiming battle and Dare's sacred moon's blood oath with a legendary dagger. When this was done she would make Bodhan take them to Aaru, so she could tell her everything.

When this was done. When the queen was safe.

They reached the lake again as the sun began to set. Had so little time passed? It felt like they had been gone for days.

The male voice ahead was loud with relief. "There you are. I left the others guarding the ship so I could look for you. I just checked those trees, I was sure I did. Where did you run off to?"

Captain Amaranthe tapped her booted foot, waiting for Stacy to finish. Phina tugged Cyrus impatiently, knowingly, wanting a closer look at the exchange.

"Mr. Stacy, did I tell you that if you were needed we would light our beacon?" Her voice was cold.

James Stacy swallowed. "Yes, Captain Amaranthe."

"And did I also order you to stay with the ship until and unless that beacon was lit?"

Phina smiled as they came to stand beside Wulf and Freeman.

"Yes, Captain Amaranthe." James Stacy was looking decidedly green around the edges.

The captain tilted her chin toward Dare and Bodhan, her dark hair gliding like silk along the back of her long jacket. "Bodhan, hand me your pistol."

Phina chuckled. It was soft, but the men around her heard it.

"I enjoy sport at the expense of others as much as the next man," Wulfric mumbled through the side of his mouth, taking off his shaded spectacles to rub them on his vest. "Not sure why you're laughing, though. I like James, myself."

Phina leaned in and caught his pale green gaze as Bodhan argued for his young guard's life in playful banter with the captain. "You still haven't learned have you, Wulfric the Modest?" she said. "She *likes* our young Jamie. If she didn't, she would not say a word. And he would already be dead."

"Fascinating."

Phina pretended she did not see Freeman's uncharacteristic glare at Wulf's besotted tone while James Stacy was sent back to the ship, his boots near flying across the ground.

Wulf chuckled. She wondered how long Bodhan's friend was staying on board. Too much longer and there would be trouble. She knew it. Freeman would make sure of it.

Cyrus's hand was warm on her back. Comforting. He smiled at her and shook his head. "What?"

"Nothing," he assured her. "Just pondering the fact that I have claimed a handful of a woman. You do love trouble. I can see I'm going to have to keep a close eye on you."

She lifted her chin in mocking defiance. "You can try, Sword. At least you'll enjoy the view while you work."

Seraphina was distracted from their interplay when the Felidae the matriarch had sent with them walked to the edge of the lake and knelt beside it.

Her hand slid out of Cyrus's and she walked forward to join the captain and Dare, who'd both moved closer to see what the guide was doing.

He lifted several small stones, none of them looking any different to Phina than the others that rimmed the unique lake. She saw heat waves coming up from beneath them and she crouched beside the Felidae. "What is it?"

The young man looked up at her with sparkling black eyes. "It is a different kind of spirit veil. Older than our time. The way to the lotus."

His hand disappeared into a hidden compartment in the soil. His arm twisted forward, then back again.

He removed his hand and began to replace the rocks and pebbles until they looked as undisturbed as the rest. Was that it? She thought he was taking them to the tower.

Dare's voice startled Phina into glancing up. "Look there! In the middle of the lake."

Phina saw a device rising from the lake's center. A thick rod as big as a tree with several slender rods attached to its sides. A large globe-like piece was fastened at the apex of the contraption, its function unclear. She did not readily recognize the metal, a feat that should be simple for her considering her formative years in the mines. It was like iron, but not. Like silver, but not.

It began to spin slowly and she saw that the rods were churning the water, exciting the glowing algae that dwelt in the lake.

They shone, growing brighter and brighter. She could see the energy rising off the lake, forming ripples in the air.

Then she felt it.

The ground beneath her feet shook. She looked toward their Felidae guide for assurance, but he was gone. He'd disappeared and left them to—whatever this was.

Her claws came out and her stance widened. "The earth is quaking. We should get to safety."

Dare gripped Phina's hand with her own, their shared scars soothing her in a way. "We are fine." She'd raised her voice to be heard over the noise erupting from the ground. "I believe this is supposed to happen."

Phina, careful of her extended natural weapons, squeezed Dare's hand. "Fair Dare of the bright blue hair is comforting me? Will the wonders never cease?"

She heard Dare laugh, heard the sadness in it that Phina wished she could take away from her. "Not any time soon, my friend. Not if the queen's stories were true."

"The hillside."

Phina followed the captain's gaze. The Deviant hovered beyond the single rocky rise around the green sanctuary that housed the Lake of Light. And now, it seemed, that rise was moving. Shifting, but in a slow, controlled manner that seemed . . . impossible. They had walked over that ground only hours before. James Stacy himself must have trod it on his way back to the ship.

Segments of the rise separated in a way that reminded Phina of the first time she had seen the cargo lift on the Deviant. One moment a deck, the next, a lift. What was the hillside becoming? What was waiting for them inside?

An enormous white oval dome, its color reflecting off the charged plant life in the lake, began to rise from the black rocks. Higher and higher until it looked like the bud of a ship-sized flower.

It settled with a mechanical *thunk*. This was a machine? How large must it be to have moved the very ground beneath their feet?

The churning rods, Phina saw from the corner of her awestruck gaze, had stopped spinning and begun to sink beneath the water's surface once more.

"What on *Theorrey*?" Cyrus sounded as bewildered as the others looked.

But it wasn't over.

What had looked to be a sealed bud had long, perfect petals. The odd building of white metal bloomed in the sun's dying light. A lotus tower.

Phina could detect now the telling sound of machinery as its silvery petals spread out to frame a more recognizable building with windows, a large set of double doors, and a dome roof made entirely of glass.

Tower Orr.

The clapping had Phina and the others turning toward Wulf.

"What?" He shrugged off their confounded expressions, his smile transcendent. "The marvel of invention must be praised. In a few days I have gone from an airship with a dual steam and theorrite engine, to a tribe of Felidae who live in trees but somehow have the capacity to power their dodge, as you call it, without an obvious source of energy. Now cleverly concealed hydraulics reveal what is obviously an astronomical observatory instead of common rock." He turned to Bodhan. "This impresses no one else? Apparently I need to spend more time topside if this is normal to the rest of you."

Bodhan grinned ruefully and patted Wulf on the shoulder. "This is not normal, friend. And around here, neither are you."

Phina watched Freeman bite his cheek to suppress his grin and she met Cyrus's gaze. "I believe we found the tower."

Dare nodded beside her, a wistful smile on her lips. "The tower was a lotus and the lotus held the universe inside its petals."

"The queen's fairy tale," Cyrus added. "But we do not need the universe. We just need answers. More, it seems, than we did before."

A voice broke through the quickening darkness. "You found what He wanted you to find. The only answers you need are His."

A man with his arm in a sling and his hair wild stepped out from another large outcropping of rock between them and the tower. Phina snarled, taking several steps toward him, instinctively protecting Dare and the others. "*Stet.*" She spat his name. "Your people do not want you, and I will kill you if you come closer."

She cocked her head and grinned malevolently, jangling her bracelet. "In fact, I would take pleasure in killing you. Almost as much pleasure as I took when I watched my Sword beat you unconscious."

His laugh was an ugly growl. "You have ruined yourself with a false queen's Wode. I can smell him on you. A Felidae whore is not worthy of my time." He turned to the others. "The Lord of Blood has a message for you. I merely pleaded with him that I be here when it was delivered. To smell your fear."

Phina could hear something coming closer. Climbing up from behind the jutted rock. That it was not human or Felidae was unmistakable to her senses. The squeaks and clang of metal, the gears and greased bolts. She could hear them easily. What form of automaton could make that much noise?

It came out of the shadows and she heard Dare gasp. Heard the song of Captain Amaranthe's sword as she drew it and prepared for battle.

The Khepri had not made this.

It almost looked like a marsh cat. Phina hated the marsh, but she had been in it more than once. She'd seen the feline beasts up close.

But marsh cats had no hair encircling their head like the rays of the sun. Their tails were wide and flat for pushing through the water, not slender with a sharp tuft of fur on the end. Marsh cats were nowhere near as intimidating as this nightmarish creation.

Bodhan drew his pistol and aimed, causing Stet to step back with a bloodthirsty grin. "Your weapons won't hurt him or anything that belongs to him. You will only make him stronger."

The creature crouched on top of the rocks, clinging to them with steel claws that more than rivaled her own. It opened its mouth and a strange sound emerged, a tinny roar that was not as frightening as the razor rows of teeth that glinted threateningly from inside its gaping jaw.

Bodhan took a step closer. "Let us test your claim."

The emerald blast of light from his theorrite pistol hit the automaton directly in his side. The beast staggered with the force of the jolt but Phina saw its eyes. The eyes were glowing brighter.

She lifted her hand. "He's right. You're giving it more energy."

How was that possible?

A small gear-like object flipped out onto the creature's metal tongue from deep inside its maw. As the gear spun, Phina knew. It may not be the Khepri's creation, but whoever had done this had his knowledge.

"I could not let this continue." The strangely polite male voice coming from the beast's mouth filled the tense silence around it. "Not without shedding some light on your dark escapade. You are working from a state of ignorance, which, while blissful, is going to end up destroying all of you. Since I am on a very specific timetable, I have no wish to kill your beloved Idony until everything is in place. No wish, but every intention of doing so should you persist."

This was the man who had the queen? His voice? Phina studied the deadly automaton and felt dread climb her spine. This was what they were up against?

His voice was condescending. Pitying. "I know you believe her as innocent as a child. She has been this way for over three hundred years, so do not let her sweet smile fool you, Seraphina Felidae."

She jolted at the mention of her name.

The voice continued. "I know who all of you are, the important ones at any rate, and I am honestly saddened that you would think ill of me. Seraphina should be with her people, preparing for my return and the rule of the Felidae over Theorrey. Vengeance and blood and all the goods you can steal will be yours. All that you are owed for what they made you suffer in those cages." The automaton rotated its head as it spoke in a disturbingly lifelike way. "Captain Amaranthe, I would have someone of your skill truly *using* your blade instead of keeping it polished. As to your other training, well, let us just say I would not mind seeing you kneeling and collared at my feet. I believe I would make a good master for you."

The captain took a few steps closer, her sword raised, but Stet lifted his gun, aiming it in her direction. "He is not finished."

The captain's voice was venomous. "He will be soon."

The recording, heedless of the confrontation, continued. "The Sword and the Chalice. My arrangements for you went surprisingly wrong. I knew the Senedal was special, is special, despite her clever disguise. Honestly, I can hardly contain myself, I am looking *that* forward to meeting her in person. But the Arendal? I underestimated your skill for survival, Cyrus. Your family is not known for . . . well, anything really. Yet, here you are, determined and bold as ever. Upsetting my *takwin* queen so much that I was almost compelled to replace her, but as previously stated, I am on a schedule. And work of that magnitude takes time." The automaton shook its head, its copper-wired hair tossing with its movements. "I could kill you now, all of you, but I am merciful. I have *always* been. I only want a better world, as do you. I offer you this chance. Cease your search. Give Stet the moonfire dagger and return to your lives. Soon they will be better. You have my vow."

The ground beneath the metal creature's paws, along with its mechanized body, exploded in a blast of brilliant pink fire and energy. It happened so fast Phina did not know what to make of it. Had it self-destructed? Had lightning struck it? The smoke cleared and a terrified, singed Stet was running as fast as a Felidae could, leaving behind the shattered pieces of brass, copper, theorrite, and stone still raining down on the lake's shore.

A cheerful voice had Phina whirling, claws out, ready for anything. "I do apologize. His recordings are often filled with long bouts of dialogue, and on occasion it can be helpful. Not this time, however. I decided to let him finish basking in his ego before I formally introduced myself."

A young woman, around Dare's age, was standing in the doorway, the light bouncing off the tower from the lake revealing her image in stark relief.

Hair streaked with golden brown and blonde had been pinned up in a sort of bun that had tilted at some point during the course of her day. The silken curls escaping the pins perfectly framed her heart-shaped face. Her eyes were a sparkling blue. Not indigo or ice, but the blue of the sea, and her smile was so bright it near equaled the light coming up from the lake beside them.

Phina narrowed her gaze and took a deep breath. What she'd

thought were freckles or spots on the woman's face were actually spots of grease. How interesting.

She had a curvaceous figure, from what Phina could tell, but it was hidden behind a noble's long gown, complete with bustle, and topped with a floor-length leather apron.

She smelled delicious. Like warm queensfruit tarts and explosives.

Though the latter scent may not be coming directly from her. It may, in fact, have something to do with the canon-sized weapon she was hefting against her hip.

Wulf was the first at her side.

"May I help you with that?" Wulf bowed formally. "I would love to know what you call it. I assume it is your own invention? How did you create that marvelous pink hue with a theorrite power source?"

She handed it to him with a beaming smile and dipped her head. "Thank you for noticing. Yes, it appeared to be very effective against that theorrite-absorbing autonomous creature. It is the Scarlet Lord's latest irritant, and one we now have a defense against. As to the color, every lady should have her secrets." She patted the pockets on her apron. "I need to make a few notes."

She noticed the others watching her and shook her head. "Apologies again." She walked down toward them and shook Bodhan's hand firmly, then Cyrus's and the captain's. "I am Aurora Steele, formerly of Queen's Hill, currently of Tower Orr." She stopped in front of Dare. "You may know my father, Scholar Steele?" She batted her hand carelessly as if to push the question away. "I won't be insulted if you don't recognize me. I was a bit of a thorn in his side and he rarely introduced me at functions. I, however, know you, Dare Senedal. All of you. The Khepri's told me so much about you, and when he said you were coming for my help, Lady Theodora and I were over both moons. I have been dying to get on that ship and get my hands dirty in the engine room."

Captain Amaranthe sheathed her sword, a bemused expression replacing her usual look of cynicism. "Your help? He told you we were coming for your help?"

Aurora sighed. "He forgot to tell you? Weapons for the Deviant? Light refractors to detect the Scarlet Lord's ship? Lady Theodora's skills? Nothing? Did he at least tell you about the quintessence? The elements? Or have you all just been wandering about with no idea as to what was going on?"

Bodhan recovered first. "We received a recording from the queen to come here. We weren't told why."

"Of course you weren't." She blew a golden curl out of her eye, flustered. "That man *is* frustrating. But, as Queen Idony always said, he is almost as clever as I am, so I should let him get away with his eccentricities."

Wulf's voice held a trace of disbelief. *"Almost* as clever?"

She smiled. "Come inside. I've been here at least two astronomical seasons and have yet to uncover all the tower's secrets." They looked at each other, unsure, and she opened the door. "As long as you are inside Tower Orr nothing can hurt you. Your crew can take shifts if they like, we have plenty of food, and the bedrooms are ready for company. Though I would stay away from the parlor at the moment. One of my experiments caused the smallest of explosions."

Phina chuckled. Aurora Steele had knocked the captain for a loop. The usually unflappable slayer of men was flustered, walking speechlessly toward their new host.

She inhaled again, the scent of Aurora and queensfruit tarts too tempting to resist. "I am definitely going to like her."

Cyrus appeared beside her and slid an arm around her waist, tugging her against him. Phina's body curled instinctively against his in remembered pleasure. She kissed his neck and a growl rumbled in his chest.

"Like her all you want, Seraphina." He slid his hand past her tail to caress her hips. "As long as you remember you belong to me."

In his eyes she saw no judgment, only love. She would always be a little wild. He had to know that. Just as she knew he would always be a little protective.

They might bring each other to the brink of sanity and back every day, but for her, it would be worth it. "I will. Are you ready for what comes next?"

Cyrus laughed softly and started walking with her toward the tower's open door. "I have no idea. As long as you are with me, and I can get my hands on one of Ms. Steele's weapons, I think I can handle anything."

Her tail caressed his thigh. "We shall see who gets their hands on whose weapon first, Sword. I have a skill or two you've not seen yet."

"Something to look forward to."

The soothing consistent hum around him was not clearing his mind the way it always had before. He set down his tools, adjusting the layered lenses of his scopularia until he could see normally in the dim light of his workspace.

All the preparations they had made, the decades of readying themselves . . . none of the risks were worth the jeopardy Idony was now in.

It had happened. The Scarlet Lord had decided he needed more than his desert domain. Much more. Any mistake made now would have disastrous consequences, not just for Idony, but all of Theorrey.

He opened his journal, his brass finger tracing a page it could not feel as he studied what had occurred until now.

Every curse held a blessing. It was a phrase his mother had uttered long ago. Perhaps she was right. They were coming together, at last, as he had known they would. The women and, he supposed, their men, who would shape the world. Elements that were stronger to-gether than they could possibly be apart.

The quintessence.

A scarab landed tumbling on his desk and he smiled. "What news today, my friend? What exactly is that island dictator up to now?"

Before he could find out, a familiar, rhythmic clicking had him spinning his chair around. His cryptograph. Other than his creations, it was his favorite device. He had made it take the shape of a large open tome made of brass and steel. On one page, four rows of clockwork typeset with pictographs that only he knew how to decode. On the other, a wheel of conductive coil that began to turn when a message was being sent or received.

The device had only one duplicate, meaning the message could only be from her. "Aurora."

He watched the type lift one image after another, never reaching for paper or a writing implement. There was no need since he could decipher the code in his sleep.

His shoulders slumped in relief. "They made it. They are at Tower Orr."

He watched as she relayed the information about the dagger and the automaton, as well as her successful testing of her latest weapon. "Little braggart," he muttered, unable to stop the feeling of pride and affection from leaking out in his grumbling.

All together now. Nearly ready.

He would hate that. The Scarlet Lord would hate knowing he would have to use a replica of the moonfire dagger if he wanted to move forward with his plan. Just as he was using an imitation queen. That he had been denied the Chalice, as well, would infuriate him.

The next steps would be crucial. But for now, at least, the captain and her crew were safe.

Time for the real work to begin.

Printed in the United States
by Baker & Taylor Publisher Services